THE PROMISE
of MORNING

Books by Ann Shorey

AT HOME IN BELDON GROVE
The Edge of Light
The Promise of Morning

AT HOME IN *Belden Grove*
BOOK 2

THE PROMISE
of MORNING

ANN
SHOREY

Revell

a division of Baker Publishing Group
Grand Rapids, Michigan

© 2010 by Ann Shorey

Published by Revell
a division of Baker Publishing Group
P.O. Box 6287, Grand Rapids, MI 49516-6287
www.revellbooks.com

Printed in the United States of America

Library of Congress Cataloging-in-Publication Data
Shorey, Ann Kirk, 1941–
   The promise of morning / Ann Shorey.
      p.   cm. — (At home in Beldon Grove ; bk. 2)
   ISBN 978-0-8007-3333-9 (pbk.)
   1. Infants—Death—Fiction. 2. Family secrets—Fiction. I. Title.
 PS3619.H666P76 2010
 813'.6—dc22   2009046653

Scripture used in this book, whether quoted or paraphrased by the characters, is taken from the King James Version of the Bible.

 10 11 12 13 14 15 16   7 6 5 4 3 2 1

For Richard—with love and gratitude

1

Beldon Grove, Illinois
March 1846

Ellie Craig brushed the last leaf from the surface of a granite marker embedded in the soft earth. "There, Lizzie." She crooned her daughter's name. "Isn't that better?"

She dropped an empty tow sack in front of the next stone to protect her skirt, then lowered herself to her knees. "Mama's here, Susanna."

While her hands busied themselves pulling out dead grass that surrounded the gray-flecked slab, Ellie tried to remember what Susanna had looked like. Two months old she'd been, and never strong. Just like Georgie, who rested next to his sisters under the third inscribed stone.

Tugging at the muddy sack, she moved to her son's grave. She shook her head and let the tears fall. "Ah, Georgie, my precious little boy." Ellie kept her voice to a whisper. "Such hair you had—so bright, like a new penny. But you left me too, didn't you?"

Meager sunshine washed over the three rectangular stones lying in a neat row in front of her muddy boots. A cool breeze blew past, slipping with little sound through the still-leafless hickory trees surrounding the cemetery. Ellie shivered and tucked her arms under her shawl.

Her husband, Matthew, called from the wagon where he waited with ten-month-old Julia. Using the folded sack, she rubbed mud from her hands while she picked her way back to the road. Melted snow, followed by heavy spring rains, left some of the burial mounds looking like small islands in a boggy marsh. Ellie's foot slipped, and she grabbed at a cross-topped obelisk inscribed "Beloved Parents" with the names and dates of birth and death of the deceased couple listed on the sides. For a moment she stood motionless, buffeted by painful memories.

"Ellie?"

"Coming."

Matthew stood next to their wagon, bent over to hold Julia's hand. He glanced up at Ellie, his face lit with pleasure. His eyes still held the warmth that had drawn her to him fourteen years ago.

"Look—she's been standing and walking while we waited for you."

Ellie gasped and ran to the toddler. She snatched her off her feet and glared at Matthew. "She could have fallen under the horse's hooves and been trampled. Whatever possessed you?"

Frightened by the sharp words, Julia wailed.

"Now see what you've done." Ellie flounced past Matthew's waiting hand and attempted to climb into the wagon with the child in her arms.

"Stop it." He placed his broad hands at her waist and lifted her onto the step. Once she was settled he held her in his steady gaze. "Don't you think I'm just as careful as you are with this one?"

He climbed up, sat next to her, and took Julia in his lap, dangling his pocket watch in front of her face. She stopped crying and grabbed for the golden prize.

Ellie kept her head down and picked at a thread in the skirt of her cinnamon-colored wool dress. "You don't know what it's like to watch her as each day goes by, praying she will live to grow up."

"I do know. And I can tell you exactly how many more days she has lived than Lizzie did—sixty-three. And tomorrow it will be sixty-four." He handed Julia back. "Every hair on her head is precious to me. But so are our other children." Matthew wrapped the reins around his hand, but left the brake locked in place. "Look at me."

She turned toward him.

"You must let some time pass before we come here again. With every visit you leave more of yourself behind." He raised his hands in a gesture of helplessness and then let them drop to his thighs. "I'm afraid one day I won't get you back at all." The horse stirred in its traces, rocking the wagon.

Ellie heard Matthew's words as though they came from a great distance. She hugged Julia tighter and studied her husband's face. His brown eyes reflected distress. She slid next to him, leaning into the warmth of his body. "I'm sorry. I shouldn't have snapped at you. It's just . . . among the graves . . . I think of everyone I've lost."

He squeezed her knee with his free hand. "All the more reason to stay away from here." He flicked the reins over Samson's broad back.

The wagon rolled north on the track that led toward the community of Beldon Grove. Afternoon light glinted off windows of a new house being built at the corner of Cemetery Road and Adams Street.

Matthew cleared his throat. "Do you still want to go to Molly's to work on her quilt?"

"Yes. Jimmy and Johnny can take care of things at home a little longer. One of them can always go get Aunt Ruby if they need help."

"Can't imagine what kind of help two thirteen-year-olds would need from your aunt."

A smile lit Ellie's face. "You're right. More than likely, she'd be sending for them."

Chuckling, Matthew headed for his sister's house. When the wagon rolled to a stop, Molly's oldest daughter, eleven-year-old Luellen, dashed out to greet them.

"Mama! Uncle Matthew and Aunt Ellie are here," she called.

Molly appeared in the doorway, wiping her hands on her apron. "I thought I noticed you driving by earlier."

After Matthew helped Ellie and Julia from the wagon, Molly joined them, slipping an arm around Ellie's shoulders. "You went to the cemetery again."

Ellie nodded, her momentary good humor submerged by a fresh wave of grief. Grateful for Molly's understanding, she followed her indoors.

"Sit." Molly pointed at one of the chairs that lined the plank table in her kitchen. She patted Ellie's back, then turned toward the work counter. "Karl set up the quilt frame in the back room for us. I put the top in, but it'll wait. There's coffee left from dinner and I just took a tin of tea cakes out of the oven."

Ellie noticed the tiny grin that hovered at the corner of Molly's mouth. "It seems you're enjoying your new range."

"I am. Karl says I'm going to make us fat with my baking, but it's such a pleasure to have a real oven after cooking over an open hearth all my life." Molly moved to the brickset range that had been built into the former fireplace recess. She lifted a towel from a hook on the wall and used it to protect her hands when she removed the coffee boiler from one of the range eyes.

Matthew sniffed the air. "Smells good in here." He stepped behind Molly and grabbed two of the warm tea cakes. "I'll take these to Doc. Does he have patients with him?"

"No. Lily's back there, though." Molly smiled as she mentioned her youngest child. "He told her she could help him this afternoon—doing what, I can't imagine." She pointed down the hallway at the office door. "Go on back. He'll be glad to see you."

Ellie watched her husband enter Karl's office. Once the door closed behind him, she turned back to Molly. "You've been blessed to marry someone who's so good to your children. It doesn't always work out that way."

Luellen spoke up before Molly could reply. "It's hard to remember when Papa Karl wasn't our papa. James and Franklin remember our real father, but I was too little when he died." She straightened, clearly pleased to be part of the women's conversation.

"It has been a long time," Ellie said, standing Julia on the floor.

Luellen jumped to her feet and clasped the toddler's hand. "Can I take her in the back room? I'll let her play with my dolls."

Ellie fixed a cautioning glance on her niece. "Mind you, don't let her hurt herself."

"You can trust me. I'll be careful."

Molly placed pewter mugs of coffee on the table and pushed a tray heaped with tea cakes in Ellie's direction. "Have one. You'll feel better."

Ellie picked up one of the soft cakes and nibbled at one edge. The rich caraway-flavored treat melted on her tongue. *Mmm.* She finished it and reached for another. When she picked up a third cake, Molly leaned across the table and touched her arm.

"What's wrong? It's more than just the visit to the cemetery, isn't it?"

11

Ellie returned the sweet to the tray, arranging it into a spiral pattern with the others. Not looking up from her task, she said, "Being at the cemetery, seeing all those headstones . . . I thought about my mother and father. They were gone before I knew them. And now my babies . . ." Ellie glanced up, then stacked three cakes in the center of the spiral. She tilted her head to study the effect.

Molly cleared her throat to speak.

Ellie ignored her. "I was so lonely growing up. Aunt Ruby and Uncle Arthur were good to me—and still are—but it wasn't like having real parents." Her voice trembled, and she fought to get it under control. "I've always wanted a home where no one would ever leave me. I used to dream—" Heat flooded her face. "I'm sorry. I don't know what's got into me today."

"You never told me you felt like this."

A tear slipped down Ellie's cheek. "Why did my babies have to die? And my parents?"

"Only God knows the answer."

"You've no idea how it feels to lose three infants, one after the other. I spend every moment watching Julia and praying the Lord will let her live."

"All your children need you, not just Julia. Maria's only eight. You shouldn't leave so much of the cooking and cleaning in her hands."

"Matthew's been talking to you, hasn't he?"

Molly's silence answered for her.

"Well, he's wrong. The boys help, too. And of course Aunt Ruby comes whenever I ask her."

"Who's at home with them now?"

Ellie stood, her chair screeching against the pine floor boards. "I'm managing fine. It's easy for you to criticize, you with your comfortable life and new husband." Her voice choked.

"Ah, Ellie." Molly opened her arms.

"Forgive me." Ellie sniffled and wiped at her wet cheeks with the back of her hand. "I know Samuel's passing was a dreadful blow, but it's over for you, don't you see? You have Karl and a wonderful new life."

"It's never over. There will always be a part of me that loves and misses Samuel. But we have to go on." Molly stepped back, leveling her gaze on Ellie. "It's been nearly three years since your Lizzie died. Things will get easier. I just know they will."

The door to Karl's office opened, and he and Matthew walked the length of the hall to join the women, Lily skipping between them. When they reached the kitchen, Karl bent to kiss Molly's forehead.

"Came to get a couple more cakes before you ladies eat them all."

Ellie noticed Karl's glance sweep over her and knew Matthew had been sharing his concerns with him. Wishing he'd keep their family troubles to himself, she dismissed her own tendency to burden her Aunt Ruby. After all, Ruby listened and sympathized. Karl tried to fix things.

"So, Ellie, how's Maria doing? Over her sniffles?"

"She's fine." Ellie pasted on a smile. "She's a big help to me in the kitchen and with Julia. I don't know what—"

A thud and a howl sounded from the next room.

"Julia!" Ellie turned and ran from the kitchen in time to see her baby being helped to her feet by Luellen. Molly's quilt frame stood behind them, each corner resting on a three-rail ladder-back chair. Loose pieces of fabric, cut into hexagon shapes, were piled in one corner of the muslin top.

Grainy sunshine flowed through the south-facing window. Its

light reflected off Julia's blonde hair and the tears on her round cheeks, making her look like she was made of spun glass.

Luellen turned frightened eyes on Ellie. "She just took a tumble and bumped her head on one of the chairs. She's fine."

Ellie hugged Julia to her chest, feeling a pulse of fear at the sight of an already-purpling lump on her forehead. "How do you know she's fine? She could be concussed." She patted the baby's back, trying to shush her.

Luellen hurried to Molly. "Mama, I was watching her. She just fell, all by herself."

Karl joined them and touched Ellie's shoulder. "You know toddlers fall. Don't take on so." He looked at Luellen, who was on the verge of tears. "Come here, Lulie. It wasn't your fault." He slipped an arm around her.

Ellie followed Karl out of the room. When they reached the kitchen, Matthew took Julia from her arms. Her sobs had subsided to an occasional hiccup.

"I know what will make her happy again." Luellen clapped her hands. "Yesterday James found a bee tree in the woods between us and the cemetery. It was full of honey, even after sitting all winter." She opened a cupboard and brought out a stoneware jar. "He took most of it to Mr. Wolcott's store to sell, but left us a fair bit." She placed the jar on the table and looked at Molly. "Can I give them some?"

"Of course."

Luellen bustled to a shelf on the far wall and selected a square crockery dish. She used the side of a basting spoon to cut a chunk of honeycomb, dropping it into the empty container. Then she picked up a teaspoon and scooped it into the honey jar.

"Here's a taste for Julia." She held the spoon out and Julia's mouth opened like a baby bird's. "She likes it. See, no more tears."

Ellie felt a pang of remorse for losing her temper with Luellen. "Thank you. We'll all enjoy this treat." She looked at Matthew. "We'd best be getting along. You've got a sermon to work on for tomorrow."

Clouds scudded across the sky as they settled themselves for the trip home. Karl stood next to the step. Ellie braced herself, expecting him to say something more about their older children.

Instead, Karl rested one hand on the side of the wagon, his eyes on Matthew. "Did you see the handbill at Wolcott's store about a traveling repertory group coming to town? They're going to do a Shakespeare play."

Surprised at the change of subject, Ellie shot a glance at Matthew. A play? She waited for the explosion. He'd never bothered to hide his opinion that stage actors were people of loose morals.

His jaw tightened. "When?"

2

Matthew turned the horse onto Monroe Street and headed for Wolcott's Mercantile. "I have to see that notice for myself. I can't believe Ben would allow such a thing on his storefront."

Their wagon rolled past bare trees framing the town square. A group of young boys wearing paper hats and waving wooden swords played soldier in the center of a grassy area. Ellie turned her head, watching their game. "If Georgie had lived, he could be playing with them."

Matthew glanced at the children, then looked at his wife. "Ellie, please. Let's talk about something else." His tone sounded sharper than he'd intended.

She stiffened her shoulders and looked away, resting her chin on top of Julia's bonnet.

When he rounded the corner onto Jefferson Street, he pulled the wagon to a stop in front of the store. "You can wait here if you want. I won't be long."

"No, I'll come in. I want to look at the dry goods. Julia's going to need a new dress for summer."

"Maria will need one too. We have two daughters." He strove to keep the annoyance out of his voice.

While Ellie walked into the building, Matthew stopped at the front wall to examine the posted notices. The wind lifted a black and white handbill near the door.

THE FORSYTHE TOURING COMPANY PRESENTS
WILLIAM SHAKESPEARE
"The Bard of Avon"
His Celebrated Play
MACBETH
!! Entirely New Scenery and Costumes !!
Coming to Beldon Grove Friday, May 15th
Watch for Future Information Regarding Time and Location

Matthew stepped back and read it again. How could Ben do this? He strode into the store, noting that Ellie was busy looking at rolls of printed calico displayed on a table near the back of the building.

Ben Wolcott stood in front of a counter near the window, sorting cured animal hides into two piles. His center-parted gray hair shone with Macassar oil. Matthew suppressed a smile at the sight of his longtime friend's singular vanity. He looked like a dandy.

He glanced up when Matthew entered. "Brother Matt. It's a pleasant surprise to see you and the missus on a Saturday afternoon. Thought you'd be home stirring up some powerful words for us to chew on tomorrow."

Matthew walked to the counter. "I came to talk to you."

"Aye-yuh?" Ben's New England roots flavored his reply. "What is it you need?"

Matthew took a deep breath and held it a moment before responding. "What I need," he said in measured tones, "is for you to take that sign off the front of your building."

"Sign?" Ben dropped the hide he was checking. "There's at least a dozen bills posted out there. Which one do you mean?"

Out of the corner of his eye, Matthew saw Ellie turn to watch them. "The one advertising that play."

"*Macbeth*? That's not simply a play. It's Shakespeare." Ben moved behind the counter and faced his friend.

"Doesn't matter who wrote it. If it's going to be performed on a stage, it's a play and folks in it are actors." Matthew's jaw tightened. "We've been friends long enough for you to know what I think of such people."

"I believe it'll be good for the town. Back where I came from, we enjoyed Shakespeare whenever a troupe came through." He squared his shoulders, drawing himself up to his full height, which still left him several inches shorter than Matthew. "Our young folks learn reading and ciphering, but they don't know anything of the world beyond our county."

"'Love not the world; neither the things that are in the world.'"

Ben didn't blink. "This isn't any more worldly than teaching youngsters to read. The handbill stays where it is."

Once they were in the wagon headed home, Matthew let Samson lead the way while his thoughts traveled back to his argument with Ben. He hated confrontation, and now he and Ben were at odds. *He's bound to see it my way after I tell him what happened in Kentucky.*

After several moments he realized Ellie was talking to him. "Mr. Wolcott had a double pink with a tiny check pattern that would be so pretty with Julia's fair skin." She cleared her throat. "And Maria's too, of course."

It took him a few seconds to switch his thoughts from actors to his wife's comments about cloth. "Did you tell him you wanted it?"

Ellie looked sideways at him from under the brim of her bonnet. "I thought I should ask you first."

"We still have credit with Ben from last year's crops. There's more than enough to cover new dresses for my girls."

18

"Good. Then next time you take me to the mercantile I'll get enough to make one for each of us. Thank you." Ellie settled back on the seat, a pleased smile on her face.

"Maybe Ruby will help you with the sewing." He flicked the reins over Samson's back, relieved to see her focus on something besides Julia.

◯

After supper, Matthew rode to Wolcott's farm. The issue of the play roiled his stomach like tainted beef.

Ben opened the door at his knock, spilling yellow lamplight over the wooden porch. "C'mon in and warm yourself. Feels like it's fixing to snow out there."

The lingering aroma of bread cooling on the worktable, mingled with steam issuing from the spout of the coffee boiler, filled the air.

Ben's wife, Charity, bustled forward. "I just made fresh coffee. Want some?"

"Yes. Thanks." Matthew followed Ben to the table. Charity placed filled mugs in front of them and then slipped from the room.

A moment of silence passed between the two men.

Ben leaned back, resting his elbows on the arms of his chair. His gaze locked on Matthew. "What brings you out on a Saturday night? Must be serious."

Matthew leaned forward. "Been thinking about that play all afternoon. You've got to cancel the show. I don't want actors in this town. They're a low form of humanity."

"A low form of humanity? How can you say that?"

"Let me tell you about actors." Matthew shoved his chair away from the table and stood with his back to the open hearth. "Before

19

I left Kentucky, a riverboat brought a group of them from Louisiana to Marysville, where I lived. They set up a tent and commenced plays and dance frolics—some doings every night for two weeks." He clenched his fists. "One afternoon while they were there, I cut through the woods to visit my sweetheart. On the way I thought I heard crying. I followed the sound . . . and saw her . . . on the ground with one of those . . . actors." He spat the word. "He was doing things to her that are only proper between man and wife."

Ben watched him, pity written on his face. "You don't need to tell me more."

"Yes, I do." Matthew walked to the table. Placing his hands flat on the surface, he met Ben's gaze. "He debauched her. Then when the weeks were up, he was gone with the rest of them."

"What happened to—?"

"She hung herself."

Ben placed a hand on his shoulder. "I'm sorry. But that was a long time ago. You can't judge all performers by what happened back then. It was a different place, with different people. It won't happen here."

"You can't be certain."

"No, I can't. But I'm not dropping my support of this play. This is the first time an acting troupe has traveled this far from the Mississippi. I think it will be a good opportunity for the towns-people to see more of life than a dusty farm village in the middle of a prairie."

"You're my oldest friend. I respect you. Nevertheless, I plan to oppose this. My sermon topic tomorrow will be on avoiding the evils of the world."

Concern wrinkled Ben's forehead. "If you preach against a Shakespeare play, you'll just stir up trouble for yourself—and sound like a fool."

"I don't think so." Matthew slung his coat over his shoulder and banged out the door.

When he stepped outside on Sunday morning, Matthew discovered the temperature had dropped below freezing overnight, turning the muddy farmyard into a sheet of ice. The clouds that blew in late Saturday afternoon now covered the sky. A brisk wind gusted from the southwest, bringing a threat of snow. Matthew harnessed Samson in haste and drove the spring wagon around to the hitching post at the front of the house.

He hurried up the porch steps and pushed open the door. "Ellie. Get the children ready quick as you can. It'll take longer to get to church today and I want to be early."

Maria clattered down from upstairs and grabbed his hand. "I'm all dressed, Papa."

He looked her over. The buttons on her blue wool dress didn't line up with the buttonholes, and her braids had loose blonde hairs sticking out of the plaits. "Didn't Mama help you with your dress?"

"No, I did it all by myself while she took care of Julia."

Matthew felt a pang at her eagerness to please. Dropping to one knee, he placed his hands on her shoulders. "Let Papa fix this." His fingers moved down the row of small china buttons that marched from beneath her chin to her waist. Taking a second look at her braids, he decided they wouldn't show under her bonnet. "You look very pretty." He hugged her and kissed her cheek.

The twins emerged from the kitchen, followed by eleven-year-old Harrison. "Please help Maria with her cloak, then bundle yourselves and get in the wagon." Matthew turned toward the stairs. "I'll go up and hurry your mama along."

When Ellie stepped onto the porch carrying Julia, Matthew tucked his Bible under one arm and offered a hand to assist her down the steps. She took one look at the ice-covered ground and planted her feet like a balky mule.

"We can't take the baby out on a morning like this. What if the wagon upsets?"

"As long as I can see where we're going, we'll be fine."

She frowned at him but inched down the stairs and allowed him to help her into the wagon.

Matthew climbed in next to her. "Cover Julia with your cloak. We'll be there before you know it."

The horse stepped carefully along the ice-covered road. As the two miles between farm and church rolled by, Matthew turned his mind back to his sermon. He'd been awake most of the night formulating points to lead his flock to the inevitable conclusion that plays were sinful and that they were to have nothing to do with people who performed in them.

Lulled by Samson's rhythmic pacing, Matthew missed seeing an ice heave in the roadway. The horse stepped over it, but the wagon wheels slid sideways when they hit the frozen bump. Ellie screamed and clutched Julia to her chest.

Matthew gripped the reins and pulled hard as they swerved back and forth across the track. One of the back wheels caught in the shallow ditch beside the road. The wagon tipped, then righted itself with a thud that rattled the traces.

Heart pounding, he turned and looked at Ellie. Her mouth was pinched tight. Her eyes clearly said "I told you so."

Matthew slid an arm around her shoulder and pulled her to him. "I'm sorry. I wasn't paying attention."

She shrugged him off. "We're almost there. Just go on."

From his position on the raised platform, Matthew gazed over his congregation, pleased to see a good turnout in spite of the cold. Upturned faces, glowing in the warm yellow light, lifted their voices singing "A Charge to Keep I Have." The candles lining the walls flickered with the movement in the room.

With one hand directing the music, Matthew sang the familiar hymn along with the standing worshipers. Part of his mind kept to the words while he checked the benches to see who might be missing. As he scanned the back row, his eyes were arrested by the appearance of a couple he'd never seen before. The man stood well over six feet tall. He was large in every way, without appearing to have the slightest measure of fat on his body.

The stranger wore a well-tailored suit, and his shirt front bore a cascade of ruffles over which draped a broad golden watch chain. The woman next to him wore stylish clothing but something seemed amiss in her posture. She looked like she had not completely unfolded when she stood to sing. He made a mental note to introduce himself before they left.

The hymn ended. Matthew knelt for opening prayers, enjoying as always the soft rustle in the room as the congregation knelt with him. He prayed long and earnestly for God's anointing on his message. Standing, he resumed his place behind the pulpit.

"It has come to my attention that we are in grave danger of attack by Satan." The people straightened on the benches. "My text today is, 'If any man love the world, the love of the Father is not in him.' Ours has traditionally been a plain religion. We believe we are set apart so others may see and turn from their worldly ways." Matthew raised his open Bible in one hand, its soft leather cover sagging over the sides of his palm. "We most definitely do not allow our children to attend dances or public entertainments. These amusements allow them to come in contact with unsavory individuals."

He gestured in the direction of Ben Wolcott's mercantile. "There's a sign on the wall in the center of town. It's an enticement to all who read it. I believe it is an open door to an attack by Satan." Matthew raised his voice. "Do not offer him a foothold by falling under the spell of those who promise education in the guise of entertainment. You'll be opening a door to the sort of people we don't want in Beldon Grove."

He glanced at the congregation to gauge their reaction. Some looked puzzled, others stone-faced, most were closely attentive. In the back, the stranger's expression remained neutral, his eyes half closed, as though he were bored by the topic.

After lengthy exhortation, Matthew concluded, "I call on every one of you to take a stand for what is right. Turn your backs on this temptation. You have your Bibles. Read them."

Every soul saved was a spiritual child to him. This room was filled with such children, people he had labored with in prayer through many long meetings. Clutching his Bible, Matthew sank to his knees, noting Ben Wolcott's sorrowful expression as he did so. He averted his gaze.

"Let us pray for deliverance."

When the closing hymn had been sung, Matthew walked to the back of the church to greet the visitors. When he stood next to the stranger, he felt power exude from the man. Here was someone who would automatically command attention when he entered a room. His trunklike legs strained at the fabric of his trousers. When Matthew put out his hand, it was engulfed by the bigger man's.

"Name's Marcus Beldon. This is my wife, Zilphah."

He judged Marcus Beldon's age to be somewhere near his own. Forties. Zilphah Beldon appeared older than her husband. Mousy brown ringlets dangled under her lavish bonnet. She extended a twisted hand to Matthew. "Please do not grip me firmly. I suffer from much pain in my extremities."

Gently, he clasped her fingers. His impression from the pulpit had been correct. Standing, the woman was curled over as though a heavy burden rested on her back. "A pleasure, Mrs. Beldon."

"Thank you." Her icy tone matched the morning's weather.

Stung by her dismissive manner, Matthew turned back to Marcus Beldon. Hazel eyes set beneath dark eyebrows accented the man's clean-shaven face. A mass of salt-and-pepper black hair fell across his forehead and curled around his ears.

Ellie joined them carrying Julia. "My wife, Eleanor." Matthew placed a possessive hand on her shoulder.

A spark lit Beldon's eyes. He bent in a half-bow toward Ellie. "Mrs. Craig. You are clearly the mother of this beautiful child in your arms. She could have no other."

Ellie blushed. Lifting her gaze to meet Marcus Beldon's, she stammered her response. "This is our Julia. The other children are over by the stove."

Beldon's glance flicked across the room. "A handsome group, indeed."

Matthew felt a stir of irritation at the man's patronizing tone. "We've been blessed, sir. And yourselves? Are your youngsters not with you today?"

"Alas, we have neither chick nor child." Beldon looked down at his wife. "My poor wife is barren."

"Marcus!" Her cheeks turned a mottled red.

"It's the plain truth, my dear. Let's not prevaricate in the presence of the good preacher."

Matthew realized he'd trod on hostile ground. To turn the conversation, he asked, "Is it a coincidence that you bear the same name as that of our community?"

"No coincidence at all." The golden fobs on his watch chain glinted in the candlelight when Beldon replied. "My father Jeremiah founded this settlement before the Black Hawk War. At the time of the uprising, he thought it prudent to take his family back to Virginia." He glanced down at his wife. "Now that things are more civilized here, Zilphah and I decided to return to the town which bears our name. A place where I can make my mark, so to speak."

"Beldon Grove is a growing community. What skills do you bring us?"

"Marcus is a lawyer." His wife answered for him in a nasal voice. "The town needs one, it would seem."

"Besides reading law, I was educated at Harvard for the ministry." Beldon threw his shoulders back, tucking his fingers into the front pockets of his trousers. "But it appears that job is filled."

3

After the family finished Sunday supper, Ellie sat near the long plank table in the kitchen and rocked Julia. Overhead an oil lamp hummed, settling its warm light over her family.

Under the window, Maria and Aunt Ruby stood in front of an oiled wooden shelf. Aunt Ruby washed dishes in a tin basin and then handed dripping plates to Maria for drying. While they worked, Aunt Ruby kept up a running argument with Matthew about the Shakespeare play.

Only half listening, Ellie let her mind roam back to the newcomers at church that morning. His wife had said he was a lawyer. She wondered how long he'd stay in their small village. She recalled the spark that lit Marcus Beldon's gaze when he looked at her. Warmth rose in her cheeks. Uncomfortable with the direction her thoughts were taking, she refocused her attention on her aunt's comments.

Aunt Ruby's hands rested on the rim of the basin. "I still think you're making a big to-do over nothing. Mr. Wolcott said lots of towns back east have acting troupes come to present Shakespeare." She scooped up a handful of forks and dropped them into the water.

Matthew looked up from the game of checkers he was playing with Uncle Arthur and pinched his lower lip between thumb and forefinger. Ellie smiled inside. She'd seen him do this countless times when he wanted to stop himself from making a quick rejoinder.

He jumped one of Uncle Arthur's checkers, then responded. "Did you see the notice at the mercantile?"

"We were there last Thursday when the rider came through and put it up. Isn't that right, Arthur?"

"Yup. Didn't look evil to me—just a regular person. No horns or tail." He aimed a teasing smile at Matthew.

Startled, Ellie looked at her uncle. She was accustomed to deferring her opinions to those of her husband because of the sixteen-year difference in their ages. But if Uncle Arthur saw nothing amiss, maybe Matthew was wrong about actors.

"The man said there would be an introduction before the play started, so we'd all know what the story would be about," Aunt Ruby said. "That doesn't sound so bad."

"I didn't say the play was bad. It's having actors loitering about town that worries me. It's well known that they're people of loose morals."

Uncle Arthur raised an eyebrow and jumped two of Matthew's checkers, then leaned back in his chair. "Your move."

Matthew frowned at the board, then at Aunt Ruby. "You and Arthur never allowed Ellie to attend dance frolics or entertainments when she was a girl. Why have you changed your thinking?"

"There's dancing and then there's schooling. Mr. Wolcott says Shakespeare is schooling."

"Then let's teach it in school and that'll be the end of it."

"Humph." She lifted the basin from the counter and moved to toss out the dirty water.

As soon as she opened the back door, smoke curled out of the firebox and drifted across the room. Julia wrinkled her nose and exploded in a series of sneezes.

Ellie threw a corner of her apron over the baby's head. "We're all going to catch our death. Hurry and shut that door."

The latch clicked. "That only took a moment, child. No need to get in an uproar." Aunt Ruby sat at the table and pinned Matthew with her gaze. "Times are changing. We don't live in the backwoods anymore. I, for one, am pleased to have the opportunity to improve myself."

Matthew stood. "We'll see." He took his coat from a peg next to the door and shrugged his arms into it. "Time to do the milking."

Once the door closed behind him, Ellie turned to Aunt Ruby. "He cares about the folks in town, you know that. You never used to disagree with him." She handed Julia a wooden spoon to play with. "In fact, you seemed to think he was well-nigh perfect when he came courting."

"He's a good man, I don't deny that." She tucked stray wisps of faded blonde hair behind her ears. "But I think he may have jumped in here without checking to see how deep the water is."

Aunt Ruby and Uncle Arthur both believed Matthew was wrong. Ellie rested her cheek on Julia's curls. *Is he?*

Apparently misinterpreting Ellie's silence as anger over her criticism of Matthew, Aunt Ruby said, "I know your place is at your husband's side." She spoke in a placating voice. "But I don't have to follow his lead. I hope the play does come to Beldon Grove."

Intrigued in spite of Matthew's disapproval, Ellie leaned forward. "Where do you think it would be performed?"

That night, while Ellie readied Julia for sleep in their upstairs bedroom, Matthew stepped across the hall to settle a wrestling match that erupted between Jimmy and Johnny. She heard thumps and bangs as the twins rolled each other back and forth on the bare wooden floor.

In a few moments the commotion subsided and Matthew entered the room grinning. "I think Jimmy won that one." He walked over to the bed and tickled Julia's round belly.

The baby laughed and wiggled, her feet flying free of her linen nightdress. Ellie picked her up and carried her to an oak crib placed against the back wall of the room.

"Time to settle down." Once she had Julia covered, Ellie leaned on the rail and watched her. "She's blinking long blinks. She'll be asleep in a moment."

Matthew put an arm around Ellie's waist and pulled her to his side. "Come over by the light. I need to show you something."

"What is it?"

He didn't answer, so she followed him to a small table near the door. Using a wooden stool at the side of the bed, she climbed up and sat beside him on the feather tick.

"I'm waiting."

Matthew removed an envelope from his shirt pocket. "This came on Wednesday."

"You've been carrying a letter around for five days? Why on earth did you wait until now to show it to me?"

An apprehensive expression crossed his face. "I didn't want you to see it at all, but then I figured you had to know."

"Know what?" Her heart thumped. "Tell me."

Matthew lifted the flap and took out two folded sheets of paper. Clearing his throat, he read, "'Dear Brother Craig. I propose dropping you a line for the first time, though not for want of respect for you. The circumstance of my writing is to give you some information . . .'"

The letter went on through many polite formalities, until Ellie interrupted. "Matt. Who's this from? Why are you being so mysterious?"

He turned to the second page and read, "'It is my sad duty to inform you that my son, George Long, died December last on his homestead land in Brazoria County, Texas. We are looking into any inheritance rights which might pass to the family.'" Matthew handed her the papers. "It's from your Grandpa Long."

The room grew dark. Matthew receded into the distance, becoming smaller and smaller. "He's writing about my father." Ellie leaned forward to stop the dizziness that threatened to engulf her. "How can this be? He died twenty-five years ago."

4

Ellie moved the tall candlestick to the edge of the table and reread the message, using her index finger to follow the tightly spaced words. Matthew slid his arm around her waist and pulled her closer.

His initial plan had been to destroy the letter. It would only upset Ellie, and to what end? She believed, as he did, that her father had died when she was a small child. The message promised to bring nothing but turmoil into their lives. He studied Ellie's face, wondering what she was thinking.

She folded the pages and laid them on the table next to the candle. "You haven't said why you waited so long to show this to me."

"I didn't want to see you hurt." He cleared his throat. "No, that's not the reason." Matthew studied her, praying for understanding. "I was afraid. Afraid of what this might mean to you. To us." He choked on the words.

Her voice took on an edge. "Then why show me at all?"

"Your grandfather said they're looking into an inheritance. I decided there was a chance more might come of this and you wouldn't be prepared." He lifted her onto his lap. "I'm sorry."

He rested his cheek against the top of her head, savoring the fragrance of the rose oil she used to dress her hair. After a few seconds, she looked up. The candle glow turned the tears on her cheeks into pearls of light.

"They told me my mother and father were in heaven. If this is true, my father gave me away—like a *puppy*—so he'd be free to go adventuring." Ellie's voice broke.

He rocked her back and forth. "I know. I don't understand any of it."

"They lied to me. They've lied to me all my life." Ellie slid off his lap and marched across the room to the clothespress. She flung the doors open and dug around inside. "Where'd I put my boots?"

"What d'you want with your boots at this hour?"

"I'm going to Aunt Ruby's right now and make her tell me the truth."

"Wait until morning. We'll both go."

When Matthew woke at daybreak, Ellie wasn't in bed next to him. He pushed himself up on one elbow to check the crib. No Julia. His breath caught in his throat. He jumped out of bed, grabbed his pants, and slipped them over his long underwear. After shoving his sockless feet into boots, he hurried out of the room, laces dragging the floor behind him. As he clattered down the stairs, his nose caught a whiff of boiling coffee.

His heart slowed its frantic beats. "You're still here."

Ellie turned. "Of course. Why aren't you dressed? I want to leave right after breakfast."

Julia toddled about the room, touching the walls to keep her balance. Matthew scooped her off the floor and cuddled her against his chest. Her chubby hands tugged at his beard.

He pried Julia's fingers loose while answering his wife's question. "I thought . . ." His voice trailed off. He didn't know what he thought. Instead, he walked over and kissed her cheek. A skillet filled with salt pork and apples bubbled on top of the stove. "Smells good. I'll go finish dressing." Still carrying Julia, Matthew turned toward the steps.

"Hurry the other children along, will you? We can take them to school before we go to Aunt Ruby's."

Matthew nodded, grateful for a diversion into the commonplace. "They'll be happy they don't have to walk."

He swallowed around the knot of dread that formed in his throat at the prospect of a confrontation with Ruby and Arthur. No matter how he studied on it, for the past twenty-five years they'd kept them from knowing Ellie's father was alive.

Matthew turned right on the street in front of Bryant House Hotel. He passed Wolcott's store and stopped at the school just as Molly's four children walked toward them.

Her oldest son, James, paused and waited. "Pretty rich, riding to school," he said to the twins and Harrison when they scrambled out of the wagon.

James's brother, Franklin, followed him into the school yard. Watching him, Matthew recalled the time eight years ago when Franklin had been held captive for several months by the Fox tribe. He still moved like an Indian. Matthew doubted he'd ever outgrow his careful way of placing each foot before taking a step.

He waved at the boy and then jumped down to help Maria out of the wagon. She slipped free of his grasp and squished across the thawed ground toward Lily and her older sister Luellen.

"How can you walk and read at the same time?" she asked Luellen when she reached her side.

Franklin turned. "That's what I'd like to know. I think we should put a rope on her and lead her to school so she won't get lost."

Luellen lowered her book and directed a scornful glance at him. "Don't worry about me. I know where I'm going."

"Matt?" The sound of his wife's voice jerked Matthew back to the reason they'd come to town. "Are we going to sit here all morning?"

"Just waiting to be sure the children get inside all right."

The front door of the hotel opened as they turned south on the stage road toward Arthur and Ruby Newberry's farm. An unfamiliar voice boomed through the crisp air.

"That you, Reverend?" Marcus Beldon walked to the edge of the porch, dressed in a fur-collared black overcoat. The bulky knee-length garment made him look like a bear standing on hind legs.

Pleased to have another delay, Matthew reined the horse to a stop. "Morning, Mr. Beldon. You're out early." Even at a distance he could sense the power in the big man.

Beldon tipped his beaver hat. "Mrs. Craig. This cold air has put roses in your cheeks."

"It's cold indeed. Surely you'd be more comfortable indoors next to the fire."

"That I would." A bland smile rested on his lips. "But I saw you folks pass by a few minutes ago and wanted to have a word with your husband."

Ellie poked Matthew in the ribs. "Stop dallying," she said under her breath.

Marcus Beldon faced Matthew. "I hope you can make time in the next few days to meet with me. I have some questions." He paused. "About the community. I'm sure you know most of what goes on around here."

Matthew nodded. "I'd be pleased to do that. Where do you suggest?"

"Why not right here?" Beldon gestured at the building behind him. "There are two fairly comfortable parlors off the reception room."

"I'll be back later in the week. I'll see you then."

Beldon pulled his hands from his pockets and rubbed them together. "Excellent. I will make it a point to be available."

Matthew pushed down a surge of irritation at the man's condescending tone. What could Beldon want from him that he couldn't learn just as easily from the hotelkeeper?

Ellie nudged him again.

"If you'll excuse us?" Matthew lifted the reins. "I want to get the baby out of the cold."

"But of course." Beldon raised his hat. "Mrs. Craig. A pleasure to see you."

Ellie nodded, but anything she might have said was buried in the rattle of the harness as Matthew urged Samson toward Arthur and Ruby's farm. The horse's hooves tossed up chunks of muddy ice, splattering the front panel of their wagon.

Ellie snugged the lap robe around herself and Julia. "I'm worried about what to say to them. Did you bring the letter?"

"Certainly did." Matthew touched the front of his thick woolen coat. "Right here in my pocket." He patted her knee. "I'm worried too. I switch between anger and puzzlement." They rode in silence for a few moments. "Perhaps there's a good explanation." He couldn't imagine what it might be, but he could hope.

Once past Ben Wolcott's land, Matthew slowed the wagon and turned onto the lane that led to the Newberrys'. Shifting Julia on her lap, Ellie reached out and gripped his hand. He felt her fingers tremble. "Do you want to go home?" he asked. "I can talk to them."

She straightened. "No. This is something I must do."

The wagon rolled around to the rear of the tidy whitewashed house. Bleached linen curtains at the kitchen window were drawn open, revealing Ruby's back as she stood at the stove.

According to their custom, Matthew tapped on the back door, opening it at the same time. A cloud of soapy-smelling steam enveloped them when they walked inside.

Ruby turned from the wash boiler, eyes wide. "Matthew. Ellie." She looked at her niece. "It's Monday. Why aren't you home tending to your family's washing?"

"We have something that couldn't wait."

Ruby hurried over. "Well, take off your things and sit down." She took Julia from Ellie's arms. "Yesterday you were worried that she'd take a chill sitting in your kitchen, and now you're out running her around the countryside in the cold. Her little cheeks are like ice." She moved a chair close to the stove and settled the baby on her lap.

Ellie glanced at Matthew and held out her hand. Without a word, Matthew reached into his pocket and gave her the letter.

"What?" A puzzled expression crossed Ruby's face.

"We got a letter from your pa," Matthew said.

"Forevermore! He never wrote me. Why'd he send you a letter?"

Ellie removed Julia from Ruby's lap and handed her the folded pages. "Read it."

The only sound in the kitchen was an occasional hiss as water condensed under the lid of the copper boiler and dripped onto the stove top. The flush in Ruby's cheeks deepened as she read. When she turned to the second page, her eyes widened and she pressed her fingers over her mouth. After a moment, she refolded the letter and returned it to Matthew with shaking fingers. Her gaze slid to Ellie and then quickly moved away. Silence hung in the air.

"Well?" Ellie asked. "He's writing about my father, isn't he?" Her voice rose. "All these years you've let me believe he was dead and he wasn't. I could've seen him, known him, but you kept me from it." Julia started to whimper and Ellie thrust her at Matthew, then faced Ruby. "Why?"

Ruby stood and extended her arms. "I can explain. You need to understand how things were."

Ellie took a step back. "I understand that you and Uncle Arthur have lied to me. How can you expect me to believe you now?"

Footsteps sounded from the front of the house. Arthur entered and flicked an apprehensive glance around the room. "What's all the shouting about?" He directed the question at Matthew, one man to another, rather than seeking a reply from his wife or niece.

Ruby raised her head. Defeat wrote itself across her features. "She knows about George. Pa wrote them a letter."

"Your brother's in Texas. After all this time, why would your pa write them about that?" Arthur stepped between Ruby and Ellie. Lowering his voice, he said, "I thought no one would mention George. That was the agreement."

"He's dead. He died last December." Ruby pointed at the letter dangling from Matthew's fingers. "Pa seems to think there may be an inheritance concerning the land down there—that's why he wrote."

"That'd be your pa. If it comes to money, he'll stir hisself." Arthur tugged at his short white beard, then glanced at Ellie. "For your sake, I hope it's not another of his harebrained—"

"We didn't come here about money." Ellie snatched the sheets of paper from Matthew's hand, wadded them into a ball, and threw them at Ruby's feet. "Let Grandpa Long have whatever's down there. I don't want it." She glared at her aunt. "We're here this morning because you lied to me."

Matthew stood Julia on the floor and slipped an arm around Ellie. "She trusted your word. Can you imagine what a shock this is to her? To us?"

Arthur's face lost its usual benevolent expression. "Yes. I can." He laid a hand on Matthew's arm. "Sit down." He pointed at the wooden table in the center of the room. "Ruby, pour us some of that coffee. We have a story to tell."

Keeping his arm around Ellie's shoulders, Matthew led her to a chair. They watched in silence while Ruby took four pewter mugs from a shelf and filled them. After placing them on the table, she sank into a chair next to Arthur. Tears welled in her eyes.

He nudged her side. "You tell them."

"Well, after your ma died—"

"Did she really? Or is this another untruth?" Suspicion cut through Ellie's words.

"She did. You were about three, going on four. Anyway, your pa was sore upset. We could see he wasn't taking good care of you." Ruby's lower lip trembled and she turned to Arthur. "You tell her."

"He was letting you wander loose," he said. "It was wintertime, and sometimes you wasn't even wearing a wrap. You'd come to our cabin, hungry, wanting something to eat. Things went on like that for a spell." Something in the memory caused him to smile briefly, then the smile disappeared.

Ruby picked up the narration. "We didn't mind looking after you. Most of my brothers and sisters had young'uns of their own and Arthur and me didn't. Come spring of 'twenty-one, some men rode through full of big news about this fellow Stephen Austin getting a contract from the Mexicans to settle three hundred families down there in Spanish Texas. Nothing would do but that your pa had to go with them—"

Arthur broke in. "You can imagine we tried to talk him out of it. I mean, living under foreign rule? Hadn't even been fifty years since their pa fought in the war against England, and now here was George throwing away his independence. I tell you, Pa Long was dead set against the whole plan."

Ellie folded her arms over her chest and looked across the table at her aunt and uncle. "This is interesting, but I don't see any reason not to tell me about him from the beginning." She pushed back her chair. "I don't even know if this is a fact, or something else you're making up."

Matthew hoisted Julia onto his lap where she babbled and grabbed for his coffee. "Let's hear them out." He pushed the mug out of Julia's reach and quirked an eyebrow at Ruby. "Go ahead. Tell us the rest."

"I just need for her to get a picture of what it was like in those days." Ruby gazed at her niece. "Your pa said he'd go down there, get himself a land grant, then come back for you. We doubted it, seeing as how he wasn't doing much of a job of looking after you as it was. But when spring wore on, he packed up your things and brought you to us. Said it'd only be for a year or so."

Ellie leaned forward, shoulders hunched, head down.

"My pa, your Grandpa Long, raved and threatened, but off George went. Time went on. Months. Then a year. Nary a word.

We thought, 'Well, no sense bothering the child with all this. We'll just tell her he died.' For all we knew, it was the truth."

Ellie made a small whimpering sound. Matthew slipped an arm around her shoulders and pulled her close. Part of him could understand the reasoning behind letting Ellie believe her father had died, but he'd seen, as Ruby and Arthur had not, the tears she'd shed after reading the letter. It was bad enough knowing she'd been given away. Learning that her father had been alive for many years and never returned for her doubled the pain.

Arthur scraped his chair away from the table and stood. "Don't say 'we.' I told you from the beginning that we should be honest with her. Now see what it's come to?"

Ruby looked from Arthur to her niece. "It seemed best at the time." Her eyes pleaded for understanding. "I never meant to hurt you."

Water drops on the stove hissed in the quiet room.

Finally Ellie drew a deep breath. "It doesn't matter now whose idea it was." Tears spilled from her eyes. "What I don't understand is how could he walk away from his own child?"

5

Ellie wrung her mop over a pail of lye solution and scrubbed at grease spots in front of the cook stove. Physical activity helped work off the anger and hurt that accompanied her waking hours. Over the past five days she'd dusted each room, even the seldom-used parlor, taken down and washed the kitchen curtains, and hauled ashes out of all the fireplaces.

In spite of her resolution not to, she walked to the kitchen window and peered down the lane to see if her aunt and uncle might be coming toward the house. They weren't.

Ellie's mind churned with questions about her father. Nobody would talk about him when she was a child. What did his voice sound like? Was he tall and burly, like Uncle Luke? Or skinny, like Uncle Elwood? She plunged the mop back into the bucket with more force than necessary, splashing the hem of her apron. Ellie eyed the watery evidence of her afternoon's labors, and sighed. Now she'd never have answers.

She gazed out at the lane again. Matthew passed by, driving his team of Belgians harnessed to the box wagon he used for spreading manure. His return signaled suppertime. She hurried out the back door and emptied the bucket beside the steps. Then, drying her chapped hands on her apron, she ran up the stairs to check on Julia.

The baby's cheeks were pink with sleep when she rolled over and sat up in her crib. Ellie's heart lifted at the sight of Julia's radiant smile. "Mama's here." She swung her in the air, kissed her, then laid her on the bed to change her diaper. After dropping a fresh gown over Julia's head, Ellie carried her to a low chair next to the bedroom fireplace. Once settled she unbuttoned her bodice. "Let's get you fed before Papa comes in for supper."

While Julia nursed, Ellie watched the glowing coals. A single tongue of flame rose and bobbed from side to side, as though scouting for companions. Her mind jumped to her father's life in Texas. Did he regret leaving her? Was he lonely?

Then a new thought intruded. Maybe he remarried. Eyes wide, she stared unseeing at the flame. She could have brothers and sisters.

Ellie stood at the worktable in the kitchen and cut leftover venison into chunks for a meat pie. Each whack of the curved chopper emphasized her frustration with the unknowable portions of her father's life. She dropped the pieces into a deep crockery pan, then added salt pork, flour, and cold gravy. A crust, already rolled, waited next to the wooden cutting board.

She looked up when Matthew entered. "This'll be ready by the time the children are home from school." Ellie surveyed his manure-splotched trousers. "At least you left your boots outside. After you change, you can throw those pants on the wash pile by the door."

Matthew nodded. Glancing around the room, he said, "Looks mighty bright in here. You've been busy."

"I always clean on Fridays. You know that."

"Yes, but you usually have Ruby to help." He cupped a hand

around her shoulder. "I thought by now she'd be over her ruffled feelings."

"Aunt Ruby's ruffled feelings are the farthest thing from my mind at this moment." She stepped back and placed her hands on her hips. "I thought of something else this afternoon—what if my father remarried while he was in Texas? I could have family down there."

Matthew shook his head. "You don't."

"How do you know?"

He placed his hands on her shoulders, pressing hard as if to hold down her hopes. "Your Grandpa Long wouldn't be figuring to inherit anything if there'd been a wife and children."

Ellie shrugged his hands away. "Molly didn't inherit when her husband died. She was all but penniless when you brought her here from Missouri."

Matthew settled into a chair and pinched his lower lip. After a moment he said, "That was different."

"I want to know if I have brothers and sisters." She folded her arms across her midriff. "Will you help me?"

"It would be a fool's errand. You'll only be disappointed." He used his patient father voice. "I don't want to see you hurt. No good will come from digging around down in Texas for relatives who don't exist."

Ellie turned her back on him. No matter what he said, she was going to find out. She slid the meat pie into the oven and banged the door shut.

After the meal, the children remained at the cleared table to do their schoolwork. Matthew held Julia while helping Harrison memorize the names and capitals of all twenty-eight states. Jimmy and Johnny had their heads together over their arithmetic assignment, and Maria painstakingly copied the letters of the alphabet onto her slate. Ellie shook out the dishtowel and hung it on a peg near the stove, all the while listening to the soft murmur of her children's voices. At the same time, part of her mind wrestled with questions about her father's life. Questions that refused to go away.

She slipped into the chair next to Matthew and lifted Julia onto her lap. Looking over Maria's shoulder, she pointed to a reversed letter.

"Small dee and big dee have their backs to each other." She wrote the two letters on the slate. "Like this."

Maria beamed and copied her. "This way?"

"Exactly so."

When Harrison finished reciting, Matthew turned to Ellie. "I need to go to town tomorrow."

Mentally she started a list of things she wanted to do in Beldon Grove, beginning with a visit to the cemetery. Then she'd go to Molly's and see if Molly had heard of Brazoria County in Texas.

When she opened her mouth to speak, Matthew held up his hand to stop her. "It'd be best if I went alone." He pushed back his chair and stood. "I clean forgot about calling on Marcus Beldon this week. What with everything that happened on Monday—"

Imperceptibly, Ellie shook her head.

"What happened on Monday, Papa?" Harrison asked.

"Never mind." Matthew turned back to Ellie. "I won't be gone long."

Ellie sighed, disappointed. "Will you bring Molly back with you?"

Matthew took special care with his appearance on Saturday morning. No sense offending Marcus Beldon by showing up looking like a farmer.

When he came downstairs, Ellie had her sleeves rolled up and was kneading dough for the day's baking. She brushed a stray wisp of hair from her forehead with the back of her hand. "You promise you'll bring Molly and Lily to visit when you return?"

"If they can come." He looked at Maria who sat watching Julia play with a ball of yarn. "That all right with you, young'un?" He knew it would be. Five months younger than Maria, Lily was an infant during the time Molly lived in their home following her husband's death. The two cousins had grown up as best friends.

"Oh yes, Papa." Maria's eyes shone. "We'll have such fun."

Smiling, Matthew left the kitchen. A gust of cold wind caught him when he stepped out of the shelter of the house. He grabbed at his hat, looking up at the deceptively blue sky. "March is going out like a lion this year!"

By the time he stopped the wagon in front of Bryant House, a handful of clouds had bunched on the western horizon. Pausing on the steps of the hotel, Matthew brushed stray bits of straw from his black trousers and straightened his hat. Then he turned the polished brass knob on the heavy oak door and entered the reception area.

Like most of the townspeople, he'd watched the hotel being built. He heard snatches of conversation regarding plans for its cosmopolitan fittings, but once the building was complete, he'd had no reason to visit. Now he noticed how the shining bead board wall paneling harmonized with a tan-colored floor cloth. An intricately designed fretwork arch curved over the hotel keeper's desk at the rear of the room.

A man dressed in a russet-colored jacket and checked waistcoat walked around the desk when Matthew entered. "Are you in need of accommodations?"

His haughty tone grated on Matthew's nerves. "Would Mr. Beldon be available?"

"Ah yes." The clerk smoothed the burgundy cravat tied around his neck. "The Beldons are in room four. Would you like me to announce you?"

"If you don't mind."

The clerk pointed to a room that opened to their left. "You may wait in the parlor." He strode down the hallway that led to the rear of the first floor.

Matthew entered the area indicated, again taking in the richness of the appointments. A large divan faced a screened fireplace, in which burned a low fire. Two matching lounge chairs covered in moss green velvet sat under the heavily draped windows. Glancing at his boots, he noticed to his horror that a rim of mud encircled the sole of his left boot. He grabbed his handkerchief and was trying to clean the grime when he heard voices approaching from the reception area.

He tucked the soiled cloth into his back pocket and turned in time to see Marcus Beldon enter the parlor.

"Reverend Craig." He sounded annoyed.

"Mr. Beldon." Matthew held out his hand.

Beldon grasped it with the same enthusiasm he might use if he were offered a dead catfish. "I expected you to come sooner."

"I apologize. Family matters kept me at home."

Marcus Beldon led the way to the seating in front of the fire. Choosing one of the lounge chairs, he lowered his bulk into it. "Sit down, Reverend. I'll try not to take up too much of your time."

He seemed completely at ease in the comfortable surroundings. No, not at ease—in charge. Matthew sat at one end of the divan. For a long moment, the two men regarded one another in silence.

Matthew leaned forward and rested his hands on his thighs. "You wanted to talk about Beldon Grove?"

"In a way." The big man cocked his head and studied Matthew. "I found your choice of sermon topic curious. I take it you're opposed to a performance of Shakespeare being held here?" He leaned forward, smoothing the finely woven fabric of his dove-colored trousers as he did so. "Do you think it's your place to stand against a cultural event taking place in this town?"

Matthew's mind flashed to Ben's warning. *If you preach against a Shakespeare play, you'll sound like a fool.* His cheeks warmed.

Beldon's fingers drummed against one knee. "My father's intention was to establish an outpost of eastern refinement here on the prairie."

"Obviously, your father abandoned that vision when he left here fourteen years ago."

"He left, true." Beldon's fingers continued drumming. "But he did not abandon his dream. On his deathbed he instructed me to come here and see that it's carried out."

"With all respect, sir, it doesn't matter who your father was. You are a newcomer here and cannot be expected to begin imposing your will against that of the community."

"The community's will? Or yours, Reverend Craig?" Beldon stood, hulking over the seated Matthew. "So that there's no misunderstanding between us, you must realize that the future of Beldon Grove is my rightful heritage. You'd do well to remember it."

Matthew pinched his lip and forced himself to remain calm. "Are there any other items you wish to discuss? If not, I must be about my business."

"I won't keep you, then. Mrs. Beldon and I look forward to

attending your church again tomorrow." He smiled. "It's such a change from what we were used to in Virginia."

Matthew noticed Zilphah Beldon near the entrance to the parlor staring at her husband with a puzzled expression. She didn't look pleased at what she'd overheard. He wondered how long she'd been standing there.

When Matthew left the hotel, he fought the urge to slam the door behind him. His temper didn't improve when he noticed a printed broadside attached to one of the porch supports. In elegant script it announced that Shakespeare's *Macbeth* would be performed in the Bryant House ballroom on Friday, May 15. His mouth turned down, remembering Beldon's words. His father's vision indeed. His rightful heritage. As though the community had been waiting with bated breath for him to arrive.

He urged Samson northward, past the blacksmith's forge and out onto the prairie. Matthew's hands shook with suppressed rage. More than anything, he wanted to go back to the hotel and drag Marcus Beldon out the door and onto a coach heading east. He hadn't felt this strongly about anything since arguing with his father over the older man's refusal to free his slaves. Then, Matthew had stormed off his family's Kentucky farm on his eighteenth birthday, and turned his passion toward the saving of souls, both black and white.

Now he slowed Samson to a walk and turned him onto a frost-blasted verge of dead grass. The chill wind made his eyes water. Matthew climbed off the wagon and swiped moisture from his cheeks. His heart pounded. *Lord, take away my anger. I know it's wrong.* He waited, drawing slow, deep breaths until his pulse settled to a normal rhythm.

Other thoughts filtered into his mind. He knew Ellie would ask him what Beldon wanted. Considering all the events of the past week, he decided she didn't need any more worries. He'd keep the conversation to himself.

True to his earlier promise, Matthew stopped at his sister's before going home. When he opened the door, he saw Molly and Luellen busy with bread making.

"Matt." Molly hurried over and wrapped him in a floury hug. "Where's Ellie?"

"Waiting for you." He grinned at her vivacity. Her home was filled with laughter and activity no matter what time he happened by. "Want to come out for a visit?"

"Yes indeed. Just let me tell Karl where I'm going." She wiped her hands on her apron and hurried down the hall toward his office.

Matthew walked to the work table where Luellen stood shaping dough into loaf-size chunks. The rich aroma of flour leavened with warmed yeast filled his nostrils. His niece gave him a welcoming smile and returned to her task.

"Those look just right." He patted her back. "Your mama's doing a good job of teaching you."

Luellen blushed. "Next week she said I could do the whole job by myself if I wanted to."

"You be sure to bring a loaf to church then. I'll look forward to sampling your work."

Eight-year-old Lily ran across the kitchen. "Can I go with you, Uncle Matt?"

"Sure can. Maria wouldn't let me in the house without you." Smiling, he tweaked one of her dark braids. He looked up when Molly returned, carrying a shawl. "Ready?"

She nodded, then paused next to Luellen and pointed at the

loaves arranged on a baking pan. "As soon as those are doubled, pop them in the oven. Be sure you get it plenty hot first."

"I will. I know how."

Molly leaned over and kissed her cheek. "I'll be back before suppertime." She turned toward the door, then stopped. "I almost forgot. James brought in a washtub full of honey again this morning. I want to take some to Ellie and the children." She pulled the tub out from under the table. "I swear that boy has learned to think like a bee. I just pray he doesn't . . ."

"What?" Matthew asked.

Molly cast a meaningful glance at her daughters. "Nothing."

With a long-handled spoon, she dug a thick wedge from the honeycomb and placed it in an empty stoneware container. When she pulled the spoon away, a golden thread of syrup remained at its tip, spinning downward in a slow spiral.

6

Ellie and Molly sat across from each other at the kitchen table, the aroma of baking bread swirling around them. The first browned loaves had come from the oven and cooled on a work surface against the back wall.

At the far end of the table, Maria and Lily pushed their chairs together to form a mutual lap on which baby Julia bounced and wiggled.

"Mama, can I give Julia a bite of bread and honey?" Maria asked, looking at the plate of fresh bread resting next to Molly's container of honey. "She'd like it."

"You would too, I expect." Ellie smiled at her.

"And some for Lily?"

"Of course."

Ellie walked over to the girls. She spread two soft slices with honey, cutting off a tiny corner and trimming the crust for Julia. "When you finish, you can take the baby upstairs—but be very careful with her."

Holding the triangle of bread toward her sister's mouth, Maria said, "We will, I promise."

Ellie resumed her seat and bit into her own piece of honey-soaked bread. Its heavy sweetness filled her mouth and trickled down her throat. Sighing with satisfaction, she swallowed and took another quick bite. "What were you saying about James?" She pitched her voice low so the girls wouldn't overhear.

"He wants to enlist in the militia and go fight against Mexico." Molly's expressive green eyes clouded with worry as she spoke.

Ellie dropped her unfinished slice onto her plate. "You can't let him. He's too young."

"He's sixteen. He thinks he's old enough." A tear formed in the corner of Molly's eye and slipped down her cheek. "Karl thinks if we wait, he'll forget about it, but I don't believe he will. You know how stubborn James is when he's fixed on an idea."

Ellie nodded, remembering James's accident several years earlier and his subsequent determination to overcome the loss of sight in his left eye. "But Mexico? I thought that was all settled. Matthew hasn't said anything about a war."

"James saw an article in last week's *Illinois Monitor*. President Polk says it's the United States' destiny to enlarge her borders." Molly shook her head. "Men and their wars!" She swiped at her tears with a corner of her apron. "According to the story, the Mexicans haven't stopped fighting us down in Texas, despite its becoming a state last year. The President thinks we should send them packing once and for all."

Texas. Ellie opened her mouth to tell Molly about the letter from Grandpa Long, then closed it. She'd wait for a better time.

Molly drew her mug toward her with quivering hands and stared into its depths. "After enduring all the months when Franklin was missing, I can't face the thought of losing James. It's too much to bear." She cupped her hands over her mouth and rocked back and forth, shoulders hunched.

Ellie reached for Molly's wrist. "Let's pray—"

Loud giggles interrupted her. She swung her head toward the girls.

"Mama, look at Julia! She's got her hands stuck together." Maria pointed at her baby sister, then collapsed into a fit of laughter.

Julia struggled to pull her clasped hands apart. Her face was coated with a layer of honey. Tendrils of hair had plastered themselves to her cheeks. Ellie ran around the table but stopped short of lifting the sticky child from the girls' laps.

She glared at Maria, hands on hips. "Whatever did you do?"

"I didn't do anything. We were feeding Julia spoonfuls, and she just reached into the dish and scooped up some of the comb." On closer inspection, Ellie detected flakes of beeswax embedded in Julia's curls.

Molly joined her, eyes still shiny with tears. "Quite a mess. Lily, you're as much to blame as Maria. You're both supposed to be watching her."

Ellie leveled her index finger at Maria. "You and Lily get a basin and warm some water. Now. You're going to spend the rest of your visit washing Julia and getting all that honey out of her hair."

The following Saturday, Ellie worked at her baking with an anxious ear tuned toward the upstairs bedroom. Over the past few days Julia's appetite had disappeared. This morning Ellie noticed that when Julia lay on her back her legs flopped apart like a frog's. Nothing she tried had helped—not even her never-fail spring tonic laced with honey.

She shoved the last loaves of bread into the oven and hastened up to the bedroom. When she peeked into the crib, Julia's heavy-lidded blue eyes stared up at her. Ellie fought to keep rising panic at bay. She felt the baby's forehead. No fever.

Ellie lifted her from the crib, supporting the child's blonde head with her left hand as she would for a newborn. Julia drooped in her arms like a heavy rag doll. She sat in the rocking chair and untied her bodice for the baby to nurse. Julia hadn't eaten since yesterday, and Ellie's engorged breasts ached. Julia mouthed at the nipple, then rolled her head to one side.

Cold prickles coursed over Ellie's body. She tugged her bodice closed. Cradling Julia, she ran down the stairs to the kitchen.

"Maria. Run get Papa." She pointed toward the barn. "He's out there. Tell him Julia's worse. He needs to fetch Dr. Karl right away."

Maria dashed out the back door, leaving it standing open. A cloud of smoke issued from around the firebox on the stove. Ellie kicked the door shut with one foot and paced the room while she waited for Matthew.

"Please, oh please, God, make her well," she murmured as she walked between stove and table.

Julia whimpered, her usual alert expression muted. She looked half asleep.

Ellie stopped pacing when Matthew pounded into the room. His eyes locked on Julia. "How is she?"

Shaking her head, Ellie blinked back stinging tears. "She's weaker than she was this morning. We need Karl to come out."

Matthew put an arm around Ellie and the baby and pulled them close. "I'll be back quick as I can." His beard scraped her face when he kissed her temple.

"Hurry!" Ellie knew it would take almost an hour to ride the two miles to town, fetch the doctor, and return. "Please, God, let Karl be in his office." Her stomach clenched as she fought fear-induced nausea.

She slumped in the kitchen rocker. "Mama's here," she whispered against Julia's silky hair. "Uncle Karl's coming to take care of you." Her foot tapped against the floor as the chair rocked back and forth. "You're going to be right as rain in no time." After she ran out of words, she hummed a lullaby.

Maria busied herself around the room, taking baked bread from the oven and sweeping spilled flour off the floor. Between chores she paused beside Ellie's chair and dropped kisses on Julia.

Ellie's eyes rested on her older daughter. "You're my good right hand. Thank you for helping."

Maria's blue eyes shone at the compliment. She ducked her head. "You're welcome, Mama." After a pause she said, "Julia's not going to die, is she?"

"No! Don't even think it."

The words had no sooner left her mouth when they heard a hesitant tap at the door. Maria opened it to find Aunt Ruby on the threshold.

Ellie gasped. The sight of her aunt broke the dam that had been holding her tears at bay. "I'm so glad to see you," she choked between sobs.

Aunt Ruby tossed her shawl over a peg near the door and bustled to the rocker. "Matthew stopped by and told us about Julia. Arthur's tying the horse to the hitching rail. He'll be right in."

She bent over the chair and kissed Ellie's cheek. Her arms reached out to take the baby, but in an unthinking reflex Ellie pulled Julia closer to her chest.

"No."

A shadow of hurt darkened her aunt's face. "I won't harm her. Surely you know that."

Ellie brushed at her tears and gazed down at the baby in her arms. Even the commotion of having someone new come into the room failed to attract Julia's interest. Her head lolled against her mother's shoulder.

Ellie spoke in a ragged whisper. "I can't let her go."

After an impulsive stop at the Newberrys', Matthew urged his horse to a gallop. He hadn't planned to detour to their house, but when he approached their lane he felt impelled to ask Ruby's help. The question in Ellie's eyes when he left spoke more clearly than words.

Now he slapped at his horse's side, trying to get more speed out of an animal that was already running full out. Christ's words on the cross filled his mind. *My God, my God, why hast thou forsaken me?*

"I've served you faithfully since I was eighteen years old." Matthew bargained over the thumping of hooves. "Please. Don't take this child from us." Sky the color of sharpened iron closed over his head. If there was comfort from heaven, he didn't feel it.

When he reached town he turned his horse right on Adams Street and reined to a stop in front of Spengler's house. A quick glance at Karl's horse standing in the stable told him the doctor was probably there, and not out on a call. Matthew sprinted around the corner of the house and burst into Karl's office.

Startled, Karl turned away from a microscope poised over a rectangular slip of thin glass. "Matt. Take a look at—" He stopped. "What's wrong?"

"It's Julia. She's taken a bad turn. Can you come?"

He pushed his chair away from the low table at which he had been working. "Of course." He opened the door leading to the living quarters and hollered down the hall. "Molly. I'm off to Matthew's. Baby's sick."

She hurried down the hallway, concern in her eyes. "Oh no. What is it?"

"We don't know." Matthew crushed his hat brim in his hands.

"Shall I come with you?"

"Best stay with the children," Karl answered. "I'll come get you if it's needful."

He seized his brown leather satchel and followed Matthew into the chill April afternoon.

◦

When the two men stopped their horses in the Craig farmyard, Matthew noted with thankfulness the presence of Arthur Newberry's horse and buggy tied behind the house. He hadn't been altogether sure whether Ruby would be willing to mend the rift between them and make the trip to see her niece.

Karl dismounted and followed Matthew through the back door.

Ellie raised her head, desperation in her eyes. "Thank God you're here." She held Julia toward Karl, still supporting the child's head.

Matthew saw that nothing had changed in the time he'd been gone. Their baby drooped in her mother's grasp, her blonde brilliance dulled.

Karl crossed the room and took Julia in his arms. "Someone bring a cloth for the table. I want to examine her here where the light's good."

Ruby ran upstairs and returned carrying a dark blue coverlet, which she flipped over the tabletop. She looked at the doctor. "Anything else?"

"Not now." He laid Julia on her back, pulling her nightgown up to her chin. The child's legs flopped open. "How long has she been sick?" he asked Ellie.

"It started a couple of days ago with her not wanting to eat. Then I noticed that she wasn't . . . uh, needing her diaper changed."

Ellie put out a shaky hand and stroked the blonde wisps that fell across Julia's forehead.

Karl raised the baby's knee and then let go of it. As soon as he moved his hand away, her leg dropped back into its sprawled position. "What about this?"

"Just since this morning." Ellie's voice quavered.

Matthew moved closer and put an arm around her. Arthur and Ruby stood behind him, Ruby's hands resting on Maria's shoulders. As one, they searched the doctor's face for a sign of good news.

Karl ran his hands over Julia's body, lifting each arm in turn. He tested her vision by moving his finger in front of her face. Placing his ear against her chest, he listened to her heartbeat. Finally he pushed one of his knuckles gently into her mouth.

"Why are you doing that?" Matthew asked.

"To see if she'll suck it." He shook his head. "She didn't."

He drew Julia's gown back over her feet. "She didn't get into anything outdoors, did she? Maybe putting leaves in her mouth?"

Ellie looked offended. "Of course not. I watch her very carefully. You know that."

Matthew studied his wife's face. She looked more pale than Julia. Her blue eyes were reddened with fatigue.

He knew he'd have to be the one to ask the question. "Well, Doc?"

"Could be brain fever—I don't know."

"Is she going to get better?"

"I don't know that, either." Karl scrubbed his fingers across his face. "I'm sorry."

After Karl left, Ellie carried Julia upstairs to the bedroom and sat with her in the low chair next to the fireplace. Laying her head

59

against the baby's soft curls, she rocked and hummed. Julia's eyes drooped shut. Her body relaxed.

The door creaked on its hinges. Ellie glanced up and saw Aunt Ruby hesitating on the threshold.

Ellie lifted a finger to her lips and whispered, "She's sleeping."

"That's good." Aunt Ruby kept her voice low. "Doc said rest would be the best thing to bring her around." She tiptoed into the room and perched on the edge of the bed. "What can I do to help? Do you want me to sit with her?"

Ellie shook her head. With the baby's eyes closed, and her body tight against Ellie's, she didn't look sick at all. But as soon as she was placed in the crib, the illusion disappeared. Julia's head rolled to one side, her limbs splayed as though she had no bones.

Fear rose in Ellie's throat like bile. She turned toward the door, motioning Aunt Ruby to follow.

When they were in the hallway, Aunt Ruby opened her arms and Ellie pressed into her embrace, clinging to her the way she had as a little girl. "I'm so frightened. I just can't lose Julia."

"Don't talk nonsense, child. You know how quick young'uns come back from sickness."

Ellie backed up a step. "I know how quick they succumb too." Memories of her three precious babies filled her mind—tiny, pale bodies laid in small coffins. So quiet, so cold.

Aunt Ruby nodded, sympathy written across her face. "Yes, dear, I know you do." She took both of Ellie's hands in hers. "But for your sake, you need to trust that she's going to be perfectly restored."

Seeing her aunt's reassuring expression, Ellie allowed herself to feel a sliver of hope. Aunt Ruby's pragmatism annoyed her at times. Now she saw it as full of promise.

"I'll go down and cook supper. You stay here if that's what you want. I'll fix you a tray." Briskly, with a "that's settled" air, Aunt Ruby trotted down the stairs into the kitchen.

Before Ellie closed the bedroom door, she heard a clamor of voices as the boys returned from woodcutting. It sounded like they were each talking at once, asking about Julia.

"She's sleeping nicely," Aunt Ruby said, her voice clipped. "If you boys will keep quiet, she'll be able to continue."

Ellie shut the door on her family and took up her vigil beside the crib.

7

Ellie stood close to the open grave, her aunt and uncle on one side and her husband on the other. Their four children clung together next to Matthew. She heard them sniffle while Mr. Wolcott read a brief funeral message from a thick Bible held in his right hand. Matthew's body shook with silent sobs, but Ellie hadn't been able to cry since the night Julia died.

"'Suffer the little children to come unto me, and forbid them not: for of such is the kingdom of God,'" Mr. Wolcott read. He turned toward Matthew and Ellie. "Julia has been spared all the pain that goes with life on this earth. She's safe in the arms of Jesus."

His words buzzed in her ears like so many bees. She couldn't follow the service. Her only thought was to get home and crawl into bed, away from the reach of the well-meaning townspeople who surrounded them.

Mr. Wolcott handed her a small spade, a gesture signifying the close of the service. Ellie pushed the spade into the pile of earth in front of her, quivering both with emotion and lack of food. She flung a shovelful onto the white wooden coffin resting at the bottom of the grave. The damp soil landed with a hollow thunk.

She turned to hand the tool to Matthew and couldn't find him. A blanket of gray obscured everything around her. The hole in the earth disappeared, and she felt herself float away to someplace warm and quiet.

☙

When Ellie opened her eyes, she lay on the front seat of their wagon. Matthew's worried face stared down at her. "The sun shouldn't be shining today," she said. "Funerals are meant to be dark."

He turned his head, speaking to someone out of her range of vision. "She's awake."

Behind him, Aunt Ruby's voice responded. "Glory be." The wagon jiggled as she climbed up beside her niece. "You like to scared us half to death, child."

Ellie pushed herself up on one elbow. Her children were clustered on the rear seat.

"Mama?" Maria leaned forward. "Are you all right now?"

She reached up and touched her daughter's cheek. "Yes, I think so. I don't know what happened."

Aunt Ruby hovered next to her. "You caused quite a stir. You've been out for some time."

"I have?" It felt like mere seconds had passed since she held the shovel at the burial site.

"At least five minutes."

Ellie noticed a knot of townspeople lingering nearby. Matthew's fists clenched when Mr. Beldon detached himself from the group and walked to the wagon.

"Reverend Craig. I wonder if I may be of assistance." He gestured toward the edge of the cemetery, where a plum-colored phaeton waited in the dappled shade of a hickory tree. "Mrs. Beldon and I would be pleased to carry your wife home in our conveyance. It's far more comfortably appointed than your wagon."

The links on his golden watch chain shot sparks of light across Matthew's face. "At such a time, I'm sure her well-being is foremost in your mind."

Ellie listened to him, dazed. Why would a stranger intrude on a family matter? She glanced in the direction of Beldon's carriage. The phaeton's folding cover had been raised, hiding his wife from view.

Matthew cocked his head toward the man. "Thank you for your kind offer. Mrs. Craig is fine right where she is." His voice sounded as cold as the gravestones surrounding them.

Mr. Beldon nodded. "As you wish." He lifted his hat toward Ellie. "Please accept my condolences." He strode toward his carriage, not pausing to speak to any of the few families still gathered in the cemetery.

"It was nice of him to offer," Aunt Ruby said.

Shooting her an annoyed look, Matthew untied Samson and guided their wagon toward home.

Ellie sat up in bed and gazed around the room. Afternoon sunshine fought its way through closed curtains, highlighting the rocking chair resting next to the empty crib. Head aching, she stood and walked to the west-facing window, noting the path her gown left in the dust where it brushed the wooden floor. Below her, several pairs of boys' pants flapped on the clothesline. She closed her eyes and rubbed her forehead. Laundry on the line meant it was probably Monday. What had happened to Saturday and Sunday?

She opened the bedroom door and stepped into the hallway. The house smelled faintly of soap and warm turpentine. Ellie crept to the top of the stairway and peered down into the kitchen. The copper wash boiler steamed unattended on the rear of the stove. Floorboards creaked on the porch. Curious, she descended the stairs to open the back door.

Aunt Ruby turned from the wooden tub where she'd been scrubbing what looked like one of Matthew's shirts. "What're you doing out here in your nightdress? And barefoot?"

Looking down, Ellie saw her aunt was right. "I don't know."

Aunt Ruby dropped the sodden garment into the washtub. "Let's go in." She wiped her hands on her apron. Sliding an arm around her niece, she guided her to the table. "Sit. I'll bring you a cup of broth."

Ellie obeyed, the fog in her head beginning to evaporate. "Where are the children?"

"Molly has them at her house. They've been there since . . . since we laid Julia to rest." Aunt Ruby folded her arms together, squeezing them across her middle. "Matthew's out with Arthur. They're doing the plowing."

Ellie glanced around the familiar kitchen, noticing that Ruby had set the milk to rise under the window instead of on the worktable. The pans were covered with one of Ellie's best linen towels.

When Aunt Ruby set the cup in front of her, Ellie asked, "How long have you been here?"

"Just today? Or since the burial Saturday?"

"Both," Ellie said, half afraid of the answer.

Her aunt slid out a chair and sat. "Two days, off and on. Today, since midmorning. Sunday, all day."

"I don't remember anything about Saturday afternoon or Sunday."

"You slept. That's all. Just slept. Best thing for you, if you ask me." She squeezed Ellie's hand.

Ellie lifted the cup and took a sip of broth. The hot liquid burned her lips. She blew on the surface and tried another swallow, then pushed it away. "I shouldn't be down here like this. Someone might come." She jumped to her feet. "I'll get dressed, and be back in a few minutes."

"I'll be here."

Ellie paused on the bottom step as memories flooded back. She swayed and gripped the newel post. Little Julia. Her inability to protect her from illness. Her blonde baby lying in the cemetery next to her three other infants. Ellie thought of the children staying at Molly's. Guilt swept over her. She wasn't even being a proper mother to the ones God allowed her to keep.

Matthew removed his straw hat and wiped sweat from his forehead. "Looks like Ruby got the wash hung out." He glanced at Arthur. "Don't know what I'd of done without her these past couple of days." He glanced at the bald man bobbing along beside him. "Or you either, truth be told."

"Glad to have a chance to help out." Arthur lowered his voice, although they were still several yards from the house. "Me and Ruby've been heartsick at the way things turned out for you and Ellie. Losing Julia wasn't in no way a blessing—don't get me wrong." He glanced anxiously at Matthew. "But it did give us a way to make it up to you for deceiving her about her pa."

Tears stung Matthew's eyes at the mention of Julia. Right now he felt he'd lost his whole family. He missed the clatter of the older children in the house, but most of all he missed his wife's soft voice and smile.

Arthur spoke as if he'd been tracking Matthew's thoughts. "D'you think she's better today?"

Matthew shook his head. "I couldn't see any change when I looked in on her before dinner."

When they walked past the clothesline, a gust of wind caught at a damp shirt. One sleeve brushed against Matthew's beard. He put his hand over the spot, remembering the feel of Ellie's fingers on his face. He longed for the comfort of her touch.

They stopped at a bench beside the back door to remove their muddy boots. From the kitchen they heard women's voices. Matthew's head jerked up. He kicked off his boots and strode into the house.

Ellie stood beside the stove wearing a clean apron over her black dress. Her face looked thinner, and smudges like purple thumbprints stained the skin under her round blue eyes.

"Dearest." He drew her to him.

She leaned against his chest, and for a moment he stood motionless, the better to absorb her presence. But when he kissed the top of her head, she jerked away.

"Supper will be on the table in a minute." Her voice quavered. "Then would you get the children from Molly's? They belong here."

The following week, Matthew drove to Ben Wolcott's store with Ellie beside him. He stole glances at her as they traveled, hoping a peaceful trip away from the farm would rekindle a spark of affection between them. Over the past several days, she had stayed busy from sunrise to sundown, shining each room in the house, fussing over the children, cooking large meals. At night, she'd fall into bed exhausted and go right to sleep. He wished she'd recognize that he mourned Julia too.

When they reached the store, the first thing he noticed was a prominent handbill tacked to the front of the mercantile.

THE FORSYTHE TOURING COMPANY
PRESENTS
WILLIAM SHAKESPEARE'S
MACBETH
Friday, May 15th
!! Stagehands and Seamstresses Needed Now !!
Apply at Bryant House Hotel

He'd paid little attention to community affairs during Julia's illness. But now his fears about the play came rushing back. He'd let Ben preach for two Sundays and this was the result. Ben had completely ignored his wishes.

The door opened. Two women left the building deep in conversation, and didn't look up until they almost collided with Matthew and Ellie.

"Reverend. Mrs. Craig," one of them stammered. "So sorry for your loss."

The second woman nodded, and they hurried down the steps leading from the board sidewalk to the street.

Ellie stared after them. "They act like we've got the typhoid."

"That's the Sims sisters. You know how they are." Matthew pushed up his hat and rubbed his forehead. "I'll pay a call on them next week and find out what the trouble is."

When they entered the store, Ben greeted them from behind the counter. "Good to see you out, Mrs. Craig. What can I get for you today?"

"I'm looking for some calico to make a summer dress for . . ." Ellie's voice faltered.

Concerned, Matthew rested a hand on her shoulder.

She swallowed audibly. "For Maria. And I need some kitchen

supplies, as well." Ellie handed Ben a list and moved toward the back of the store where the dry goods were kept.

Matthew realized he'd been holding his breath, as though by not breathing he could direct all his energy on helping his wife through a painful moment. He exhaled with a whoosh and turned to Ben. "I see we're still in disagreement over those folks bringing a play to Beldon Grove. You have a new handbill posted outside."

"Aye-yuh." Ben placed Ellie's list beside the cash box. He met Matthew's gaze. "Figured you had more important things on your mind than a fight with me over something that's only going to last one night. Few more weeks they'll be gone and none of us will be the worse for it."

"Maybe the play will last one night, but what about the folks who'll be exposed to evil beforehand with all this stagehand and seamstress folderol? Young girls could be led astray."

As Ben opened his mouth to reply, Ellie called from the back of the room. "Mr. Wolcott, I need two dress lengths of this double pink calico."

Ben shook his head at Matthew and lifted a long-bladed pair of shears from under the counter, then walked back to where rolls of fabric were displayed.

Matthew folded his arms and watched while his friend measured and cut the patterned cloth. No matter what Ben thought, Matthew knew he was right.

8

"Will you stop at Molly's?" Ellie asked after Matthew untied Samson from the rail at the front of the store. "I don't feel I've properly thanked her for keeping the children for us after . . . well, for keeping the children." She blinked back tears, grateful that the broad brim of her bonnet hid her face.

"Be glad to." He turned Samson east toward Adams Street.

Ellie relaxed on the wagon seat, relishing the sunshine's warmth soaking into her shoulders. A light breeze carried the scent of lilacs from beyond a picket fence fronting a white clapboard house at the corner. She made a mental note to ask Mrs. Carstairs for a start off her lilac bush. She'd plant it as a memorial—without mentioning that fact to Matthew. His refusal to talk about Julia told her more strongly than words that he blamed her for their baby's death.

After tapping on the frame of the open door to signal their presence, Matthew and Ellie entered the Spengler cabin. The kitchen was deserted. An open box containing a cake of stove polish rested on the table, next to scattered brushes and a rag.

Agitated voices came from the direction of the room that housed Karl's medical practice.

Ellie cocked her head. "That sounds like Molly. Let's go around to the office."

"I don't know." Matthew hesitated. "Maybe we should leave them be."

"No. We're here. I want to see Molly." She turned just as the door at the end of the hallway banged open and Molly dashed toward them, sobbing. Karl strode a few paces behind her, distress written on every line of his face.

For a moment, Ellie stood rooted in place. Then she took a step toward her and laid one hand on her arm. "What's wrong?"

"It's James. He's run off to enlist in the militia."

"No." Ellie's hand flew to her mouth. "Are you sure that's where he's gone?"

Karl replied for his wife. "No doubt about it. This week's *Monitor* said Mexicans attacked our troops near the Rio Grande. As soon as James read that, all he could talk about was joining up." He grasped Molly's shoulders and drew her to his side. "Show them the note."

Sniffling, she took a wrinkled sheet of paper from her apron pocket and handed it to Ellie.

> Dear Mama and Papa Karl.
> I can't abide seeing our great country threatened. Me and two other fellows are heading to Texas to join in the fight against Mexico. Please don't be worried. You know how good I am with a rifle. I will write to you when circumstances allow.
>
> Your son James

"Oh, Molly." Ellie gazed into her sister-in-law's anguished eyes, then read through the note once more, hoping she'd missed

71

something. Texas again. It takes men and doesn't give them back. She returned the note to Molly. "How long has James been gone? Maybe you could catch up to him, bring him home."

Karl shook his head. "He's got a goodly start on us. He told us he was going to help with the planting on Russells' farm and wouldn't be home for a couple of days. Then a few minutes ago Molly found that message under the stove black." Karl's eyes narrowed. "James knew she wouldn't be cleaning the stove until today. He and Billy Russell must've had this planned. I'm surprised Billy's pa didn't stop them."

Tears slid down Molly's cheeks. "He probably told them he had our permission."

Ellie closed her eyes and fought off the desire to weep with her. Once started, she was afraid she wouldn't be able to stop.

"Your other children will be home from school soon," Matthew said. "You'll only upset them, carrying on like this."

Karl rested his chin on the top of Molly's head. "That's what I told her."

Matthew's remonstrance grated on Ellie's ears. Leaning close to Molly's ear, she whispered, "I know how you feel. Go ahead and cry."

Molly cast her a grateful glance, but took a handkerchief from her sleeve and wiped her eyes. She looked at Matthew. "Karl knows the girls will be upset anyway. Luellen in particular. She idolizes her big brother."

"I'm afraid Franklin will think he's already a hero," Karl said. He stroked Molly's hair. "We'll have to find some way to take the glory out of James's enlistment without overly frightening our daughters." He seemed to be talking to himself as much as to the group.

Matthew moved next to Karl. "There's nothing we can do right now to make James come home. But we can all join together in asking the Lord to be with him and protect him."

Ellie's mind slid sideways while he prayed. Besides considering James's whereabouts, she thought of her possible brothers and sisters living in Texas. *Lord, keep them safe if the fighting comes to their door. Give me the chance to know my family.*

◯

A week later, Jimmy and Johnny banged into the kitchen after school, their auburn hair wet with sweat. Ellie turned from the stove and smiled at the twins. Their enthusiasm for life lit the room like a row of candles.

"You look like you ran all the way home. Where's Harrison and Maria?"

Between gasps for breath, Johnny said, "They're down the road a ways. We wanted to be first to tell you."

"Tell me what?"

Jimmy pushed in front of his twin. "Franklin's got a job."

Elbowing him to one side, Johnny said, "As a stagehand."

"For that play," both boys said together. They made the word "play" sound like their cousin had hired on in Hades itself.

"Oh my word." Ellie dropped into her rocking chair.

"What do you think Papa will say?" Johnny asked.

"I have no idea."

Yesterday's sermon had hit on the evils of make-believe, and stage plays in particular. Matthew had thrown in references to the temptations performers placed in the path of vulnerable young people. She leaned forward in the chair and contemplated his possible reaction. Was the play really all that important to him? Or had he got himself out on a limb and was too stubborn to back down? She wished she knew.

Ellie paced to the window and stared out, arms folded across her chest, while the twins each dipped a cup of water from the crock next to the wall. Waiting for Matthew's response was like seeing clouds on the horizon. A storm was coming—she just didn't know how serious it would be.

Jimmy pulled a chair out from the table and straddled it, facing her. "Papa told us to help him with the corn soon's we got home. D'you think we should tell him?"

Ellie shrugged. "I don't see why not. He'll hear about it sooner or later."

After the boys bolted down slices of bread and honey and finished their water, they loped off to the cornfield with more eagerness than they might normally show. Ellie returned to the stove, wondering what could have motivated Molly and Karl to allow Franklin to become a part of a production that Matthew so vehemently opposed.

When he came inside for supper, his eyes snapped with anger. "The twins told me about Franklin. How could Karl and Molly do that to me?"

Ellie turned. "To you? I doubt you entered into it. This must be something Franklin wanted. They have to consider their children first."

"Since when do we do what our children want? We're the parents." His damp hair stood out from his scalp.

"Matthew, calm down."

"I am calm." He combed his hair back with his fingertips, then slid his chair away from the table and sat.

The children took their seats, eyeing their parents. Ellie placed a bowl of rabbit stew on the table, then thumped a pan of cornbread in front of Matthew.

"Will you say grace?"

While Ellie cleared the plates, Spenglers' buggy rolled to a stop behind the house.

Maria ran to the door and flung it open. "Did you bring Lily?"

Molly and Karl climbed the steps to the porch. "Not this time," Karl said. He poked his head inside the door and looked at Matthew. "I expect I need to throw my hat in first."

"Won't be necessary. You're welcome." His voice sounded gruff.

Ellie glanced from one man to the other. Matthew's jaw was set in a tight line and Karl looked equally determined.

"Bedtime, Maria." She watched while her daughter dawdled her way up the stairs and then turned back to their guests. "Do sit down, please. There's coffee left from supper if you want some."

Karl shook his head. "Not now. Thanks."

Matthew waited in silence until they were settled, then focused an outraged glare on Molly. "Of all people in Beldon Grove, how could you, my own sister, allow your son to be a part of this . . ." He grappled for a word. "This offense in God's sight."

Karl sat beside his wife, silent but obviously ready to speak up if she wanted him to.

Molly leaned forward, resting her forearms on the table. "First of all, I don't agree with you about this play being an offense. I've listened to you, and I've listened to Mr. Wolcott, and find I agree with him." She clasped her hands together. "Shakespeare is educational. They teach his works in colleges, Mr. Wolcott says."

A muscle twitched at the corner of Matthew's mouth. "By the time a young man is in college, he knows right from wrong. Franklin is, what? Fourteen? Hardly old enough—"

"We had to do something. He's been talking of running off to fight alongside James."

Ellie gasped. "Franklin going to war! God forbid."

"I agree," Karl said. "That's why we said yes when he asked if he could take this stagehand job." He tucked an arm around Molly's waist. "He'll unload wagons and drag props around until he's worn out, and maybe it will help him settle down."

Molly reached across the table and grasped Matthew's hand. "I'm sorry. I know how strongly you feel about this, but we're talking about *my* son. I'll do anything to keep him at home."

"We hoped you wouldn't take it too hard," Karl said, "seeing as Aunt Ruby is already involved."

Matthew jerked as though he'd been struck. "Ruby?" He turned to Ellie. "Did you know about this?"

Hand to her throat, Ellie shook her head. "She hasn't said a word to me." She frowned, recalling. "But I haven't seen much of her lately, either."

"How involved?" Matthew asked Karl.

"She's the seamstress. Ben says she's been at the hotel every afternoon since the notice went up."

9

After Molly and Karl left, Matthew strode to the edge of the corn-field. He leaned on the top rail of the fence and inhaled the earthy fragrance of freshly turned soil. Ordinarily he took pleasure in evening trips to survey his newly planted crops, but tonight he saw the furrows through a haze of dismay. His family acted as though it was his reaction they needed to worry about. He was just the messenger. Lifting his eyes to the indigo sky, he focused on the evening star. One star among thousands. He'd never felt more alone.

In better times, he'd have taken his worries to Ellie. She'd listen, and whether or not she offered advice, talking it out would have helped him. Matthew shook his head. Over the past month, he'd avoided broaching any subject that would cause her distress.

Several days after Molly's visit, Matthew sat at the kitchen table studying for Sunday's sermon while Ellie worked in the sitting room sewing Maria's dress. A plum-colored phaeton clipped past the window on its way to the front door. He recognized Beldon's vehicle. No one else drove a carriage that grand.

Matthew jumped to his feet, tucking his loose-fitting linen

shirt into his waistband. The thought crossed his mind to dash upstairs and change from his stretched-out black felt slippers into his Sunday boots, but he stopped himself. If it were Ben at the door, he wouldn't worry about his slippers. Why shine himself up for Mr. Beldon?

Ellie set her sewing aside and joined him at the door. Her blonde hair was braided and drawn back in a neat circle at the nape of her neck. A crisp white apron covered her black dress. With pride, he put an arm around her shoulders and opened the door at the first knock.

"Reverend." Marcus Beldon swept his hat from his head with a flourish. "And Mrs. Craig." He bowed in her direction. "I trust I'm not intruding. I wanted to exercise my team, and found myself out in your part of the county."

"We're pleased you stopped by." Matthew opened the door to the parlor and gestured toward twin upholstered settees positioned at either side of the cold hearth. "Please come in and rest yourself."

He waited for Beldon to be seated, then sat facing their caller. Ellie stood behind him. "Would you like some tea?" She directed her question toward Marcus Beldon.

"No, thank you. Anything from your lovely hands would be a delight, but I'll only be staying a short while."

Matthew glanced up to see a flush bloom on Ellie's cheeks at the man's flattering tone. "I notice Mrs. Beldon isn't with you."

"Unfortunately, she suffers from a sick headache and asked that I go out without her." The settee creaked as he shifted his weight. "She sends her regards." He paused, moistening his full lips with the tip of his tongue. "We are both extremely sorry for the loss of your beautiful child."

Matthew swallowed hard. The mention of Julia brought tears

to his eyes, which he fought to conceal. He darted another glance at Ellie.

Her eyes clouded. "Thank you. She *was* beautiful, and such a joy to me."

Beldon studied Matthew and then looked back at Ellie. "I understand this is the fourth time the Lord has called one of your children home." His features melted in sympathy. "What a tragedy for you."

Matthew stood and moved next to his wife, resting a hand on her shoulder. "Yes, it is tragic. But we must let the Lord do what seems good in his eyes." He cringed inwardly. *That sounded so pompous!*

Ellie tipped her head and scowled at him. At the same time, she shrugged her shoulder free of his grip. "It's kind of you to call," she said. "I'm sure the two of you have more to discuss than our personal losses." She nodded at their guest. "If you'll excuse me?"

He rose and bowed in her direction. "Certainly. Always a pleasure, Mrs. Craig."

After Ellie left the room, Matthew studied Beldon for a moment, uncertain how to proceed.

His guest saved him the trouble. "From last Sunday's sermon, I gather you're still opposed to culture in our little community?"

Matthew bristled. "If you call consorting with stage performers 'culture,' then yes, I am. I'm concerned that our young people will be led into a life of corruption, or worse."

"That's hardly likely to happen. My father—"

"Your father's not here. You are. Please speak for yourself."

Still standing, both men took a few steps from side to side like prizefighters facing off. Beldon's immaculately pressed suit and dove-gray silk waistcoat gleamed in the soft light that flowed through the uncurtained windows. He focused his dark-lashed eyes directly on Matthew.

"Very well then. I'm concerned that you are not the person to be leading a congregation. In addition to your misguided attempt to deny Beldon Grove the opportunity to see a classic Shakespeare performance, I noticed at church last week that you spent considerable time greeting your flock personally." He raised one eyebrow. "Are you sure that's proper? In the churches we attended in Virginia, the common people kept a respectful distance between themselves and men of the cloth. How can you expect to influence anyone to your way of thinking if you're no different than they are?"

Matthew bit the inside of his lip. "It's not my way of thinking, it's the Lord's way." He stalked to the front door and held it open. "I'm sorry you don't approve of how I treat my parishioners. What is suitable in the eastern states doesn't always travel well."

"Propriety always travels well, Reverend. You'd best keep that in mind."

After Beldon left, Matthew strode back to his papers and Bible on the kitchen table and flung himself into a chair. He stared at the page spread open before him. A red haze of anger blurred the printed words. He placed his elbows on the tabletop and buried his face in his hands, wondering what Marcus Beldon could possibly have against him.

He startled when Ellie spoke from the doorway.

"Wasn't it nice of Mr. Beldon to take time from his law practice to pay a condolence call?" She walked over to the worktable and poured cream from the morning's milking into a crock. "He's such a gentleman."

A faint smile rested on her lips.

Ellie leaned across the top of the cookstove and brushed blacking onto the cold surface as though she could scrub away the argument she'd had with Matthew the previous night. Each stroke of the brush protested his refusal to listen to her plea for help. She stopped polishing and stood motionless, trying to decide how to proceed.

Across the room, Aunt Ruby sat at the kitchen table with a swath of crimson fabric draped over her knees. As she plied a needle through the cloth she said, "Guess what I heard at the hotel yesterday?"

Ellie forced her attention to her aunt. "I expect you're going to tell me."

"Well . . ." The older woman shifted in her chair. "You know Mr. and Mrs. Beldon live there, don't you?"

Ellie nodded.

"Mr. Forsythe told me, in confidence of course, that it's Mrs. Beldon who holds the purse strings in that family. She's the one who pays the rent on their suite and on the parlor he uses for his solicitor work."

Ellie dropped the rag she used to polish the stove and faced her aunt. "How would he know that? Surely Mrs. Beldon doesn't confide in him." An image of Zilphah Beldon came to her mind. A mousy woman with a hunched back and a sharp tongue. It had crossed her mind more than once to wonder why a man as magnetic as Mr. Beldon married such an unattractive woman.

"Mr. Forsythe says her father sends bank drafts addressed to her for their keep. The desk clerk told him." Aunt Ruby's reply sounded defensive. "He's staying right there in the same hotel, for pity's sake. He can't help but notice how she orders her husband around." She lowered her voice to a confidential whisper. "Mr. Beldon's law practice in Virginia failed. She's giving him one more chance to make good."

Mrs. Beldon reminded Ellie of the biblical proverb, *"It is better to dwell in the wilderness than with a contentious and angry woman."* She turned to her aunt. "I feel sorry for Mr. Beldon. His wife seems . . . difficult. We shouldn't listen to empty gossip."

"I don't think it's merely gossip. Mr. Forsythe seemed quite sure."

Aunt Ruby's voice dropped to a softer pitch whenever she mentioned the owner of the touring company scheduled to present *Macbeth*. For a moment, Ellie studied her. Aunt Ruby's faded blue eyes were lit with fresh color and snap. Even her hair looked different. Instead of a severe center part with wings of hair slicked back over her ears, she had pulled some strands loose and curled them near her face.

"You look happy."

"I'm having a good time." Aunt Ruby anchored the needle in the fabric. Her eyes sparkled. "I feel part of something bigger than myself—important, I guess you'd say. I'm forty-six years old, and never done anything but be Arthur's wife. Down there at the hotel, Mr. Forsythe goes out of his way to include me in all their preparations." She flipped the cloak out in front of her and folded it while she talked. "You should see how busy everyone is. Those props are so heavy. It takes two men to tote them to the second floor. And the wardrobe. So much sewing to do. Mr. Forsythe says I'm the best seamstress they've ever had."

Ellie returned the brush to a box that held the cake of stove polish and screwed the wooden cover tight. She'd hoped for an opening to share her thoughts, but so far her aunt had done nothing but talk about Mr. Forsythe and the goings-on at the hotel.

Ellie cleared her throat, then blurted, "I have something to tell you."

Aunt Ruby set the cloak on the table. "What is it?"

Ellie hesitated. What if she sided with Matthew? "Uh, well, nothing."

"Come on. You can talk to me. Are you and Matthew having troubles?"

Ellie's cheeks warmed. "Why do you say that?"

"Things haven't been the same between you since . . . Julia passed on."

"It's more than Julia." She moved a chair forward and sat facing her aunt. Her words poured out, tripping over each other. "I believe my father remarried. I'm sure I have brothers and sisters somewhere in Texas. But Matthew won't listen when I talk about it."

Aunt Ruby closed her sewing basket and stared at Ellie. "What on earth makes you think he remarried?"

"A man needs a wife. Especially if he's homesteading land. He settled there twenty-five years ago. Surely in all that time he found someone to marry."

After a long moment, Aunt Ruby sighed and reached for Ellie's hand. "We would have heard. Besides, the letter didn't say anything about a wife." She squeezed Ellie's fingers. "Your family is right here. There's no need to pretend you have another one."

"I'm not pretending." Ellie pulled her hand away and stalked to the window, her back to her aunt. "I see it does no good to talk to you, either."

Footsteps clattered on the porch. Ellie turned at the sound of children's voices, glad of the distraction. She hurried toward the stove. "I need to get a fire going. They'll be wanting to eat soon."

Her children roared into the room, followed by Matthew. Harrison led the pack. "We did it, Mama. The last two acres are planted."

Jimmy pulled the dipper from the water crock and gulped several swallows. "Got done before noon too."

On her knees, Ellie poured live coals from a bucket into the firebox. "Good," she said, her voice muffled behind the stove door.

After the tinder caught and blazed, she placed kindling over the flames and stood. Out of the corner of her eye, she saw Matthew frown when he spotted the folded garment Aunt Ruby held.

She grasped the cloak to her chest and stood. "Time to head home. Arthur'll be wondering about his dinner." She pursed her lips. "One thing I can count on with Arthur—he's always hungry."

Maria ran to her. "Are you coming to hear us recite this evening? Mama made me a new dress and I memorized a *very* long poem."

"We'll see, precious. Might be I'll be busy at the hotel." Aunt Ruby laid the folded cloak on the table and hugged her great-niece.

After she left, Maria leaned against Ellie's side. Her blue eyes were wide with hurt. "Aunt Ruby always comes to Spring Recital. Doesn't she love me anymore?"

"Of course she does, but . . ." She stopped, at a loss to understand Aunt Ruby's actions. Bending, she kissed Maria's dirt-streaked face, then patted her bottom. "Go clean up. Dinner will be ready soon."

Ellie watched her daughter dash to the washstand on the porch, her thoughts still on her aunt's puzzling behavior.

The next afternoon, Matthew dropped Ellie off at Wolcott's Mercantile. "I'll stop by for our order after I call on the Sims family." His voice sounded distantly polite.

Ellie nodded, matching his distance with coolness of her own. "I'll be at Molly's working on her honeycomb quilt." She stepped onto the board sidewalk without waiting for his assistance.

After the wagon rolled away, she watched until he had turned the corner and headed north. Prairie wind blew dust from the wheels into her face, stinging her tear-filled eyes.

Blinking hard, she walked into the busy store. Conversation ceased the moment she entered. Several women turned their backs and busied themselves scrutinizing the merchandise. Ellie remembered the cool greeting she and Matthew had received from the Sims sisters the previous week.

She stepped up to the counter, keeping her head averted from the other customers, and handed Mr. Wolcott her list. "Nothing special today. Just flour, vinegar, and such. Matthew will pick it up later."

"I'll take care of it, Mrs. Craig." His gaze lingered on her. "You all right?"

"Just a little tired. We were late getting home last night."

Mr. Wolcott smiled. "Those youngsters of yours did themselves proud. Didn't miss a lick, no matter what the teacher threw at them."

Ellie warmed, remembering her children's perfect recitations. "Harrison had me worried once, but he came through." She met the storekeeper's eyes. "It was good of you and Mrs. Wolcott to be there."

"Wouldn't miss Spring Recital for the world. Without young'uns of our own, me and Charity kind of take an interest in all of them."

Tears threatened again at his kind tone. If she didn't leave soon, she'd break down in front of everyone. Wrapping her shawl tighter across her chest, Ellie backed away from the counter.

"Matthew will pick up our things later," she repeated, then hurried out the door.

The wind blew steadily from the west, pushing her along Jefferson Street in the direction of Molly's cabin. She clutched her swirling skirts as she passed Carstairs' picket fence and turned the corner onto Hancock.

"Mrs. Craig!"

Penelope Carstairs waved at her. "I have the slip you wanted from my lilac bush. Can you stop in for a moment?"

Ellie turned. "Of course. Thank you for remembering."

As she followed the buxom young woman, she glanced over at aromatic purple flowers covering the bush in one corner of the yard. A vision of a similar planting outside her kitchen window filled her mind.

Stopping on the porch, Penelope lifted a leafy shoot wrapped in wet burlap from a crock next to the door. "It's started to root. I hope it does well for you."

Ellie extended her hand to take the dripping bundle. "This will be lovely. I'm going to plant it as a memorial for our little Julia."

A closed expression came over Penelope's face. "Yes, your loss is most unfortunate. Surprising such a thing could happen in a preacher's family, isn't it? Makes one wonder."

A pain started near Ellie's heart and filled her chest. She stepped back, gripping the lilac shoot. "Wonder what?"

"Well, a preacher and all. Is it . . . a judgment?"

Darkness filled Ellie's vision. "Who's saying such things?"

Penelope's face reddened. "Uh, different folks. I don't believe it, of course."

Somehow Ellie got down the steps and out of Carstairs' yard. Walking as fast as she could without breaking into a run, she headed for her sister-in-law and sanctuary.

10

Ellie held her needle between trembling fingers and studied Molly's face. "You've already heard? Why didn't you tell me what people were saying?"

Molly's expression showed dismay but not surprise. "I didn't think it was worth repeating." She shook her head and gazed at Ellie across the quilting frame. "There've just been a few remarks here and there, far as I know. Karl and I wonder who started it."

Ellie knew her husband didn't deserve this poisonous accusation. He'd always been steadfast in his devotion to the ministry of their church. "Do you think Matthew knows what's being said about him?"

"I couldn't say. Why don't you ask him?"

"I can't."

"Why ever not? That's the best way to tackle a problem—head on." Molly's gold-flecked eyes shone with love and concern.

A moment's silence fell between the two women.

Ellie poked her needle into a six-sided patch of flowered cloth and joined it to an indigo hexagon already pieced to the quilt top. Then she sighed, abandoning her stitching. "Matthew and I seem to be at odds with one another right now."

"Is it about Julia?"

"That's a big part of it . . . but there's more." She tilted her chin upward and took a deep breath. Beginning with the letter from her grandfather, Ellie related how she learned of her father's recent death, the confrontation with Aunt Ruby, and then her own conviction that her father had left a wife and children somewhere in Texas. "Matthew thinks he's protecting me by refusing to make inquiries. And Aunt Ruby called it a fantasy." She noticed Molly's dumbfounded expression. "You don't believe they exist either, do you?"

"I . . . suppose it's possible." Molly tucked her needle into the fabric and pressed her fingers to her mouth, forehead wrinkled in thought.

"Possible, but not likely. Is that what you mean?"

"No, not at all." She leaned back, lips curved in a half smile. "Why don't you write your grandfather?"

Ellie's heart sang a song of gratitude.

Molly drew her chair closer to the frame. "Do you still have his letter?"

"No." The admission silenced the music in her heart. Ellie slumped and stared at her boots. "I threw it on the floor at Aunt Ruby's. She probably burned it weeks ago."

"Then ask Matthew if he kept the envelope." Molly sounded ready to take up the challenge. "Your grandfather's address will be on that."

"I told you. I can't. Matthew doesn't want to talk about my father."

"Maybe you can soften him up. You know, nice supper, early to bed. Then after . . ." Molly's face reddened. "Well, then ask him about it. When he's in a good mood."

Blood pounded in Ellie's ears. "I can't do that, either." She lowered her head and focused on joining a double pink hexagon to the growing pattern on the quilt top. "I haven't . . . been a wife to Matthew since Julia died. I'm afraid to. I couldn't bear to lose another baby." Dropping her voice, she looked at Molly. "How do you and Karl keep from having children? You've been married over six years."

"We don't keep from it." Molly bit her lower lip. "I just haven't conceived. We don't know why."

During the ride home, Ellie's mind circled the events of the afternoon. Molly's support of her theory about her father gave her new courage to pursue the quest for brothers and sisters. But her suggestion to inveigle Matthew into helping them left Ellie in despair. As sorry as she felt for Molly following their conversation, she felt sorrier for herself. She'd hoped for some answers, not more problems.

Matthew followed Ellie up the stairs, admiring the way light from the candle she carried accented the curves of her body. At twenty-eight, the promise of beauty she'd had when he married her had ripened into a lush, appealing softness.

He'd been patient for weeks, hoping Ellie would show some sign that she'd welcome his advances. Tuesday evening, when she claimed exhaustion yet again, he'd lost his temper with her and lashed out, accusing her of not being a proper wife to him. She huffed that if he was a better husband, he'd understand, then turned toward the wall and pulled the covers tight around her neck. Matthew shook his head at the memory.

Once in the bedroom, he stripped off his trousers and shirt and waited beneath the chilly linen sheets. Ellie stood with her back to him, dawdling with the buttons on her dress. At last she pulled the garment off and dropped her nightgown over her shift. Hands clasped behind his head, Matthew savored the vision of his wife's long blonde hair rippling across her shoulders. With practiced skill, she wove it into a long braid, then slid beneath the covers. His pulse quickened.

Rolling away from him onto her side of the bed, she emitted a deep sigh. "It's been a long day." The pillow muffled her voice.

"All we did was go to town." Matthew pressed near her, warming from the heat of her body. He turned toward her back and rested his hand on the roundness of her hip, waiting to see how she would react.

Ellie neither moved toward him nor away. Emboldened, he caressed her side gently from waist to knee. This time she tensed and resettled herself at the extreme edge of the bed tick. Drawing a deep breath, he moved closer. The feathers inside the tick ballooned up between them.

Pushing them flat with his arm, he again placed his hand on her hip, curving his fingers against her pelvic bone. "Ellie, dearest, it's been long enough."

She put her hand over his, squeezed his fingers, then slapped his hand down on the sheet. "Please. Stop it." She sprang up and faced him, her white gown illuminated by the moon glow that fanned across the room. "Can't we just share a bed, without . . . ?" He heard tears in her voice.

"How can you ask that of me? Of us?" He pushed himself upright, resting his back against the headboard. "It's not just me, Ellie. Be honest with yourself. Could you really be happy if we no longer shared physical love?"

"What else can we do?" She brushed a tear from her cheek. "I'm afraid if we have another baby, it will die too."

"Aren't you putting yourself in God's place? Whether we're blessed with more children or not is in his hands."

Her head jerked up. "Don't preach at me. I feel guilty enough as it is."

He looked at her, ethereal in the moonlight. His mind captured memories of their wedding night; his surprise at her willingness to become one with him. Matthew recalled a stolen time down by the creek shortly after Maria had been born, Ellie laughing as he pulled her down into the grass, her soft hair falling across his face. Pain twisted inside like a curved blade. He must have moaned aloud, because Ellie came to him and took his hand.

"If having me in the same bed is too difficult, I can share Maria's room," she whispered.

"You've given this a lot of thought, haven't you?"

"Yes."

"There's no need for you to leave. I promise not to approach you again."

During the night, moonlight surrendered to an oncoming storm. Heavy raindrops burst against the windows. Wind rattled the panes, trying to force its way into the house. Matthew sighed and rolled onto his left side, glancing at Ellie, who lay on the edge of the bed with her back to him. He listened to the rhythm of her breathing. It didn't sound like she slept, either. Flopping onto his back, he laced his fingers together behind his head and stared at the ceiling, wondering how much longer it would be until daybreak.

When he opened his eyes again, Ellie was no longer beside him. Her voice came from across the hall. "Stop fidgeting, Harrison. Let me fold your collar over your roundabout."

Despite his weariness, Matthew had to smile at the weekly struggle she had getting their youngest son buttoned into his short jacket and tidied for the Sabbath.

As he opened the bedroom door, Ellie moved past with her

hand resting on Maria's shoulder. She gave her husband an impersonal smile. "Breakfast is almost ready."

"I'll be right there." He watched her descend the stairs, thinking that to an outsider's eyes they would appear to be a normal family. Matthew sighed. If only they were.

The journey to church would have been quiet under any circumstances. Ellie and the children crowded together on the rear seat of the covered buggy in an effort to stay dry. Attempts at conversation blew away in gusting wind. Bundled in an oilcloth greatcoat, hat pulled low on his head, Matthew kept a tight hold on the reins as the horse splashed through muddy ruts in the road. He cast worried glances at his neighbors' plowed fields, trying to see whether the storm might be carrying off newly planted seeds. So far, the ground seemed to be absorbing most of the rainfall.

Although still stunned by his wife's decision, now a segment of his mind worried over the possibility that he might lose a good part of his spring planting. *Lord, your Word tells us not to be surprised by trials that come. You promise to lift us up again. Please let it be soon.* Rain drummed steadily on the top of the buggy, drowning out his prayer.

Pale light seeped through the narrow windows of the church. The room smelled of wet wool and leather, mixed with tallow smoke from candle sconces along the walls. Surveying the assembled townspeople, Matthew noted an unusual number of empty spaces on the benches. While he pondered whether to wait for latecomers, the door opened and Marcus Beldon ushered his wife inside, removed her cloak, and hung it on a peg in the vestibule.

Glad he'd delayed the extra moment, Matthew stepped to the pulpit and opened his Bible, then noticed five strangers had entered behind the Beldons. They were dressed far too elegantly to be locals. The man nearest to Beldon wore a suit the color of a raven's wing over a pearl gray waistcoat. A plum and gray cravat wrapped his shirt collar and ended in a bow tied under his chin.

By now, heads were craning toward the rear of the church. Making a conspicuous stir, Marcus Beldon ushered his guests to an empty bench. While they seated themselves, he crossed the aisle and found two vacant spots for himself and his wife. Curious whispers filled the room. From his seat, Beldon smiled and acknowledged glances sent his way with a royal nod.

Matthew cleared his throat, trying to direct the attention of the room to the morning's service. Gradually, people turned forward and an expectant silence filled the church.

"My text today is taken from the first chapter of Joshua. 'Be strong and of a good courage . . .'" Matthew's voice faltered. How could he exhort these people when he felt anything but strong and courageous? He glanced toward the rear benches. Beldon had his hand cupped over his mouth and was whispering something to his wife.

Swallowing, Matthew tried again. "'. . . for unto this people shalt thou divide for an inheritance the land, which I swore unto their fathers to give them.'" His voice grew stronger. "To the south of us, in the new state of Texas, we have brave citizens lining up to fight for land the Lord has already given into our hands." As he listed the similarities between the fight with Mexico and the Israelites' struggles to gain the land of Canaan, he felt lifted onto the Old Testament battlefields. Mothers in those days must have wept too, he told them, but their husbands and sons were fighting the Lord's battles.

Looking over the congregation as he spoke, Matthew saw Karl take Molly's hand. His gaze again drifted toward the strangers seated in the back.

Quickly, so he wouldn't be caught staring, Matthew returned his attention to the notes he'd placed next to his Bible. "The thing I want you to remember from this portion of scripture is that God gives the success. We don't do it on our own." He quoted other verses in Joshua to strengthen his point, expounding on how each one fit the country's current situation. The minutes slipped by. Then, pushing his notes aside, he said, "Locally, we are also involved in a battle. Not for territory, but for the moral purity of our citizens."

The group at the back sat up straighter, giving him their full attention. Beldon's chin jutted into the air and he folded his arms across his chest.

Matthew faltered at the hostility in the man's eyes. He hadn't planned to add these comments to today's sermon. Somehow, they were out of his mouth before he could stop them. He put both hands on the sides of the pulpit and leaned toward the congregation. "You have less than a week to make up your minds about this . . . perfor- mance that's going to take place at the hotel." He invested the word "performance" with as much scorn as he could. "Will you go the way of the flesh, or will you resist the devil?" He flipped to another verse in Joshua and concluded, "'As for me and my house, we will serve the LORD.'" Closing the Bible, he slapped the cover for emphasis. When Matthew knelt to deliver the closing prayer, he heard feet shifting and throats clearing at the back of the sanctuary.

Ruby was the first person to reach him after the service. "Mat- thew! How could you ride roughshod over those folks? They're visitors, for pity's sake."

He stared at her. "What do they have to do with anything?"

Instead of answering, she took his arm and tugged him toward the back of the church. A group had already formed around Marcus Beldon, seeming to hang on his every utterance. The five men who had entered with him stood to one side.

Ruby marched over to the dark-suited one Matthew had noticed from the pulpit. "Reverend Craig is my niece's husband." She sounded apologetic. "Matthew, this is Sorrel Forsythe. He and these other gentlemen are here to present *Macbeth* to our community."

Matthew had already put out his hand when she began her introduction. It hung in the air between himself and Sorrel Forsythe a moment too long.

"A distinct pleasure." Forsythe took Matthew's hand and gave it a limp shake. "We've heard much about you from Marcus, and now we finally meet." His hand felt soft, like a child's.

Glancing up, Matthew saw that Beldon and the other four actors had gathered behind Mr. Forsythe. Beldon watched him with a smirk on his face.

As he cast around in his mind for an appropriate response, Mrs. Beldon joined the group. To his surprise, her brown eyes conveyed sympathy.

"Thank you for giving us such a thought-provoking look at the conflict with Mexico." Her voice rang out clearly enough to be heard beyond their small gathering. "I can tell you've given it much consideration."

Her husband's face was a study in confusion. "Mexico? I thought he preached on the evils of Shakespeare."

She tapped his arm with a crooked forefinger. "You hear what you want to hear, Marcus."

Matthew took her hand. "Thank you for the kind words, Mrs.

Beldon. Mexico is a subject that has come close to our family these past weeks." He nodded at the coterie surrounding her husband. "Gentlemen. So glad you came to hear God's word."

As he walked toward his wife and children, Matthew heard Beldon snort, "Craig's word is more like it."

Trembling with suppressed anger, Matthew joined his family gathered next to the woodstove. His sermon sounded hollow to him now. *Trust in God and he will give the victory? I'm trusting. Where's the victory?* Glancing over his shoulder, he saw several members of the church listening to Beldon. Some darted quick looks in his direction, and as quickly looked away. Normally he enjoyed lingering after the morning's service to visit with townsfolk, but today he wished they'd all hurry home so he could leave.

Ruby appeared at Ellie's side. "Come with me for a moment, child. I want you to meet Mr. Forsythe."

Ellie raised her eyebrows questioningly at Matthew.

He folded his arms over his chest. "Go ahead. I'll wait here."

Arthur stood behind Jimmy and Johnny, warming his backside at the stove. A frown creased his normally placid expression.

When he caught Matthew looking at him, he shrugged. "Can't tell that woman anything. This seamstress thing is a passing fancy."

Matthew shook his head. "Having Ruby involved is an embarrassment—opposing something my wife's aunt has jumped into whole hog." Ben's warning echoed in his mind. *If you preach against a Shakespeare play, you'll sound like a fool.*

Arthur shoved his hands in his pockets and rocked back on his heels. "Don't worry over it. The whole thing will be over soon."

11

At breakfast Monday, Matthew glanced out the window, startled to see Ben drawing his buggy to a halt near the back porch. Behind him, fence posts steamed as they dried out from the previous day's soaking. Their neighbor jumped over several puddles on his way to the steps.

"Did Ben say anything to you about coming by this morning?" Matthew asked Ellie.

She shook her head. "He'll be late opening the store. It must be important."

He pushed back from the table and met his friend at the door. "Come on in—coffee's still hot."

"No thanks. I stopped by to walk your fields with you to see how much of your crop you've got left." Pointing at his mud-caked boots, he continued, "Just finished with my own. Don't look too bad, Lord be thanked."

Matthew stepped onto the porch, shoved his feet into his boots, and paused to tighten the laces.

Ben waited at the top of the steps. "Nice morning."

"Yup." Matthew led the way around the fence and out to his fields. Their footsteps squished over the sodden ground as they walked between muddy furrows of newly planted seed. "Looks like everything stayed put. I'd just as soon not walk the whole place. We'll do more harm than good, wet as it is."

"Aye-yuh, I think you're right."

The two men backtracked to the fence and leaned on the top rail. "Why are you really here? You've never dropped by to check my crops before."

Ben studied the toes of his boots for a long moment. Then he turned and met Matthew's eyes. "Something's happening in town that you should know about. Wish it wasn't me had to tell you."

Splinters of alarm pricked Matthew's skin. "I'm listening."

Ben pulled off his hat. The Macassar oil on his hair glistened in the sunlight. First he fiddled with his hat brim, then pulled a handkerchief out of his pocket and wiped his forehead.

"Are you going to tell me or not?"

"Folks are getting stirred up against you. I heard some of them talking about you in my store."

"Stirred up? Because of that play?" Matthew slapped his leg. "Good. They should be. Proves I'm doing my job."

"It's not the play, though maybe that's some of it." Ben kicked at a clump of grass.

"It's not like you to beat around the bush. Spit it out."

Ben stepped away from the fence. "They're saying Julia's death, and the other children before her, are a judgment from God. That you're not fit to preach his word."

Matthew's stomach rolled and he gulped hard to keep his breakfast down. He clutched Ben's shoulder. "Who? Who's saying that?"

"I've heard it from several people. Not to my face, of course, because folks know we're friends." His hazel eyes filled with anger. "I'm going to find out who's spreading this calumny."

Thoughts racing, Matthew backed away, vaulted over the rail

fence, and strode toward the barn. He heard his father's voice in his ears. *You're deluded if you think you're called to be a preacher. Stay home where you belong.* Flinging open the barn door, he went to the nearest stall and led his horse out to be saddled.

Ben followed him into the barn. "Where are you going?"

"I don't know." Matthew rested his forehead against the animal's warm hide. "I really don't know."

Ellie watched Matthew and Mr. Wolcott ride away. Matthew had never left without saying good-bye before. Heavyhearted, she turned back to the stove and grated lye soap shavings into the wash boiler, then dropped in an armload of her sons' grimy shirts. The water changed from clear to muddy gray. *Just like our lives.*

The house was quiet. The children were at school, and now Matthew was gone too. She could put her plan into action. Ellie stepped back from the stove and wiped perspiration from her forehead with the hem of her apron, then climbed the stairs.

She headed straight to the clothespress in their bedroom. Even knowing she was alone, Ellie still checked over her shoulder before kneeling to open the drawer that held Matthew's personal possessions. Her heartbeat pounded in her ears.

The fragrance of stored sunshine rose from her husband's clean shirts and underthings when she opened the drawer. With trembling hands, she reached beneath the stacks of clothing and drew out a slim walnut document box.

Ellie groped around the bottom of the drawer, her fingers searching for the small brass key that fit the lock. Nothing. Defeated, she sank back onto her heels. *Now what?* She lifted the box and shook it. The contents teased her with rattles and whispers.

She tipped it on its side and shook it again. This time the hinged lid flew open. Folded papers sifted onto her lap. Several pen nibs rolled under the clothespress and two wooden pen holders clattered past her knees.

She'd intended to look through his papers without disturbing their order, but that was impossible now. Ellie bent over and fished under the clothespress for the runaway nibs. She gathered four of them and prayed none were hiding next to the wall. Once the nibs and holders were back in the walnut box, she turned her attention to the pages in her lap. A letter from the presiding elder, appointing Matthew to the Beldon Grove church. Several drawings of the church building in various stages of construction. A credit receipt from Wolcott's Mercantile for last year's corn crop. Then a sheet of yellowed paper, folded inward on all four sides, caught her eye. Ellie'd never seen it before.

It was too old to be from Grandpa Long. Curious, she unfolded one side of the letter, then stopped, a tingle of guilt prickling her throat at the idea of spying on her husband. A voice inside told her to put everything back and leave the room. Instead, Ellie opened the fragile document carefully, so as not to tear the paper. A lock of auburn hair tied with a blue cord nestled in the center of a sheet covered with faded script.

Ellie traced the silky curl with her index finger. Matthew had told her about the sweetheart he'd lost years ago in Kentucky. But he hadn't told her he'd kept a lock of her hair. An arrow of jealousy impaled her heart.

Angry, she pushed the auburn curl to one side and started to read.

Dear Brother Matthew,

Since we don't know where you are, we are

sending this to the Elder of your conference
and pray it reaches you.

Our dear Mother went to the arms of her
Lord on Monday last after a brief sickness. She
asked for you at the end. I'm sending a lock of
her hair for you to remember her by.

Pa is worse than usual. Sister Molly
has been a blessing to us boys. We all send
greetings and hope this finds you well.

Y'r Brother Adam

Ellie lowered the paper and blinked back tears. The date written at the top of the sheet was March 11, 1825. His mother. He'd kept this, and his grief, hidden for over twenty years. She lifted the lock of hair, seeing it with fresh vision. His mother's hair was the same color as the twins'.

She stood and walked to the window, staring out at their cornfields. For the moment she forgot the distance that had crept between herself and Matthew and concentrated instead on the kindhearted man who'd won her love when she was still a girl.

She turned back to the clothespress, where the contents of the walnut box lay strewn across the floor. Ellie placed the curl back in the center of the paper and closed the sides over Matthew's memories. Praying she wouldn't be found out, she replaced the contents of the box as she hoped they'd been arranged and tucked the polished container into the drawer.

Not until later did Ellie remember she hadn't found the envelope from Grandpa Long.

That afternoon Ellie pegged Matthew's laundered shirts onto the clothesline with special care. She smoothed his white cotton Sunday shirt, then took one hand and pressed a sleeve to her cheek. *Lord, help me to be kind-spoken to Matthew—even though I can't be all that he wants in a wife.*

A breeze ruffled the hanging garments, reminding her of the scripture that compared the Spirit of God to the wind. Comforted, Ellie lifted the empty basket just as Matthew rode into the yard.

She hurried toward him, smiling. "I'm glad to see you. Where'd you and Mr. Wolcott go?"

His gaze met hers, then dropped to the saddle horn. "No place special. Ben went to town. I rode a ways east, looked over the countryside."

"What for?"

"Do I need a reason?" He tapped Samson's sides with his heels and rode on to the barn.

Deflated, Ellie stared after him. She spun around and stalked toward the house.

On Thursday afternoon, the kitchen door opened and Uncle Arthur called Ellie's name.

"I'm in the sitting room." She dropped the shirt she was mending for Harrison into the basket beside her rocking chair and walked to the hallway. "If you're looking for Matthew, he took the children out to help replant the acre next to the creek."

"Nope, looking for you." His fringe of hair lay flat around his scalp, bearing the marks of the hat he held in his hand. "Ruby sent me to see if you'd come help her this afternoon."

Ellie chuckled. "Now that's something new—Aunt Ruby asking for *my* help. What does she need done?"

"Sounds like one of them actors tore his stage getup real bad and she's got to make him a new costume before tomorrow." Uncle Arthur looked uncomfortable in his role as go-between. "Said to tell you she's got it all cut out, just needs another pair of hands to help with the sewing."

She wondered what Matthew would say to the request. He hadn't spoken much for the past few days. She knew he was upset with her decision not to risk having more children, but it was unlike him to retreat into silence the way he had. She flicked a glance out the kitchen window toward the creek. Matthew's broad-brimmed straw hat was barely visible beyond the branches of the willow trees. She hoped he wouldn't be too perturbed—after all she was doing a favor for Aunt Ruby.

She smiled at her uncle. "I'll get my sewing basket."

Pairs of flirty-tailed wrens darted in and out of the hedgerows as Uncle Arthur's buggy rolled toward the Newberry farm. Bubbling birdsong drifted through the warm afternoon.

Ellie leaned back against the seat, lifting her face to the sun. "It's good to be out on such a lovely day, Uncle. I'm glad you came to fetch me."

"Ruby'll be happy you could help." He flicked the reins over the horses' backs. "Git on there."

Surprised, Ellie realized they were passing the lane that led to her aunt's house. "Why aren't we stopping?"

"Ruby's at the hotel. Seems like she does everything but sleep there these days."

The hotel! Ellie felt the thrill of forbidden fruit. She'd never have dared visit the place on her own, but the decision had been taken out of her hands, hadn't it? Pent-up curiosity won out over her sense of duty to her husband. She leaned forward in anticipation when Bryant House came into view.

While Arthur escorted her to the sewing room, she stole quick glances around the hotel. Green velvet drapes outlined windows in the parlors they passed as they walked down the ground floor hallway. In the center of one room, a display of iridescent plumes in a brass vase rested on a round, marble-topped table.

She drew a breath. "Oh, Uncle, can we stop for a moment?" Not waiting for an answer, she stepped over to the table and touched one of the feathers. "How beautiful!"

"As are you, Mrs. Craig." She jumped at the sound of Mr. Beldon's voice. Ellie had forgotten he lived at the hotel. Had she trespassed?

Flustered, she acknowledged him with a nod. "I'm just leaving."

"No need." He came toward her, impeccable in a fawn-colored suit. "These are public rooms. Stay as long as you wish."

A spicy smell, reminiscent of cloves, drifted over her. Mr. Beldon's nearness caused Ellie's heart to beat in her throat. She loved Matthew. She did. So why did she feel drawn to this dark-haired man who caused her husband such discomfort?

"These feathers." She tried to control her voice. "What are they?"

"Why, peacock tail feathers, my dear. Have you never seen a peacock?"

She shook her head.

"Truly one of God's wonders. When the male wants to attract a mate, he spreads his tail until he has a spectacular fan of color on display." He smiled, demonstrating by spreading his broad fingers apart in a fan shape. "It's quite a sight. Makes one want to take a closer look."

Uncle Arthur moved next to Ellie, taking her arm. "If you'll excuse us? My niece is here to help her aunt."

"Of course." Mr. Beldon bowed in her direction. "Always a pleasure. Until next time."

Her uncle hustled her to an unadorned room at the rear of the hall, where she found Aunt Ruby sitting in a low chair, sewing what looked like a dark gray pair of men's trousers.

"Here she is," he announced.

Aunt Ruby jumped to her feet. Ellie noted that rather than her usual linsey-woolsey work skirt and apron, her aunt wore what Ellie knew to be her second-best dress. Although the over-dyed green fabric had faded back to yellow, the black flowered calico pattern in the wide skirt still looked bright. The full sleeves flared like wings as Ruby hugged her niece.

"Thank goodness you could come." She thrust several cut pieces of gray fabric into Ellie's hands. "These need to be joined into a tunic. On the stage it will look like chain mail."

"Chain mail?" Ellie's mind still felt fuzzy from her unexpected meeting with Mr. Beldon.

"It's what soldiers wore way back when—kind of like knitted armor."

Settling onto a chair, Ellie asked, "How do you know all this?"

"Mr. Forsythe has been explaining things to me. It's a pure wonder how smart that man is."

Completed garments piled up on one end of the table. Ellie mimicked her aunt's speed, her needle racing along seams and across hems. When she snipped off a trailing thread, she glanced up and noticed Sorrel Forsythe standing in the doorway. His deep-set brown eyes seemed to bore through her.

"Have you brought a spy into our midst?" When he raised an eyebrow, the lines at the corners of his eyes stretched tight and disappeared.

Ellie froze at his question.

Aunt Ruby laughed and glanced at her niece. "Sorrel's sense of humor takes some getting used to." She turned to him and said, "I told you this morning I needed help to get done on time."

"So you did." He walked over to Aunt Ruby and rested a hand on her shoulder. "From the looks of things you've accomplished your task magnificently."

Her cheeks pinked. "It was nothing." Shining eyes betrayed the outward modesty.

Mr. Forsythe nodded in Ellie's direction. "Would you be interested in seeing the stage sets? We're doing our dress rehearsal this evening—not that I don't know this play inside and out." He flicked the fingers of one hand as if to show that it didn't matter to him whether he rehearsed or not. "But we do need to practice our marks. The stage upstairs is much smaller than anything we're used to."

Practice our marks? He might have been speaking a foreign language. Ellie glanced out the window and noticed that the sun had slipped halfway down the western sky. She stood, holding her sewing basket in one hand. "I don't think I'd better take the time. My family—"

"Nonsense, child." Aunt Ruby took the basket and placed it on the table. "You can't leave until Arthur fetches you, so you might as well go upstairs with us."

Still she hesitated.

Mr. Forsythe held out his arm, crooked at the elbow. "Come

106

along. The devil's not crouching at the top of the staircase, I assure you."

"Go on with you. You know you're curious." Her aunt gave her a gentle shove.

Giving up her show of reluctance, Ellie allowed herself to be escorted from the room. Instead of using the main staircase she'd noticed when passing through the reception area, Mr. Forsythe headed for the rear entrance.

Aunt Ruby explained the layout of the hotel as they walked. "These are the stairs the actors use. That way the audience can't see them in their costumes before the curtain opens."

Their footsteps echoed in the enclosed stairway as the trio climbed single file to the stage. When she entered the ballroom of the hotel, converted to a theater for Friday's performance, Ellie blundered into a heavy piece of canvas hanging from a rope stretched across the stage.

"Careful. Paint's still wet on that one." Mr. Forsythe pulled her back. "Come around here and you can see how it'll look from the audience." He guided her past hanging ropes, their ends coiled on the floor.

Walking from the back of the stage to the front, Ellie thought the musty-smelling canvas backdrops resembled laundry hung out to dry, but when she turned around to look from below the stage, she caught her breath in amazement. A crenellated stone edifice had been painted on the heavy cloth. Green brush strokes along the bottom edge gave the appearance of grass and shrubbery.

"Why, it's a castle, isn't it?"

Mr. Forsythe smiled. "But of course. The opening scene takes place outdoors." He pointed at the tops of the other backdrops hanging behind the castle, enumerating each one in turn. "A banquet room, a sleeping chamber, a battlefield."

Ellie closed her eyes for a moment, imagining the story as Aunt Ruby had told it to her. She turned to her aunt. "Oh, I wish I could see the play!"

"I wish you could too."

On the ride home, Ellie clutched her sewing basket to her chest. The smell of oil paint clung to her nostrils the same way the image of the makeshift theater stayed in her mind. The thought of people crowding the second floor of the hotel to see *Macbeth* filled her with envy.

She forced herself to focus on family and home. Next to her, hands on the reins, Uncle Arthur whistled a tuneless ditty and tapped his toe on the floor of the buggy. The sun had dropped low on the horizon.

"Would you like to stay to supper?" Ellie asked.

"Don't mind if I do. Ruby's been leaving me to fend for myself lately. A home-cooked meal will go good."

Surprised, Ellie glanced at him. "She's not home by suppertime?"

"Nope. Not for the past several days anyhow. Eats at the hotel with them actor folks."

Ellie felt mild shock. She hadn't realized her aunt had taken up so completely with the theater troupe. "Don't you mind?"

"Sure I do, but Ruby's Ruby. It'll be over tomorrow night, and she'll be back home, making me hop to it." He grinned. "Been kind of peaceful, come to think on it."

When they crossed the bridge spanning the creek that bordered the Craig farm, Ellie looked over the cornfield, hoping Matthew was still at work and hadn't noticed her absence. But when they entered the kitchen, he was seated at the table.

He glanced behind their backs. "Where's Ruby?"

"Left her at the hotel," Uncle Arthur answered.

One of Matthew's eyebrows dipped in a half frown. He turned to Ellie, his voice rising. "Your note said you were going to Ruby's. You were at the hotel all this time? With those people?"

Her heart fluttered in her throat. "I didn't know that's where we were going."

Uncle Arthur came to her defense. "S'true. Guess she figured Ruby was to home when I came to fetch her. But Ruby's been working at the hotel for some days now." He glanced out the window in the direction of town. "Makes sense, I guess. Easier than packing everything back and forth."

"At the hotel." Matthew looked down at the floor, fingers pinching his lower lip.

Ellie knew he was trying to control his temper. She placed the sewing basket on the table and lifted her apron from its peg on the wall. "Supper won't take long." She kept her tone light. "Just have to fry up some sausages to go with the beans. I asked Uncle Arthur to stay."

Matthew stared at her for a long moment, his eyes dark with anger. "How could you?" The words burst from his mouth. "Week after week I've preached against this play. How do you think it looks when my wife parades into the hotel and lends a hand in putting it together?"

"It wasn't like that. I did it to help Aunt Ruby." Ellie blinked hard to hold back tears. "She asked for me. After all she's done for us, how could I refuse?"

"She's right," Uncle Arthur said. "It was the Christian thing to do."

"Christian!" Matthew snorted, glaring at him. "I don't know what that means anymore."

Stunned at her husband's reaction, Ellie put her hand on his arm. "What's wrong?"

He stepped out of reach. "What isn't?"

12

Matthew woke at daybreak Saturday. His first conscious thought was one of relief that Friday night's play was now a thing of the past and life could settle back to normal. He stirred on his side of the bed, careful to keep an open space between himself and Ellie on the feather tick. He longed to roll over and draw her close, but instead slid out from under the coverlet. As his bare feet touched cold floorboards, he heard banging at the back door.

Ellie heard it too, and sat up, rubbing her eyes. "Who'd be here at this hour?"

"Someone must be sick and calling for the pastor." Matthew snatched his pants from a peg on the wall, slid them on, and tucked his nightshirt into the waistband. "I'll see who it is." Barefoot, he hurried from the room.

Ellie followed him down the stairs. When Matthew opened the door, Arthur flung himself inside.

"Is Ruby here?" His eyes cut to the corners of the kitchen, as though he might find her hidden behind a chair.

"It's barely dawn." Matthew placed a hand on Arthur's shoulder. "Why would she be here?"

Arthur turned to Ellie. "Did she say anything to you on Thursday?"

"No." Her jaw dropped. "Do you mean she's gone?"

"She's gone all right."

"Something must have happened to her." Matthew walked to the stove and tossed several pieces of wood on top of the previous night's coals. "Did you check along the road to town?"

Arthur stumbled to a chair and sat, covering his face with his hands. "Did more than that. It was just an old man's foolish hope that she'd be here with you."

Ellie moved close to Matthew's side. He grasped her hand and turned to Arthur. "Start at the beginning and tell us what's happened."

"Went to that play last night, like half the folks in town, then afterward Ruby said she had to stay and help them pack up. Said she'd have someone bring her out after they was done." Arthur sighed. "So, I went home to bed. Well, I woke up a couple hours ago, and she still wasn't back." He looked at Matthew. "I thought the same thing you did—something happened along the road and she was out there hurt. Saddled up the horse and rode to town, slow-like, with a lantern so's I could check the hedgerows. Nothing."

Arthur pivoted in his chair and peered out at the brightening day. When he turned back to them, his eyes were deep pools of pain. "At the hotel, that namby-pamby clerk was all in a dither. Seems them actors packed up and left in the middle of the night without paying their bill." He paused. In the heavy silence, they could hear the iron surface of the stove tick as it heated.

Tears formed at the corners of Arthur's eyes and trickled down his round cheeks. "Ruby went with them."

Matthew waited while Arthur settled onto the seat of the buckboard. He'd already tied Arthur's horse, King George, to the back of the wagon.

"You don't have to do this. I can ride home."

"Course you can. Just thought you might like a little company."

Arthur stared straight ahead as the buckboard rolled out of the farmyard and crossed the wooden bridge over the creek. "I feel like I been trampled by a team of draft horses. All these years with Ruby and never a notion she'd do something like this."

"We don't know what really happened. Maybe she's been taken against her will."

"Hah! Against her will, my foot. You don't believe that, and neither do I. If you could've heard all the 'Mr. Forsythe this' and 'Mr. Forsythe that' the woman's been prattling, you'd know it was him turned her head." His voice shook. "You was right from the beginning. That play brought no good to this town—Ruby's gone, and Jack Bryant is out food and lodging for all the time them folks spent in his hotel."

In a corner of his mind, Matthew couldn't help but feel vindicated. But even his greatest fears hadn't included Ellie losing her aunt, the only mother she'd known. He considered reassuring Arthur that God had a plan in this for everyone's good, then rejected the idea. Instead, he glanced around at the sprouted corn in fields lining the road. The downy leaves reflected the soft gold of the morning sun. "Feels sticky already. Going to be a hot one."

Arthur ignored the remark. He sat with his hands clasped on his knees, fingers clenching and unclenching. He shook his head like someone trying to wake from a dream. "Thirty-one years. You'd think you'd know a person after all that time."

Matthew nodded, holding the reins lightly while Samson trotted down the dirt track. "Yup. You'd think so."

"She was such a pretty little thing when I met her. Old man Long, her pa, had a passel of daughters, but she was the best looking of the lot." His voice trailed away. They rode without speaking for several minutes, then Arthur cleared his throat and continued. "Anyways, she said she'd marry me when I came calling. We settled down there in Flint County. I figured we'd have a houseful of young'uns, but it didn't happen. Ruby kind of watched over her nieces and nephews, but it ate at her, not having any babies of her own."

"So you ended up with Ellie when her pa took off." Matthew fought down impatience at hearing the familiar story once again.

"The way she doted on that child, I figured she was enough for Ruby." More to himself than to Matthew, he continued, "But now that I think of it, she never seemed satisfied-like."

Matthew thought of countless occasions when he'd heard Ruby harangue her husband about one thing and another. Unsatisfied was a good way to put it. "Um-hmm."

"Like she was after something just out of reach. Well, guess she's found it." Arthur's voice faded.

Holding the reins with one hand, Matthew guided Samson onto the lane leading to the Newberrys' house. When they reached the barn, Arthur climbed out of the wagon and untied King George, then led the animal toward its stall.

Matthew followed.

Turning, the older man jutted out his jaw. "There's no need to hang around me. I ain't going to kill nobody."

"I know that." He gentled his voice. "Thought maybe there might be something I could do to help."

"Help what? Bring Ruby back? We don't even know which way they went." Arthur pulled off his hat and rubbed a hand over his bald scalp. "Just let me be for a while. I got to think on it before I decide what to do."

Matthew's feelings of inadequacy taunted him. His father told him he'd fail, and here was the proof. He couldn't even help his own family. He shoved his hands into his pockets. "I'll come by later today."

"No need. See you tomorrow in church."

He raised his hand in a half wave and walked toward the buckboard.

When Matthew arrived home, Ellie looked up from her kneading, the rolled-up sleeves of her black dress bordered with flour. "How's Uncle Arthur?"

"Poleaxed." Matthew dropped heavily into a chair.

"I know how he feels." Her hands stopped moving, and she rested them on the edge of the bread trough. "I can't believe this is really true. Seems like any minute now she'll come through the back door to lend a hand with the baking." Ellie glanced at him, a frown sketched across her forehead. "Now that I think about it, she hasn't been here to help in quite a while." She returned to her task, rocking back and forth as she pushed and folded the mound of dough. Tears trickled down her cheeks.

Matthew walked to the worktable and put his arms around his wife's waist, lightly, so she'd know he wasn't thinking of anything but comforting her. "I don't know what to say. I can't even guess how you must feel right now."

She turned and pressed her face into his chest, sobbing. "How could Aunt Ruby go away and leave me? She knows how much I need her." Matthew held her, his heart aching as she poured out her grief. Finally, she drew a long breath. "I thought about this the whole time you were gone." She looked up at him with red-rimmed eyes. "It's worse than a death, Matt. Aunt Ruby had a choice, and she chose to go."

"Maybe she'll have second thoughts and come back." He stepped away.

Ellie slid a chair from beside the table and sank into it. "You know what I keep wondering?"

He shook his head.

"Did I drive her to this because I was so angry about my father?"

His heart constricted. "No. Of course not." He tried to think of the right thing to say. Knowing how weak his words sounded, he repeated what he'd said before. "Maybe she'll come back."

Ellie wiped her eyes on a corner of her apron. "Do you think Uncle Arthur would take her in?" She pulled a handkerchief from her pocket and blew her nose. "It would be like Hosea and Gomer in the Bible."

Matthew thought a moment. "I don't know. Hosea took his wife back because he had a word from the Lord." He stroked Ellie's hair, gazing out the window in the direction of the Newberrys' farm. "Guess we'll have to wait and see what kind of a word Arthur receives."

Dismayed, Matthew surveyed the few worshipers gathered in church for Sunday services. Several benches were unoccupied. He had to confess to himself that he'd anticipated many congregants returning with their tails between their legs after the news of the acting troupe's ignominious departure spread through town. Then he remembered the rumors about God's judgment on him. The palms of his hands felt clammy at the thought. He wiped them on his trousers.

Ellie sat with their four children on the first bench. In spite of Arthur's promise, he hadn't appeared in his usual place right behind Ellie. That worried Matthew.

His eyes traveled to Molly and Karl who sat with their children on the other side of the center aisle. Ben and Charity Wolcott were also present, as well as a dozen or so of the most faithful worshipers. At the rear, Marcus Beldon sat next to his wife with an expression on his face that could only be described as smug.

With a start, Matthew realized people were looking at him, waiting for him to begin the service. He knelt next to the pulpit. "Let's pray for the Lord's anointing on this meeting."

As soon as the final hymn had been sung, Molly hurried toward him, wide-eyed. "Is it true that Aunt Ruby left town with the Shakespeare troupe? And that the hotel bill wasn't paid?"

"That's what I understand. I talked to the clerk at the hotel myself, and he said they must have slipped out sometime after midnight Friday." Matthew glanced at Ellie. "It's been a blow to all of us."

"Poor Arthur." Molly shook her head. "You know I think that woman is a trial and a sufferance, but he never seems to notice." She looked behind her at the bench where Arthur would normally be sitting. "He probably didn't want to face folks today."

"Not that many folks here to face." Matthew glanced toward the back of the room. Beldon and his wife were already gone.

Ben joined them and clapped Matthew on the back. "One of your best sermons. 'If we confess our sins, he is faithful and just to forgive our sins—but the first step is confession.' Food for thought." He grinned. "Speaking of food, why don't you and the family take supper with us today?"

Matthew wasn't fooled by Ben's cheerful manner. He saw concern in his friend's eyes, and knew the invitation represented Ben and Charity's attempt to compensate for the emptiness of the church. "Be glad to. I want to look in on Arthur first. Would you mind if we brought him along?"

"We thought he was at your place." Ben's voice registered surprise. "We stopped in to take him with us this morning and he wasn't there. Buggy was gone too."

Ellie clutched Matthew's sleeve. "You've got to find him. There's no telling what he'll do, upset as he is."

Matthew looked at Ben. "Will you go with me? There's still plenty of daylight left."

Following a fruitless afternoon's search, Ben and Matthew left again at dawn the next morning. Ben planned to ride north to New Roanoke, on the remote possibility Arthur would have passed through there heading for Chicago.

Matthew traveled east as far as Industry Township, asking about his wife's uncle at every settlement and farm along the way. No one had seen a plump, middle-aged man driving a buggy pulled by a chestnut roan.

Late in the day Matthew followed the scarlet rays of the setting sun back to Beldon Grove. He'd done all he could think of to do. The image of Ellie's stricken face burned in his mind.

After stopping at Ben's and learning his search had also been unsuccessful, Matthew turned toward home. Once there, he didn't need to tell Ellie anything.

She took one look at his expression and dropped into a chair. "Do you think he's got himself lost on the prairie?"

Matthew pinched his lower lip. "I pray not."

"No one saw him? You didn't find any tracks?"

"No."

Ellie rested her elbows on the tabletop and buried her face in her hands. Matthew laid a hand on her shoulder, waiting for the sound of sobs, but none came.

After a moment, she raised dry eyes and studied his face. "I'm tired of crying. I'm tired of being left. I'm going to locate my father's family in Texas and bring them here."

He stared at her, mouth agape. "What does that have to do with your aunt and uncle? There is no family in Texas. Please. Be realistic." He lifted his hands. "Besides, if we can't find Arthur right here in Illinois, how on earth can you expect to track down people hundreds of miles from here?"

"I'll find a way."

Matthew stood next to his upended plow inside the barn. Stray bits of hay blew along the packed earth floor at his feet. He dipped a brush into a pail and painted the green moldboard behind the plowshare, covering areas scraped bare by spring plowing. The smell of linseed oil rose to his nostrils after each brushstroke.

The familiar sound of his horses crunching hay in their stalls formed a soothing counterpoint for his tumbling thoughts about Ellie and Arthur.

Sighing, he laid his brush to one side and picked up a narrow paddle, stirring the paint to keep it from separating. As he watched green pigment swirl through the oil base, he heard his children approach the barn.

"You ask him."

"No, you."

"What do you boys want?" he asked, recognizing Jimmy and Johnny's voices. When the twins stepped into the dim interior, he saw Harrison and Maria tagging behind them.

"We want to know . . ." Johnny's voice trailed off.

Jimmy poked him in the ribs. "Come on. You said you'd do it."

Matthew placed an arm around Johnny's shoulder. "It must be important to bring the whole pack of you out here." Harrison and Maria edged closer, and he used his free hand to give one of Maria's braids a playful tug. He quirked an eyebrow at the twins and waited.

Johnny took a deep breath. "What's an adulteress?" The words tumbled out with barely a pause between them.

Four pairs of eyes watched him as he fumbled for a response. Without asking, he knew the term had most likely been overheard after church the previous Sunday. He turned to his daughter. "Maria, you go help your mama get supper on the table. Harrison, you go with her." As he spoke, he bent over and dropped a kiss on his daughter's head. "This is grown-up talk."

Reluctantly, the two youngest children left the barn. Arms folded, Matthew watched as they passed the black walnut sapling between the barn and the house and climbed the back steps. He couldn't help but smile. If they walked any slower, they'd be moving backward.

Then he leaned against the side of a stall and answered his sons. "An adulteress is a married woman who lays with a man who is not her husband."

"Told you so." Jimmy said to his brother.

Matthew frowned at them. "Now tell me why you asked such a question."

"One of the town boys said that's what Aunt Ruby is." This time Johnny spoke up with no hesitation.

"Listen to me. We don't know for certain what happened to your aunt. It's best not to stoop to name-calling, do you understand?"

"But isn't that why Uncle Arthur went away? Because his wife is a bad woman?"

Putting an arm around each of his sons, he hugged them to him. "You miss your uncle, don't you?"

They nodded.

"So do I. And I'm worried about him. But listening to gossip and repeating it will do more harm than good. You know what the Bible says about being a talebearer."

Jimmy's face reddened. "Yes, Papa."

"We're sorry," Johnny added.

Matthew pulled his watch from his pocket and snapped the lid open. "More than an hour before supper. Plenty of time for you to hoe a couple rows of corn."

He watched the boys as they walked to the cornfield, his lips pressed in a tight line, wishing that he could protect his children from life's hurts.

The following week, Matthew drove his family to his sister's house so Ellie could join Molly and Charity Wolcott for their Thursday afternoon quilting session. Maria sat between them on the front seat, and their three boys rode in the rear, legs dangling over the open back of the buckboard. Taking the children allowed the youngsters an afternoon of play with their cousins while Ellie visited with the women.

She hadn't brought up the subject of her possible Texas family since the day he'd returned from searching for Arthur. He hoped it had been a passing fancy, brought on by the shock of Arthur and Ruby's disappearances. "It's good to see you so pert."

"I've been looking forward to this. I miss having other women to talk to." She gave him a sideways glance over the top of Maria's head. "Sundays aren't as good for visiting as they used to be."

"No, they're not," he said, glad she'd brought the subject of his eroding congregation into the open.

They'd tiptoed around it long enough. Last week, even the Beldons were missing. Matthew intended to seek Ben's advice while his family spent the afternoon at Molly's.

When Matthew entered the mercantile, the customer at the counter glanced at him, then dropped his eyes. Matthew walked over to him and put out his right hand. "How've you been? I've missed seeing you in church."

After a moment's pause, Orville Carstairs shook his hand without enthusiasm. "I'm fine. We've been, uh, worshiping somewheres else."

As far as Matthew knew, the church he pastored was the only church in Beldon Grove. Across the counter, Ben lifted his index finger in a "wait a moment" motion. Glancing between the two men, Matthew realized there was something Ben wanted to tell him, and he didn't want to do it in front of Orville.

"Well, give my best to your wife." He laid a hand on Orville's shoulder. "Tell her the lilac start she gave Mrs. Craig is flourishing."

"I'll do that." Clutching his parcel, he fled the store.

Ben closed the cash box and led the way to the back room. Matthew saw two chairs pushed against a wall, dwarfed by flour and vinegar barrels, crates of merchandise, and stacks of pots and lanterns.

With a sigh, Ben sank into one of the chairs and pushed the other one toward him. "Take a load off, Matt."

Without preamble, Matthew launched into the reason for his visit. "Any idea what's happening with the church? Last Sunday I could count attendance with my fingers and still have a thumb to spare."

Ben nodded. "It's Beldon. He started a Wednesday night prayer meeting over at the hotel, and he's got folks convinced that God doesn't want you preaching his word."

Matthew felt like he'd just fallen through a hidden trap door. "But . . . folks around here are my friends. You know how hard we worked on the church building. How could anyone convince them God doesn't want me as their pastor?"

"Beldon hasn't tried it on me, but I hear he uses scriptures like the ones where God casts down unworthy priests like Eli's sons."

"What does that have to do with Beldon Grove? There's no point of comparison."

Shaking his head, Ben said, "I know that, and you know that. But take a person like Orville Carstairs, for instance. I doubt he's able to read the Bible for himself, so he takes the word of someone like Beldon. Lots of folks in this town can't read much more than their name. Many of them don't even have Bibles." He shifted in his chair and looked directly into Matthew's eyes. "I think when Ruby and then Arthur disappeared, that's what drove the final nail in your coffin. Scripture says a church leader should be one who rules his own house well, and Beldon is holding Ruby and Arthur up as proof that you can't even maintain order in your own family."

13

Ellie faced Molly and Charity across the quilt frame. While she worked her needle around a piece of blue calico, she studied the progress they had made over the past months. The quilt top resembled a flower garden in riotous bloom. Yellow, pink, blue, green, and violet pieces joined together like the cells of a honeycomb. "Why isn't Luellen in here helping with the stitching? This is for her bridal chest, isn't it?"

Molly shook her head. "She said she'd rather read. She's not interested in being a bride."

"At eleven years old, I expect she's not," Charity said. When she smiled, her expression gave a hint of the carefree girl she'd once been. Eyes twinkling, she continued, "But she needs to learn to quilt right along with baking and cleaning—and reading."

"I know that," Molly said. "It's Luellen you need to convince." She focused her attention on stitching a double pink piece to the background fabric.

The women worked in silence for a few minutes, then Ellie turned to Molly and said, "It's been over four weeks since James left. Has he sent word?"

"Nothing yet. But I've found a way to learn where he is."

Charity and Ellie both stopped sewing and stared at her. Almost in unison, they asked, "How?"

"I happened to see Mr. Beldon outside the mercantile one day. Somehow he'd heard about James's leaving and asked about him." Molly tucked her needle into the quilt top and laced her fingers together. "He offered to contact officials in Decatur. Turns out James was a bit hasty—the militia hasn't been officially called up yet."

"How can you remain so calm? I'd be frantic." Ellie looked at Charity. "Wouldn't you?"

Charity tilted her head to one side. "After what happened with Franklin, perhaps she's learned to trust."

"I have, indeed. But another part of what I learned is that the Lord sends help from unlikely sources. And I believe Mr. Beldon will be able to tell us where James is, and perhaps persuade him to come home."

Ellie leaned forward, intrigued. "When will he let you know?"

"He said to come to his office in a couple of weeks. There should be a reply by then."

The colors of the quilt top danced in front of Ellie's eyes. "You would go to the hotel . . . alone?"

"It's perfectly safe. I'd be in one of the parlors, not his private rooms, for goodness' sake."

"I'm not sure that's wise," Charity said.

Molly lifted her chin. "I'll do anything to find out where James is."

Ellie nodded, a plan forming in her mind.

By the time Matthew arrived to take Ellie home, the women had finished the section they had been working on and scrolled the frame to the next. Molly draped a linen sheet over their work to keep it clean until the following Thursday.

"Supper's almost ready, Matt. How about you stay and eat before your trip to the farm?"

Ellie glanced up at him, hoping he'd agree. The rich aroma of stewed meat and onions had been making her mouth water all afternoon.

"We're having cider cake," Molly added.

Matthew shook his head. "Not today, thanks. I want to get back." His skin had lost its ruddy color. His lips were bloodless.

"What's wrong?" Ellie scrutinized her husband. "You look like you've seen a ghost."

"Nothing. There's nothing wrong." He stepped outside the house and called the children. "Hurry up. We're leaving."

Ellie and Molly exchanged glances. It wasn't like Matthew to be so abrupt. Whatever happened during his visit with Mr. Wolcott had left him profoundly upset.

They rode home without speaking. Ellie longed to pry information out of him, but knew he'd want to wait until the children couldn't overhear their conversation. In the back of the wagon, the boys made screeching noises with whistles they'd hollowed out of sticks. About the time she thought she couldn't stand another piercing squeal, the buggy rolled over the plank bridge and into the farmyard.

Once the wagon stopped, Matthew looked over his shoulder at their sons. "You boys get to the milking." He turned his head to include Maria in his commands. "You help Mama with supper."

Ellie frowned at him, irritated by his peremptory behavior. "Supper won't be much. I was counting on eating with Molly and Karl, so I didn't leave anything on the stove."

"Doesn't matter. Cornbread and milk will do." Matthew took her hand and helped her from the wagon. "I'll see to the horse." Without another word, he led Samson toward the barn.

126

That evening, once they had donned their nightclothes, Ellie perched on the edge of the rocker next to the bedroom fireplace and folded her arms across her chest. "Something dreadful happened in town today, and I want to know what it is."

Matthew sat on the bed. The candle on the nightstand cast shadows across his face, hiding his deep-set eyes. "Looks like my ministry here is finished."

"No."

"You've seen the attendance the past few weeks. I found out today that Beldon is behind it. He's telling people that I'm not fit to preach God's word—and they believe him."

"That sounds like pure gossip to me. Why would someone like Mr. Beldon care about you or your church? Surely an important man like that has bigger things on his mind."

Anger flashed across Matthew's face. "You'd defend him? Against me?"

She walked to the bed and laid a hand on his shoulder. "I'm not defending him. I see what's happening in the church, and my heart breaks." Ellie took a deep breath and held it for a moment. "I just think you're wrong when you blame Mr. Beldon. It's not like you to be so unfair. What proof do you have?"

Matthew shrugged her hand away. "Is it fair when all my years of pastoring the Beldon Grove church are ignored, like so much chaff after harvest?" He moved to the window and pulled the curtain aside. The blackness of the night reflected his face on the windowpane. Even in the imperfect image Ellie saw the anguish written across his features.

"I'm leaving for Quincy tomorrow to talk to the presiding

elder of our district." Matthew spoke into the void. "I'm going to resign."

Shock rolled through Ellie. She couldn't imagine Matthew as anything but a preacher. His devotion to his calling had been one of the things that had drawn her to him when they first met. She loved sitting at the front of the church and listening while he taught from the Word of God. Ellie had seen many lives changed under his caring guidance. He couldn't throw it all away.

She clasped his limp hand in both of hers. "Matt, don't. Please don't. This will pass, you'll see."

"And in the meantime I go to a near-empty church and preach to my family? I'd look like a bigger fool than I did preaching against the play. You saw where that got me." He pulled his hand free and walked to the bed. "Let's get some sleep. I want to leave early."

The sound of creaking floorboards awakened Ellie. She opened her eyes and saw Matthew bent over the blanket chest, pulling something out of its depths. Pale gray light filtered through the curtains.

"What are you doing?" she asked, keeping her voice low so she wouldn't rouse the children.

He startled. "I'm sorry. I didn't mean to wake you." When he turned he held his saddlebags in one hand. "Getting things together for the trip to Quincy."

Ellie rubbed the sleep from her eyes. "It's way before sunrise. Why not have a good breakfast and think things over? There's no need for you to go tearing out of here."

Matthew flopped the saddlebags onto the bed, stuffed a few items of clothing into one side, and pulled the buckle tight. "Sooner I leave, sooner it'll be done."

"Matt—"

"Don't start in on me. I've been awake most of the night thinking and I keep coming back to the idea of just being a farmer." His mouth twisted sideways. "Least that way our livelihood won't depend on what people say about me."

Fear rode up Ellie's spine. She slipped out of bed and hurried to her husband's side. More than anything she ached to wrap her arms around him, but she knew how unfair that would be considering the bargain they had drawn. Instead, she reached out and slid her hand over his cheek, his beard coarse beneath her fingers. Everything they'd built over the past fourteen years trembled in the air between them.

"You don't know what Brother Meecham will say. Maybe he won't release you."

He captured her hand in his. "When he hears what's happened to the Beldon Grove church, it's likely he'll expel me from membership." He brushed his lips across her fingers. "I'm going. I expect to be back by this time next week."

Desperate to keep him with her, she asked, "But what about Sunday's service? You can't just ignore it."

"Already talked to Ben. He'll open the doors and preach to whoever shows up."

Until that moment Ellie hadn't realized how much of herself was bound up in the respect that came with being a pastor's wife. "But what about me? Don't you care what I think?"

He turned, one hand on the latch. "I care, but I won't let it stop me."

Frustrated and angry, Ellie spent the hours after Matthew's departure scrubbing floors as though she could scour away the events of the past several weeks. But her usual cure-all for misery failed her this time. Somehow Matthew's presence made itself known even when he was in the barn or out in the fields. Today had a hollow feel, like answering a knock and finding no one there. In her heart she cherished the hope that he would change his mind en route and be back before supper.

But supper came and went, and once the children were in bed Ellie faced her first night without Matthew since he went to Missouri to get his sister Molly after her husband died. Then she'd had Aunt Ruby and Uncle Arthur. Now they were gone too. She walked out onto the back porch in her wrapper and slippers and gazed at the sky. A crescent moon hung overhead, surrounded by a wilderness of lights.

I wonder if Matthew is counting stars tonight. In their early days together they used to sit outside on summer evenings, competing to see who could spot the first glittering pinprick overhead. How long had it been since they'd sat and watched the heavens? Ellie couldn't remember.

Banners of gauzy clouds unfurled above her head. A slight breeze rustled through the cornfield and slid over her bare legs. Even after the wind shifted and the air chilled, she remained huddled on the top step, reluctant to go indoors and face the empty bedroom.

Ellie leaned into the kneading trough, folding the heavy mass of dough toward her and then pushing it away. She wondered how much longer they would have the luxury of wheat bread. The small salary Matthew received from the conference wouldn't have supported them without their farm's production, but it did allow a few extras such as coffee, sugar, tea, and wheat flour. Giving the dough one last fold, she wiped her hands on her apron and placed a linen towel over the trough.

Harrison wandered in the back door. "Sure is quiet without Papa."

"It is."

"When's he coming back?"

"In a few days." Ellie looked at his dusty brown feet. "You can't be finished with the hoeing so soon."

He slouched over to a chair. "Jimmy and Johnny were making fun of me. They said I'm too slow to be any help."

Ellie planted her hands on her hips. "Does Papa think you're slow?"

"No."

"Well, neither do I. There's acres of corn to be hoed. If the twins are bothering you, go down by the creek and work. Maria and I will come out and help you after dinner."

She brushed a trickle of sweat from her forehead. The morning already felt hot and sticky. Once she heated the stove for bread-baking, the kitchen itself would turn into an oven. Ellie gazed out the window at clouds piling up in the western sky, hopeful that a good rain would clear the air.

Harrison dipped a cup of water from the crock next to the door and took his time drinking it. Then he headed back to the fields, his lower lip protruding in a sulky pout.

At mid-afternoon Ellie and Maria donned sunbonnets and walked through foot-high corn plants to the place where Harrison labored at his task. Maria was too young to safely handle a hoe around the tender stalks, so Ellie gave her a bushel basket to use to pick up fallen weeds.

Harrison looked at his little sister critically. "Papa never tells us to pick up the weeds."

Biting her lip, Ellie gazed at her younger son. "Do you want help or not?"

"Yeah." He kicked at the dirt.

"All right then, be nice to your sister."

Ellie pulled her skirt up past her bare ankles, tying the extra fabric into a knot. Gripping one of the hoes, she chopped at the spindly weeds filling the rows between corn plants. Working in silence, they completed a row and started down the next one. Ellie's back ached. Sweat stung her eyes. She leaned on her hoe for a moment, fanning her face with her hand. In the distance, she noticed a cloud of dust growing larger as it approached the farm.

Dropping the hoe, she ran for the road. "You children keep working," she called over her shoulder. "I'll be right back."

Once Ellie got close enough to see who it was, she wished the corn were high enough to hide her completely. She'd hoped to see Matthew, but Mr. Beldon drove over the plank bridge, his stylish carriage spraying dust as he entered the farmyard. Rooted to the ground, she watched in dismay as he tied his horse to the rail and walked toward her. Dripping with sweat, dress hiked up to reveal dirty bare feet, she'd never felt less like entertaining a visitor, especially one as sophisticated as Mr. Beldon. Ellie felt her face grow hotter than it already was.

"Mr. Beldon," she squeaked. "I . . . I thought you were someone else."

He walked toward her as though he greeted damp, dirty women as a natural course of life. "Mrs. Craig." He bowed slightly. "I apologize for the interruption. I came by to have a talk with your husband."

"He's not here."

"Indeed." His glance swept over her. "That would be why you are working in the fields?"

"We can't let the weeds get ahead of the corn."

Ellie didn't want to tell him the reason for Matthew's absence. Grabbing at the knotted fabric of her skirt, she managed to pull the extra length loose and let it drop to cover all but her toes.

Reaching for composure, she said, "I'm sorry you drove all the way out here for nothing. Could I offer you a cool drink before you start back to town?"

"That's kind of you. Yes, I'd like that."

She pointed to two caned rockers sitting on the covered porch. "I hope you'll be comfortable there."

"Quite comfortable. Thank you." He followed her up the steps.

"I'll just be a moment."

She whisked inside, tugging off her limp sunbonnet as she sped through the kitchen and up the stairs. In front of the pier glass in her bedroom, she ran a comb through her damp hair to smooth back straggling tendrils. After brushing dirt off her feet, she shoved them into leather slippers and hurried back downstairs. Quickly she dipped two cups of water from the crock and arranged them on a tray with a plate of gingerbread cakes she'd been saving for the children's supper.

Mr. Beldon stood when she emerged, taking the tray from her hands and placing it on a low table between the chairs. "This is very kind of you. I fear I've come at an awkward time."

"Not at all." She settled herself and picked up a cup of water. Dirt showed under each fingernail. Hastily, she put the cup down and folded her hands in her lap. "Where is Mrs. Beldon?" she asked, more out of politeness than any real interest.

"Unfortunately, she's plagued with severe rheumatism. She's having an especially pain-filled day today."

"I am sorry. Does she mind being left when she's so ill?"

"I wouldn't call it 'ill' precisely." He turned, fixing dark-lashed eyes on her face. "In fact, she'd rather be left alone than fussed over." Mr. Beldon picked up one of the cakes, dwarfing the slice with his broad fingers. Taking a bite, he closed his eyes and smiled. "Delicious. Reminds me of sweets my mother made when I was a boy."

A pulse pounded in Ellie's throat. She squeezed her hands between her knees, then drew a deep breath and blurted, "Mr. Beldon, I'm glad you stopped by. I have a favor to ask."

14

After two days in the saddle, Matthew's body felt like it had been run over by a hay wagon, reminding him why he'd requested a church assignment following twelve years of riding circuit. The closer he drew to his destination, the more his resolve weakened. If he quit, he'd be running from God just like Jonah did. Tall prairie grass snicked against his boots as the horse followed a narrow track leading to what Matthew hoped was the ten-mile point—a grove of cottonwoods that oriented westbound travelers toward Quincy and the Mississippi River. He began to wonder if requesting a different church would solve things.

His mind shied away from thoughts of Ellie's reaction to leaving the community where their children were buried, not to mention what she'd say about the prospect of starting anew after they'd worked so hard to build up their farm.

He'd been so absorbed in his thoughts he hadn't noticed shadows stretching across the rolling prairie. Fingers of dusk had filled in the hollows. Matthew removed his hat and surveyed the grassland, hoping to spy a settler's cabin nestling nearby where he might seek shelter. Nothing. He wasn't eager to spend a night in the open with only a shotgun to protect him from prowling wolves.

When he crested the next rise, he spotted a narrow creek winding its way across the landscape. The horse saw it too, and veered toward the water. Upon reaching the sandy bank Matthew slid out of the saddle, still holding the reins.

"Guess this is as good a place to stop as any," he said to the sturdy Morgan, patting his smoky mane.

After tethering the horse, Matthew removed his bedroll from one saddlebag and spread it about twenty yards from the creek. In the growing darkness he rummaged in the other bag until his fingers found the package of corn cakes and dried venison he'd tossed in for his supper.

He lowered himself to the ground, using his saddle for a back rest, and chewed his makeshift meal. Tilting his head upward he searched for familiar constellations—Little Bear, Hercules, Leo. *I wonder if Ellie remembers when we used to sit together and count stars?*

At first, Matthew thought he was dreaming about the big spring on the hill above his father's farm. Cool water dripped on his face as though falling from leaves that hung next to the rushing cascade he remembered from childhood. But at the first crack of thunder he sat bolt upright, now fully awake. Streaks of lightning stalked through the blackness. *Samson.* He groped for his boots, then hurried toward the spot where he'd tethered the horse. A flash of lightning lit the area, illuminating the Morgan's wide, fear-filled eyes.

Matthew reached the trembling animal and laid a gentle hand on his neck. "Whoa now. Settle down."

Samson shuddered under his touch.

"I'm just going to get my oilskin." He spoke in a soothing tone as he walked to his saddlebags.

Matthew slipped the waterproof garment over his already

damp clothing and stowed his bedroll. The next burst of lightning showed him that the tiny creek had overflowed its banks and now crept toward them. If he stayed where they were, he'd risk getting washed away. But heading for high ground would tempt the lightning. He decided on the high ground.

Samson stamped and circled when Matthew tried to throw the saddle blanket over his back. Gripping the lead rope to hold the head still, he dropped the blanket over the horse. He had to let go of the rope to lift the saddle high enough to place it on Sampson. As soon as he did, the animal sidestepped.

"Blast it, hold still!"

A crackle of lighting flared. Matthew lunged forward and lowered the saddle onto the blanket, then grabbed the front cinch and snugged it around the horse's belly. After waiting out another flash and boom, he fastened the back cinch and hoisted the saddlebags over his shoulder. Then, keeping a firm grip on the lead rope, he untied it from the stake. Samson pranced and tossed his head, but followed Matthew through the sodden grass to the top of the swale where they would wait out the storm.

Toward daylight the clouds thinned and scudded east. As sunrise flowed over the prairie, Matthew saw he was surrounded by sheets of water. Brooks and rivulets had swollen into roaring torrents. The grass lay flattened on the ground, obliterating the trail he'd followed the previous day. When he stared due west, he saw ragged shapes against the horizon. He tamped down misgivings at the prospect of riding across open prairie with no trail for a guide. While crossing through low places, he'd be out of sight of the grove completely. What if he lost his way?

He put a foot in the stirrup and swung onto the horse, grimacing when he hit the soggy saddle. Turning his back on the sunrise, Matthew rode toward what he hoped was the landmark he sought.

His progress through muddy water and across soft ground took far longer than he'd figured. His stomach growled, reminding him that he'd eaten the last of the venison for supper the night before. Angry at himself for not bringing more food, Matthew kicked a heel into Samson's side.

"Giddup."

The horse trotted faster, his hooves splashing fans of mud in every direction. As the sun rose, the cottonwood trees ahead seemed to ascend from the prairie and move toward him.

Encouraged, Matthew settled back in the saddle and allowed his mind to wander to his planned conversation with Elder Meecham. Suddenly the horse stumbled and pitched forward. Before Matthew could grab the saddle horn, he flew over Samson's head and hit the ground, landing on his right shoulder. For a moment he lay in the mud fighting dizziness, white lights pulsing behind his eyelids. Searing pain tore down his arm and across his chest.

When he tried to stand, his feet slid on the slippery grass and he dropped to his knees in the muck. Drawing as much breath as he could into his lungs, Matthew managed a faint whistle.

"Come here, boy."

The horse turned his head and looked at him, but didn't move.

He whistled again. "C'mon. Here."

Samson took a few steps in his direction. By crawling on his knees and using his left arm for balance, Matthew reached the animal's side and grabbed a stirrup.

He dragged himself upright, gasping as pain wrapped itself around his upper body. Swaying, he waited for a wave of blackness to pass, then shoved his left foot into the stirrup and swung into the saddle.

"Aaah!" Cold sweat prickled his forehead. "God, help me. Give me strength."

He fought the temptation to rest his head on the horse's neck and sit without moving. Instead, he urged Samson into a slow walk. Every footfall sent knives through his upper body. He had to hang on.

❀

Sunset had flared across the sky by the time Matthew reached the outskirts of Quincy. With gratitude he noticed a sign proclaiming the whitewashed clapboard building directly in front of him to be a livery stable. Once he passed the livestock pen, Matthew gingerly pulled back on the reins to stop his horse.

"This is as far as you go, Samson." He patted the animal's neck. "Now you get your oats."

A husky man wrapped in a stained leather apron met him at the doorway. "By thunder, if'n you don't look done for! What happened to you?"

"Fell off my horse out there past the ten-mile point."

"And you rode all this way? Gol dang! You're a tough one."

Matthew slid off Samson's back. "Not so tough," he gasped. "No choice." He cradled his right elbow in his left hand. "Could you take care of my horse? Rub him down, grain him?" He stopped to catch his breath. "And tell me where I might find Barton Meecham?"

Brown eyes peered at Matthew from behind an explosion of beard. "From the looks of you, I'd best take you to him myself." He thrust a grimy hand in Matthew's direction. "Name's Elijah Dawson. Folks around here call me Eli."

"Matthew Craig." He surrendered his left hand to the big man's grip, wincing as pain shot through him.

"You wait there." Eli pointed at a bench next to a watering trough. "Soon's I get your animal stabled I'll bring a buggy around."

139

Matthew sank onto the wooden bench and rested against the wall of the livery. While he waited for Eli, he looked down the muddy main road that ran through town. Various businesses lined the street, among them a tobacconist, a saloon, and a post office. On a hill to the east he saw a cross-topped church steeple. From his vantage point in the shadow of the building, it seemed to him that the glow from the fading sunlight bathed the spire in gold. Weariness cloaked him and he let his mind drift into a state of semi-sleep. Shadows crept across the road and up the hillside, as though a curtain were being drawn over the town.

Roused by the sound of horse's hooves, Matthew looked up to see Eli rounding the stable driving a low-slung black buggy.

"There's a doc north of town. How about I take you there first?"

Matthew shook his head. He was primed to meet with Elder Meecham. Seeing a doctor would only delay matters. "I'm bruised pretty bad is all. Nothing a doctor can fix."

He staggered to his feet and stumbled through the slurry of mud and horse droppings to mount the buggy step. Using his left hand he hauled himself onto the seat beside the stable owner. His injured side screamed a protest of pain.

"I put your gear in back." Eli pointed over his shoulder at Matthew's saddlebags lying on the floor. "Figured you'd need it."

"Thank you." Matthew squeezed the words out using as little air as possible. The buggy turned at the corner and started up the hill. After crossing two intersections, they stopped in front of a rambling one-story dwelling that looked like it had been cobbled on to at a whim rather than by any clear plan. It stood near the church Matthew had noted from the road below.

Eli jumped down and picked up the saddlebags. "I'll tote these for you. Don't look like you're in any shape to carry them."

"Thanks."

"Want me to wait?"

Matthew glimpsed a lighted window in one of the added-on sections of the house. "No need. Looks like he's here." He fumbled in his pocket for a coin, but the burly man held out a palm to stop him.

"We'll settle up when you come for your horse." Eli flashed a white smile out of his bushy whiskers and climbed back into his buggy.

Matthew watched for a moment as he drove away. Now that he stood at Elder Meecham's door the determination that brought him to Quincy fled. He'd pastored in Beldon Grove for so long. He lifted his hand to rap on the doorframe, then hesitated. Did he really want to leave his church? He shook his head. He didn't see any way he could stay.

A tall, cadaverous-looking man opened the door at Matthew's knock. Thick curly hair grew low on his forehead, beneath which a pair of dark brown eyes looked him up and down. "Do I know you, sir?"

"My name is Matthew Craig," he said, conscious of his mud-encrusted boots and bedraggled clothing. "I'm pastor of the church in Beldon Grove. I've come to talk to you."

Barton Meecham's eyes widened. "Craig! You look like you've been drug behind a horse. No wonder I didn't recognize you." He turned his head and called over his shoulder, "Ma, come here." Returning his attention to Matthew, he held out his right hand. "We're not doing any talking until we take care of you. Is that blood on your shirt?"

Blood? Matthew didn't remember bleeding. Meecham slipped a hand under Matthew's left arm and guided him to a chair in the warm room. A low fire burned in the hearth. In the shadows he saw that one wall was entirely given over to bookshelves.

Footsteps sounded from the back of the house, and an older woman hurried in carrying a lamp, placing it on a table next to Matthew. Her hair was covered with a white cap, which framed the lines and wrinkles in her face. From her slat-thin build to her dark-lashed eyes, she was undoubtedly Barton Meecham's mother.

"This is Reverend Craig, from Beldon Grove," Meecham told her. "Appears he's going to need a little tending-to, and a hot meal."

Mrs. Meecham bent over the chair where Matthew sat. "Think you could manage a little beef soup? There's plenty left from supper."

Matthew could hardly think beyond the persistent pain in his side, but he mustered a polite smile. "Sounds mighty tasty, ma'am. I haven't had beef in a very long time."

After Matthew had eaten what he could, Meecham and his mother insisted that he let his injuries be cleaned and dressed, then he must get a good night's rest before getting down to the business that had brought him across the prairie. The two of them cleared a space on the cluttered kitchen table for a basin of hot water and then helped him remove his shirt and undergarment.

To his surprise, he learned that the blood on his shirt had come from a sizable gash in his scalp, which had bled down the back of his neck. As gently as she could, Mrs. Meecham sponged his wound with hot water, then smeared it with thick, smelly black creosote. Matthew flinched when the ointment contacted the open wound.

"There, there." Mrs. Meecham made soothing noises. "It's bleeding a little. We've got to get it to quit. I'll be done soon and you can get some sleep."

Blue and purple bruising covered the right side of Matthew's torso. When he focused on his shoulder, he realized that it hurt too much to simply be bruised. He sucked enough air into his lungs to allow him to speak. "Feels like my shoulder's broken."

Mrs. Meecham looked at her son. "You'd best see to it. I can wash him, but I don't know about setting bones."

The tall man bent over Matthew, peering at his shoulder in the yellow lamplight. His callused fingertips probed the joint, each touch a jolt of pain.

Then Meecham stepped back, dropped his hands to his belt, and unfastened the buckle. He pulled the leather strap from around his waist, handing it to Matthew. "Put this between your teeth and bite down. This is going to hurt considerable."

Matthew clutched the still-warm leather in his left hand, wishing he'd accepted Eli's offer to take him to the doctor before conveying him to Meecham's. He glanced around the low-ceilinged room, noting food spots crusted on the surface of the cookstove and the stack of unwashed crockery piled on a side table.

He dropped his gaze to the belt coiled in his hand. "Uh, think maybe we should fetch a doctor?"

Meecham leaned against the table, his face a picture of wounded pride. "I set many a woodsy's bone in the old days when there wasn't a doc for a hundred miles. You don't think I'd lay a hand on you if I didn't believe I could help, do you?"

Two choices lay before Matthew. Leave the house and find a doctor, which seemed an impossibility given his physical state, or submit to Elder Meecham's ministrations and hope for the best.

He picked up the belt and bit down on it. "Go ahead," he mumbled around the leather.

Meecham lifted Matthew's right arm, gripping it above the wrist.

Sucking in his breath against the pain, Matthew waited. The

room was so quiet he could hear water bubbling in the kettle on the stove.

Meecham raised the arm the way a blacksmith would open a bellows, then jerked it straight out from the shoulder.

Matthew screamed, the belt dropping from his mouth. Beads of sweat dotted his forehead.

"Don't hear no crackling. I think it's just dislocated," Meecham said, retrieving the leather strap. "Bite down again. We're going to put 'er back in place." He manipulated the arm until the shoulder joint popped together.

Matthew's eyes swam with tears. He let the belt fall from his mouth and rested his head against the back of the chair. Although his shoulder did feel easier, the throbbing in his ribs intensified and the wound on his scalp burned. "Are you done? I don't think I can take much more."

Meecham examined his bruised torso. "You could have some broken ribs." He glanced at his mother. "Would you fetch a roll of bandages, please, Ma?"

Once they had Matthew's chest wrapped and his right arm secured to his side, the Meechams led him to a small room that opened off the kitchen, and helped him settle onto a narrow quilt-piled cot.

Mrs. Meecham propped the sagging door with a stick of firewood. "I'll leave this open so's heat from the fire can get at you. Don't want you taking a chill."

The pain in Matthew's shoulder and ribs alternated between agonizing and unbearable. He closed his eyes and let his thoughts drift homeward, knowing how worried Ellie would be when he didn't return by Friday.

15

Ellie sat on the shaded back porch, her mind on the conversation she'd had with Mr. Beldon earlier in the week. She picked up a pencil and stared at the blank sheet of paper on the table next to her. "List everything you can think of," he'd said. "You never know what might be important."

Humidity coiled around her like ground fog. Ellie dropped the pencil and wiped sweating hands on her apron. Through the open kitchen window she heard the oven door creak and Maria dragging pans of bread out to cool. A thump told her they'd been set on the worktable. From the cornfield, voices of her sons carried up to the house.

She retrieved the pencil and leaned over to write.

Name—George Long
Born Cape Girardeau County, Missouri. Don't
    know the date.
Had fair hair and blue eyes.
Father—Andrew Long. Possibly living
    somewhere in Missouri?
Went to Texas 1821 as part of Stephen Austin's
    company.

Would have married there sometime after 1821.

Children probably 18 to 22 years old.

Died in Brazoria County, Texas, December 1845.

Her hand stuck to the paper and she peeled it free. Eight lines on a page. Loss washed over her. Ellie bowed her head. Her children could fill eight pages about herself and Matthew. She sucked in a breath, glad she'd asked Mr. Beldon for help. When he found her family, they would answer all her questions.

Ellie wiped her tears on her apron, folded the paper, and tucked it into her pocket. Guilt niggled at a corner of her brain. She knew Matthew would be furious if he learned she'd taken her request to Mr. Beldon, of all people. She dismissed the thought by reassuring herself that if Molly could consult him about James, there was no reason he couldn't help her too. Matthew would never need to know.

That night Ellie lay awake, thoughts of Matthew and Mr. Beldon warring in her mind. Matthew had told her not to pursue the notion of her father having other offspring. Now, in the worry hours before dawn, she wondered if he might have been right. The little bit of information she possessed surely wasn't enough for anyone to use to locate records of her father's life. Any children born of a later union would now be adults themselves. Why would they want to travel the long distance from southern Texas to Illinois? It would be better if she were just to forget the whole thing. And yet . . .

The feather tick crackled. In spite of the open window, the air felt sticky. She missed the comfort of Matthew's steady breathing. The chirping of crickets and the occasional hoot of an owl filled the night.

"Please, God, don't let anything happen to him," she whispered. "If you bring him home, I'll—" *No, I can't promise that.* She amended her prayer. "Please bring him safely home."

Ellie scooted upright and leaned against the headboard. All her life she'd leaned on others to carry her through difficult times, and now every support was gone. Her mind skittered away from the possibility that Matthew wouldn't return.

She swung her feet to the floor and padded to the window, as though at this moment she might see him riding into the yard. A half moon soaked their acres in dim gray light. Shadowed shapes lurked at the edges of the cornfield, but no matter how closely she watched they didn't take the form of a horse and rider.

The following morning, Ellie hurried the children toward the door as soon as Mr. Wolcott's Dearborn wagon rolled into the yard. "Don't keep him waiting. We're already late." She took Maria's hand and followed the boys down the back steps.

Charity beamed at them as they approached. "Don't you two look lovely in those pink dresses. Maria, you're going to be as pretty as your mama some day."

Maria dipped her head and blushed. Harrison shot her a scornful look. "She ain't pretty. She's just a fool girl."

Clamping a hand on her son's shoulder, Ellie gave him a gentle push toward the wagon. "That's enough. Get in." She turned to Mr. Wolcott. "Will coming to pick us up make you late for preaching today?"

"The trip out here makes no difference." He sounded upset. "I went in early to open the church and found Marcus Beldon already there. Seems he's intending to take care of preaching from now on."

Charity touched his arm. "Now, Ben, he didn't say that. He told you he'd be pleased to fill in whilst Reverend Craig was away."

Away. So far Ellie hadn't told anyone but Molly and Karl about her husband's intention to resign the pastorate. She placed her hopes on the presiding elder refusing to let him go, or possibly suggesting he set aside some time to rest.

"Who does Beldon think he is, I'd like to know," Mr. Wolcott said under his breath.

Ellie remembered the day she'd first met Mr. Beldon and his wife at the church. "He did tell us he'd been educated for the ministry."

"Educated! What have all these educated ministers ever done for the world? Sit in their classrooms and memorize scripture. Did Jesus ever go to a university?" He flicked the reins over the horses' backs, jolting the wagon forward. "All this fancy learning is going to ruin the church. We need more men who answer a call and are willing to ride from place to place, spreading the gospel."

Charity leaned over and whispered into Ellie's ear, "Now you've got him started. We'll hear about this all the way to town."

"Matthew's of the same opinion," Ellie whispered back. "I wonder if that's why he doesn't care for Mr. Beldon. He's never said as much, but I can tell by the way he acts when the name comes up."

When they entered the church, Ellie sought a space for herself and the children on one of the rear benches.

Mr. Beldon had been walking toward the pulpit when he glanced over his shoulder and noticed the Craig family entering. He came straight down the center aisle and clasped both of Ellie's hands in his.

"I can't tell you how happy it makes me to see you here. I've been concerned that you would take it wrong to have me preach today, but your presence completely reassures me." He continued to hold her hands while smiling down at her. "I hope you'll accept my humble efforts on Reverend Craig's behalf." Then he bent his head and whispered, "I'm looking into the matter we spoke about the other day. Did you bring any more information?" He stood close enough for Ellie to see the thick lashes that framed his dark eyes.

The warmth of his grasp burned into her skin. Both attracted and frightened by his nearness, she swallowed in an effort to push her pounding heart back down her throat.

She slid one hand into her reticule and offered the folded list. "Here's everything I could think of."

Mr. Beldon palmed the paper, slipping it into the breast pocket of his jacket. "I'm sure it will be a great help." He kept his voice pitched low.

Aware people were watching them, Ellie drew back. "Thank you." She spoke loudly enough to be heard by those around them. "My husband would be pleased at your willingness to serve, did he but know of it."

He tipped a bow in her direction and strode to the pulpit, while Ellie sank onto a bench, weak-kneed.

"Papa wouldn't be pleased at all," Johnny whispered. "Why did you say he would?"

"Hush. You don't know what Papa thinks."

"I know what he thinks about Mr. Beldon."

Heads turned and curious eyes rested on them.

Ellie ignored them, squeezing her son's knee none too gently. "Enough. You know not to talk during church."

Johnny came as close as he dared to giving her a hard look, but settled back with his arms folded across his chest and his jaw jutted forward.

While Mr. Beldon expounded on the scriptures, using words Ellie was sure some in the congregation were at a loss to understand, she glanced around at the filled benches. She hadn't seen many of the people present for more than a month.

Standing alone after the service, Ellie realized Mr. Beldon's welcome hadn't influenced those who felt that she, too, was under judgment. Few people stopped to greet her on their way out the door. When she lifted her eyes, Ellie spotted Hettie Sims moving in her direction, her turkey wattle chin bobbing as she closed the distance between them.

Fixing a polite smile on her lips, Ellie held out her hand. "How nice to see you here, Miss Sims. I know Reverend Craig would be pleased."

Hettie Sims sailed past her as though Ellie was part of the wall, the scent of rose water and musty wool trailing her out the door.

Ellie dropped her hand, face burning. *Old biddy. I hope she falls down the steps.* She glanced after Hettie's retreating back, disappointed to see her navigate the front steps without a stumble and glide toward the street. Ellie turned to see if anyone had noticed the snub, and saw Molly and Karl coming toward her. She hurried to join them, eager to be with people she loved and who loved her.

Molly hugged her. "You and the children come to dinner, won't you? We haven't seen you all week." She glanced at the Wolcotts. "Karl already invited Ben and Charity, so you're stuck waiting for a ride unless you come." Her tone teased.

Spirits lifting at the prospect of a pleasant afternoon, Ellie teased back. "You leave me no choice." She glanced outside at her boys, who were already huddled with Molly's son Franklin. Maria and Lily sat together in Karl's wagon, looking impatient.

She linked arms with Molly. "Let's go."

Once Ellie left the prying eyes of the congregation and settled next to her sister-in-law, she dropped the mask she'd worn during the service. Sighing, she leaned back and closed her eyes.

"Are you all right?" Molly asked.

"I'm trying to be." Ellie squeezed her hands together. In a low voice, so the children wouldn't overhear, she continued. "I'm worried about Matthew. He's had more than enough time to go to Quincy and return."

Karl leaned around his wife. "Perhaps the presiding elder detained him on church business. Isn't there a general conference coming up?"

"No. Matthew wouldn't be going anyhow."

"Give it a few more days. I'll come by midweek to check on you."

That night Ellie sat at her kitchen table reading Karl's copy of the latest *Illinois Monitor*. She'd borrowed it to read news of the conflict with Mexico and possibly gain some inkling of where Molly's son, James, might be. After combing through the densely printed columns of type, she had no more idea than Molly and Karl did. She hoped Mr. Beldon had more luck.

Her heart beat faster at the memory of his reassurance that morning that he hadn't forgotten her own request.

She was ready to fold the paper and set it aside when a small notice near the bottom of a page caught her eye. "Divorce. Ruby Newberry vs. Arthur Newberry. Filed by Ruby Newberry. Sangamon County." Ellie's hand shook. She'd never known anyone who had been divorced. She stared at the printed page and tried to absorb the news. This would create another scandal. Then a second thought struck. Would people hold this against Matthew too?

Ellie grabbed the paper, pushed her chair away from the table, and hurried to the stove. She shoved the *Monitor* into the firebox, watching as the edges browned on the banked coals. A spurt of flame appeared in one corner. Then remembering the paper belonged to Karl, Ellie jerked the *Monitor* out of the stove, singed but intact, and slapped at sparks worming along the edge. She glanced around the kitchen, looking for a place to hide the ugly announcement. She opened a cupboard, pushed cheese molds out of the way, and tucked the newspaper behind them.

She latched the door and started for the table to blow out the lamp when she realized how nonsensical her actions were. *If the notice is in the* Monitor, *anyone can read it. It's not like a wound I can hide beneath a bandage.*

Ellie squatted to reach for the folded paper when she heard footsteps on the back porch. She hurried toward the sound, leaving the cupboard open. The footsteps outside stopped.

She paused, hand on the latch. "Who's there?" She took a step backward.

A voice rasped, "It's me. Arthur."

Ellie flung open the door. "Uncle! I thought we'd never see you again." She wrapped her arms around him, feeling evening dampness on his coat.

He patted her shoulder. "Don't take on so. I'm here." He followed her into the kitchen and flopped into one of the chairs.

In the lamplight, Ellie saw purple hollows under Uncle Arthur's eyes. His face had gaunted up during the month he'd been away. His beard, which he'd always kept trimmed, was a mass of white whiskers that bunched under his nose and straggled across his cheeks. The characteristic expression of perpetual good humor had disappeared.

"I'll build up the fire. You must be chilled to the bone."

"Thank you. A little heat would help these shakes." His teeth chattered between words.

"My goodness, you're sick. I'll brew a pot of tea, then get you to bed. There's a cot ready in the extra room."

He nodded. "You're a good girl. Your aunt would be proud."

At his statement, Ellie stiffened. She slipped in front of the cupboard and pushed the door shut with one knee.

While she fed wood into the fire, Uncle Arthur said, "I figured on sleeping in your barn tonight, but when I saw your light I reckoned you and Matthew was still up." He glanced around the room. "He gone to bed?"

"Matthew's not here." Ellie answered over her shoulder, still arranging firewood on the coals. "He went to Quincy Friday last and he's not back yet."

"Q-q-quincy?" Uncle Arthur stuttered the question around the tremors that shook his body.

Alarmed, Ellie shot a sharp look at him. She left the firebox door ajar to allow heat into the room, then laid a hand on his forehead. "Fever. You must have the ague. In the morning, I'll send one of the boys to Karl to get some quinine pills." She took his arm and tugged him to his feet. "We'll talk tomorrow—for now you need rest. I'll bring the tea when it's ready. Do you think you can make it up the stairs?"

A spark of his old humor lit Uncle Arthur's eyes. "Made it this far, didn't I?"

Late the following afternoon, Uncle Arthur sat at the kitchen table, this time wrapped in quilts. Karl and Ellie sat across from him. His skin remained pale and yellowish, but the tremors had abated.

He cupped his hands around a mug of hot broth. "Thought I could find Ruby if I headed for St. Louis. Seemed a likely place for actors to be. I must of got the ague from them river swamps down along the way."

Karl nodded. "That's rank air, especially if you're not used to it."

"Never give it much thought when I started out. All I could think of was catching up with your aunt." He gazed at Ellie while he spoke.

She darted a glance at the closed cupboard door, unable to meet his eyes.

Uncle Arthur took a sip of broth. "Come to think on it, I don't know what would've happened if I'd come across her." His shoulders slumped. "Anyways, I didn't find no sign nowhere."

Karl rose from his chair. "Afraid I need to get back. I've got office hours on Monday evenings, and folks usually come in." He handed a tin pillbox to Ellie. "See he takes these three times a day, at least for the next week."

"A week?" Uncle Arthur's head snapped up. "I'm going to my place after supper."

"No. Your farm's waited this long. It'll wait a few more days. Get your strength back first."

"I don't want to burden Ellie—she's got enough worries with Matthew gone."

Ellie bent and dropped a kiss on the top of her uncle's head. "How could you be a burden after all you've done for me?"

The light behind his eyes dimmed. "I must be a burden. My own wife doesn't want me."

"She'll be back. You wait and see." Karl put on his hat and turned to Ellie. "Can you come out to the buggy for a minute? Molly sent a ginger cake for the young'uns."

Once out of earshot of the house, he asked, "Want me to go looking for Matt? I don't like the idea of him being away for so long. I can't think what might be keeping him."

She shook her head. "You've got too many people depending on you. Quincy's a long ride." Then fear overrode stoicism. "But if you know of someone who might go . . ."

Karl removed his hat and combed his fingers through his blond hair. After a moment's thought he said, "I'll ask Griffiths' son Daniel. That fellow could track a snake over a pile of rocks." He reached into the buggy and handed her the cake. "He'll find him."

Ellie brushed moisture from her forehead and placed the cooled flatiron on the stovetop, exchanging it for a heated one. She looked longingly out the open back door at the balmy June afternoon, then glanced at the pile of clothes still waiting to be ironed. If she could get through her chores before suppertime, she'd go out and sit with Uncle Arthur. It was too pretty a day to spend indoors.

She'd sent Maria and Harrison to the cornfield to pick worms from the stalks. Jimmy and Johnny were mucking out the barn. Ellie sighed and smoothed another dampened garment over the short-legged board resting on the kitchen table. Curls of steam rolled out under the path of the hot iron, scenting the room with the clean smell of the outdoors.

Dust rising from the road caught her attention. *Matthew?* Ellie dropped the iron back on the stove and hurried to the porch in time to see Mr. Beldon's phaeton rattle across the plank bridge and into the farmyard.

Upon seeing Ellie, he pulled his team to a halt and jumped from the carriage. "I came as soon as I heard."

He strode toward her. As usual, he wore a well-tailored coat and trousers, which emphasized his muscular physique. He didn't look like a man who ever rushed anywhere.

"Heard what?"

Behind Mr. Beldon's back, Ellie noticed her twin sons walking toward them. Both were almost as tall as Matthew, and already possessed a goodly share of his strength. They covered the distance between barn and house and stopped next to her.

Mr. Beldon's eyes met Ellie's. "About your husband's disappearance. I came to see if I could be of any help."

Johnny stepped closer to his mother. "Uncle Karl's already got Daniel Griffith out looking. You're not needed, sir."

"Don't see what a city man could do, anyhow," Jimmy muttered.

Shocked, Ellie's mouth dropped open. "Boys! Remember your manners."

"It's quite all right." Mr. Beldon took her hand, ignoring the twins. "Children tend to get overexcited when their normal routine is disrupted." He spoke in a soothing tone. "My offer stands, if you need me." He squeezed her hand, then turned and strode toward his carriage.

16

The morning after Matthew's arrival at Meechams', he overheard Barton Meecham and his mother talking in the kitchen.

"What do you reckon brought him clean over here?" Mrs. Meecham asked.

"Don't know. He said he wanted to talk to me, so we'll find out soon enough."

"I've said this before, Son. You need to visit the churches in your district more often. This poor boy had to ride all this way to talk to you."

"Ma."

Matthew heard exaggerated patience in the man's voice.

Meecham continued, "In the first place, Brother Craig is hardly a boy. He's near to my age. And in the second place, if he'd stayed put, I'd of gotten to him in another month or two."

"Humph. Maybe what he has to say couldn't wait until you got around to traveling."

Matthew pushed himself up on the cot with his left arm, grunting at the pain that flared down his right side.

"You awake in there?" Meecham called.

"I am. I'll be out directly."

The door swung wide and Meecham entered, carrying a garment over his arm. "Let me help you get a shirt on. Likely you aren't wanting to move that arm any more than you must."

"Thanks, but I can manage."

The smell of fried ham filtered in from the kitchen. Matthew's stomach growled, reminding him how hungry he was.

Ignoring his objection, Meecham leaned down and slipped one sleeve onto Matthew's left arm, then draped the shirt over his right shoulder. No one had helped him put his clothes on since he was a child, and the intimacy of the act embarrassed Matthew. Further, the difference in their height left him feeling like the boy Mrs. Meecham had said he was. He grabbed his pants before Meecham could think of helping him with those too.

When Matthew entered the kitchen, platters of fried ham and eggs waited on the table, next to a pan of steaming biscuits.

Mrs. Meecham glanced at him. "Dig in, young man. We always eat good for breakfast—you never know what a day might bring."

He didn't need to be told twice. He tugged a chair away from the table with his left hand and lowered his weight onto it. Mrs. Meecham filled his plate, cutting his ham into bite-sized pieces while he watched, half amused. Dressing him, cutting his food. The next thing he knew, they'd offer to feed him.

She pointed at his plate. "Want me to help you with that?"

Matthew shook his head, awkwardly manipulating his fork with his left hand. "Sooner I get the hang of this, the better."

Once he'd wiped the last of the egg yolk from his plate with a biscuit, Matthew eased his body back in the chair. Feeling strengthened, he decided to divulge his mission before his courage deserted him. "Brother Meecham, I came to ask you to assign me to another church in the Quincy district."

He looked surprised. "You don't beat around the bush, do you? Want to tell me why you're giving up on Beldon Grove?"

"It's the other way around. Beldon Grove is giving up on me."

Meecham shifted in his chair to allow his mother to clear the table, then leaned toward Matthew. "Start at the beginning."

Matthew told him about Marcus Beldon's arrival in Beldon Grove and the man's belief that the community was his rightful heritage. He related the deaths of his and Ellie's four infants and the whispering campaign that had sprung up in town, claiming that the deaths were God's judgment against him as a preacher.

Mrs. Meecham turned from the basin. "Don't you believe it, young man. Barton's papa and me lost all our babies 'cept this one." She pointed a soapy hand at her son. "Wasn't a judgment. God weeps when his little ones pass on, but he weeps for us, not them. They're in a better place."

Tears formed in Matthew's eyes at her gentle tone. He looked at the ceiling and blinked hard to keep them from spilling. "Yes, ma'am, I believe that too, but there's plenty of folks in Beldon Grove think otherwise right now."

Meecham's expression softened. "I understand this has been hard on your family. But it doesn't sound like enough reason to give up your church. Is that all?"

Matthew started to lean forward, but the pain in his ribs stopped him. Drawing a thin breath, he again rested against the chair back. "There was one other matter. About the same time Beldon got to town, handbills went up about a Shakespeare play that would be coming."

"All the way to Beldon Grove? Which one? I'm quite fond of Shakespeare myself."

Nervous sweat prickled Matthew's forehead. "Uh, *Macbeth*." If

159

it weren't for his sore ribs, he would have squirmed in his chair. Ben was right. Everyone was right. He felt his skin flush under his beard. Why hadn't he listened?

"*Macbeth*. One of my particular favorites. And how was the performance?"

Matthew gulped. "I didn't go."

At Meecham's look of surprise, he told him the whole story of his opposition to the play, how Beldon had used it against him, and how eventually it had split his congregation. "But it wasn't the play itself. I worried about actor folk corrupting our young people." He jutted his chin forward. "Turns out I was right. My wife's aunt ran off with one of the performers."

"How does that make you right? Your wife's aunt is probably old enough to know what she's doing. You can't blame the acting troupe for her decision. Might've happened another time with someone else."

Speechless, Matthew blinked. He hadn't considered that possibility.

Meecham tilted his head, a skeptical light in his eyes. "I'm wondering if you're exaggerating your problems with this Mr. Beldon, as well."

"No. I'm not. He claims her adultery proves I can't manage my own family." Matthew's left hand curled into a fist. "I need to leave the Beldon Grove church for the good of the body."

One eyebrow raised almost to his low hairline, Meecham folded his arms and studied Matthew for a long moment. "The good of the body? Sure it's not your wounded pride that's making you run?" He pushed back his chair and paced the length of the room. Then he turned toward Matthew, shaking his head. "You owe fidelity to your congregation. You've led them for years. Now you want to leave when things go sour?"

Matthew felt like a child being scolded by an angry parent. He stood. "What's to be gained by my staying? Beldon has most of the congregation gathering at the hotel now. No one comes to the church on Sundays." In the background, the stove brush scratched as Mrs. Meecham scrubbed the surface of the squat range.

After glancing at his mother, Meecham stepped next to Matthew, placed a gentle hand on his left shoulder, and directed him toward the parlor. "Let's go in here. It's quieter."

Cold air in the unheated room struck Matthew's face like a damp cloth. Rather than sit in the chair Meecham pointed out, he walked over to the bookshelves and leaned against them. If his ribs hadn't been so painful, he'd have crossed his arms over his chest. As it was, he slipped his left hand in his pocket and waited.

"No one comes on Sundays?" Meecham repeated Matthew's statement back to him. "Your family is there, and you mentioned several other people in the community who are standing with you. Are they of no consequence?"

"They'll understand. They've seen what's happened."

"So you're leaving them to worship at a hotel? Have you thought about that?"

In his mind, Matthew saw a vision of his family and friends smiling up at him as he stood behind the pulpit. He bowed his head. "Maybe you could trade me to another station, and someone else could minister in Beldon Grove." Put into words, the idea sounded lack-witted, even to him.

Meecham's dark eyes flared. "Uproot two families to salve your wounded pride? Brother Craig, I expected better of you. You were recommended for the Beldon Grove church based on the strength of your good work on the circuit. No one mentioned you'd cut and run when you encountered difficulties."

"I believe I'm doing what is best." A nagging thought surfaced.

Like opposing the play was for the best? His ribs throbbed, and he sank into a chair. He'd run out of arguments. He only knew he'd lost most of his congregation to Marcus Beldon, and all of Meecham's persuasive words wouldn't bring them back.

Frowning, Meecham walked across the narrow room and stared down at Matthew, regret in his eyes. "There are seven missions in the Quincy district, and except for Beldon Grove now, all the pulpits are filled. I have no place to send you."

Matthew opened his mouth to reply, but Meecham cut him off. "If you really feel you have to leave, you can go back to riding circuit. There's a need for an itinerant preacher in the southern part of the state."

Riding circuit was the last thing he wanted. How could he look after his family if he was gone all the time? He remembered long days in the saddle in all sorts of weather. No set place to sleep most nights. Poor food.

Trapped, he choked out, "What are the boundaries?"

"We can go over that later, when you're fit to travel." Meecham opened the kitchen door and spoke to his mother. "I have calls to make this morning. You look after Brother Craig."

After the front door closed, Matthew continued to sit in the unheated parlor. He'd won the argument, but at a high price. How would Ellie react when she found out he'd be riding circuit? He shook his head. What had he gotten himself into?

As the days of Matthew's recovery slipped by, Elder Meecham treated him with restrained courtesy. Occasionally, Matthew would sense that he was being watched and look up to find Meecham studying him with a speculative expression. But the subject of the Beldon Grove church was not raised again.

The following Sunday he felt well enough to walk to church with them and attend services. As they covered the distance, Matthew's thoughts were far from the steepled building down the lane. Instead, they centered around his wife and family—they were bound to be frantic at his prolonged absence. If only he had a way to get word home quickly.

When he stepped into the sanctuary of the Quincy church, he noted the differences between the small building in Beldon Grove and this one. Where his church had benches, the Quincy meeting house had high-backed pews. One of the windows had been set with tiny panes of stained glass, which scattered drops of color over the heads of the worshipers. A simple cross was carved into the front of the tall pulpit. He made a note to himself to have someone carve a similar cross on his pulpit in Beldon Grove. Then heaviness filled his chest as he remembered. It wasn't his church anymore.

His gaze fell on a blonde woman seated near the aisle. She held a sleeping infant wrapped in a blue blanket. Next to her sat three children, stairstepped in age. Her husband sat at the other end of the pew. Matthew groaned. His loneliness felt like physical pain.

"Are your ribs hurting?" Mrs. Meecham whispered. "You don't have to stay if it's too painful."

He shook his head. "I'll be all right. Please don't worry." Once seated, Matthew opened his Bible, flipping to the Psalms for comfort. It was time to go home.

When Matthew reached the grove of cottonwoods marking the ten-mile point from Quincy, he turned his horse due east and plodded toward home. Although his ribs and shoulder had begun to heal during the nine days he'd spent at Meechams', every step Samson took sent a jolt of pain through Matthew's right side. He gritted his teeth and rode on, determined to reach Beldon Grove before nightfall.

In the distance, he saw a rider coming toward him. Tall grass concealed the horse's legs, making it appear the rider was sailing across the prairie. Several minutes passed before Matthew saw the man's face clearly. *Daniel Griffith.* He tugged on Samson's reins and stopped to wait.

Daniel pulled his hat off and hollered, "Reverend!" A wide grin split his tanned face. "Wish all my tracking jobs was this easy."

"Someone sent you to find me? Did something happen to Ellie? One of the children?"

"Naw, nothing like that. You was gone so long Doc asked me to go looking for you. Miz Craig's been sore worried."

Matthew pushed his hat back and rubbed his forehead. "Fell off my horse the day after I left." He shifted in the saddle so Daniel could see that his right arm was bound to his side. "I've been in Quincy being tended to. I knew my wife would worry, but couldn't find anyone to take word back."

Daniel affected a world-weary expression. "Well, you know how women are. The least little thing throws them into a tizzy."

The image of young Daniel as an expert on women amused Matthew. Although Daniel was twenty-four years old, he'd never left his parents' home, nor showed any interest in the girls who shined up to him. Matthew figured it had something to do with his older brother running away when the boys were in their late teens. Since then, Daniel had done all he could to reassure his mother that he had no plans to desert her.

Matthew suppressed a smile and said, "That being the case, I'd best hurry along."

Daniel swung his horse around and rode next to him. "I'll stick with you, Reverend, 'til you get to your farm. Wouldn't want nothing else to happen to you out here." He pointed to the east. "Saw some wolf tracks back yonder. We need to keep a bright lookout."

Alarm prickled through Matthew. "How many, do you think?"

"More than a few. Heard they've been killing sheep."

The image of his wife and children alone on the farm rose in his mind. Before Matthew left Quincy, Elder Meecham gave him the names of settlements to visit on the southern Illinois circuit. Matthew knew the assignment would keep him away from home for weeks on end.

"I expect you to get started just as quick as you can," Meecham had said. "You're leaving me hard pressed to fill the pulpit in Beldon Grove—don't shirk on the circuit too."

Matthew's gaze locked on his horse's tangled mane while a fresh wave of anger washed over him. *Lord, you know I'm not shirking. Help Ellie and Meecham to see it too.*

Daniel interrupted his thoughts. "Say, how come you were in Quincy? Have business there?"

"Yes." Matthew drew a shallow breath. "I'm leaving the Beldon Grove church."

Daniel gaped at him. "Because of what people are saying about you and the missus having them babies die on you?"

"Mostly."

"Never figured you for a quitter, Reverend."

17

Ellie opened both the front door and the sitting room window, hoping for a cooling breeze while she stitched her way through the week's mending. She sewed patches on the knees of Harrison's pants, but her mind remained preoccupied with Matthew. Karl had assured her Daniel could find him, but she didn't see how. It had rained twice since he left. Any tracks would have been washed away. She thought of Mr. Beldon's offer to assist in the search, wishing the twins hadn't been so rude to him. The more help they had, the sooner Matthew might be found.

Hooves clattered on the plank bridge.

She startled at the sound, her needle stabbing the soft flesh of her index finger. Ellie swiped at the drop of blood with her apron and hurried to the back door in time to see Daniel Griffith ride into the yard. And behind him, Matthew.

She dropped her mending on the porch floor and dashed down the steps. "You're safe!"

"Yes." Matthew eased off his horse. Deep creases lined his face, making him look older than his years. His right arm was bound to his body.

"Oh my word. What happened?" She went to him and nestled close to his left side, breathing in his special Matthew smell. Having him close brought the frayed edges of her life back together.

"I'll tell you when we get inside. I need to sit on something that's not moving." Matthew's face showed surprise when Uncle Arthur shuffled onto the porch. "Looks like you have news for me too."

Daniel turned his horse toward the road. "Be seeing you, Reverend. I hope." He tipped his hat and rode out of the farmyard.

Ellie watched him go, puzzled. "What does he mean, 'I hope'? Why wouldn't he be seeing you?"

"In a minute. I've got to rest." Matthew climbed the stairs, drawing a breath between each step.

Once in the kitchen, the children came running as he made his way to Ellie's rocking chair. Matthew sat carefully, tipping the chair so that his weight rested against the back. "Helps to get pressure off my ribs."

Maria slipped next to his left side and patted his hand. "What's wrong with your ribs?"

Matthew's mouth twisted in a half smile, half grimace. "I think they're all broke. The ones on my right side, anyway."

"Oh, Matt." The words flew from Ellie's mouth. "And you rode home like that?" She slid into a chair facing her husband. "When did it happen?"

The family gathered around the kitchen table and listened while Matthew told of his accident and stay in Quincy. "I knew you'd be worried." His eyes met Ellie's. "But there wasn't any way to get word back quick enough. When Daniel showed up, I guessed you must have thought I was a goner."

"Daniel found you?"

"We met on the trail. I wasn't lost, but he stayed with me. Said he was worried something else would happen." His lips stretched in a wry grin. "Can't say I was sorry for the company."

"And Elder Meecham? What did he have to say?"

"Plenty of time for that later." Matthew nodded in the direction of their children. He tilted his head and sniffed the air. "Something smells good. What's for supper?"

Ellie recognized a deliberate change of subject. "Stewed prairie hens. The boys snared two this morning." She moved toward the stove. "It'll be on the table in a few minutes."

During the meal Matthew focused his attention on Uncle Arthur, peppering him with questions regarding his whereabouts during the past several weeks. Ellie listened, fingers drumming impatiently in her lap, while he took Matthew through every mile of his search for Aunt Ruby.

As soon as he wound down, Ellie turned to the children. "Bedtime. You need to be up early to start your chores."

Matthew laid his fork on his empty plate and took a swallow of coffee. "Don't hurry them. They can stay up a few extra minutes tonight."

Ellie bit her lower lip. "Fine." She seized a stack of plates and plunked them in the basin. "Maria, come help me."

"But I want to talk to Papa."

"So do I." After nearly two weeks alone with her children, at that moment Ellie felt ready to lock them in the root cellar. She set her jaw and poured steaming water over the supper dishes. What happened at Meechams'? Frustrated, she plunged her hands into the cloudy water. A sharp pain shot across the base of her thumb and she jerked her hand out to find blood trickling from a gash in her palm. A moan escaped her lips as she wrapped the wound in her apron.

"Ellie." Matthew struggled from the chair and crossed the room. He lifted her hand. "Let me see."

"I can take care of it myself." She jerked her hand free. "Maria, please wash those dishes. Watch out, there's a knife in the water." Ellie stalked toward the stairs. "Good night. I'm going to bed."

When she climbed the steps, she was aware of her family's stunned expressions, but she was beyond caring.

✑

Matthew closed the bedroom door behind him. Ellie sat up, pushing one of the feather pillows against the headboard for a backrest. He walked around to her side of the bed and scrutinized her bandaged hand. Faint traces of blood showed through the linen strips. "How's your cut?"

"I think the bleeding's stopped. It's not as bad as it looked at first." She disengaged herself from his grasp.

"Maria can wash dishes for you while your hand heals."

"Yes." Silence settled between them. After a moment, Ellie cleared her throat. "Well? What happened in Quincy? Did you resign?"

The candle flame on the bedside table guttered as Matthew sank into the chair beside the fireplace. "No, I didn't resign . . . exactly."

"What's that mean?"

"It means I'm still a pastor in the church." He dropped his head and began fiddling with the buttons on his shirt.

"Our church? Oh, that's wonderful. I've been praying that's what you'd decide." She threw the covers back and slid to the floor, ready to wrap her arms around him. Before she reached the rocker, however, he held up a hand to stop her. Ellie stood still, floorboards cold beneath her feet.

"Not in Beldon Grove. I told him I couldn't go back there."

"What?"

"I asked to be assigned to a different church."

"But we can't leave this farm after all the work we've—"

"We're not leaving. He's assigned me to the southern circuit."

The room swayed. Ellie pushed herself back up onto the bed and stared at her husband. Her frustration flared into hot anger. "When we got married, you said you were finished with circuit riding. You promised."

His shoulders drooped. "Try to understand. This was my only choice. It was either go back to the circuit or leave the ministry altogether."

Heart pounding in her throat, Ellie spit the words at him. "It wasn't your only choice. You could've stayed right where you are. Beldon Grove needs you. You always said God put you here. How can you walk away from his will?"

"Now you're God's messenger? Leave me be." Matthew rubbed his eyes. "I have to work this out for myself."

"No, you have to work this out for all of us. How do you expect me to take care of the house and crops and children without you?"

"Arthur's here, isn't he?"

Before she realized what she was doing, Ellie had flung herself from the bed and raised her hand to slap him across the face.

Matthew seized her wrist and stared at her, shock in his eyes. "What's come over you?"

"I don't need Uncle Arthur. I need you." She crumpled to the floor at his feet, sobbing. Blood from her cut oozed onto her nightgown.

"Stop it. Please." With difficulty he rose from the rocking chair and helped Ellie stand, then led her to the bed. "Get some sleep. We'll talk tomorrow."

He left the room, taking the candle with him. When the door closed, Ellie wrapped her arms around her middle and rocked back and forth in the silent darkness. Tears of remorse slid over her cheeks.

◯

After a sleepless night, Ellie rose at daybreak and tiptoed downstairs, searching for Matthew. When she slid open the parlor door, she saw he'd propped himself into a half-sitting position on the divan. Soft snores whistled through his beard. Her heart tripped in her chest at the sight. They'd never slept in separate rooms before. She eased the door shut and moved into the kitchen, praying the children hadn't overheard last night's quarrel. She stirred coals in the stove, adding several sticks of kindling to start the fire.

"Mama?"

She turned at the sound of Johnny's voice, forcing a smile. "Good morning. Your turn to milk the cow, is it?"

He nodded, a troubled expression on his face. "I heard you and Papa last night." His voice cracked. "You can't let him go."

Ellie pursed her lips. "If you overheard us last night, you know there's precious little I can do about it." She knew her tone was sharper than it should have been, but the last thing she needed was a thirteen-year-old boy telling her how to deal with her husband. "Perhaps you can change his mind. I can't." She turned her back, the cut on her hand stinging as she dragged a heavy iron skillet into place on the stovetop. "Best go milk that cow."

As soon as the door closed, Matthew appeared in the room, his left arm clasped around his right.

Tension prickled up her spine. "I'm—"

"If you're going to say you're sorry, there's no need. I knew you were bound to be upset. It wasn't my intention to provoke you." He stepped close and placed his left hand on her shoulder.

Ellie warmed at his touch. "If you'll just stay home, things can go back to the way they were."

Matthew looked at her for a long moment. The sadness in his eyes spilled across his face. "The way they were? How far back are you remembering?" He dropped his hand. "Too much has happened. A stream doesn't run backward, and neither will our lives."

His words sounded like the tolling of a funeral bell. Part of her mind agreed with him, but his rationalization didn't stop her from wanting him to stay in Beldon Grove. Wordless, she turned toward the stove to hide the tears that rolled down her cheeks.

"Ellie?"

She didn't look at him. "I'm listening."

"Today's Thursday. I haven't forgotten that this is the day you go to Molly's to work on her quilt. I want Doc to take a look at my ribs anyway." Matthew cleared his throat. "I'm planning to ask him to keep an eye on things out here while I'm away." His hand grazed her shoulder. "This would be easier with your co-operation, but with or without it, I have to go. I wish you'd try to understand."

His footsteps receded. Once he left the room, she turned away from the stove. Why should she make it easy for him? She was the one who was going to suffer. She opened the breadbox and cut a thick slice from one of the loaves. Spreading it with crabapple preserves, she gobbled it down. The sugary taste of the preserves left her with a momentary feeling of comfort. Maybe if she ignored his plans, he'd give them up.

The first thing that caught Ellie's attention when she entered Molly's cabin was the sweet almond fragrance of Scotch shortbread.

The air in the room felt heavy with a combination of June humidity and heat radiating from Molly's oven.

Ellie had intended to share her frustration over Matthew's plans with Molly and Charity. But now that she had the opportunity, she hesitated. What if they thought he was leaving because she'd failed as a wife? She remembered her outburst the previous night and flushed. She *had* failed.

She moved to the kitchen table and lifted one of the diamond-shaped sweets from the rack where they were cooling. The warm shortbread melted over her tongue. She sighed with pleasure and took another bite.

From behind her, Molly teased, "If you were one of the children, I'd scold you. We usually wait to have our treats until after we're done quilting."

Ellie spoke around a mouthful of crumbs. "Sorry. I know better." She wiped her lips with her handkerchief and followed Molly into the next room where Charity sat waiting at the quilt frame.

Once settled onto their chairs, the women worked in silence for several moments. Five rows of uneven stitches near the roller testified to Luellen's reluctant participation. Charity pointed at them and glanced at Molly, a question in her eyes.

Molly shook her head. "Leave them. She has to learn."

Ellie concentrated on drawing her needle through layers of fabric and batting without disturbing the bandage wrapped around her palm. With each stitch, she considered how to present Matthew's decision in a way that wouldn't cast her in a bad light.

Charity broke into her thoughts. "Aren't you going to tell us what happened between Matthew and Elder Meecham in Quincy?"

"I'm not sure what happened. Matt didn't say exactly." Ellie bit her lower lip. "All I know is he's leaving the pulpit here and taking up a southern Illinois circuit." She studied her companions' faces, waiting for their reactions.

Eyes wide, Charity leaned across the frame as she spoke. "But he's needed here."

The memory of last night tingled across Ellie's fingers. Her face burned with shame. "I don't know how to stop him." She avoided Charity's gaze by concentrating on her stitchwork. "I think it's too late."

Charity exhaled, her breath making a puffing sound in her nostrils. "I can't imagine Matthew leaving the Beldon Grove church. Why, he and Ben built it—stick by stick and member by member." She lowered her voice. "Maybe you can change his mind in the bedchamber, if you know what I mean." Her fair complexion turned rosy.

Ellie stared at the bright colors honeycombed across the top of the quilt. Their outlines blurred through threatened tears. She'd told no one about her decision not to risk another pregnancy, and now wasn't the time to blurt it out. Charity's suggestion might have worked once. *All our decisions have consequences.* She remembered Matthew preaching on that subject, and teaching it to their children. Was this her consequence? Her husband didn't want to live with her?

Molly patted her shoulder. "Matt's always been stubborn. Once he makes up his mind, it's as good as done." She looked from Ellie to Charity. "I'm sure Ellie has already tried everything she knows to get him to stay."

Her kind words sent a knife into Ellie's heart. What would have happened if she'd kissed him instead of trying to slap his face? Regret sent a tear slipping down her cheek.

Charity's face softened. "Oh my dear, I'm so sorry. I didn't mean to upset you. I should know better than anybody how impossible it is to change a man's mind. The good Lord knows how hard I tried to talk Ben out of conducting on the Underground Railroad." She shook her head. "I cried, I begged, I . . . did everything. You can see how much influence I had. He's been involved for nearly a decade."

"Molly told me you care for escaping slaves who arrive injured." Ellie dabbed at her tears with her handkerchief.

"I do now. But I must confess I balked at first." She smiled faintly. "Remember the scriptures say that a house divided against itself cannot stand. We're to be helpmeets for our husbands, not adversaries."

Ellie sucked in a deep breath, feeling more like a failure every minute. "At least the church will be in good hands. Mr. Beldon preached well last Sunday. It's just hard for me to see him in Matthew's place."

"The church is in good hands?" Charity jabbed her needle into the quilt top. "What makes you think that? Marcus Beldon's a Judas."

Ellie blinked, surprised at the outburst. "He has the town's best interests at heart. You know his father founded Beldon Grove. And he's always been very concerned and polite to me."

"Perhaps that's how he seems to you, but Ben says Marcus Beldon is the person who's been casting doubts on Matthew's fitness as a preacher."

Molly shook her head. "I can't believe he'd do a thing like that. He's got such a kind heart." She laid her hands on the edge of the quilt frame and smiled at Charity. "He's going to get news of James for us. He has connections with someone in President Polk's cabinet."

"So he says," Charity muttered.

Ellie gazed in wonder at Charity, all thoughts of Matthew's

departure forgotten for the moment. "It's not like you to be so suspicious-minded. Whatever happened to 'judge not, lest ye be judged'?"

"She's right," Molly said. "How does your husband know what's in Mr. Beldon's mind?"

"You girls are being led into a snare." Charity lifted her sewing basket onto her lap, inserted her needle in its case, and snapped the lid shut. Then she stood and leveled her index finger at Molly and Ellie. "Mark my words. If Marcus Beldon succeeds in driving Matthew away, you'll have to ask yourselves—who's next?"

18

Through the window in Karl's office, Matthew watched Charity stride across Adams Street and head down Hancock toward the center of town. He slipped his watch from his left-hand pocket and fumbled the latch open. The hands read two o'clock. At that moment the inner door swung wide and a young boy stepped out with a wooden splint wrapped around his arm, his face tearstained. His mother followed, gushing her thanks to the doctor as she exited.

When they left, Karl leaned against the entrance to his examination room and grinned. "Sorry to make you wait, my friend. That little lad thought he was big enough to ride one of his papa's plow horses." He shook his head. "Short ride."

Matthew eased himself from a sitting to a standing position. "I know something about falling off horses." He headed for the inner room. "I want you to take a look at my ribs and shoulder. Had them tended to in Quincy, but not by a doctor."

After spending several minutes probing Matthew's side and checking the rotation of his right arm, Karl wrapped the ribs in clean cloth strips. "You'll need to take things easy for a couple more weeks. They won't heal if you don't hold still."

"Can't spare that much time. I need to head for Adams Station soon's I can."

"So Daniel had it right. You're leaving. I didn't believe him."

Matthew imagined he saw condemnation in his friend's eyes. "It's for the best." He braced for argument.

"You could stay right here and fight for your church. You're letting a lot of people down."

"It'll be easier all around if I leave. How can I minister to people who think God himself is against me?"

Karl slid a chair away from the wall and gestured for Matthew to sit. "Remember when we first met, and you got me to talking about why I'd come west from Philadelphia? You listened then, and you listened every time I came to you with questions. It was you brought me to salvation." His blue eyes bored into Matthew's. "That's your ministry. There's a lot of people in this town who'd be looking at the fires of hell if it weren't for you."

Matthew shifted in his chair. Karl hadn't been around when people he'd converted crossed the street to avoid talking to him. His friend hadn't felt the sting of rejection.

"Where are they now? All these people you say I helped. Like sheep, they've flocked to a new shepherd."

He'd known Ellie would be opposed to his decision, but he'd counted on support from Karl. Matthew had never felt more alone.

After breakfast the next morning, Matthew looked at his sons. "Let's go out to the cornfield. I want to see what you've done while I was away." He stood and took a shallow breath, his lungs fighting for space against his tightly bound ribs.

Ellie stood with her back to him, scrubbing at something on the stovetop. Except for a cool "good morning" when he emerged from the parlor, she'd said little. Seeing her distress, and envisioning his children's reactions, left him shaken. Was his decision the mistake everyone said it was? His heart quailed at the idea of confronting Beldon for the leadership of the church. He pictured the big man with his impeccable suits, his impressive vocabulary, his commanding presence. The thought made him feel small and insignificant. He couldn't stay. That's all there was to it.

The twins were already on their feet and at the door. "We worked every day," Jimmy told him. "Me and Johnny did most of it. Harrison's slow."

Matthew dropped a hand onto his youngest son's shoulder and squeezed reassurance. "I'm sure you each did your best."

He followed them around the rail fence and into the waist-high corn. Hoed soil was still visible between the plants, but the bare spots were shading in. Matthew squatted to check the moisture in the earth, grunting with the discomfort of lowering his body to a crouch. He scooped a handful of dirt and allowed it to trickle through his fingers. "Dry. We need more rain."

He glanced at his hayfield. "But not right now. You boys will have to start cutting while this clear weather holds." He focused his attention on Jimmy and Johnny. "You've helped me with the haying before. Think you can do it by yourselves this time?"

Johnny straightened his shoulders, pulling himself to his full height. "You can count on me."

"Me too," Jimmy added. "Don't know how much good Harrison'll be though."

"Well, you'd better be grateful for his help the next few days. I'm sending him home with Uncle Arthur when he leaves next week."

"Really?" Harrison's eyes brightened.

Matthew nodded. "Your uncle's place needs attention. He can't do it alone while he's getting over the ague. Mind now, you'll probably be doing the same work you do here—weeding the garden, mucking out the barn, splitting wood—and you'll have to do it without your brother's help."

Harrison shot the twins a triumphant look. Uncle Arthur was a treasure trove of stories and games and a great favorite with his niece and nephews. Matthew knew his children had figured out that if they asked questions about the early days, when settlers came down the Ohio on flatboats and had to fight Indians, Arthur could talk for hours about his adventures. Chores were forgotten and often postponed for another day. Time spent with their uncle was a treat indeed.

He felt a pang as he watched his sons' lively faces. They were changing so fast. He cleared his throat. "Come to the barn. I'll show you the best way to sharpen a scythe."

Later, as he climbed the back stairs to the porch, Matthew felt the bottom step rock slightly under his weight. Looking down, he couldn't see anything wrong with the board. He promised himself he'd check it later. Right now he needed rest. The effort of walking over the uneven ground of the cornfield, then later working in the barn, set up an unmerciful throbbing in his ribs.

When he stepped into the kitchen, Maria hurried over to him, a broom in her hands. She wore a ruffled cap over her blonde hair the way Ellie did when she cleaned house. "Are you done working outside? Will you tell me a story?"

Floorboards creaked overhead. Ellie was probably busy shining furniture, a Friday chore. "Didn't your mama tell you to sweep the kitchen?"

"Well, yes."

He smiled at her. "I'm going to rest on the divan for a short while. When you finish, come on in and we'll have a story time."

Maria's face shone. "I'll hurry."

On Sunday, Matthew woke before sunrise. Dull pewter light sifted through the parlor windows. As consciousness returned, it brought nervous clenching to his stomach. He felt the palms of his hands moisten as he considered his plans for the day. *Father, please be with me. This is the hardest thing I've ever done.*

He pushed himself to a sitting position and listened, thinking he heard a sound in the kitchen. When it repeated, he realized Ellie was up and busy with breakfast

He'd found her surprisingly amenable the previous evening when he told her of his plans. Now that he considered it, she'd been less argumentative ever since they returned from Molly's on Thursday. Maybe she was starting to see things his way.

Matthew stood, intending to go upstairs and put on his church clothes. When he opened the parlor door, Ellie came down the hall toward him, a concerned frown wrinkling her forehead.

"You don't have to do it." She rested her hand lightly on his arm. "What are you hoping to accomplish?"

He ran his fingers through his sleep-spiked hair. "I'm not sure, but I know it's the right thing. I can't leave otherwise."

Ellie slid her hand away. "Then you'd better get ready if you still intend to arrive early." She stepped aside so he could pass. "Breakfast will be waiting when you come downstairs."

By the time he arrived at the table, the twins were up and had clattered into the kitchen. "We want to go with you." Fully dressed, Johnny stood beside his father's chair.

"We can help," Jimmy added.

Matthew shook his head. "I'm riding Samson. You wait for Uncle Arthur to bring you in the buggy." He speared a griddle cake from the platter in the center of the table and dropped it onto his plate. His stomach rebelled at the prospect of food, but he knew he needed to eat.

"You boys haven't washed or combed your hair," Ellie said from the other side of the room. "Go finish cleaning up, then wake Harrison and Maria." When they left, she picked up the platter and carried it back to the stove. "Want some ham?"

"No, this was plenty." Matthew scraped his chair away from the table, leaving his meal half eaten. "It's time to go."

Ellie wiped her hands on her apron. "We'll be there in another hour." She opened her mouth to say something else, then apparently changed her mind.

He wished he knew what lay behind the expression in her eyes. Support? Or pity?

Coolness hung in the air as Matthew pushed open the doors of the church. He wanted time to walk through the building and memorize its details while he was alone. His footsteps echoed on the wooden floor when he moved down the center aisle and stepped onto the platform in front. Sunlight from east-facing windows made the well-worn pulpit gleam. He laid his Bible down, opening it to the passage he'd selected for his farewell message. Again the palms of his hands moistened. He'd put out no announcement. No one in the community knew he'd be there that day.

"I heard you were back. Going to try it again, are you?" Marcus Beldon strode up the aisle.

Matthew's heart drummed in his throat. "It's still my church." Leaving the platform, he faced his adversary.

Beldon pulled his jacket open, throwing out his chest and tucking his hands in his pants pockets. He rocked back on his heels, looking at Matthew with one eyebrow raised. The gold watch chain across his waistcoat glistened in the light. "That's not the story that's going around. Word is you're headed south to be an itinerant preacher."

Matthew retreated a step. Standing next to the immaculately groomed Beldon never failed to make him feel like a bumpkin. "I'm going to be riding circuit, yes. But I think I owe it to the people here to say a proper farewell before leaving."

"Very commendable. And don't worry about this church. I'll see it goes on." Beldon clapped him on his right shoulder.

Matthew gritted his teeth to hide the pain that shot down his side. "It's not up to you, is it? You can't just take over the pulpit of a church without an appointment from the elders."

Beldon narrowed his eyes. "I have a divinity degree from Harvard College. Once you're gone, I'll present myself to whoever's in charge over in Quincy. They'll jump at the chance to get a man with my qualifications."

At the sound of voices, both men looked toward the back of the church. Several townsfolk entered together. When they saw Beldon standing with Matthew they stopped, apparently confused.

Beldon hurried toward them. "Come in, come in! The good reverend and I were just discussing the sermon."

Matthew pinched his lips to keep from being provoked into a public argument. Instead, he returned to the pulpit and closed his Bible. He'd speak what was in his heart.

Gradually, the church filled with people, more than Matthew had seen there in months. Many of them looked at him and then seemed to search out Beldon for assurance. But others hurried forward, welcoming him. When Arthur led Ellie and the children to their accustomed spot on the front bench, he noted worry lines around his wife's eyes.

Matthew surveyed the congregation, heart swollen with sadness at the thought of leaving.

He held up his hand to silence the buzz of conversation in the room. "Let's seek the Lord's presence."

Using the side of the pulpit for support, he lowered himself to his knees and offered a fervent prayer asking the Lord to guide not only his words but the ears and hearts of his listeners.

When Matthew stood, he rested his hand on his worn leather-covered Bible, its pebbled surface a comfort. "Today's service isn't going to be what you expected. I know most of you are surprised to see me here. Some of you heard I was leaving. Some of you thought I'd already left." Taking as deep a breath as his ribs would permit, Matthew continued. "Two weeks ago I went to Quincy and resigned as pastor of this church."

A collective gasp sucked air from the room.

He focused his gaze on the people that he knew had supported him—Ben and Charity, Molly and Karl, a few neighbors and friends from various homes in the community. "But I couldn't leave without saying good-bye."

Startled murmurs reached his ears. "It's true then."

"He's going."

A voice called, "Don't leave, Reverend. We want you here."

Matthew tried to see who'd said it, but couldn't be certain. In the back of the room, Beldon sat with his arms folded across his chest, face unreadable.

Matthew swallowed. *Lord, this is harder than I expected. Help me find the right words.* "There's been too much dissension here for me to feel useful to you. Some of it's been my fault. I made far too large an issue over the performers in *Macbeth*, even though one of them did end up bringing upheaval to my family." He glanced at Beldon and his covey of supporters. "Other whispers have reached my ears. I won't give them credence by repeating them now." In the front row, Ellie sat with her head down, shoulders bowed.

Matthew's eyes filled with tears and he blinked them away. "I'll be leaving soon for Adams Station, the first stop on my circuit. God bless you all. I pray you will put your differences aside and work to make this a united church body. Outsiders look at us quarreling among ourselves and see no reason to convert to Christianity. Let that not be so in Beldon Grove."

Heart pounding, he left the platform and walked to the rear of the church. Hands reached out to touch him as he went past. To Matthew's surprise, one of the hands belonged to Zilphah Beldon.

She gripped his coat sleeve with her twisted fingers. "You're making a mistake, Reverend," she whispered. "Don't go."

19

Ellie stood under the clothesline watching the twins at work in the hayfield. Johnny took the lead, bending at the waist and swinging his scythe, dropping hay onto the ground in a wide swath. Jimmy followed with his own blade, a dozen feet behind and to one side. Slowly they worked their way across the first acre. They weren't able to cut as big a swath as Matthew did, so it would take them longer to finish. She scanned the few wispy clouds trailing overhead, praying they wouldn't get caught by a thunderstorm while the hay was down.

She realized she'd been standing motionless, observing, while the wet garment she held in her hand dripped onto her apron. Quickly, she pegged it to the line.

Harrison ran between rows of hanging laundry and planted himself in front of her. "We're ready to go. I came to say good-bye."

Ellie's heart turned over at the sight of her younger son's freckled face shining up at her. She reached out and pushed his springy dark hair out of his eyes. He looked so much like Matthew. Her hand slid from his forehead to his shoulder and then she clasped him to her in a fierce hug. "I'll miss you so much. You be a good help to Uncle Arthur, now, you hear?"

He wrapped his arms around her waist and held on for a

moment, then backed away. "Uncle says he has lots of work for a strong boy like me."

"I don't doubt it, Son."

"And maybe he'll teach me to play his fiddle. He says he learned when he was my age."

Ellie followed the eager boy to the buggy where Uncle Arthur waited. Wooden clothes pegs in her apron clicked together as she walked, sounding like she had a pocket full of crickets. Matthew stood there giving Arthur last-minute instructions.

"Did you get the hamper I packed for your supper?" Ellie asked.

"Right here." Arthur pointed behind him.

She stood on tiptoe to look into the back. "Where are your things, Harrison? I don't see your box."

"It's under the seat." He climbed up next to Uncle Arthur.

Ellie glanced between Matthew and their son, trying to think of another question that would keep him near her for a few more moments.

Matthew met her eyes. "He'll only be a mile away, and Arthur has promised to come by every few days."

She squeezed her hands together, feeling the cut on her palm that scrubbing and wringing wet clothing had irritated. She forced a smile. "See you soon, then."

The buggy rumbled over the planks bridging the creek, and rolled off down the road toward the Newberrys' farm. Dust rose and settled in its wake. Ellie walked to the porch and sank onto the top step, where the overhang from the roof provided shade.

"Ellie?"

She raised her head and looked at her husband.

Matthew waited at the foot of the steps, chin raised in the

stubborn gesture she knew so well. "It'll be good for the boy. He's often left out of the twin's activities. You baby him too much."

Ellie turned her head away and stood. "I need to finish hanging the laundry."

The bottom step gave slightly when she trod on it, throwing her off balance. Matthew reached out and caught her arm. She held her breath, hoping he'd pull her close and end their estrangement. Instead, they gazed at each other for a silent moment, then he dropped her arm and walked toward the hayfield.

"I need you to look at this," Matthew said from his seat at the kitchen table, a large book open before him. The twins had dragged themselves to bed soon after they ate supper, and once Maria finished helping her mother with the dishes, she too climbed the stairs to her bedroom.

Ellie wiped perspiration from her forehead with a soap-reddened hand, then slid into a chair next to Matthew. She frowned at the colored map on the open page. "Where'd you get this?" She traced a finger over the gilt-edged pages. "It must've cost dearly."

"Ben made me the loan of it. It's a universal atlas. There's a map here for every one of the states." Matthew turned the book around so that Illinois was right side up in Ellie's vision. "I want to show you where I'll be while I'm gone." He indicated a point near the western center of the state. "Here's Beldon Grove." His finger moved toward the bottom of the page. "This is Adams Station. Southeast a ways you see Tylerville." Matthew's hand traveled, tracing an invisible line. "From Tylerville, I swing north to Arcadia Mills, then back home."

"That's half the state." She lifted her head and studied his face. "How can you cover that much ground when you can barely saddle your horse without help?"

He ignored her question, jabbing a finger at Adams Station. "I'm reckoning a week for each stop, including travel, should have me back here in a month or so."

But then he'd just turn around and leave again. The strain of Matthew's imminent departure, coupled with the end of a fatiguing day, brought quick tears to Ellie's eyes. She looked down at her palm, absently fingering the cut across the base of her thumb. "You're leaving me to take care of this farm with two half-grown boys and a little girl."

"Arthur will be here every few days. He'll take you to town whenever you need anything." Matthew stood, slapping the atlas shut with one hand. "My saddlebags are packed and ready. I'll be off at first light." He moved down the hall toward the parlor.

Ellie sat at the table after he left, watching light patterns cast by the oil lamp jump over the tabletop. Moths crashed against the glass chimney. They fluttered away, then flew back to the lamp and crashed again. She could see herself in their frantic actions, pounding away at Matthew to stay in Beldon Grove, but never getting past the glass wall that surrounded his decision.

Ellie stood and extinguished the light. "Get on with your lives," she said to her fuzzy-winged companions. "You'll never get through the glass, and you'll only hurt yourselves trying."

Ellie passed the first two days after Matthew's departure following her accustomed routine. She spent most of her time on housework, with Maria's help, while Jimmy and Johnny trudged out to cut hay. The skies remained clear, but the ever-present fear of rain while the hay was down added a sense of urgency to their task.

Thursday noon when the boys dragged in for dinner, they were sweating, sunburned, and exhausted. Ellie watched as they devoured the fried ham and boiled beans she'd prepared. By the time they started on the dried-apple pie, she'd made a decision.

She removed her apron and threw it over a chair. "I'm coming out with you. Maria and I can turn the hay over while you cut."

Her sons stared at her as if she'd announced she was going to shoe their team of draft horses. "You don't know how to rake hay." Jimmy's adolescent voice squeaked in protest.

"Then you'll show me. Get your sunbonnet, Maria. No one's going to see the inside of this house but us, so who cares if we clean it or not."

Her children gaped at her while she tied her skirt in a knot above her ankles and looped her bonnet strings under her chin. When Ellie strode to the barn to get a rake, the twins hurried past her to open the heavy door. Once she and Maria were equipped, the boys walked with them to the edge of the field. Stubble crunched beneath their boots as they approached the first sweet-smelling swaths of cut grass.

Jimmy took one of the rakes and let it drop as far out as the handle would reach so that the curved tines fell into the drying hay. "Let the weight of the rake do the work," he said, clearly proud to have something he could teach his mother. "Drop it over the hay like this, then drag it toward you. It should turn up for drying while you pull." He demonstrated. "Then do it again.

Make nice rows." Grinning, he offered Ellie the wooden rake. "Now you try it."

After a bumbling start, she felt the rhythm of the work. "Thank you, Son. I'll help Maria while you get back to cutting."

By the end of the day, blisters had formed across her palms and the cut at the base of her thumb threatened to break open. Ellie'd never felt so tired. At the same time, she'd never felt such a sense of accomplishment.

She looked down at Maria, who struggled beside her. "Time to stop for supper."

Her daughter dropped her rake and leaned against Ellie's side. "Look at all we did, Mama."

The pride in her young voice echoed Ellie's emotions. Rows of hay stretched behind them, fluffed and golden.

"I'm proud of you. You did grown-up work today."

In truth, Ellie had manipulated her own rake so Maria only had to turn small amounts at a time. Nevertheless, she had done a heroic job merely to stay at the task in the sun all afternoon.

Ellie turned to where Jimmy and Johnny worked, and whistled to get their attention. "Suppertime," she called when they looked her way.

Maria's blue eyes grew round. "I didn't know you could whistle."

"I'd forgotten I even knew how. Uncle Arthur taught me, but he wouldn't let me do it around Aunt Ruby." Ellie chuckled at the memory. "It's unladylike, you know."

"Would you teach me?"

She picked up her daughter's grubby hand and kissed the blistered palm. "Of course. We'll practice tomorrow while we rake."

Early Saturday evening, Ellie glanced out the open kitchen window and noticed dumpling-shaped clouds bobbing on the western horizon. A breeze fluttered the red gingham curtains, ushering the promise of rain into the room. *Not now! The hay's still down.* Her mind worked frantically. Tomorrow was Sunday. Matthew never allowed anything to interfere with church attendance, but Matthew wasn't here. She and her children had accomplished the backbreaking task of cutting the hay, and now she couldn't let it get soaked before they stored it in the haymow. Moisture would cause it to mildew, which sickened the animals. Or the worst might happen—stacked wet hay could heat and spontaneously burst into flame.

Her children sat at the cleared supper table. Maria's head drooped with fatigue. The twins both slumped in their chairs, eyes half closed.

Ellie surveyed the clouds again. "Rain's coming. If we're going to save our hay, we'll have to get it into the barn as quick as possible."

Jimmy and Johnny looked at each other. "Not tonight!" their expressions said.

Ellie's back ached, and in spite of the cloth strips padding her hands, she had raw and oozing blisters. She pushed Matthew's vacant chair away from the table and sank into it. "I know how tired you are, but this has to be done. If we work fast, we can get at least one load picked up and in the barn before dark."

She rested her gaze on Maria, noticing the dust that streaked her fair skin. "You wait in the barn and push the hay back in the mow. It will be easier than raking it up in the field." Ellie patted Maria's hand.

She turned toward the twins. "If God is willing, the rain will hold off so we can get an early start and finish tomorrow."

Their faces mirrored their shock. "Tomorrow's Sunday. What would Papa say?"

"I imagine he wouldn't like it. But if he'd stayed home, we wouldn't be facing this problem, would we?" She raised her eyebrows and studied both boys. "We need every stem of that grass to feed the stock through the winter. I'm not going to take the chance of losing it after all the work we've done this week."

Ellie awakened at first light the next morning, slid her aching body out of bed, and hurried to the window to check the weather. Clouds had continued to pile up during the night, their bellies dark with unshed moisture. "Thank you, Father, for holding off the rain." She smiled to herself at the irony of thanking God for making it possible for her to spend Sunday hard at work instead of in church.

She dropped her sweat-stiff work dress on over her shift, and rolled clean stockings onto her feet. When they were finished, they'd each have a long bath. She didn't care how much water she had to heat.

Crossing the hallway, she opened bedroom doors and roused her children. "Daylight. Let's get to work."

As their team of Belgian horses hauled the second wagonload of hay toward the barn, Ellie noticed a covered buggy coming toward the farm. Uncle Arthur, with Harrison. She clapped a hand over her mouth. She'd completely forgotten they were coming to take her and the other children to church. Feeling like a guilty child, she climbed off the hay wagon when it came to a stop and waited for her uncle.

Harrison bailed out of the buggy first and ran to her. "Mama!"

Ellie held out her arms and hugged him. "My goodness. You look bright and shiny this morning." She rested her cheek against his still-damp hair. "Are you minding Uncle Arthur?"

After tying his horse to the rail, Uncle Arthur joined them. "He's been my good right hand." He tilted his head and frowned at her disheveled appearance. "Did you forget it's Sunday, Eleanor?"

Ellie swallowed. Her uncle hadn't taken that tone with her since she was Harrison's age. She reached out and clasped both of his hands in hers. "No, I didn't forget." She gestured toward the clouds that massed overhead. "The four of us have worked all week cutting and raking hay. We need it too much to let it spoil now. I figure if we keep going we should be able to get it under cover before the rain comes."

Uncle Arthur turned one of her hands over and unwrapped the rag tied around it. Raw open blisters pocked her palm. Gently, he touched the wounds with his fingertips. Pushing his hat back on his head, he looked up at the twins, still sitting on the wagon seat. "Why didn't you send for me and Harrison?" He drew her to him for a brief hug. "This is too big a job for you."

She stepped back, brushing at the dust marks her dress left on his black Sunday coat. Placing her hands on her hips, she replied, "We did it, didn't we? Besides, you're not up to heavy work yet."

"I can drive a hay wagon." He unbuttoned his coat and handed it to Harrison. "Put this on the buggy seat, and go change your clothes. We've got to get this feed in the barn."

Humidity from the approaching rain gathered under the ridge-line of the barn roof, carrying with it manure smells from the stalls below. Ellie bound a kerchief around her head to keep sweat from trickling into her eyes while she and Maria pushed hay toward the back of the loft. The stack grew higher and harder to manage with each wagonload. She'd lost count of the number of times Arthur had driven the wagon into the barn and her sons pitched the hay up to her.

Now Ellie sat at the edge of the loft and dangled her legs, waiting for the next wagonload. She held out a hand to Maria. "Come sit. Let's rest a moment." In the silence that ensued when they stopped raking, she noticed a tapping sound on the roof. All her senses prickled. Rain. She hurried to the ladder and climbed down. Dark circles of moisture splattered on the dusty ground outside.

The wagon rumbled toward her, piled high with stacked hay. Arthur stood in front of the seat, urging the horses forward. "Git up! Go!" The haystack swayed, threatening to topple onto the ground.

Ellie ran toward the rail fence separating the barnyard from the fields. "Slow down!" She hoped he'd hear her voice over the noise of wagon wheels and rattling harness. "It won't do us any good if the hay's scattered from here to breakfast." Raindrops peppered her chaff-covered sleeves.

Arthur checked the reins and the horses slowed to a walk. Ellie stepped aside as the wagon rolled past her and through the open barn door, then hurried after it. Once inside, her sons grabbed pitchforks and threw the feed into the loft.

Ellie joined her uncle on the wagon seat. "How much is left on the ground?"

"Little more than half an acre."

"That's a terrible amount to waste."

"If this rain goes by quick enough, we can turn it and dry it again."

Ellie closed her eyes, remembering the amount of work that had gone into turning it the first time. Her aching muscles protested at the idea of repeating the task. "We'll have to, won't we? Matthew counts on using all the hay so we don't have to buy feed."

The gentle spatter of rain changed to a steady drum roll.

20

Matthew dismounted and stood next to his horse. The stream that lay between him and the track continuing south had overflowed its banks, and he couldn't see a safe place to cross. Should he continue, or turn back to the last cabin he'd seen? He pulled his watch from his pocket and clicked open the case. It was still early. Everything in him cried out to stop. His right side throbbed. A week had passed since he left home and he hadn't yet reached Adams Station. He knew he was traveling far more slowly than he did as a young man on the circuit, but by late afternoon the pain in his ribs overwhelmed him. All he could think of was rest.

Holding Samson's reins, he walked along the water's edge looking for a spot shallow enough to cross on the horse's back and avoid getting his gear soaked. As he traveled east, the freshet grew broader and deeper.

He tried the other direction. Although it wasn't raining, the air carried the scent of recent rainfall and the threat of more to come. Around a bend, Matthew came upon an uprooted cottonwood lying across the stream. Water swirled on both sides of the trunk, foaming as it pushed through dead branches. On the opposite side, he noticed a stand of timber. If he could get there, it would provide shelter for the night. Better yet, he might spot another settler's cabin nearby.

Matthew studied the fallen tree, then leaned against Samson and removed his boots, tying the laces together and shoving his stockings inside. He stepped out of his trousers and hung the boots and britches around his neck. Wearing only drawers and his linen shirt, he lifted the saddlebags off the horse and draped them over his left shoulder. After tying the animal to a tree root, he climbed onto the trunk and took a few tentative steps toward the opposite bank. Rough bark scraped at the soles of his feet. When he neared the top, with its tangle of dead wood, he reached down and tested a limb. The cottonwood shifted under his weight, but the limb didn't break.

Matthew paused for a moment to be sure of his footing, then picked his way between boughs until he saw the grassy creek bank below. As he looked for a safe place to descend, his foot slipped. Without thinking, he grabbed for one of the branches with his right hand, then groaned in agony as pain tore through him. He dropped, straddling the trunk, and waited until the spasm passed.

When he clambered down, the spongy ground gave way and he sank over his ankles in the muck. Mud tugged at his feet with each step until he reached a dry cut where he could stow his gear and return for the horse.

Climbing back through the branches added more scratches to his bare calves. Travel hadn't seemed this tough when he was eighteen. He shook his head at his own folly. If only he hadn't tied Samson, perhaps he could've called and the horse would have come over on his own. Teetering on the rough surface, Matthew returned to the other side of the stream.

After untying the animal, he mounted and rode him downstream past the fallen cottonwood. Matthew had to kick his heels into Samson's side to urge him into the swift-moving water. The horse floundered as the bottom dropped away, then steadied himself and swam toward the southern edge. The sun had moved toward the horizon, washing the prairie in golden light.

When Matthew had dressed and secured the saddlebags to the horse, he remounted and turned toward the grove of trees. He'd never make it before nightfall. A slight breeze blew from the west, carrying with it the fragrance of burning wood. He scanned the prairie, hoping to see a trail of smoke that might indicate a cabin hidden in a swale of grass. Nothing showed against the rain clouds boiling overhead. Matthew continued south, resigned to having to spend a night in the open.

Halfway toward the trees, he topped a rise and spotted a squat shanty crouched beyond a bend in the trail. A wispy string of gray smoke rose from the chimney. Matthew's heart quickened at the prospect of spending the night out of the weather.

When he'd ridden close enough to see an open door and paper-covered window, he drew Samson to a halt. "Halloo the cabin! Anyone home?"

A scrawny man wearing buckskin clothing appeared in the doorway. He shaded his eyes with one hand and peered up at Matthew. "What're you wanting?"

"A meal and a place to lay my head, if you've got such to spare."

The fellow left the cabin and approached Matthew. His spot in the doorway was immediately filled by a weary-looking woman with two small children hanging onto her faded homespun skirts. From the look of her, she'd soon add another child to their family.

"Come in, and welcome," she called.

Her husband wiped his hand on his pants leg, then extended it toward Matthew. "I'm Billy Sikes. That there's my wife Melinda, and our two boys, Jacob and Richmond."

"Matthew Craig."

Billy held Samson's reins while Matthew dismounted, then led the animal around the side of the cabin where a rough corral had been formed by anchoring stacks of tree limbs between posts. He called over his shoulder, "Your horse'll be safe in here." Two spavined mules lifted their heads when Samson joined them, then went back to chewing the sparse grass that grew at their feet.

When Matthew entered the cabin, the youngsters scurried back into the shadows, watching him with eyes too big for their small faces. Melinda bent over the hearth, stirring something in a blackened pot.

She darted a shy glance at Matthew. "What brings you clean out here? We don't never see a soul from one week to the next."

Matthew looked around for someplace to sit, and finally settled on a crooked chair with worn-out caning in the seat. "I'm a preacher, ma'am. I'm headed for Adams Station to hold a meeting there."

Her husband came inside, dropping Matthew's saddlebags next to the wall. "A preacher, eh? We don't hold with such truck. You're welcome to stay, but keep your praying to yourself."

Melinda's shoulders tensed. "Billy."

"You hush." He looked at Matthew, and then gestured around the room at the puncheon table and the cross-pole bed. "You can see we ain't got extra space, but you can spread your blanket in front of the hearth when it's time to sleep."

Matthew's mind slid back to previous nights on the trail, where he'd been greeted warmly by settlers. Somehow he'd expected the same reception wherever he went. After all, wasn't he bringing the gospel to people who were perishing? *You didn't have to come all this way to find people who need the gospel.* The voice in his ear sounded as clear as though it were spoken aloud. *I sent you to Beldon Grove and I have not changed my mind.*

He remembered Zilphah Beldon's words, uttered as he left his church building for the last time. "You're making a mistake . . . don't go." He felt a flush rise from under his collar and cover his face. Bowing his head, he stared at the dirt floor. What else could he have done?

In Adams Station, Matthew stood in the back of a wagon that had been pressed into use as a speaking platform and looked out at the assembled congregation. Since none of the cabins in the settlement were large enough to hold a gathering, people sat outdoors on benches, chairs, and blankets brought from their homes. Grateful for the shade offered by a grove of red oak trees, Matthew gazed over the tops of heads and focused on a square log building near the end of the single road that ran through the community. Several young men loitered around the doorway passing a jug back and forth. One of them pointed in his direction and said something to the others. They all guffawed.

Nothing ever changed. Trouble waited wherever a meeting was to be held. Matthew turned his attention back to the sixty or so people gathered below the wagon. "We're going to have preaching here today."

"Amen, brother!" shouted an elderly man near the front.

"Those rowdies out there aren't going to stop us, are they?"

"No!" cried several voices.

Matthew knelt in the wagon bed and waited until the assembly before him went to their knees. "Lord, give me the words thou wantest me to say this afternoon. Grant thy hearers open ears and hearts." He lifted his head and stared straight at the disruptive group in front of the groggery. "And please keep thy hand of protection over this meeting."

He used his left arm to lever himself to his feet, opening his Bible after he stood. "It seems fitting to take my text from the Acts of the Apostles, chapter seventeen. Those of you who know the Word know that this is the recounting of the apostle Paul's declaration to the idolaters in Athens." He held the book open in the palm of one hand, and lifted it so that even the louts standing at the end of the street could see. Raising his voice, Matthew continued, "Paul preached to people who worshiped at an altar named 'To The Unknown God.' It would seem that the fear of the God who made the world and all things therein is also missing among some of you."

Heads nodded agreement.

Following scripture, Matthew read each verse and then expounded on it. He felt himself to be in familiar territory. This topic was one he'd chosen often during his early years as an itinerant preacher. From experience, he knew there were always hearers who came out of curiosity mixed in among the believers who held services in their homes when a minister wasn't available. He wanted to reach the hearts of the curious.

After coming to the end of the passage, Matthew eased down from the wagon bed and faced the rapt gathering. Running his finger along a line of print in his Bible, he spoke each word in a clear voice. "'And the times of this ignorance God winked at; but now commandeth all men everywhere to repent!'" He paged over to the Epistle to the Hebrews. "And here we are warned, 'Take heed, brethren, lest there be in any of you an evil heart of unbelief, in departing from the living God.'"

Matthew closed his Bible and laid it behind him in the wagon. "Has anyone here departed from God? Will you come back to him now?" He lifted his hands and held them, palms open, toward his audience. "He's waiting." A dozen or so of his listeners came forward and pressed in on him in their eagerness to respond to the message. He grasped their extended hands, at last feeling justified in his decision to leave Beldon Grove.

Among those crowding up to him was a man near Matthew's age who had his arms around the shoulders of two lads who, judging by their round red cheeks, were obviously his sons. The three of them were dressed in hickory brown tow-cloth trousers, tan checkered shirts, and woven straw hats.

"I'm Nathan Clyde." The ruddy-faced man pushed the boys toward Matthew. "These here are Boone and Lafayette. I want you should take supper with us and explain to them more about the Lord."

Matthew looked at Nathan's sons and felt a stab of loneliness for his own boys. The image of the twins working in the hayfield came to his mind. His mood of justification faded.

He heard Nathan clear his throat and realized he hadn't responded to the man's invitation. "I'd be pleased, and thank you."

"We're just down the road a piece; it's the cabin with a real glass window. You can't miss it." Nathan turned and made his way through the gathered worshipers.

As Matthew watched him go, he noticed that the young men from the groggery had entered the meeting ground.

One of them pushed through the crowd and faced him. "How 'bout me, Preacher? Think you can cure my unbelief?" His whiskey-laden breath assaulted Matthew's nostrils. The others followed him, snickering.

"I can't, but God can." Matthew straightened his shoulders, noticing that most of the worshipers had backed away, leaving him alone with his antagonist.

"You're the one standing here. I'm askin' you."

The man's followers roared with laughter, slapping each other's backs. "You tell him, Jason!"

Glancing around, Matthew saw that if there was to be a resolution, it would have to come from him. People who had eagerly listened to his preaching now stood back, watching the drama. Apprehension choked him. He felt as he did when he faced Beldon before his congregation. He looked at the ringleader and his three grinning cohorts. Good-sized young men, any one of them could beat him in a fair fight.

All the frustration and anger he'd suppressed over the past months boiled to the surface. He grabbed Jason by the front of his shirt, using the coarse fabric as a handle to pull the fellow closer. "I will not have the Lord's word mocked." He jerked the shirt, staring directly into his tormentor's bloodshot eyes. "Do you understand me?"

Jason shoved Matthew's hand away. "Get your hands off'n me."

Before Matthew could react, Jason swung at him and landed a wicked blow to his jaw, splitting his lip. The flat, metallic taste of blood flooded his mouth. Gasping in shock, Matthew threw his arms up to protect his ribs. He wasn't quick enough. Jason landed a solid punch to his belly, then hooked a foot behind Matthew's knee and sent him sprawling. Matthew turned his head in time to see Jason draw his leg back and aim a kick at his face. Curling into a ball, he rolled to one side. The boot grazed his head, throwing Jason off balance.

His assailant stumbled backward. Cursing, he came at Matthew again, right hand knotted in a fist. Voices penetrated the roaring in Matthew's ears. "Stop! Let's git outta here." The other three louts seized Jason's arms and dragged him away. Then the four of them turned and fled the meeting ground.

Matthew heard their retreat between his gasps for breath. He lay on his side in the dirt, dust prickling his face. Blood trickled across his chin from the cut on his lip. His head pounded where Jason had kicked him.

"Reverend." Nathan Clyde squatted beside Matthew. "You all right? I didn't see what they was up to until I was almost home. I come running fast as I could." He put his arm around Matthew's back and helped him to a sitting position.

Humiliated, Matthew took a mental inventory of his injuries and decided his swelling lip was the worst of it. "Yes. I'm fine. Nothing feels broken." He looked around. Most of the crowd was drifting away, some glancing over their shoulders. A few watched from a safe distance. Would they remember his message, or his beating?

A white-bearded individual walked over to him. "Don't know why they sent ye down here. Something bad happens every time a preacher shows up." He worked his lips and spat a stream of tobacco juice next to his boots. "Last one got his horse stole." The old man leaned over. "Here. Let me give you a hand."

"Obliged." Matthew tottered to his feet. He shook his head, trying to clear it.

Nathan studied him. "Think you can make it down to my place?"

"If you get me on my horse."

When he slid off Samson's back, he hoped fervently that an invitation to spend the night would come with the promised meal. He ached everywhere.

Nathan appeared at the open door. "Come on in, Reverend. My wife'll get you a basin so's you can wash that blood off."

Matthew followed his host inside, noting the table set with seven wooden bowls, and a tray of spoons at one end. Looking around the single room, he spotted Nathan's sons, Boone and Lafayette, sitting on a bench in the shadows beyond the open hearth. Two little girls who both looked to be under five years old played on the floor at their feet.

Nathan walked to his wife. She stood at least a head taller than he did and looked like a collection of long sticks wrapped in a homespun apron. "This here's Lizzie."

Lizzie dipped a curtsy in Matthew's direction, then turned to the hearth. She drew the iron crane toward her and tipped some water from a kettle into a washbasin. "You can use the bench outside the door there to clean up."

Matthew followed her, thanking her when she set the basin down and handed him a towel. He couldn't recall ever seeing a woman as tall as Lizzie Clyde. The top of her ruffled cap rode only a few inches below the low ceiling.

"I feel just terrible about them boys attacking you, a reverend and all." Golden brown eyes shone out of her freckled face like two stars. "Supper's near ready. You set and rest yourself when you're done washing."

After the meal, Matthew sipped his coffee and tried to sort out his thoughts. Did Elder Meecham know the community's reputation when he sent him here? He longed to return home, but Meecham's parting words held him in place—*Don't shirk on the circuit too.*

He stared at the flames crackling on the hearth. In his imagination he pictured them as a thicket of fiery trees. Like a forest, the only way around his dilemma was to go straight through.

Nathan cleared his throat, breaking the silence. "Got a question for you, Brother Craig."

Matthew nodded, glad for a diversion from his gloomy speculations. "What is it?"

Leaning his arms on the tabletop, Nathan gazed at him over the flickering light of a candle. "Stranger rode through here the other day, said he heard talk there was going to be a play put on up north in New Camden. By someone named Shakespeare. The play's called *Macbeth*, I think he said."

From her stool next to the fire, Lizzie bobbed her head in agreement. "That's right. *Macbeth*. I remember because it reminded me of old man MacBride, down the road."

Nathan's eyes searched Matthew's face. "I was raised up not to hold with plays and suchlike, but the fellow said this one's taught in fancy schools out east. Anyways, do you think such a thing is wrong?"

Like dust clouds following a stampede, painful memories swirled in Matthew's mind at the mention of the play. "Do I think it's wrong?" He stood and took a breath. "No, I don't. You folks want to travel to New Camden to see it, go ahead."

21

Uncle Arthur tied his horse to the hitching rail in front of Molly's house, then helped Ellie step down from the wagon. She squeezed his arm. "I'm glad I decided to come with you today. At first I thought I'd just give you my list and you could pick up our supplies."

"Why?"

"It hurts to have people who used to be part of Matthew's congregation pretend they don't notice me in the mercantile."

"I think they're ashamed of their part in what happened. I'd wager there's more than a few of them wish they could undo it."

"Doesn't look that way to me. The church was full on Sunday. People seem to like Mr. Beldon." She tugged at the tight sleeves of her best dress. "Anyway, it's a lovely day and I'm going to enjoy it."

He patted her hand. "That's my girl."

Molly dashed outside and embraced Ellie. Some of her dark hair had escaped from the crown of braids she wore and slipped down her neck in tendrils. "Come in. I have a wonderful surprise." She seized Ellie's hand and tugged her through the door. "You too," she called over her shoulder to Uncle Arthur.

Once inside, Ellie's eyes widened when she saw the figure seated at the table. Lean, haggard, skin burned black from the sun, but nevertheless recognizable. "James?"

His eyes smiled a greeting. "Aunt Ellie."

She rushed to his side and hugged him, shocked to feel his ribs prominent under his cotton shirt. "What happened to you? When did you get home? Did Mr. Beldon—"

Molly stepped next to her. "James was dropped off yesterday by a peddler on his way to Iowa. He picked him up on the road outside of Mt. Jackson." She put an arm around her son and rested her cheek on his hair. "You can see how sick he's been. But he's home. God answered our prayers."

Uncle Arthur dragged a chair next to James and sat. "Doubtless you already told your folks, but I want to know why you was able to come home, seeing as how you enlisted. Never knew the Army to be merciful."

James studied his scratched, bruised feet. "Didn't enlist," he mumbled. "Took me and Billy a couple weeks to get to Alton, then we found out we were supposed to be somewheres else. Time we got to the next place, we were too late, and had to go chasing the volunteers again." He took a deep breath. "Eventually we came to a regular camp, down near Belleville. You can imagine, by then we were tuckered."

He looked up as Luellen slipped into the room. Some of the tiredness in his face disappeared. She moved past him to the range and removed several loaves of bread from the oven. Their yeasty fragrance swirled through the kitchen. "We're celebrating," she said. "Fresh bread on a Wednesday."

James turned and smiled at his sister. "You don't know how many times I dreamed about your good bread when Billy and me were on the road."

Luellen's face flushed. "You don't know how often I prayed you'd come back safe." She touched his cheek.

James clasped her hand and held it for a moment.

"You were saying about Belleville . . . ," Uncle Arthur said. "Go on."

"Well, me and Billy camped with the volunteers for a week or so. We thought we'd eat better than we did on the road, but we were sore disappointed. All we had was salt pork and beans, and the crick water was foul. We both come down with dysentery. Lots of fellows had died there already, someone said. Anyway, after a few days a regular Army soldier arrived and spread the word that some of us weren't officially enlisted. Told us we needed to go to Peoria or Springfield and sign up before we could go to Mexico."

Ellie clasped her hands and leaned forward. "But you came home instead. Praise God. I wish Matthew could be here right now—he prayed for you nightly."

"We had to come home. We were sick and out of money. I walked the soles off my boots." He lifted his feet, showing her thick yellow calluses.

Molly stood. "He promised he wouldn't sneak off again."

"Good," Ellie said. "You're too young for soldiering."

"There were plenty other volunteers in that camp my same age. I never said I wouldn't go—just promised I wouldn't sneak off."

Molly's face tightened. She turned to Ellie. "Would you mind if I didn't go to the mercantile with you today?"

"Of course not."

Uncle Arthur stood next to the range, holding a half-eaten slice of bread. "While you're at Wolcott's store, I'll ride out to the blacksmith's to pass the time," he said to Ellie. "I'll stop and pick up your goods from Ben about four, then come back here to fetch you."

Ellie crossed Adams Street, lifting her apple green calico skirt above her boot tops to keep the hem out of the dust. An occasional breeze swirled past, creating miniature whirlwinds that twirled then settled back into the roadway. She loosened the ties on her bonnet and fanned at perspiration beading under her chin.

As she passed Carstairs' home on Hancock Street, she glanced into the yard and tensed. Penelope Carstairs sat on the shaded front porch. Turning her head away, Ellie picked up her pace along the wooden walkway fronting the house.

"Mrs. Craig! Do you have a moment?"

Ellie arranged her face in a polite expression and turned toward the woman. The two of them hadn't spoken during the three months since Penelope implied that Julia's death was somehow a judgment on Matthew.

Penelope had moved to the fence, her hand on the gate. "I'd be pleased if you would stop in for a moment."

"Well, I don't have much time . . ."

"I won't keep you long."

Ellie followed her up the two steps and took one of the slat-back chairs arranged next to a low table. Around the front and sides of the porch, a tumble of yellow and purple coneflowers thrust their mounded centers toward the sky. In the south corner of the yard, the heart-shaped leaves of the lilac bush drooped in the afternoon sun.

After a few remarks about the heat, Penelope cleared her throat. "How's the lilac start I gave you doing?"

"Beautifully. I'm keeping it well watered, and hope next spring to see a bloom or two."

"I'm thankful that something from my yard is providing you comfort."

"It's a fitting memorial to our little Julia." Ellie held her breath, wondering if Penelope would repeat her remarks about the baby's death being a judgment.

"I'm sure you weren't aware of it, but when we last spoke I was preparing for the arrival of a child."

Penelope's statement surprised her. Without meaning to, Ellie shot a glance at the younger woman's midsection. The pointed bodice of her purple and white striped dress fitted snugly at her trim waistline.

Penelope caught her glance. Tears sprang to her eyes and she shook her head. "No. I lost the baby. This is the second time it's happened."

Ellie drew a sharp breath. "I'm so sorry." She touched the other woman's hand. "I know how you must be feeling."

"Of course you do. That's why I wanted to speak with you. I owe you an apology." Tears glittered on her cheeks. "I was guilty of listening to rumors, when in my heart I knew better."

"Rumors?"

"About your babies. Since the Reverend's been gone, I've had a chance to realize the wrong we did him. Did to both of you." She squeezed her hands together and gazed at Ellie. "Do you think you could persuade him to return?"

"It's too late for that. He doesn't believe he's wanted here."

"He'll be home for a rest after traveling, won't he? Tell him we want him back."

"But you and your husband were among the first to stay away before Matthew ever left."

Penelope looked at her hands, which continued to writhe as though they had a life of their own. "We see what we've done to Reverend Craig, and to you, by spreading gossip. God didn't judge you any more than he did me." She kept her head bent. "I was so wrong, and I'm sorry." Lifting her eyes, she gazed at Ellie. Tears spiked her lashes. "Mr. Beldon's not a real preacher, leastways not the kind Reverend Craig was to us. You've heard him in church. He looks good, and talks good, but inside I don't think he cares."

"He does the best he can. We have to give him time to get to know the town." Ellie placed her hands over Penelope's. "When Matthew comes back, I'll tell him what you said. I doubt it'll make a difference, but thank you for telling me. Your words are a comfort."

Once she was back on the walkway, Ellie sighed. She wished Matthew could've heard Penelope's remarks. If the Carstairs had changed their minds, maybe others would too.

The plum-colored phaeton turned the corner, its black wheels blurred with dust. When Mr. Beldon saw her, he reined his team to a stop and set the brake. "Good afternoon, Mrs. Craig."

"Good afternoon to you, Mr. Beldon."

"You're looking well. One would never guess that you're managing a fair-sized farm all by yourself."

Flattered, Ellie smiled up at him. "My sons are a big help. I don't know what I'd do without them."

Mr. Beldon nodded. "Fine lads indeed. But if anything comes up that they can't handle, please feel free to send for me."

She looked at his hands holding the reins, and suppressed a flutter in her throat. Lately she'd been waking at night with disturbing remnants of dreams in her head. Something about those hands reminded her of a recent dream. She felt a flush cover her cheeks. "Thank you. I'll keep that in mind."

"You do that." He reached for the brake.

Ellie stepped to the edge of the walk. "Wait. Have you gained any information about my brothers and sisters?"

He removed his hat and patted his forehead with a crisp white handkerchief. "Unfortunately, no. But you must realize these things take time. The conflict brewing in Texas makes inquiries difficult." His spicy, clovelike scent drifted toward her. "Rest assured, I'm doing all I can."

"Oh, I'm sure you are. I know how busy you've been. I just came from Spenglers'. It's good to see James safe at home. Thank you for everything you did to bring him back."

Mr. Beldon looked puzzled for a moment. "Ah, yes. James. Glad I could help." He freed the brake and urged his team forward.

When she entered the mercantile, Ellie sensed a change in the atmosphere since her previous visit. Several women sent genuine smiles her way as she walked into the crowded store. Tentatively, she smiled back.

The smell of oiled floors mingled with the aroma of coffee beans, molasses, and vinegar rising from barrels near the door. She eyed her meager list. Not knowing how long it would be before the church conference sent Matthew's stipend, she kept to the basics.

Mr. Wolcott leaned around the scale on the counter. "Afternoon, Mrs. Craig. Looks like you brought me a list."

"A short one, I'm afraid. Indian meal, salt, a sack of cranberry beans—just necessities." She handed him her slip of paper. "Maybe a pint of that molasses, if we still have enough credit on the books."

"Happens I noticed your chit this morning. You've got more'n enough."

Ellie doubted it. Knowing Mr. Wolcott, he'd keep them supplied and say nothing about money owed. She felt a rush of gratitude toward their longtime friend. "Thank you. You're a blessing to our family."

His cheeks flushed. "Don't mention it." He cleared his throat. "If you've got a minute, there's something I want to tell you."

"What is it?"

Mr. Wolcott's voice lowered. "Some folks have been asking me to start Sunday preaching here at the store, and I've decided to do it. There's space in the back room."

Stunned, Ellie stared at him. "What about the church building?"

He looked around, checking to be sure they weren't overheard. "If Marcus Beldon wants to preach there, we'll let him." He met Ellie's gaze with his clear hazel eyes. "Quite a few people who were lured away have come to see through his deceptions."

Ellie recalled Penelope Carstairs' remarks earlier that afternoon. "But . . . Mr. Beldon told us he studied for the ministry. So he's qualified."

"Big difference between studying books and caring about people." Mr. Wolcott leaned over the counter. "You've got to ask yourself, why hasn't he been officially assigned to the Beldon Grove church by Elder Meecham? Far as I know, Beldon hasn't gone to Quincy to see him. The man can't just take over a vacant pulpit, like a varmint moving into a deserted cabin." He spoke in a heated undertone. "It's not my wish to stir things up with those who think Beldon's the answer to all their prayers. But, we'll be meeting here Sunday morning, if you wish to join us." He straightened, suddenly businesslike, and raised his voice. "I'll take care of your list for you. Your uncle will be picking it up, I reckon?"

"Yes. Thank you." Ellie moved away, stepping around a shopper who had materialized next to her.

"Mrs. Craig?"

She turned to see a young woman holding a baby. "Yes?"

"I'm Johanna Nielsen. Me and my husband took up a farm north of here back in May. Mr. Wolcott told me you're the preacher's wife."

"I was. I mean, I am, but my husband isn't the preacher here any more."

Johanna stroked one of her baby's fat cheeks. "I just wanted to tell you that we hope he comes back. We don't much like the new man."

The rest of what the woman said washed past her ears in the wave of emotion stirred up at the sight of Johanna's child. Wisps of pale blonde hair covered the infant's scalp. One chubby fist clung tightly to the neckline of her mother's dress, the same way Julia used to hang onto her. A visceral urge for another baby rocked Ellie's body.

On the trip back to the farm, Ellie sat in silence, her thoughts tumbling over the events of the day. It was almost more than she could take in. James's return. Penelope's apology. The baby. She wrapped her arms around her middle and squeezed, rocking forward. She looked so much like Julia. *Lord, could I dare have another child?*

The grasslands along the road drowsed in the July sunshine. When the buggy rattled over the plank bridge, she roused herself, gathered her reticule and picked up the jar filled with molasses. Uncle Arthur helped Ellie from the buggy, then reached into his jacket pocket and handed her a long envelope. "I stopped at the post office this afternoon. This came, and I'm afraid to open it. What if it's telling me Ruby's dead?"

Ellie looked at the envelope, addressed in formal Copperplate script. "Sangamon County Circuit Court" was written in the upper left-hand corner. Her conscience stirred. She knew what the envelope contained, even if he didn't. "Let's go inside. No sense standing here in the hot sun."

As he followed her up the steps, Ellie's mind jumped to the newspaper she'd shoved to the back of her kitchen cupboard. She hung her bonnet on a peg inside the door, then led the way down the hall. "We'll go in the parlor. It may be cooler there."

They sat side by side on the divan under the window. Pretending to be mystified, she picked at the seal on the envelope, taking as much time as possible before revealing the contents. When she shook out the folded papers, one glance told her they represented Ruby's divorce filing.

She offered the pages to Uncle Arthur, but he pushed them back. "You read it and give me the short version." He pointed at the closely written script. "If it's from a court, most of it's going to be legal lingo anyways. Just tell me if Ruby's all right."

Ellie's heart felt like a stone. She read through the formal script, looking for pertinent phrases while Arthur drummed his fingers on his leg. When she'd stalled as long as possible, she spread the pages open on her lap. "This is a divorce petition. Aunt Ruby has filed for a divorce, claiming you treated her with 'repeated cruelty' for the last two years."

"What!" Uncle Arthur jumped to his feet, his face so red it made his beard look like mounded snow. "Let me see that." He scanned the sheets of paper, then threw them on the floor.

"Calm down." Ellie placed a hand on his arm. "You'll have apoplexy, getting angry like this."

He shook her hand off. "Repeated cruelty, my foot! I'll show her repeated cruelty." He turned, giving Ellie a narrow smile. "I'll go to Springfield and cross-file for adultery."

Uncle Arthur stamped out of the room. She hurried after him, but arrived in the hallway just as the back door slammed. The next sound she heard was a ringing crack, followed by a thud. When Ellie threw open the door, he lay sprawled on the ground below a broken stair tread.

22

Matthew approached Tylerville, the southernmost point on his circuit, with a sense of relief. Weariness rode his shoulders like a cloak. From now on, his journey would take him back toward Beldon Grove. He'd already been traveling more than three weeks, and knew it would probably take at least that long to get home. He wished he hadn't told Ellie he'd only be gone a month. He ran his tongue over the cut on his lip. Time wasn't the only thing he couldn't predict.

Since heading south from Adams Station, he'd considered the notion that perhaps Aunt Ruby might be traveling with the troupe scheduled to perform *Macbeth* in New Camden. If so, should he delay his return home further by detouring to find the woman? And if he found her, what should he do?

Normally certain in his judgments, Matthew found himself doubting his decisions, almost to the point of paralysis. Riding in one direction, he considered going in another. Stopping for the night, he wondered if he should travel farther. And the paramount question, was he too hasty in leaving Beldon Grove?

He glanced around as he entered the scattered settlement, taking in the narrow dirt track, fronted by a collection of weathered cabins. Matthew turned his horse toward the hitching rail in front of a building with "Dr. Homer Best, Apothecary" painted on a sign next to the door. The local doctor would be a good one to ask about a meeting place. He'd likely know the community as well as anyone.

He tried the latch of the apothecary, but found it locked. A tattered curtain over the window blocked his view of the interior. As Matthew stood in the dusty street pondering his next move, a woman's voice called to him from a store he'd passed when he entered the settlement.

"You looking for the doctor?"

"Not exactly." He turned in her direction, noting with surprise her mannish attire. He felt himself flush at the sight of a woman wearing trousers, and tried desperately to fix his eyes anywhere but on her legs.

Evidently she saw his discomfort and laughed as she held out her hand. "I'm Carrie Boughten. My husband owned this store, but he died so I'm stuck trying to make a living off of it. I find it easier to do a man's work in a man's clothing."

Her height matched Matthew's. He shook her hand awkwardly, startled by the strength of her grip.

"Guess you never saw a female in trousers, eh?"

Something in her speech sounded familiar, but he couldn't place what it was. "Uh, no."

She laughed again, showing white teeth against leathery skin. "C'mon in and rest yourself." She pointed to the open doorway of the store. "Tell me what brings you to an out-of-the-way hole like Tylerville."

Once inside, she pointed to two rocking chairs next to a fireplace on the far wall. The hearth was swept bare, although a basket of kindling stood at the ready. The shelves in the store showed only a meager stock. Matthew couldn't see how she survived running such a poor business.

Carrie smiled at his expression. "Middle of the day, middle of the week." Her glance took in the store. "Got plenty of time to talk. On Saturday a few farmers and their wives come in. Then I'll be busy for a spell."

There it was again. Her words reminded him of something, or someone.

She poured a dipperful of water from a barrel into a tin cup and handed it to him. "Doc's gone out to deliver a baby," she said, as though there'd been no break in the conversation since she first asked her question. "He ought to be here tomorrow, if it's him you're wanting."

"I thought maybe the doctor could steer me to someplace where I could hold a meeting." Matthew settled into one of the rockers with an audible sigh of relief. "My name's Matthew Craig. Tylerville's one of the stops assigned to me on my circuit."

"You're a preacher?"

He nodded.

She snorted with laughter. "Well, the doc is the last person you'd want to tell you where to have a meeting. The old codger would probably be struck dead if'n he stepped inside a church." Carrie shook her head, eyes dancing with amusement.

Her laughter was contagious. Matthew couldn't help but smile as he asked, "Well, then, who around here should I see?"

"Why not me? I know ever body in town, and just happen to have plenty of room right here in back of the store." She pointed to a drooping piece of burlap tacked over a doorway. "Folks have held Sunday school here in the past. But it's been a sight of time since we had a real preacher. Never figured to see another one, for a fact."

"Why is that?"

"Town's dying." She waved her hand toward the open door.

221

"People pushing on west, looking for something better. Or flat giving up and going back wherever they came from."

In spite of her outrageous attire, Matthew felt drawn to the tall woman. He smiled inwardly. If any ruffians tried to disrupt the meeting, he'd wager Carrie Boughten could deal with them single-handed.

He leaned back in his chair and took a swallow of water. "I expect you could find me a place to sleep too."

She nodded. "There's a family down the street that's real good about taking in travelers. I'd let you stay here, but folks would talk." She tugged at the knees of her pants and crossed her ankles. A moment of silence dropped between them. Carrie broke it by giving Matthew a quizzical glance and asking, "You said your name is Craig? Where you from?"

"Up north, in Beldon Grove."

"Oh." She shifted in her chair, the cane seat creaking under her weight. "I knew a family by the name of Craig, back home in Kentucky."

Realization dawned in Matthew's mind. She was from Kentucky. That's why her speech sounded familiar. "Lots of Craigs in Kentucky. Which part are you from?"

"Marysville. It's just across the Ohio a piece."

Now Matthew sat up straight and studied her. "I'm from Marysville, but I haven't been back in over twenty-five years. I had a letter from one of my brothers a number of years ago, telling me of our mother's death. Far as I know, my pa still lives there."

"Is your pa Marsden Craig?"

"You know him?" Matthew rocked back in his chair.

"Know of him. It's your ma I remember." Carrie's face softened. "She was a saint. Anybody needed help when they was sick, your ma would do all she could to ease them through their suffering."

222

Matthew looked at the floor to hide the tears that blurred his vision. He'd been an itinerant preacher for five years when he received the letter from his brother Adam telling him of their mother's death. Given the hostility that existed between himself and his father, he hadn't returned home. When he raised his head, he found Carrie looking at him as though she could read his thoughts.

Her brown eyes locked on his. "Your pa's an old man now. Last I heard he's still on the farm with your brothers."

"And his slaves?" Matthew spit the word into the room. "They still there?"

"I reckon. Some, anyways. That what's keeping you away?"

"It's why I left Kentucky. A man shouldn't be able to own another man. It's flat wrong, and I told Pa that."

Carrie chuckled. "Bet he didn't take kindly to you telling him what's what." She gazed at him. "You don't look to be all that old—you must've been a stripling when you left."

"I was eighteen. Old enough."

"No need to get huffy. I'm just thinking maybe it's time you went back—patched things up before it's too late. Tylerville's only a couple days' ride from the Ohio."

Matthew stood and handed her his empty cup. He'd never considered returning to his father's farm, and he certainly didn't need advice from a stranger. "Thank you for the hospitality. If you'll point the way to the cabin where I'm to spend the night, I'll be on my way."

Carrie studied him through narrowed eyes. "You sleep on what I'm saying, Reverend. We can talk tomorrow about setting up for a meeting."

❧

When Matthew walked into Carrie's store the next morning, she had drawn aside the burlap curtain over the interior doorway and was raising a cloud of dust with her broom. "Been longer than I thought since we had a meeting here." She flipped her thick buckwheat-colored braid over her shoulder. "I pushed those crates aside to make space for a couple benches. You can shove a flour barrel over to the front for a preaching stand. Then help me tote the seats from my house."

"How many folks do you think will come out?"

"The Wainwrights—"

Matthew recognized the name of the family in whose cabin he'd spent the night.

"—Old Man Carter, Isabelle Dooley . . ." She leaned on the broom, thinking. "Otherwise, I'm not certain. Word will spread. I've already got it started. We'll just have to wait for tonight and see."

He'd walked the length of the settlement that morning before arriving at Carrie's and, not counting the apothecary and saloon, saw only a few cabins. There were bound to be other homesteads in the area. He figured thirty or forty people overall, including children. Somewhat less than Adams Station.

"You think there's enough space for everyone?"

A smile twitched at the corner of Carrie's mouth. "Most likely." Her grin broadened. "If not, we'll move outside. Plenty of room there."

Matthew tilted a barrel sideways. Using his left arm for support, he rolled the barrel to the front of the room. From that position, he'd be able to see gathered worshipers and watch the window behind them for any signs of troublemakers. Once he felt satisfied with the arrangement, he followed Carrie to her house next door.

Her cabin bore all the signs of femininity that she bypassed in her attire. The table in the main room was covered with a blue cloth, embroidered around the edges with daisies. The benches on both sides had been painted black and stenciled. In front of the fireplace she'd placed a ladder-back armchair upholstered in floral needlepoint. Matthew took in the intricate rose and oak leaf pattern, then turned to Carrie. He couldn't keep his surprise from showing on his face.

She met his gaze squarely. "Gives me something to do during the winters. Besides, I like pretty things. Don't have to dress like a girl in order to think like one."

Uncomfortable, he looked away. The female touches brought Ellie to his mind. He frowned, wondering if he'd ever told her how nice she looked in her new pink dress. He hoped so. "Good to see a woman's touch. Especially way out here."

Carrie's face softened for a moment, then she turned brisk. "Help me with this bench." She lifted one end and waited for him to take the other. When they had the storeroom arranged, she stepped back and surveyed their efforts. "This ought to do."

To Matthew's eyes, two benches and several packing crates barely filled half the space. "Where's everyone going to sit?"

"Expecting a crowd, are you? Well, there's plenty of room on the floor if need be. Children can always park themselves on blankets."

"How long did you say it's been since a preacher stopped here?"

"Long time. Why don't you stop worrying and go get some dinner? I'll see you back here tonight."

Dismayed, Matthew leaned on the top of the barrel and looked at the eleven people who sat facing him. No wonder Carrie had smiled when he asked if there was enough room. As she had predicted, the Wainwrights were there. Middle-aged and wearing the weary look of defeated farmers, they watched him with arms folded across their chests. An elderly man sat directly in front of Matthew, head cocked to one side to catch any words that might fall from Matthew's lips. A couple near the ages of Orville and Penelope Carstairs sat on the second bench, four scrubbed and fidgety children crammed next to them. Carrie shared space on a packing crate with a dark-haired woman who sat with knitting needles in her hands, clicking away on what looked like a pale tan stocking.

Feet shuffled. Throats cleared. "You might as well commence, Reverend." Carrie said. "Can't wait all night."

He looked out the window, saw no one else on the way, then opened his Bible to the text he'd used at Adams Station.

After an opening prayer, he took a deep breath and held it for a moment before speaking. "My text tonight is from the Acts of the Apostles, chapter seventeen." Matthew read the scripture, making application to his hearers in Tylerville. He talked on, sweating in the humid room. Occasionally he lifted his eyes to the outside, hoping to see more people coming. Each time, vacant prairie filled his vision.

Inside, his listeners gazed, rapt, as his voice rose in intensity.

After numerous exhortations and explanations, Matthew thumped his finger on an open page, concluding as he always did, "'And the times of this ignorance God winked at; but now commandeth all men everywhere to repent!' Who among you will be the first to come forward?"

People exchanged glances, and squirmed in their seats. No one met his eyes. No one moved. Knitting needles ticked rhythmically in the otherwise quiet room. Matthew bowed his head, fingers pinched over his lips. *Lord, what do I do now?*

"We usually sing a hymn before we close, Reverend."

He looked up and met Carrie's sympathetic gaze. "Which one?" he asked, grateful for her intervention.

Once the room cleared, Matthew sank onto one of the benches and lowered his head into his hands. The verse "Humble yourselves therefore under the mighty hand of God" came to his mind. He couldn't feel much more humble than he did at that moment. His face felt hot, and not from the humidity.

Carrie settled on the bench next to Matthew, saying nothing. After several moments, she folded her hands in her lap and turned her head toward him. "Don't take it to heart, Reverend. Folks around here have about given up on hope. They're just waiting for the next thing, whatever it may be." She picked at the rough fabric of her trousers. "Town just gets smaller and more hardhearted. Guess that's why no preachers stop here anymore."

He let his breath out in a heavy sigh. That being the case, why did Elder Meecham send him to Tylerville? "I'm thankful for your help. It was good of you, considering you suspected how things would turn out." He stood. "I'll help you get your storeroom rearranged, then I'll be on my way."

"Where to?"

"Arcadia Mills."

"Go see your pa first, you hear?"

23

Ellie tiptoed down the stairs into the cool kitchen, hoping not to disturb Uncle Arthur asleep in the parlor. Daylight was still a promise. The room was dark enough that she lit the lamp. After rolling the wooden churn next to the table, she poured in several days' collection of cream and set the dasher in place, then commenced the rhythmic churning that would result in fresh butter to last them for the week. Still sleepy, she yawned, her mind already on the overwhelming list of daily tasks awaiting her attention.

"Ellie? That you?" Uncle Arthur's voice interrupted her thoughts.

"Yes."

"Can you come sit with me a bit?"

Sighing, she released the dasher and stood, knowing she'd have to start all over again after she'd seen to his needs. "How are you today?" she asked when she entered the parlor.

Uncle Arthur had pulled himself to a sitting position on the divan. He grunted. "Leg hurts."

He said the same thing every morning. "I need to get back to churning. Can you lean on me and come out to the kitchen?"

"I'm too heavy for you." Self-pity crept into his voice. "I'll just sit here and wait for the twins to help me."

Dawn lightened the eastern sky, the sun a glowing fist on the horizon. Ellie perched on the edge of the divan, flexing her shoulders to ease the tension that never quite went away. "You're not too heavy if you use the crutches Karl made for you. Now come on, I've got to work up the butter before the house gets too hot." She slipped an arm around him and stood, pulling him to his feet. With her free hand, she grabbed the crutches and handed them to him. "Let's go."

Once the butter was salted and stored in a crock of cold water, Ellie and Maria started the baking. The twins had walked Uncle Arthur outside so he could sit in the shade and look at the cornfields through the morning glory vines that twined along the porch supports.

Ellie stared out the kitchen window at the corn that seemed to grow as she watched. The cornstalks were taller than the boys' heads, and tasseling. She turned when she heard Maria open the oven door and slide browned pans of bread out onto the tabletop. Heat from the stove radiated against the kitchen walls.

Instead of seeing a row of browned loaves, Ellie pictured the near-empty flour bin in the storeroom. It had been close to a month since Matthew left, and no support had come from the church conference. She didn't dare add more to what they owed Mr. Wolcott. They'd have to eat pan bread made with Indian meal once the flour was gone.

Her face flushed with heat, Maria placed the last risen loaves into the oven and gently closed the door.

Ellie walked over and hugged her. "You're doing this so well, pretty soon you'll be teaching me."

Maria giggled. "Thank you."

Ellie fanned herself with her hand. "Let's go sit out on the porch while the bread bakes. It's too hot to breathe in here."

Uncle Arthur's face lit up when he saw them emerge from the kitchen. "I can smell that bread." He looked at Maria. "How about bringing me a piece?"

"Slice up a plateful," Ellie said. "Might as well enjoy it while we have it."

When her daughter went back inside, Ellie sank onto the top step, loosening the neckline of her dress to cool off. Since Uncle Arthur's accident, she'd been busy from daylight until well past dark and still wasn't able to keep up with all the chores.

She massaged her temples in an attempt to stave off a headache. Beneath her feet, a freshly hewn hickory stair tread gleamed in the sunlight. The new step lacked Matthew's woodworking skills, but the twins had done the best they could.

Uncle Arthur's voice brought her back to the present. "You're working too hard. Why don't you visit Molly this afternoon? It's Thursday. Isn't this the day you get together for a quilting session?"

Ellie leaned back on one hand and looked up at him. "It's too hot to walk all that way. I'd rather just stay here."

"I don't mean for you to walk. Have one of the boys hitch King George to my buggy. You haven't been to town since I fell—it'll be good for you."

She thought of undone chores. "I really shouldn't . . ."

"Yes, you should." Uncle Arthur looked up when Maria returned carrying a plate of sliced bread and a bowl of fresh butter. "Soon's I have some of this bread, you call Jimmy. He's got a way with horses. I'll need to talk him through the job—George can be touchy when he hasn't been worked for a while."

Uncle Arthur rested on a wooden bench inside the barn. Ellie and the children stood off to one side, watching as Jimmy worked with the temperamental chestnut roan. "Bring him out easy, boy. Stay away from his hooves."

Inside King George's stall, Jimmy wrapped his hand around the lead rope and tugged at the horse. "He's not moving."

"Give him a swat on the rump. He's got lazy."

Jimmy smacked the animal's backside, but instead of moving forward King George sidestepped, jamming a hoof hard on Jimmy's right foot. "He's standing on me." Tears sprang into the boy's eyes. "Get him off!"

Ellie ran to the side of the stall. "Do something, Uncle."

Uncle Arthur gestured to Harrison, who stood gaping at his big brother's tears. "Help me up." Once on his feet, he crutched over to the stall. "Sometimes this'll get him moving." He twisted his mouth to one side and emitted a running series of clicks.

Ears tilted toward his owner, King George moved to the front of the enclosure. As soon as Jimmy's foot was free, he hobbled to the stall opening and escaped into Ellie's arms.

After removing his boot, she stared in dismay at the already-purpling foot. His last three toes looked like stubby sausages.

Jimmy turned pale and trembled. His teeth chattered. "I'm c-c-cold."

She stared at him in disbelief. "Cold! It's like an oven in here."

Johnny pushed forward. "I'll help him to the house."

As the two boys left the barn, Ellie turned to her uncle. "Is it safe to let Harrison take the lead rope off? Doesn't look like I'll be going anywhere today."

"Better wait 'til Johnny gets back." He leaned on one crutch and held out an arm. "Come here. You look like someone kicked the slats out from under you."

Ellie didn't move. "I don't need comforting. I need help." She shook her head and watched the twins make their way across the farmyard. "It takes both Jimmy and Johnny to keep up with the chores. Johnny can't do it alone."

Harrison tugged at her hand. "You have me."

"So I do." She surveyed her son. He took his height from her side of the family and was smaller than the twins had been when they were his age. He couldn't do Jimmy's work, but she wouldn't tell him so. "Can you help your uncle up to the house? I need to go see about your brother's foot."

He stretched himself taller. "You go ahead. I can do it."

When Ellie turned, she noticed Maria hovering in the background. "Please take a basket down to the creek and fill it with plantain leaves. They'll take the swelling down."

Her daughter ran to obey, bare feet flying across the packed earth between barn and house.

Ellie caught up with Jimmy and Johnny as they attempted to climb the back steps. She put an arm under Jimmy's shoulder and helped hoist him onto the shaded porch and into a chair. In spite of years of caring for her children when they were hurt, Ellie never lost her queasiness at the sight of wounds.

Swallowing hard, she touched her son's swollen foot. "Can you wiggle your toes?"

The bruised toes moved back and forth. Jimmy had controlled his tears, but couldn't help whimpering at the effort.

She stroked the hair back from his sweaty forehead. "I'll wrap your foot with plantain as soon as Maria brings it." Bending, she kissed the top of his head. "You're being very brave."

Johnny sat beside his twin looking pained, as though the horse had stepped on him too. "Shall we put him to bed?"

"No, it's too hot inside the house. He'll be better off out here until sunset." She turned to Uncle Arthur, who slowly took one step at a time to reach the shade of the porch. "You'll be having a companion tonight, looks like. It'll be easier to keep Jimmy downstairs until his foot's better."

Ellie gathered handfuls of long, veined leaves from the basket Maria placed at her side. She crushed them between the palms of her hands until the narrow green strips softened, then padded Jimmy's swollen foot top and bottom with plantain. She bound the leaves in place with a strip of toweling and propped his foot up on the seat of an empty chair. "Don't move about. Let the plantain do its work."

Jimmy smiled through the lines of pain drawn across his face. "I'm not moving. Don't worry."

She stroked his hair again, then sank onto the top step and leaned back on her hands. A few thin clouds trailed high across the midday sky. Scarcely an hour had passed since Arthur had suggested taking the buggy to town, and in that short time things had gone from difficult to unmanageable. She swiped perspiration from her temples.

Beyond the tree line edging the creek, she noticed a column of dust rising from the road. Johnny ran past her down the steps. "Do you suppose it's Papa?"

"Who else could it be?" Ellie stood, waiting for horse and rider to appear on the bridge over the creek. *Lord, please let it be Matthew.*

Mr. Beldon's phaeton rolled over the planks and turned toward them. If he was surprised to see all of the Craig family gathered to watch his arrival, he didn't show it. "Good afternoon."

Ellie tried not to let disappointment overwhelm her. She knew she must look hot, rumpled, and leaf-stained, but after the day she'd had, she no longer cared. "Mr. Beldon. This is a surprise."

He climbed from the buggy and wrapped the reins over the hitching rail. "You and your family haven't been in church. I began to fear something was amiss out here." His gaze traveled to the porch, where Uncle Arthur and Jimmy each sat with a leg propped up on a chair. "Appears I was right." Mr. Beldon stood close enough that Ellie could have counted the links in his gold watch chain, had she wanted to. His dark-lashed eyes were filled with concern.

She waved a hand toward Arthur. "As you can see, travel to town has been out of the question. My uncle broke his leg two weeks ago Saturday."

Mr. Beldon followed her onto the porch. "My sympathies, sir. And what happened to you, young man?"

Jimmy eyed him sullenly. "Horse stepped on my foot."

Ellie shot him a "be polite" look. "He was harnessing Uncle Arthur's horse so I could take the buggy to town."

Mr. Beldon's eyes lighted. "If you need conveyance, I'd be pleased to provide it."

"No. I only planned to visit my sister-in-law. Nothing that can't—"

"My dear, why don't you go?" Uncle Arthur said. "Take Maria with you. We men can get along here for a couple of hours."

Maria jumped to her feet. "Can I, Mama?"

Johnny moved next to Ellie. "I know I could hitch the buggy for you."

She shook her head. "Thank you, but we won't risk it." Ellie held out a hand to Maria, then looked at Mr. Beldon. "If you'll wait until we freshen up, I'd be grateful for the ride."

☙

Headed toward Beldon Grove, Ellie luxuriated in the smoothness of the black leather upholstery inside the phaeton. Maria sat between her mother and Mr. Beldon, swinging her bare feet to the rhythm of the horses' hooves. They rode for several moments without speaking. Ellie's gaze landed on the dark hairs that covered the backs of his hands, a pang of loneliness for Matthew stabbing at her heart. Her husband's hands were stronger than Mr. Beldon's—tougher somehow.

She lifted her eyes to his face. "I'm afraid I'm putting you to a great deal of trouble."

"No trouble at all." Smiling, he raised an eyebrow. "It's not often I'm privileged to escort such a charming woman . . . and a pretty little girl."

Ellie knew it wasn't right to take pleasure in his comment, but she couldn't help herself. Mindful of Maria sitting with them, she said, "What have you learned about that matter in Texas that we spoke of earlier?"

Mr. Beldon glanced down at Maria, then turned to Ellie. "From what I know of Austin's arrangements with Mexico, men with wives received more land. So you're undoubtedly correct that he remarried. But you must realize that it may have taken place soon after he arrived, so any issue from that union would be grown and possibly with families of their own by now."

"I'm aware of that."

"Also, inheritance rights could have reverted to the Colony in general, and it's so far away it would be impractical to pursue a claim."

Ellie gritted her teeth. "I told you. I'm not interested in an inheritance." She checked to see if Maria was listening to them, but she seemed oblivious. "It's the . . . issue I want to find out about."

"You need to be patient and not expect too much. Adults are not likely to want to leave their land in Texas to join you in Illinois."

"I don't expect them to." Ellie snapped her response. She drew in a deep breath and held it for a moment. "What I'd like, when you find out where they are, is a letter from one or more of them telling me about their lives and something about our papa. I'd be content with that."

"Then that's what you shall have." He moved the reins to his left hand and slid his arm over the back of the buggy seat, brushing her shoulder with his fingertips. "You can depend on me."

24

The stern-wheeler *Daniel Boone* churned through the wide blue-green Ohio River on its approach to Oakport. Black smoke from twin stacks trailed behind like banners. As Matthew looked on, a bell rang and the paddle wheel stopped, then reversed and the boat swung toward the dock.

He backed Samson away a few paces when he saw lines being thrown from the boat to waiting dockhands. His palms were clammy. He could still change his mind. His pa would be there the next time he traveled the circuit. Matthew touched the scab on his lip. If there was a next time.

The stream of people and goods being unloaded ceased and folks nearby were making their way onto the steamboat. If he didn't hurry, he'd be waiting on shore when the *Daniel Boone* turned back into the current and proceeded downriver.

Matthew touched the horse's side with his heels. "All right, Samson. Let's go see Pa."

Once near the gangplank, he dismounted and led the horse toward the cargo hold, stroking the animal's nose to calm him. The pungent odor of whiskey on its way to New Orleans escaped from barrels crowding the closed space. He slipped Samson's lead through a ring attached to the bulkhead, then walked out onto the lower deck and leaned against the railing, watching the green banks of Illinois slip away. A breeze from the river ruffled his beard. He wasn't sure what he hoped to accomplish once he reached Marysville. He shook his head. Carrie Boughten was one persuasive woman.

As Matthew traveled along the oak-lined lane leading to his father's farm, he fought the impulse to turn around and wait for the next steamboat going upriver. Part of him felt like a naughty child going before an angry parent for punishment. The other part, one that had hidden at the back of his mind since leaving Tylerville, longed to see his brothers and father.

Purple shadows striped the road, reminding him that the long journey to his boyhood home was nearly at an end. The familiar two-story frame house, with its outsized stone chimneys at each end, loomed out of a clearing ahead. As he drew closer, he saw someone sitting in the shadows of the veranda near the front door.

When he stopped his horse at the cross-pole fence, a young black boy appeared through the dusk. "Take care of your horse, Massa?"

Matthew dismounted, handing the reins to the lad. "Thank you." His voice sounded gruff in his ears. "No need to call me 'Massa.' I'm Matthew. What's your name?"

"Henry, suh."

"You lived here long, Henry?"

"Yes, suh. I was borned right down there." He pointed at the row of slave cabins.

Matthew patted the boy's head. "Thank you for taking care of my horse. I expect he's tuckered."

"You're welcome, suh."

A querulous voice called from the depths of the veranda. "Who's out there palavering? Come up here."

Matthew hesitated, trying to think of a way to announce himself. He couldn't be sure whose voice called to him. In his memory, his father invariably spoke with a bass growl, not this peevish whine. "It's Matthew," he answered, mounting the veranda steps. "Is that you, Pa?"

"Who you calling Pa? I don't have any son named Matthew."

For a moment, as he studied the old man hunched in a chair that all but dwarfed him, Matthew could believe he'd made a mistake. Someone else could've bought the place since Carrie was last here. His first reaction was relief. He wouldn't have to face the man whose harsh opinions had driven him away.

"Hattie!" the old man bellowed. "Bring a lamp."

Matthew didn't recognize the wrinkled black woman who appeared in answer to the peremptory summons. Hattie carried a lighted oil lamp, which she placed on a table next to the oversized chair. She dipped her head in acknowledgment of Matthew's presence, then slipped silently back into the house. Once the pale, lined face was illuminated, there was no doubt in his mind that he faced Marsden Craig. His father's once luxuriant black hair had disappeared, leaving his scalp shining in the lamplight. Wiry gray whiskers, too sparse to be called a beard, covered his cheeks.

"Come over here where I can see you."

Matthew complied, stepping closer to his father's chair.

The old man's yellowed eyes widened. "By dad, it *is* you." He snorted. "You come back because I'm dying? Think you might get your hands on this place?"

Fear of confrontation pounded Matthew's belly. Since childhood, he'd been cowed by his father's authority. Not this time. He wouldn't let Pa roll over him again. He lifted his head and stared straight into the other man's eyes. "No. I told you when I left that I wanted no part of anything that comes from slavery."

The woman who brought the lamp appeared in the doorway. "Master Craig, cook sent me to tell you supper's ready."

Marsden turned his head at her voice. "Tell her to set an extry plate." He looked at Matthew. "Since you come all this way, you might as well spend the night."

Matthew gazed around the spacious dining room while Hattie served their meal. The ornate furniture looked as it had when he was a boy, but the patterned French wallpaper showed signs of mildew in the corners. The heavy window coverings drooped, appearing to be long overdue for an airing. His father wasn't the only part of the farm that had declined.

"Where are the boys? I thought they were taking care of things here."

Marsden spoke around a mouthful of gravy-smothered ham. "They been nearly as much a disappointment to me as you. Adam and Eli both went up to Harrisburg to live when they got married." He pitched his voice high, imitating a woman's speech. "Their wives don't want to rusticate down here in Marysville."

"But Nathaniel, where's he?" It was hard to believe that his brothers, who had been boys when he left, were now men in their thirties and early forties.

A trickle of gravy escaped the corner of his father's mouth, winding its way through his whiskers. "He comes around when it suits him. Just waiting for me to die, I expect." Marsden leaned back in his chair and studied his oldest son. "From what I hear, you've made a success of preaching after all. Thought sure you'd starve."

Puzzled, Matthew looked at him. "How'd you come to hear that?"

"Molly's miserable excuse for a brother-in-law, Brody McGarvie, came crawling back here a few years ago. Seems he lost everything Samuel worked for up there in Missouri. Thought I'd help him out. What a fool!" Marsden belched, then took another forkful of ham. "Anyways, he told me you'd come for Molly when her Samuel died, and that you had a fine church up in Illinois someplace."

Matthew remembered Brody, and the heartbreak he'd caused Molly by taking control of all Samuel's possessions and leaving her and her children destitute. He wasn't surprised to hear that Brody mismanaged the inheritance he'd obtained by trickery. What did surprise him was the sound of pride in his father's voice at the notion that Matthew headed a fine church. Did he imagine it?

Marsden dropped his fork onto his plate. "Hattie! Where's the pudding?"

"It'll be here quick, Master. Just let me get these here dirty plates out'n your way." The woman's response had been so prompt, Matthew suspected she'd been listening behind the door.

China clinked as Hattie gathered up soiled plates and cutlery. Marsden rested his gnarled hands on his belly and looked at Matthew. "Cook makes the best sweet tater pudding you ever put a tooth to. Bet you don't get anything like it up there in Illinois."

Matthew shook his head. "Probably not."

Hattie placed bowls of golden yellow pudding, swimming in cream, in front of each man and stepped out of the room. After so many years away from Kentucky living, Matthew felt ill at ease being waited upon by slaves.

His father's hawklike gaze bored into Matthew's eyes. "You say you didn't come back because I'm dying." He pointed with his spoon, splattering the tablecloth with drops of cream. "What do you want?"

"I want to have peace between us. Nothing else." Matthew poked his spoon at the sweet dessert. "We had hot words when I left home, and it's time to make it right." He swallowed, waiting for the old man's response.

"That was twenty-five years ago. You think I've been holding my breath waiting on you?" Marsden snorted, then in the next breath seemed to shrink in his chair. "Until that useless Brody come through here, I was afraid you was dead." He mumbled the words into his pudding. His hand trembled, rattling his spoon against the lip of the bowl. "I'm glad you're back. You did good to come."

Alarmed, Matthew leaned toward him. "I'm not staying, Pa. I don't agree with slaveholding—never will. But you're my father, and I owe you my respect." Reaching out, he laid his hand on his father's arm, feeling frail bones under his fingers. The power Marsden held over him had melted away, like the ample flesh that formerly covered the man's frame. "It was disrespectful for me to shout the Word of God in your face and expect you to change. If there's anything I've learned over these years, it's that God's message has to come quietly, or not at all."

His father studied him with narrowed eyes. "Respect, is it? I suppose that's right out of the Bible."

"It is."

"That the kind of thing you preach in your fancy church?"

Matthew had hoped the subject of his church wouldn't arise. He'd rather leave without his father knowing he was back where he'd started when he was eighteen. "It's what I preach, yes."

"Tell me about this church of yours. Tall steeple, colored glass windows?"

"Nothing so elaborate." He cleared his throat. "In fact, right now I don't have a church. I'm riding circuit."

"Name of heaven, boy! Why are you back to that?"

Matthew shoved his half-finished bowl of pudding toward the center of the table. Even though he no longer had the old fear of his father, the subject of his church left him feeling defenseless. How could he explain his leaving when he'd begun to doubt his own judgment?

"A group rose up against me, led by a person of power and influence. He got folks to believe I shouldn't preach there. So I left."

"Well, by dad! I never figured you for a coward. What happened to that hothead who stormed out of here all those years ago?" Marsden's eyes blazed with the angry light that Matthew remembered from childhood. "I was proud of your spunk, even though you went about things wrong."

Hurt rose in Matthew's throat at the old man's words. Why couldn't his father have said he was proud of him back when it would have mattered? He pinched his lips to stifle a bitter response.

Marsden gripped the arms of his chair and leaned forward. "You go on back there and throw that upstart out of your church."

"You don't know him. He's—"

"I know you." A slight smile grazed his lips. "You can do it."

Matthew led Samson down the gangplank and onto Illinois soil. The idea of returning home to wrest the pulpit from Marcus Beldon filled him with dread in spite of his father's parting encouragement. It was all well and good for Pa to tell him he could do it. Pa'd never been afraid of anything in his life.

A voice seemed to speak in his ear. *What do you think it was like to carve a settlement out of the Kentucky wilderness?* Matthew remembered stories he'd heard as a boy—fear of Indian attack, poisonous snakes, children lost in the thick forests. Of course his pa had been afraid. He just didn't let it stop him. He nudged Samson with his heels. "Let's get on home." If he rode hard, he could be back in another five or six days.

Samson turned, moving past hogsheads of tobacco being unloaded from the steamboat. His hooves made a hollow sound on the wooden dock. As Matthew rode past rows of barreled pork and molasses waiting to be rolled aboard, he heard a high keening.

He tipped his head and listened. The wails turned to hiccuping sobs, now soft and muffled. It sounded like a child crying. But where? Matthew guided his horse up to the landing and wrapped the reins around a post. Then he sprinted back, searching for the origin of the cries. As he moved around the barrels, he spotted a little girl crouched on the dock. She raised a tear-streaked face at his approach and tried to scuttle backward between two barrels.

Matthew squatted on his heels and held out his hand. "Please, don't be afraid. I won't hurt you. I'll help you find your mama."

The child stopped moving. Her dark brown eyes welled with fresh tears. "My mama's been dead for a long time." She squeezed a grimy rag doll to her chest and stared at Matthew.

"Well, your papa then."

She moved her doll to her shoulder, patting it like it was an infant. "My papa died too," she whispered. "In the wintertime."

Matthew stood and searched for another adult, but saw no one. He ached to gather the child in his arms, but felt if he moved too quickly she'd run away. Judging from her size, he thought she was probably Maria's age or maybe a little younger. He stretched out his hand and touched her shoulder. She didn't move.

"What's your name, little one?"

"Graciana." She straightened. "Graciana Largo."

Matthew took his handkerchief and blotted the tears from her soft, caramel-colored cheeks, then smoothed her straight black hair away from her face. "If your mama and papa are in heaven, who brought you here?"

"Aunt Polly brought me. But some bad men found her and took her away." Her grip on the doll tightened.

Matthew dropped to one knee and put both hands on Graciana's shoulders. His eyes searched her stricken face. "I'll take you home. Can you show me the way?"

"My home is gone. Papa promised Aunt Polly would take me to his family."

25

Ellie tilted a pitcher and drizzled a stream of water around the lilac start growing next to the back porch. Fresh growth sprouted from a tender green stem near the base of the plant. The heart-shaped leaves spoke to her of future promise. She felt absurdly grateful to see evidence of new life, even if it was only on a shrub.

Smiling, she settled into a chair in the shade and let her gaze roam over their farm. Chores waited, but for the moment Ellie savored the peace of the afternoon. She jumped when the back door slammed.

The twins walked to her side. "Mama?" Johnny asked. "Can we talk to you for a minute?"

She placed the empty pitcher on the floor and turned to her sons. "Of course you can. Whatever you've done, if you tell me the truth you won't be punished."

They leaned on the porch rail and faced her. Johnny's cheeks flushed. "It's not something we've done." He gazed at her with anxious eyes. "It's . . . well, we think it's wrong for you to go riding with Mr. Beldon. You act like you have a secret with him."

Shocked, Ellie stared at them.

"We don't want people to think you're like Aunt Ruby," Jimmy said.

Heat traveled through her body at the thought that her sons

were taking her to task over her behavior. Had her hopes blinded her to her responsibilities as a wife and mother? She shook her head in denial. "People won't think that. I'm not like Aunt Ruby at all."

"Then why did you let him drive you to town?"

Ellie bent her head at his words. Being a disappointment to her children was the last thing she would ever want. "You must understand, he just took me to see your Aunt Molly. Uncle Arthur can't hitch the buggy, and you know what happened when you tried it, Jimmy."

He looked down at his still-swollen foot. "Maybe you could ride with Mrs. Wolcott," he mumbled.

She opened her mouth to respond, but Johnny stepped away from the rail and stood in front of her. His voice shook. "Why did you pass Mr. Beldon a note in church the other Sunday? I saw you. What does that have to do with rides to Aunt Molly's?"

Shame seared her heart. She couldn't let her sons believe she'd be unfaithful to their father. Ellie lifted her head and allowed her eyes to rest on each boy in turn. "I asked him to do a favor for me."

"Why not wait and ask Papa?"

"Papa already said no." She stood and clasped each twin's hand in one of her own. "So I asked Mr. Beldon."

Johnny drew his hand away. "What would you do to us if we went behind your back when you told us not to do something?"

Ellie felt she might faint. "I'd punish you," she said in a small voice. Tears burned her eyes. "I'm so sorry," she whispered. "I never meant to involve you children in my concerns."

"Don't cry, Mama." Jimmy wrapped his arms around her. After a moment, Johnny moved closer and joined the hug.

Engulfed in her sons' embrace, Ellie's memory slipped back to the morning they were born. Then she'd held them both in her arms. Now they were holding her. Their grasp surprised her with its strength.

Johnny was the first to let go. He shoved his hands in his pockets and leveled his steady brown eyes on her. "What was the favor?"

She moved to the top step and sank down. Honeybees darted in and out of the morning glory blossoms draping the porch, their hum the only sound she heard over the beating of her heart.

Ellie patted the spot next to her. "Sit with me. I'll tell you all about it."

Once they'd settled on the step, she said, "You remember when Papa and I found out that my father died last year?"

"And you thought he'd already been dead for a long time," Jimmy said.

"Yes, I did. Somehow, learning he'd been alive for so many years but never came back for me was harder than knowing of his death." It felt strange to talk to the twins as though they were adults.

"And the favor?" Johnny stuck to his question like a hound following a scent.

Ellie took a deep breath, remembering her last conversation with Mr. Beldon and the doubts it had raised in her mind. "I asked him if he could find out whether my father had married during those years in Texas, and might have had other children."

Jimmy looked astonished. "How could Mr. Beldon do that?"

"And what difference would it make?" Johnny stood and gazed down at her, his expression skeptical. "Texas is so far away we'd never meet them anyhow."

Ellie plucked a morning glory and squeezed the sticky flower between her fingers. The crushed blossom left a purple stain on her thumb. The boys were right—Mr. Beldon had no way of finding them. Realization scorched through her mind. He talked a lot, but everything he'd told her was common knowledge.

She looked up at Johnny. "At the time I thought it would make a difference. Your papa was leaving, Aunt Ruby was gone, and Julia . . ." She pulled another flower from the vine. "I felt so alone. It would have been a comfort to know I had brothers and sisters—like you do."

"We're never alone." Jimmy scooted closer. "Papa says God is always with us."

"Yes. He is."

Jimmy's words swept over her. Her obsession about relatives in Texas suddenly seemed foolish. God was with her every moment. And her family was right here. "No more rides with Mr. Beldon?" Johnny raised an eyebrow.

"No." Then she clapped her hand over her mouth. "Wait. He's coming next Thursday to take me to Molly's. I'll tell him then."

Ellie poured drained cranberry beans into a crockery pot, then pushed a few pieces of salt pork beneath the surface of the beans. She added boiling water and a drizzle of molasses and slid the covered pot into the oven.

Uncle Arthur thumped into the kitchen on his crutches. "Baked beans? One of my favorite suppers."

"Good thing." She smiled at him. "We've had them quite often lately."

He leaned on one crutch and drew a chair away from the table. The forced inactivity since his fall left her normally robust uncle pale. The skin on his cheeks sagged and the corners of his mouth drooped. "Near forgot to tell you. I had Doc ask Marcus Beldon to call this afternoon."

"What! Why?"

Uncle Arthur took a deep breath and released it in a noisy sigh. "Since I can't get to Springfield I'm planning for him to write up papers to counter your aunt's divorce petition." He tugged at his beard. "Never thought I'd see the day."

Ellie didn't know which worried her more at the moment— her uncle and aunt divorcing, or Mr. Beldon's imminent arrival. "Can't you wait? Maybe she'll change her mind."

"And maybe she won't." He pushed to his feet. "Anyways, don't fuss yourself over having a caller. We'll set in the parlor and not be in your way."

Ellie watched him crutch down the hallway and open the parlor door. She wished she could turn the clock back so none of this would have happened. Aloud, she repeated Matthew's response when she'd said something similar to him. "A stream doesn't run backwards and neither will our lives."

She walked to the open back door and leaned against the frame. "Oh, Matthew, it's been a month. Where are you?" A column of dust rose beyond the creek. She held her breath, waiting for the rider to appear.

Her shoulders slumped when Mr. Beldon's carriage rolled into view. She turned away and quickly scanned the cornfield for her sons. They'd be upset if they saw him arrive, but with the corn so high perhaps they wouldn't notice. This would be her opportunity to tell him not to come for her next Thursday. Her heart sank a little at the thought. The honeycomb quilt was so close to completion. After working on it over the past months, Ellie wanted to be there to help stitch the binding when it came off the frame. But not at the cost of hurting her family.

She ducked back into the kitchen, not wanting Mr. Beldon to

think she'd been awaiting his arrival. Ellie blushed to think of her misplaced trust in the man.

When she heard steps on the front porch, she poked her head into the parlor. Arthur sat in one of the chairs near the cold hearth, the envelope containing the divorce notice clutched in his hand.

"Mr. Beldon's here," she said.

"I'm ready for him."

When she opened the door, a smile crinkled Mr. Beldon's eyes. "How delightful to see you, Mrs. Craig." He held his hat over his heart. "Your presence makes the day even brighter."

Ellie bit her lip and surveyed his face. Drops of perspiration beaded his forehead. Although he was as well-groomed as ever, he looked slick rather than suave. She stepped back and held her hand toward the open parlor door. "My uncle is expecting you." She kept her tone brisk.

Mr. Beldon blinked. "Thank you." She caught a whiff of sweat when he crossed the hallway.

"Come on in," Uncle Arthur called. "Forgive me for not getting up."

"Quite all right—"

Ellie closed the parlor door and stepped across the hall into the sitting room. The bass murmur of the men's voices followed her as she took her seat in a low chair under the open window. She lifted one of her old aprons from her sewing box and settled back, hoping for a quiet half hour to finish altering the garment to fit Maria. The hem had already been turned up and basted. All she needed to do was stitch across the fold. Ellie threaded a needle and half listened to the sound of crows squabbling with each other in the willows while she sewed.

Her mind locked on the promise she'd made her sons earlier

in the day. Hands shaking, she realized how far she'd wandered down a forbidden path. *Oh Lord, forgive me. Help me undo the harm I've done.* She tugged at the basting thread to remove it, but it held fast. Ellie anchored her needle to one side and pulled harder at the basting. The thread snapped.

Uncle Arthur's raised voice carried into the sitting room. "Adultery and desertion. You call it a 'cross bill'?"

Mr. Beldon's voice rumbled an indistinct reply.

"Write it all down on your paper," Uncle Arthur roared. "Every bit. And put down that she will have to pay the costs too."

Mr. Beldon said something else that apparently calmed her uncle, because his voice dropped and she couldn't hear the rest of the conversation. After several minutes, their visitor stepped into the hall.

Ellie dropped her sewing and hurried toward him. "Mr. Beldon, may I have a word with you before you leave?"

He reached for the latch on the front door. "It will have to wait. I'm rather pressed for time right now." He shifted his writing case to his left hand and stepped across the threshold. "A group of townspeople have asked to meet with me this evening and I need to prepare. I'll see you Thursday." The door banged shut.

When she turned away, she saw the twins standing in the kitchen watching her, disappointment on their faces.

26

Matthew lifted Graciana's bundle and took her hand. The child's small palm was dwarfed within his own large one. "You can't stay here. It's getting late."

She nodded, clutched her rag doll, and allowed him to lead her from the dock. His heart ached at the trust in her eyes. Where could he take her so she'd be safe? His mind retraced his journey through Oakport, trying to remember where he'd seen a rooming house.

When they reached Samson, she slid her hand from Matthew's and reached up to stroke the horse's shoulder. "He's very beautiful." Samson turned his head toward her and nuzzled her neck. Graciana smiled, revealing a row of even, white teeth. "Horses like me."

"I can see that." Matthew stuffed her bundle in one of his saddlebags. "Want to ride him?"

She bobbed her head, still smiling. He put his hands under her arms and lifted her onto the saddle. Graciana's blue dress floated down around the saddle horn and her bare feet stuck almost straight out on both sides of the animal. Matthew swung up behind her, tucking his right arm around her waist to hold her in place. She smelled like the dust of the road, and under that he detected the faint aroma of lavender. Her dress wasn't any dirtier than could be accounted for by her journey. Someone had taken good care of the child. "We're going to find a place for you to stay. Are you hungry?"

"Yes, sir." Her voice trembled. "You're not going to leave me, are you?"

Matthew's mind raced. How could he keep her with him? Surely she had family somewhere. "Tell me again where your Aunt Polly was going with you."

"I don't know the name of it." Her voice choked on a sob. "Aunt Polly had papers, but those men took her anyway. She said 'hide,' so I did."

Matthew hugged her to him. "Don't cry. You're safe now." He wiped a tear from her cheek with his thumb. "I won't leave you." He tipped his head back and stared at the twilight sky, wondering how many more surprises the Lord had in store. Samson clopped along the road through Oakport. Matthew held the reins with his left hand and scanned buildings for a sign indicating a place to stop for the night. He needed time to think before heading north.

Matthew sat in the kitchen of Mrs. Singer's rooming house. Water splashed in a tub on the other side of a fan-style screen as the landlady scrubbed travel grime from Graciana's skin.

"Sir, are you there?" Graciana called, her voice anxious.

"I'm right here."

The water sluiced. "Hold still, child. We'll be finished soon." Mrs. Singer sounded impatient. After a few minutes she led Graciana, wearing a faded blue nightdress, around the screen.

As soon as Graciana spotted Matthew, she pattered to him and grabbed his hand. "You did wait."

How many times had she been left alone? He hoisted her onto his knee. "I promised, didn't I?"

"Yes, sir." Graciana's damp hair hung below her shoulder blades. Her pointed face shone. "But I was afraid you'd be gone."

"Nonsense." Mrs. Singer tucked a wisp of graying hair into the severe bun she wore at the back of her head. "He's a preacher. Of course he'd keep his promise." The screen squeaked when she folded it flat.

Matthew avoided the woman's eyes. He didn't deserve credit for keeping promises. He'd promised to pastor the church in Beldon Grove, and here he was in Oakport. He squeezed Graciana's hand. "Mrs. Singer made you a nice bed upstairs next to mine. Let's get you settled."

The child slid to the floor, still clutching his hand, and walked up the stairs beside him. The narrow bedroom was just large enough to hold a single bed and a cot. A washstand with a pitcher and bowl stood at one end and a candle burned in a wall sconce.

"Here we are." Matthew forced himself to sound cheery. "See, Mrs. Singer put your doll on the pillow for you." He turned back the gray blanket on the cot and patted the threadbare sheet. "Climb in. I'm going outside for a few minutes to check on Samson."

Suspicion clouded her eyes. "You'll come back?"

"I promise." The word echoed in his head. *A promise is forever.* He'd taught that to his children.

When he reached the foot of the stairs, Mrs. Singer awaited him. Concern wrinkled the skin around her pouchy gray eyes. "That poor little mite has seen her share of grief, I'd say."

"Did she talk to you while I was stabling my horse?"

Mrs. Singer nodded.

"What did she tell you? I haven't wanted to press too hard for fear she'd be afraid of me."

She turned and led the way to the sitting room, closing the door behind them. Folding her arms over an ample bosom, she looked Matthew up and down. "She tell you her ma's dead and her pa died this past winter?"

"Yes."

"She say anything about their neighbors helping out?"

He frowned. "No. She said her Aunt Polly brought her here. Apparently her aunt had papers directing her to Graciana's family, but the woman was abducted?"

"Aunt Polly was one of the neighbor's slaves—not blood kin. She looked after the child. From what Graciana said, it sounds like her father wanted her brought north because he thought she'd be safer with kinfolks." She cleared her throat. "If you want my opinion, I think slave catchers must've stole Aunt Polly—travel papers or no." Matthew sucked in a breath, trying to absorb the information.

Mrs. Singer drew her lips into a thin line. "That child's lost everything. I hope you meant it when you told her you wouldn't leave."

After three days of steady travel toward the next stop on the circuit, Matthew spied the tall building beside a stream that gave Arcadia Mills its name. "Tonight we won't have to sleep in the open. Elder Meecham said the miller is a hospitable soul." He gave one of Graciana's braids a gentle tug. "A nice feather bed will be welcome, don't you think?"

"Yes, sir."

Matthew cleared his throat. "What did I ask you to call me?"

"I mean, yes, Uncle Matthew."

He patted her back. "Good girl."

They rode past a deserted building with a lopsided steeple on the roof. The steps and porch were missing, as were a number of clapboards along the sides. Empty window openings gaped at him. Matthew squinted down the road but couldn't see another steeple.

The sound of water spilling over a dam grew louder as he approached the millpond. Graciana wiggled in the saddle and peered at the rippled green surface of the pond. Then she turned and looked at Matthew, an eager expression on her face.

"Can I go wading?"

"I'll ask. It's a hot day. I expect they'll say yes." He guided Samson over the grassy bank toward a house standing a short distance from the creek.

Graciana beamed. "Thank you . . . Uncle Matthew."

Once in front of the house, Matthew slid from the saddle and tied the reins to a hitching post, then swung the child to the ground. She clutched his hand as they walked toward the front door.

Before he could knock, a man hastened toward them from the grist mill.

"Welcome, welcome." He extended his hand. "I'm Jacob Bates—the miller." He paused to catch his breath, his white hair drifting around his head like a nimbus.

"Reverend Matthew Craig. This is my—" Graciana moved closer to his side. Matthew sensed she was holding her breath, waiting to see what he'd say. "This is Graciana, my ward." He felt the child's body relax.

"Well, hello to both of you. Come in and refresh yourselves." Jacob pointed to the front door. "Are you passing through, or planning to settle here?"

"I've been sent by my church conference to hold a meeting." Matthew followed their host into the house.

White curtains hung over the two windows in the parlor, and a hooked rug with a flowered pattern rested beneath a square center table. Several upholstered chairs were arranged around the room.

"Is that you, Jacob?" A stout woman wearing a black taffeta dress bore down on them from the back hallway. She stopped when she saw Matthew and Graciana.

"Guests?"

"Indeed." He turned to Matthew. "This is my wife, Hilda. My dear, Reverend Craig is here to hold a church meeting."

Her eyebrows shot upward. "Where? We have no church in Arcadia Mills."

It was Matthew's turn to be surprised. "No church? When I saw that empty building at the edge of town, I thought there would be a newer one nearby."

Jacob laced his fingers across his belly. "The preacher got in a dispute with one of the members and left in a huff a couple years back. We're getting along fine without him."

Matthew felt like he'd been punched in the stomach. "Where do you hold Sunday meetings?"

"We don't." Jacob looked at his wife. "Will you bring us some cool water? I'm sure they're parched after being out in that sun." After she left, he pointed at the chairs. "Sit and be comfortable. You and Graciana are welcome to stay as long as you need to—we have an extra room." He settled into an armchair next to the empty hearth, leaning back so his paunch rested on his lap.

Matthew dropped into one of the seats on the opposite wall. Graciana took the chair closest to him and pushed it over the polished wood floor until it abutted Matthew's. Then she climbed onto the horsehair cushion and folded her hands in her lap.

Still stunned at Jacob's revelation, Matthew groped for words.

"I can't go against my church's wishes." He steepled his fingers and studied his host. "Where do you suggest I hold a meeting?"

"I suggest you don't." Jacob's genial expression never faltered. "Folks around here haven't been much for church since that preacher left. We figure if a man of the cloth can't live by what he preaches, what chance do the rest of us have?"

Matthew blanched at the blunt truth in Jacob's words. "But—"

"Don't worry over it, young man." Jacob's eyes twinkled. "You get a good rest tonight, then head on to wherever's next on your circuit. Ain't no one going to check up on you way out here."

Matthew's shoulders sagged. "I'd know, and there's no getting around that."

Graciana fidgeted next to him and tugged his sleeve. "Ask if I can wade," she whispered.

Jacob heard her, and smiled. "Yes, you can wade. Maybe there'll be some other children at the pond. It's pretty popular on these hot days."

Before Graciana could leave, Hilda returned, carrying a tray holding four glasses of water and a plate of cake slices. Her taffeta dress rustled as she placed the refreshments on the table.

Frowning, she gazed between Matthew and Graciana, "Is this your daughter?"

"This is Graciana, my ward." The words came easier this time. "She's been looking forward to wading in your pond."

Hilda put her hands on her hips and studied Graciana with disapproving eyes. "She's awfully . . . dark. She's not an Indian, is she?"

Graciana shrank next to Matthew. Her hand crept into his.

Matthew stood. He saw Hilda's smug expression through searing anger. "It doesn't matter what she is. She's a little girl who's lost her family." He stalked to the door. "We'll be going. We have a distance to travel before nightfall."

When the front door closed behind them, Matthew took Graciana's hand. "Come." He headed across a grassy slope in front of the house.

"Where are you taking me?" A fearful quiver crept into her voice.

"Down to the pond. We're going wading."

Matthew knew the community of New Camden lay near the route he would follow to reach Beldon Grove. The performance Nathan Clyde mentioned when Matthew had visited Adams Station had probably taken place by now. He'd detour and ask if anyone had seen Ruby.

Upon reaching the outskirts, Matthew was surprised to see that New Camden far surpassed Beldon Grove in size. Its main street bustled with carriages and foot traffic. As he rode along the first block, he noticed an apothecary, a book store, jewelry and watch shop, a gunsmith, and two mercantile establishments. Crossing an intersection, he came upon a square two-story building with "American House" painted across the false front over a covered porch. A smaller sign on one side of the door read "Meals and Lodging."

Graciana leaned forward, staring at all the activity. "Is this where you live?"

"No, but it's on the way. We'll stop here tonight for a real bed and a good supper."

Turning Samson toward the hotel, Matthew checked the supply of coins in his pocket to be sure he had enough for a night's lodging and some food.

When he pushed open the door to the hotel lobby, he saw a placard propped on a triangular easel.

Shakespeare's *Macbeth*
Six o'clock Friday night
New Camden Lyceum

A clerk walked out from behind the registration desk, eyeing Matthew and Graciana. "Do you require a room?"

"Yes. Thank you." Matthew pointed at the sign. "Could you tell me where the New Camden Lyceum might be?"

"Going to see the play tonight, are you?"

"Yes," Matthew said, surprising himself. He experienced a thrill of anticipation at the thought of breaking his self-imposed prohibition. "Yes, we are," he repeated, louder this time.

The clerk waved his hand toward the north side of the reception area. "Up the road about a half mile. It's a new brick building—you can't miss it." He surveyed the two of them. "The barber across the street can sell you a bath. Folks around here wear their Sunday best for entertainments."

Matthew felt his cheeks flush. "I didn't plan to attend straight off the trail."

"No need to get stirred up. Just trying to help."

In the rear of the barber shop, Matthew sat on one side of a closed door and waited while Graciana bathed. He'd unpacked her other dress and some clean underthings from the bundle she'd brought with her, carefully tucking the lavender sachet back in with her few remaining garments. A pink calico dress now hung from a hook on the wall in the washroom.

Her voice carried through the door. "Are you there, Uncle Matthew?"

"Yes."

"Good."

He leaned back in his chair. The child's fear of being abandoned touched his soul. Was this how Ellie felt? Why was it so easy for him to see Graciana's need, yet overlook his wife's? Matthew straightened his shoulders. Once he got home, he'd stay put. Let Beldon do his worst.

Graciana opened the door and stood before him, her pink dress brushing her calves above her soft leather slippers. "I'm ready except for my braids. I need your help."

"Stand here in front of me."

He took the comb she offered and parted her hair down the center. Graciana's hair was thicker than his daughter Maria's, and easier to braid. As Matthew formed the plaits, his latest worry touched his mind. Who could he find to take her in when they reached Beldon Grove? He couldn't add any more burdens to Ellie's shoulders.

A few minutes before six, Matthew and Graciana joined a crowd of people standing in front of the Lyceum. She bounced up and down with excitement. "I've never been to a play. What do people do there?"

"I've never been to one either. But I know they act out a story."

"I like stories."

He fingered the coins left in his pocket, hoping he had enough to pay for two seats. Graciana was more animated than she'd been since he found her. Guilt drenched his conscience at spending money he couldn't spare on frivolities, but it would be worth it to make her happy—even more so if he heard news of Ruby.

Once the tickets were purchased, he found seats toward the

rear and gazed around the spacious meeting hall. It resembled the interior of his church, in that benches were arranged in rows facing forward toward a raised platform. However, it probably held twice as many people, and the stage area was curtained off by burgundy velvet draperies, trimmed in gold braid. The sound of muffled voices came from behind the curtain. Matthew checked up and down the side aisles, where some people stood under lighted sconces. Could Ruby be one of the brightly dressed women he saw? Trying not to stare, he studied their faces but didn't recognize Ellie's aunt. Graciana squirmed next to him, trying to see past the people on benches in front of them.

"When it starts, you can sit on my lap," Matthew said, and she stopped wiggling.

The curtain opened, the audience quieted, and the play began. In spite of himself, Matthew soon became absorbed in the story of Macbeth and his ambitious wife. Horror engulfed him when Macbeth emerged from the king's bedchamber carrying a bloody dagger. He startled when he heard knocking at the door of the castle and inched forward in his seat, completely captivated by the plot. To his shock, the actor who next appeared on stage was Sorrel Forsythe, playing the role of Macduff. Matthew jerked upright and looked around the hall. Ruby had to be somewhere in the building.

He lifted Graciana off his knees and stood, intending to search for Ruby, when the person behind him hissed, "Siddown! I can't see."

Matthew dropped back onto the bench, resetting Graciana on his lap. Once the drama played itself out, concluding with the rightful king of Scotland being acclaimed, Matthew took Graciana's hand. He slipped out of the row and led her to the area behind the stage.

Players in the troupe jostled each other as they pulled off headgear and removed their outer costumes. At the rear of the building, a door opened. A woman emerged, holding out a hand toward a man standing nearby.

"Give me your cloak before you tear it."

As he handed it to her, she looked up and locked eyes with Matthew. The color drained from her face. Backing up, she stepped into the room she had just left and slammed the door.

Ruby!

He looked down at Graciana, who was staring around at the backstage commotion. He needed to talk to Ruby alone. Packing crates lined the hallway. He led the child to one not far from the door Ruby had just slammed.

"Wait here. I have something to do."

Tears filled her eyes. She dropped her head and pinched the folds of her skirt. "You're going to leave me here, aren't you?" Her voice was so soft Matthew had to strain to hear her.

He lifted Graciana onto one of the crates. "See that door?"

She nodded, tears trickling down her cheeks.

"That's where I'll be. I promise I'll be back in a few minutes. If you get worried, come and get me."

He pulled her into a hug, resting his cheek on top of her head. Then, oblivious to stares and muttered complaints, Matthew shoved through the milling performers and knocked on the closed door.

"Go away."

Instead, he pushed the door open, stepped inside, and closed it behind him. He and Ruby stared at each other in silence. She looked thinner than he remembered, and her skin bore a grayish tinge.

She turned her head away. "I have work to do. We need to be packed up and on the road."

"So you can cheat another innkeeper out of the price of lodging?" He bit his tongue. Wise men turn away wrath.

Ruby's face flushed. "Mr. Bryant was paid. We sent him a draft." She looked bewildered. "What are you doing here?"

Matthew searched for a place to sit in the crowded space. Locating a closed trunk, he lowered himself onto it. "I believe it was the Lord's leading. With everything that's happened, it can't be a coincidence." He held out his hand to the woman who had been part of his life since the day he'd married Ellie. "I want you to come home with me. Your place is with your husband and family."

She clutched a crimson cloak to her chest, ignoring his outstretched hand. "Arthur's not my husband any more." Her voice caught in her throat as she said the words.

"Leaving him doesn't cancel the bonds of matrimony."

"No, but divorce does." Her lower lip trembled. She shoved a stack of clothing to the floor and sat on a chair facing him.

Matthew tried to hide his shock at her words. "Divorce?" He knew very little of the procedure, but he believed that she would have to wait a minimum of two years to sever her marriage ties. "It's only been a few months. You cannot be divorced."

"I already filed the papers." Ruby's eyes brimmed with tears. "I can't go back now."

"Yes, you can. Talk to whoever it was did the filing and tell him you changed your mind."

She broke down, burying her face in the red folds of the cloak she held. Matthew moved over to her and settled an arm around her shoulders, feeling sobs shake her body.

"I did a terrible thing," she choked. "An unforgivable thing. There's no going back."

A sharp rap sounded at the door. Sorrel Forsythe stood in the opening, surprise written across his features. "Why aren't you packing?" His jaw dropped when he recognized Matthew. "What . . . what are you doing here?"

Matthew stood. "I came to take a member of my family home with me."

Forsythe looked between Matthew and Ruby. "She's done nothing but snivel since we left that backward town of yours. It's no superstition that *Macbeth* is a bad luck play. Meeting this woman has been the worst luck I've ever had." He grabbed the cloak from Ruby's hands. "You're welcome to her."

Ruby avoided Matthew's gaze. "I can't face people. Especially Arthur. He's a good man." She glanced at Sorrel Forsythe. "Good through and through. Not just on the surface."

Watching them, Matthew recognized that Ruby stayed because it was preferable to the humiliation of returning. With a stroke of intuition, he recognized the parallel between their situations.

He cupped one hand around the back of her head and lightly kissed her forehead. "People forget, sooner than you think. Something new always comes along to catch their attention."

She pulled free of his embrace, shaking her head. "I won't go back to Beldon Grove. Leave. Please."

27

Dust rose beyond the willows. Ellie stood, her sewing basket in one hand. "Maria, Mr. Beldon is coming. Time to go."

Maria bounded down the stairs. "I'm ready." She wore her apple green dress, made from the same fabric as the frock Ellie wore. She twirled. "How do I look?"

"Very nice—but you and Lily will be playing outside. Be sure you don't get dirty."

"I'll be careful. I wore this because Mr. Beldon is driving us. He calls me a pretty little girl."

Ellie flushed, realizing that her reactions to Mr. Beldon's flattery had transferred themselves to her daughter. "It doesn't matter what he calls you. It's Papa's opinion that counts."

"But Mama—"

"The ride to Aunt Molly's this afternoon is the last time we'll be with Mr. Beldon. After this, we walk or stay home."

"Does he know that?"

"He will soon."

When the phaeton crossed the bridge, Ellie and Maria stepped onto the back porch. Mr. Beldon stopped the carriage and came toward them, a smile creasing his features.

He swept his hat off and bowed. "Don't you two look like a picture! Such pretty ladies."

"Thank you." Maria beamed at him, then glanced at Ellie and dropped her smile.

Once they were headed toward town, Ellie turned sideways and studied him. His white linen jacket looked rumpled and sweat-stained. Tired lines etched the skin next to his eyes.

His face brightened when he noticed her watching him. "What time would you like me to collect you at Spenglers' house?"

"It would be best if I had Dr. Spengler take us home. I fear there will be too much talk in town should you continue to escort me to and fro."

Anger flared across his features. He stared ahead saying nothing, a muscle twitching in his jaw. In silence they passed Wolcotts' farm, then Uncle Arthur's lane and Griffiths' pottery works.

When he didn't reply, Ellie relaxed against the seat.

Mr. Beldon turned the corner at Adams Street and brought the carriage to a halt in front of Molly's house. When he looked at Ellie, all traces of anger had left his face, replaced by his usual smile. "I hope you will allow me one last opportunity to convey you and your charming daughter to your home. As it happens, I've discovered information that will be of great interest to you regarding that matter in Texas. I'll bring it with me when I come back later this afternoon." He waited her response with one eyebrow raised.

Ellie bit her lower lip, torn between curiosity and her promise to her sons. She nodded at him. "Very well. I'll expect you some time after four." She held up her index finger. "After this, however, we will find other ways to get to town."

"Of course. I understand." He stepped to the ground and walked to her side of the phaeton. "Allow me."

Mr. Beldon took her arm and helped her down. "I'll see you at four."

❧

Molly led the way to the rear of the house. "We'll sit out here this afternoon. It's cooler."

Maria and Lily skipped ahead of her, chasing each other in circles and giggling. Ellie followed, her thoughts in turmoil. She could picture the expressions on the twins' faces when Mr. Beldon brought them home, after she promised she'd no longer ride with him.

When she turned the corner behind the house, she saw Luellen sitting at a makeshift table under the silver maple Molly and Karl had planted to commemorate their wedding. Head bent, she stitched something on the back of her honeycomb quilt.

Ellie squeezed her shoulder. "This is a pleasant surprise, young lady. I'm glad you're helping today."

"Charity couldn't be here," Molly said. She lowered her voice. "I think they have a passenger from the Railroad with them at the farm right now."

Ellie nodded understanding. "Looks like you didn't need me anyway. I see the binding's finished." She moved closer to the table. "Let's turn it over. I want to see our handiwork. Maria, Lily, come here and help." She paused and studied the words Luellen had embroidered on the back of the quilt.

Luellen McGarvie.
Beldon Grove, Illinois.
July 30, 1846.

Ellie smiled at her niece. "What a nice beginning to your bridal chest."

Luellen gripped a corner of the quilt and rolled the patterned side to the top. The colors bloomed in the light. She stroked the pattern with her fingertips. "It *is* beautiful—like flowers." Then she raised her chin and looked at her mother. "But I'm not going to be a bride."

Molly shook her head. "Don't be silly. Someday you'll change your mind." She patted Luellen's back. "Who'd like some Scotch bread?" Without waiting for an answer, she strode back into the house.

Ellie watched her go, glancing at Luellen. The girl's face was set in the same stubborn lines she often saw on Matthew's.

"I'll help you fold your quilt. We don't want to get crumbs on such a lovely piece of work."

At rest in the variegated shade cast by the maple tree, Ellie helped herself to more Scotch bread. Maria and Lily sprawled on the ground nearby, busy weaving chains from the daisies that starred the grass. Luellen had taken the quilt into the house and returned with a book. She sat a little apart from them, engrossed in the story she was reading.

"Mr. Beldon will be here soon," Ellie said to Maria. "Gather your things."

When Maria stood, Molly added, "Don't forget to take those loaves of bread with you."

Maria nodded, skipping toward the cabin door.

Ellie touched Molly's arm. "Thank you. Wheat bread is a treat nowadays."

"You and Matt have done so much for me—this is nothing." Molly shifted on the bench and lowered her voice. "I love your company, but perhaps you shouldn't accept any more rides from Mr. Beldon. I'm afraid people will talk."

"I told him so earlier. This is the last time." Embarrassment warmed her cheeks. "The twins compared me to Aunt Ruby the other day." She closed her eyes and took a deep breath. "I can't have my children thinking ill of me."

"Oh, Ellie." Compassion showed on Molly's face. "How unfair of them."

"Perhaps. Perhaps not. I explained that he's offered to help me learn about my family in Texas." The silvery undersides of the maple leaves trembled as a breeze ruffled past. "The boys scoffed at the idea."

A frown creased Molly's forehead. "I'm beginning to wonder too."

"About what?"

"Whether he has any contacts at all. He apparently had nothing to do with James's return."

Ellie brushed crumbs from her skirt. "He said he would bring me information this afternoon—that's the only reason I agreed to let him take us home."

The two women stood when they heard hooves on the dirt road.

Molly took Ellie's hand. "Let me know what he says." She kissed her cheek. "We'll come get you for church on Sunday morning. We plan to go to the service Mr. Wolcott is conducting."

Ellie massaged her temples. How could she accept Mr. Beldon's help and then not attend his church?

At that moment, he appeared around the side of the cabin. He'd changed into a fresh shirt and jacket. "There you are, ladies." Sweeping off his broad-brimmed hat, he bowed in their direction.

Molly nodded a lukewarm greeting.

"Your daughter has already seated herself in the carriage," he told Ellie. "We can be away whenever you're ready."

She hugged Molly. "See you Sunday."

Hurrying to the phaeton, she climbed inside.

When Mr. Beldon picked up the reins, Molly called, "Please give my best to your wife."

"Indeed I will." His voice was cool as buttermilk. He tipped his hat and urged the horse into a trot down Adams Street.

As soon as they were under way, Ellie leaned forward. "You said you had information for me about Texas. Where is it?"

"In a moment. Let's just enjoy the ride." He looked down at the daisy chain in Maria's lap. "You like flowers, young lady?"

She nodded, swinging her feet against the footrest.

"I'll show you some."

Once past the church, he abruptly turned the phaeton east into a section of prairie grass. Faint wheel tracks leading toward a stand of trees showed in the waist-high bluestem.

Alarmed, Ellie looked at him. "Where are we going? It's getting late—my family's expecting us."

"This will only take a few minutes." He patted the top of Maria's bonneted head. "There are some wildflowers out here your daughter will enjoy."

Tall grass whispered against the floor of the carriage. The soft soil muffled the sound of the horse's hooves. Ellie scanned the area ahead, seeking the promised flowers, but it wasn't possible to see anything but undulating prairie rolling toward the horizon.

Mr. Beldon smiled at her. "Don't look so worried. You'll be glad we stopped."

Ellie felt a vague sense of unease. Glancing over her shoulder, she noticed that the main road had disappeared behind a curtain of grass. She leaned forward again, about to say something, when they crested a rise. Her voice caught in her throat. A riot of blossoms adorned the meadow in front of them. Orange milkweed, prairie blazing star, blue asters, fireweed, and crowding the empty spaces, golden sunflowers.

He pointed the buggy whip with a flourish. "Wasn't this worth a detour?"

She clasped her hands, entranced at the sight. "Yes! It's beautiful."

Maria bounced to her feet. Her daisy chain fell to the floor, forgotten. "Can I pick some?"

"Of course. That's why I brought you here." Mr. Beldon smiled indulgently.

"Stay where I can see you," Ellie said. "And just pick a few. We must be getting home."

The carriage jiggled as Maria jumped down and ran toward the meadow. Mr. Beldon watched her go, then draped an arm over the back of the seat.

"You're too far away." His voice sounded soft, coaxing.

Ellie felt a flush rise to her face. His muscular body, which seemed so appealing at a distance, now threatened.

He dropped his fingers lightly onto her shoulder, tracing a small circle. "You're a beautiful woman." His voice thickened. Fingers caressed the side of her neck, then stroked her hair. "I've wanted you since the first day we met. I can't sleep for thinking about you." He slipped his hand down her back and urged her toward him.

Heart pounding in her throat, Ellie rose and grabbed the side of the carriage. "Mr. Beldon. Leave me alone!" She put a foot on the step, ready to run to Maria.

One hand circled her wrist, holding her in place. "Don't be afraid. No one will see us."

She tugged, trying to free herself. "No. Please."

His grip tightened, then he pressed his other hand against her waist. "Mrs. Craig," he said in a sibilant whisper. "Eleanor. Do sit down." He licked his lips, leaving a wet shine on their fleshy surface. "I apologize. I've frightened you."

Breathing heavily, he slid his hand up her leg. She twitched away from his fingers. The clove-scented pomade on his hair sent a wave of nausea through her.

"You must see we're meant for each other." His words tumbled out. "Come away with me. We can go to Texas, to your father's land. Together we'll find your family."

Horrified, Ellie stared at his sweaty face, then shot a glance at her daughter picking flowers. How far were they from the road? Could they run? She dismissed the idea, knowing the thick grass would make running impossible.

Ellie swallowed to moisten her dry throat. "Drive us to the farm, please. I . . . I'll think about what you've said." Without waiting for his response, she pulled her hand free and slid from his grasp. "Maria." Her voice cracked. She called again, trying to conceal rising hysteria. "Maria! We're leaving now." She prayed it was true.

She felt Mr. Beldon's eyes boring into her back and turned to see him watching her with razorlike intensity.

He raised an eyebrow. "You realize, Mrs. Craig, if you speak of this, the town gossips won't believe a word you say."

Ellie cringed at the truth of his words. Maria ran to the carriage, pink-cheeked from the sun and carrying an armful of flowers. Settling into the space between them, she held the bouquet under Ellie's nose.

"I'll give these to Uncle Arthur to make him feel better."

"Well, aren't you a thoughtful child." Mr. Beldon flicked the reins over his horse's back and set the phaeton moving toward the road.

A musty smell, like that of a locked room, arose from the sun-flowers. Ellie turned her head away and sat with her arms wrapped around her waist, trying to stop the trembling that rippled over her body. The sensation of Beldon's hands on her remained, like palpable stains. How could she have been so foolish?

Although the phaeton clipped along the road at a good pace, the minutes seemed to crawl until they reached the farm. Mr. Beldon reined his horse to a stop with a flourish. Before he could get out to help her down, Ellie bolted from the carriage and stood below the step, cradling her sewing basket and the two towel-wrapped loaves of bread. She kept her head down, avoiding his eyes. Behind her, she heard the back door open.

Maria's face brightened. "Papa!"

28

Matthew stood at the top of the steps staring between his wife's flushed face and Marcus Beldon's smug expression. A sick feeling gripped his stomach. In the hours since his arrival home, he'd heard from the twins how Beldon had insinuated himself into Ellie's life, offering to take her to Molly's. No one knew better than himself how naïve his wife could be.

An expression of guilt painted itself over Ellie's face.

She hesitated, then followed Maria up the stairs and hugged him. "Thank goodness you're back."

His arms encircled her, feeling her softness under his fingers. He held her lightly, resting his cheek against the top of her sunbonnet. So often he had dreamed of her during the uncomfortable nights on the circuit and now here she was in his arms. A pang of desire shot through him.

He lifted his head in time to see Beldon turn his carriage and roll out of the farmyard. Desire curdled into doubt. "I hear you've been spending a great deal of time with him."

Ellie didn't need to ask who he meant. She stared at the ground.

Matthew lifted her chin with his thumb and stared into her eyes. "Of all people, why Beldon?"

Her cheeks flamed. "He offered to take me to Molly's, so I

said yes. At the time I didn't see the harm." She drew a shaky breath, then blurted, "He said he would help me find my family in Texas."

He dropped his hand, incredulous, "And you believed him? Don't you know—"

"I do now. He's evil, Matt." Tears gathered in her eyes. "I should have listened to you."

He remembered all the times he'd decided against burdening her with the man's actions. Then he recalled that when he did tell her Beldon was spreading rumors about them, she'd argued in Beldon's favor.

Stepping away, he narrowed his eyes and surveyed Ellie. "What's changed your mind now?"

"Things he . . . said." She mumbled her reply and pushed past him into the house, colliding with Graciana, who stood just inside the doorway.

Ellie took a step backward. She put her hands on the child's shoulders. "Oh dear, did I hurt you? I didn't see you standing there."

Graciana sidled next to Matthew and slid her hand into his. "No ma'am," she said. "I'm not hurt." She clutched her rag doll with her free hand.

"This is Graciana Largo," Matthew said, answering the question in Ellie's eyes. "She will be staying with us until—" He broke off. "We have much to discuss. Let's wait for later."

Clearly tired of being ignored, Maria stepped in front of Graciana and held out her bouquet. "I picked these for my Uncle Arthur. Do you want to come with me when I give them to him?"

"No, thank you. I want to stay with Uncle Matthew."

"All right." Maria skipped toward the parlor, calling Arthur's name.

During supper, Matthew surreptitiously watched Ellie. She moved about the kitchen more than necessary, jumping up to bring one thing or another to the table. Graciana had insisted on sitting next to him. It pleased him to note that Ellie seemed to have accepted the girl's presence without objection. It wasn't unusual for families to take in orphaned children, but he'd worried that Ellie was still too obsessed with losing Julia to want another child in the house.

Ellie joined Maria and the boys in asking questions about his journey, but only half listened to his answers. Not until he told the story of going to Kentucky to visit his father did he have her full attention.

"You took a steamboat to Marysville? You were needed here. You would've been back a week sooner. And I wouldn't have—" She stopped in midsentence.

"It had to be the Lord's leading. So much happened as a result." He opened his mouth to tell her about his father, and then what occurred on the dock at Oakport, but she didn't give him the opportunity.

"I believe the Lord wanted you to take care of your family, and *you* decided to go skylarking." She pushed back her chair and gathered soiled plates. "You can't imagine how hard it's been . . ." Ellie's voice choked. "The children, Uncle Arthur, the farm—" She clunked the plates into the basin and turned her back on him.

Graciana shrank against his side and hugged her doll. Matthew glanced at her and then at the stunned faces of his children. He and Ellie never quarreled in front of them.

He'd pictured an enthusiastic homecoming. Instead, he'd arrived to find Ellie gone off somewhere with Marcus Beldon, Arthur sitting on the porch with a broken leg, and the boys filled with complaints about their mother's behavior.

He walked to the worktable. "I wrote you a letter explaining everything before I left on the steamboat. It should have arrived by now."

"Well, it didn't." She wouldn't look at him.

Arthur picked up his crutches. "Believe I'll go sit on the porch and watch the storm come in. The cool air will feel good."

Glancing at their parents, the children slipped upstairs.

Maria stopped halfway up the steps and ran back to hug Matthew. "I'm glad you're home, Papa."

"Me too." He kissed her blonde head. "Graciana will share your room. I put her things in there when I got home." He held his hand toward the dark-haired child. "You go with Maria. I'll be right here if you need me."

She nodded and followed Maria, glancing back once as if to make certain he was still there.

Wind whipped the curtains at the window, pushing the scent of rain into the room. Ellie kept her eyes focused on the stack of dirty dishes in the soapy water.

Matthew spoke to the back of her head. "I'm going to sit with Arthur for a bit. You go on up when you're ready."

She flashed a teary, blue-eyed look at him. "I'm glad you're home too."

He barely heard her whisper over the rattle of cutlery in the tin basin. He squeezed her shoulder, then walked out onto the porch. Light from the kitchen lamp shimmered on raindrops falling past the roof. Matthew stood at the top of the steps and gazed into the gray dusk, hearing water splash onto the dry ground of his farmyard.

Arthur spoke behind him. "Just in time."

"The rain?"

"That too."

Matthew turned toward Arthur, lowering his voice so it wouldn't carry through the open window. "Do you think Beldon's offers to drive Ellie to town were innocent?"

"I wouldn't have allowed it otherwise." Arthur made a derisive sound in his throat. "Course, I thought that Forsythe fellow's actions were innocent too. Guess you'd better not depend on me for good judgment."

Matthew pinched his lip. "I saw Ruby."

Arthur's jaw dropped. "Where is she? Is she well?"

"She seemed well enough—a little thin, maybe."

The older man clamped a hand over Matthew's knee. "Tell me all about it." In the dim light, his eyes looked overly bright.

"The Shakespeare troupe was in New Camden. Ruby was with them."

"How'd you find that out?"

"I went to the play."

In spite of the seriousness of their conversation, Arthur chuckled. "And you weren't struck dead, were you?"

Matthew shook his head. "I deserved that, but no, the Lord let me live through it." He smiled.

"Go on," Arthur said. "Ruby was there?"

"Yes, I talked to her afterward." His eyes held Arthur's. "She wants to come home, I'm sure of it, but she's afraid you wouldn't have her."

"She sent me divorce papers. She don't want to come back."

"Ruby's not happy, anyone could see that. She made a dreadful mistake, and now she's reaping what she sowed."

Arthur gazed out at the rain, silent. After a few moments, he cleared his throat. "I miss her. Reckon if she came back, I'd let her stay."

Matthew's heart lifted. "I hoped you'd feel that way."

"Will you tell her when you're back that way?"

"I can't. They were packing up to leave, and I don't know where they were going next." Regret tinged his reply.

When Matthew climbed the stairs to bed, he smiled at the sounds of the two girls chattering in Maria's room. He hoped they'd become friends. When they found a home for Graciana, the transition would be easier if she already had a playmate.

Wearing her nightdress, Ellie waited for him in the rocking chair. Her blonde hair hung over her shoulder in a thick braid. "I'm sorry I lost my temper," she said when he closed the door. "It's been a . . . strenuous day." Her lower lip trembled.

"Finding a strange child in your kitchen must have been a shock."

Ellie shook her head. "That's the least of it." She closed her eyes for a moment and then said, "Tell me everything. You went to Kentucky—is that where Graciana came from?"

Matthew settled on a corner of the bed and hooked one arm around the bedpost. Ellie's golden beauty moved him as it never had. He regretted all the times he'd made light of her fears of abandonment.

"I missed you so much!" he blurted.

"I missed you too." Her face softened. "Every day. Now, please, tell me about that little girl."

Raindrops pecked at the window pane as Matthew began his story with an account of his visit to his father's farm, and how his father had urged him to go back and wrest control of his church from Marcus Beldon. Then he described finding Graciana hiding on the dock at Oakport.

He shook his head. "I couldn't just leave her there. She has no one. Her mother was a Mexican woman who passed away several years ago. Her father died last winter."

"Was he from Mexico too?"

"I don't think so. She said he was light skinned and had white hair." He swallowed. "Anyway, some neighbors arranged for a slave woman, Graciana called her 'Aunt Polly,' to get her away from the border area where the war is being fought. My best guess is Aunt Polly was taken by slave catchers once they crossed the Ohio. All the child knows is some bad men took her." He massaged the back of his neck to reduce the tension crawling over his back and shoulders. "Graciana is afraid of being left again. You noticed how she sticks to me like a burr."

"Yes. I can hardly blame her, now that I've heard her story."

"We'll take care of her until we can find a family who wants her. I know you're already burdened with our youngsters."

"Mrs. Carstairs."

"What?"

"Penelope Carstairs. She recently lost a baby. Maybe they would welcome Graciana." She straightened. "And Matt, our children are not a burden. I love them. While Graciana's here, I'll show her the same love."

"You're a surprise to me at times."

Ellie eyes twinkled. "That's not all bad."

After the family finished breakfast the next morning, the boys headed for the barn to start the chores. Maria gathered the breakfast plates and carried them to the basin. Without saying a word,

Graciana pushed her chair away from Matthew's side, stacked the cutlery on the serving platter, and joined Maria. The two girls studied each other for a quiet moment, then Maria smiled and moved to one side so they could share the workspace.

Matthew watched them, the corner of his mouth quirked in a grin. He spoke to Ellie in an undertone. "I was afraid Maria'd be jealous while Graciana stayed with us. Looks like I worried for nothing."

An odd expression crossed Ellie's face. "Did you notice how much those two look alike? Maria's taller, and fair-skinned of course, but see their profiles?"

He squinted at the girls. "Hmm. Maybe. Hard to say." He pushed his pewter mug toward her. "Any of that coffee left?"

Ellie brought the coffee boiler to the table. When she leaned over him to fill his cup, her breast brushed against his shoulder. Matthew leaned away. Sleeping next to her last night had resurrected desires he'd hoped were under control.

After another glance in the girl's direction, Ellie took a chair opposite Matthew. "How are you going to spend your first day back?"

"On the farm. I want to see what the boys have done while I've been gone. And I need to check Samson. Looked like he favored his left rear hoof some before we got here." He flexed his shoulders and blew out a deep sigh. "I'm glad to be home. Riding circuit's for young sparks." Matthew shook his head. "Never again."

She reached across the table and clasped his hand. "Your decision is an answer to prayer. I need you here. We need you here. The church needs you here. Did Uncle Arthur tell you Mr. Wolcott's been holding services in the rear of his store?"

"No. When did he start that?" He lifted his mug. Did he see

a flicker of disappointment in her eyes when her hand fell away from his? He blew on the surface of the coffee to cool it.

"It's been three or four weeks now. Molly and Karl have attended, and she says that quite a number of folks from your congregation are there."

"You haven't gone?"

She shook her head and pointed toward the back porch where Arthur went to sit after breakfast. "Uncle Arthur fell just before the first meeting. There's been no way to get to town."

"You could've asked Karl when he came out to tend Arthur." He felt a surge of meanness. "Or didn't you want to hurt Beldon's feelings?"

Ellie's face reddened. "Mr. Beldon's feelings had nothing to do with it." She pushed back her chair and stood, her voice changing from friendly to curt. "If you're going out to check on Samson, you'd better get started."

Matthew saw the hurt in her eyes, and regretted his gibe. "Ellie, I . . ."

"What?" Her lower lip trembled.

He couldn't think of anything to say to turn things around. "Uh, I'll come in at dinnertime."

29

"Are you still hungry, Graciana?" Ellie asked. "There's plenty more corn mush."

"No, thank you, ma'am."

Ellie covered the pot on the stove and walked back to the table. "You've been with us for a week now. Why don't you call me 'Aunt Ellie'?" She smiled. "That's friendlier than 'ma'am,' don't you think? After all, you call Reverend Craig 'Uncle Matthew.'"

"Papa said for me to call grown-ups 'sir' and 'ma'am.'"

"I was taught that too. But adults who are friends can be uncle and aunt—even if they aren't your real relatives. So . . . can I be 'Aunt Ellie'?"

"Yes, ma'am." Graciana blushed. "Yes, Aunt Ellie."

"That's better." She patted the child's shoulder, then pulled out a chair opposite Matthew. Leaning her forearms on the tabletop, she studied his face. His eyes flicked away, then met hers.

She took a deep breath. "You haven't left the farm since you got home. We didn't even go to church Sunday." Her heart pounded. She felt a flush rise in her cheeks. "What are you hiding from?"

"I'm not hiding." A muscle twitched in his jaw. "Ben stopped by last week. He knows I'm home."

"Did you tell him about your decision not to go back on the circuit?"

"What is this? Have you suddenly become my conscience?"

Graciana glanced from Matthew to Ellie. "Can I go visit Samson?"

"Certainly." Matthew's expression warmed. "He looks for you every time I go into the barn."

"I like him." She skipped out the back door, her doll tucked under one arm.

Grateful for the diversion, Ellie watched the child run past the black walnut sapling and disappear into the barn. "She certainly has a way with animals. She could probably harness King George and not get stomped."

"Not that I'd want her to try." Matthew turned his attention back to Ellie, his jaw tightening. "There's no need for you to tell me what to do. I planned to go to town today. Ben and I discussed me preaching at the meetings behind the store." He frowned.

Ellie squeezed her hands together in her lap. Since Matthew'd been home, they'd done nothing but snipe at each other. She longed for the days when they could resolve their differences with a kiss.

She reached for his hand across the table, but he stood and headed for the door.

"While I'm in town, I'll pay a call on Mrs. Carstairs. We need to find a home for Graciana before she becomes too attached to us."

The idea of losing Graciana brought unexpected tears to Ellie's eyes. The child already felt like a member of the family.

Ellie stood on the porch and watched as Matthew rode past the willows and over the bridge. Graciana came out of the barn and watched him too. She held her doll by one arm, its head brushing the dusty ground, its owner looking forlorn.

Ellie walked down the back steps. "Why don't you go wading in the creek with the others? They'd be happy to have you join them."

"Not right now, thank you, ma'am—Aunt Ellie." Her lips curved upward. "Maria already asked me. I wanted to visit Samson, but now he's gone to town with Uncle Matthew."

Graciana's round brown eyes brightened when she mentioned the horse. Ellie studied her, trying to think of a way to keep her busy during Matthew's absence.

The girl took a step backward. "Did I do something wrong?"

"Oh, no." Ellie bent over and drew Graciana into her arms. "You haven't done anything wrong at all. It's a joy to have you here." She dropped a kiss on the top of Graciana's head, then released her. "Come in the house with me. I think there are a couple of Maria's outgrown dresses that might fit you. They're upstairs in the storeroom."

Ellie took Graciana's free hand and walked toward the house, talking as she went. "By the time clothes have passed from boy to boy, there's nothing left but rags. But Maria doesn't have a little sister—" She stopped and swallowed sudden tears, then took a new breath. "A little sister to hand things down to."

"I don't have a little sister, either." The doll's head bumped on the risers as they climbed the back steps. "It was always just me and Papa, as long as I can remember."

"All seven years." Ellie smiled down at her, teasing.

"Yes." The child nodded, a serious expression on her face. Her lip trembled. "Now, no Papa."

Ellie squeezed her hand. "I don't have a papa, either. Uncle Arthur is my papa." She pointed to him, dozing in his chair on the porch. His white beard curled beneath his round pink cheeks. A tiny snore escaped his open mouth.

Graciana giggled and whispered, "He looks like Papa. White hair and a beard."

They stepped into the kitchen.

"While we're in the storeroom, we can do a bit of cleaning." Ellie collected a broom and a damp rag before heading upstairs.

Graciana followed her over the threshold of the room and then stopped, her eyes taking in the collection of wooden boxes and trunks stacked against the far wall. After a moment's hesitation, she moved to the carved walnut cradle Ellie had used for each of her babies. Kneeling, she placed her doll on the red blanket tucked under the hood.

When she looked up, her face shone with pleasure. "Papa made a cradle for my doll, but it was too big to bring with me." She stroked the carving on one side, setting the cradle to rocking.

Ellie stood, transfixed. Her first impulse was to snatch the doll from the bed. She bit her lip to keep from saying anything.

She paused until she could control her voice. "Let's look for Maria's clothes. They must be near the front of the stack." Ellie leaned the broom against the wall and dusted the top of a box with the damp rag.

The first box she opened revealed cloth strips she'd collected to braid into a rug—a winter project. She dropped the cover shut, then tugged a blue-painted trunk away from the wall. After wiping dust from its surface, Ellie lifted the lid.

"Here they are. Come see."

Graciana joined her and peered into the trunk. The top garment was an indigo print dress with cuffed sleeves. She touched the yoked neckline with one finger. "This is pretty."

"Yes, it is. The color's still bright too." Ellie measured it against

Graciana's back to gauge the length. It fell at mid-calf. "Just right. We won't even need to shorten the hem."

She laid the dress aside and lifted the next one from the pile of folded clothing. "This was Maria's Sunday best, so it didn't get much wear." The sleeves of the butternut-colored wool dress flared when Ellie held it up. "It will look nice with your brown eyes."

Graciana's shoulder brushed Ellie's as she bent to retrieve the next garment. "This one looks too small."

Ellie knelt next to the trunk, resting on her heels. "Most of these are from when she was younger. But two dresses are plenty for now." She shut the lid and gathered the clothes under one arm. "I'll rinse the blue one and hang it in the sunshine to freshen it. We'll air the brown dress and save it for Sundays."

A trickle of perspiration wound its way down her temple. She grabbed the broom and rag. "It's too hot in here to clean today. Let's go downstairs where it's cooler."

After retrieving her doll from the cradle, Graciana joined Ellie at the doorway. "Thank you for my new clothes, Aunt Ellie."

Ellie took her hand and squeezed it. "You're welcome." She reached for the doll. "May I?"

Graciana handed it to her. Up close, it bore signs of hard travel. One of the embroidered eyes had frayed, and the fabric was grimy. The doll's middle had been stiffened with what felt like a round stick inside the padding to hold it firm. The stuffing in its arms and legs had shifted, so that the limbs were lumpy.

Ellie placed the doll on top of the clothing she carried and headed for the stairs "How about if I give her a bath when I wash your new dress? I can fix her eye and give her new stuffing."

Graciana frowned and looked between her doll and Ellie. "Can I watch? Papa told me to keep her with me always." She patted the doll's firm center section. "Papa's love is in here."

"What do you mean?"

"When Papa got sick, he gave Aunt Polly something to sew inside Nora—that's my dolly's name. Papa told me it would remind me he'd love me forever." Graciana's voice wavered.

She collapsed on the top step and buried her face in her hands. Sobs shook her shoulders. "I miss my papa."

Ellie dropped the clothing and the broom and sat next to Graciana, holding her close. The child snuggled against her chest, weeping. They rocked back and forth, Ellie's cheek against the top of Graciana's head.

"I know you miss your papa. God is looking after him now, and he's looking after you too. He brought you to us, didn't he?" She bit her lip. Better not promise anything.

After a few more moments, Graciana drew a shuddering breath. Her body relaxed. Ellie slid a handkerchief from her apron pocket and wiped the child's tears from her cheeks.

"Let's go downstairs and give Nora her bath, shall we? We'll make her look new."

Graciana nodded and started down. Her bare feet pattered on the wooden steps with a sound like hands clapping.

Ellie gathered Nora and the dresses into her arms and followed Graciana into the kitchen. In a few minutes, she'd know what was inside the doll.

Uncle Arthur called through the open door. "Carriage coming. You expecting anybody?"

"No."

Apprehensive, she placed the doll on the table and went to the door. Graciana trailed her onto the porch. A covered buggy crossed the bridge, but Ellie didn't recognize the driver.

Uncle Arthur sat forward. "Looks like a hired hack. Didn't know we had such around here."

The buggy stopped at the hitching rail and the driver stepped down. A black-draped woman descended.

Ellie couldn't see who it was through the heavy veil covering the stranger's face. The woman stood next to the carriage while the driver pulled a carpetbag from the back and placed it beside her. Tipping his hat, he clambered onto the seat and drove out of the yard. If any words were exchanged between him and his passenger, Ellie didn't hear them. She moved toward the steps, wondering who on earth would come to their farm, with baggage, unannounced.

The visitor stood below, looking up at them. She pulled the veil away from her face. "I've come home, if you'll have me."

Ellie stared. "Aunt Ruby?"

"Don't you know me, child?"

Ellie flung her arms wide and rushed down the back steps. "I thought I'd never see you again."

Aunt Ruby allowed herself to be hugged, then drew back. "Don't. I'm not worthy."

Her tear-bright eyes settled on Uncle Arthur. He got to his feet and stood balanced on his crutches, mouth agape.

"I didn't expect to find you here." Aunt Ruby picked up her bag. "I can leave."

"No. Stay." A play of emotions crossed Uncle Arthur's countenance. Shock gave way to hurt, then what seemed to be anger settled over his normally benign features. He took a step backward. "Come up on the porch so's I can see you better."

Once in the shade of the sloping roof, Aunt Ruby removed her bonnet and appeared to notice Graciana for the first time.

"Do you have visitors?" She seemed to shrink inside herself. "I shouldn't have come. I can't face people." Her cheekbones stood out below sunken and red-rimmed eyes. The once blonde hair looked dull and showed streaks of gray.

"This is Graciana," Ellie said. "She's joined our household for a time." She patted the child's shoulder. "Take Nora out front and play under the oak tree for a while, please."

"Yes, ma'am."

Using the end of one crutch, Uncle Arthur pushed a chair in his wife's direction. "Sit."

She slumped into the chair and bowed her head. "I couldn't go through with it. I've had no peace since I left."

"This is between the two of you." Ellie moved toward the kitchen. "I have no business listening."

"Don't go," Aunt Ruby said. "You both need to hear me out. Then you can decide what to do next." Her voice broke.

"How about fetching some water for your aunt?" Uncle Arthur asked. "I expect she's thirsty."

Ellie nodded and fled to the kitchen. Once inside, she leaned against the worktable for a moment and waited for her hands to stop trembling. Having Aunt Ruby back felt like seeing someone return from the grave. When her hands steadied, she dipped water from the crock and carried it to the porch.

Silence hung between the three adults until Aunt Ruby cleared her throat. "I haven't been able to eat or sleep for weeks. Not that I expect you to feel sorry for me—this is all my doing." She kept her eyes on the floor as she spoke. "When I left with the troupe it seemed so romantic. Sorrel made me feel like a girl again." She glanced up and met Uncle Arthur's implacable gaze. "I told myself I deserved to be happy. But once the excitement passed—" Her face flamed and she ducked her head.

Ellie fidgeted in her chair. Aunt Ruby's words roused the uncomfortable memory of her own attraction to Marcus Beldon. She shrank at the thought of what might have happened had she been open to his advances. Realizing she was twisting her hands together, she made a conscious effort to stop.

Aunt Ruby turned to her. "I don't deserve anyone's kindness, but I came to you and Matthew because I hoped you'd take me in. I'll do anything you want done, just give me a place to stay." She took a sip of water and placed the mug on the floor beside her chair.

"You've got a home of your own." Uncle Arthur's voice sounded harsh. "No reason you can't go there."

"How can you? After all I've done?"

"I told your pa I'd take care of you, and I reckon the promise still holds." He turned his head toward Ellie. "Soon's Matt comes back, he can hitch the buggy for us. No need of me staying underfoot long as Ruby here can take care of things."

Ellie noticed a glint of satisfaction in her uncle's eyes and felt a ripple of shock at his expression.

Matthew's surprise at seeing Aunt Ruby showed on his face when he rode into the farmyard. After tying Samson, he ran up the steps and clasped her shoulders. "I've prayed for this moment."

She pushed his hands away. "Please don't. We all know what I've done. Where else could I go?"

"But—"

Uncle Arthur spoke from inside the kitchen door, where he had his belongings wrapped in a bundle and resting next to his crutches. "I'd be obliged if you'd hitch up my buggy. We'll be going to my place straight away."

"Stay for supper, at least."

Ellie stepped to Matthew's side and placed a hand on his arm. "I've already asked and been refused."

His eyes reflected bewilderment.

"Things don't always happen like in the Bible, Matt." Uncle Arthur moved onto the porch. "We won't be killing no fatted calf."

"I sent the twins to the barn to clean out Uncle Arthur's buggy," Ellie said to Matthew. "It got covered in dust and hay sitting there these weeks."

Aunt Ruby had told her of Matthew's visit in New Camden and how his plea had eventually convinced her to return. Now as she watched him leading Samson toward the barn, Ellie felt an overwhelming sense of love for her husband.

She felt heat rise in her face at the direction her thoughts were taking. She wanted to tell him how much she missed being a wife to him. How she was willing to put her fears aside so they could be close again. But could she face rejection?

After the evening meal, Ellie stood at the window staring into the twilight. Matthew sat at the table writing a report to Elder Meecham. His pen made scratching noises in the quiet room. Outside, the children played hide-and-seek among the lightning bugs that twinkled around them.

Ellie smiled at the sight of Graciana running and shouting with the others, her doll tucked under one arm. Aunt Ruby's homecoming had pushed all thoughts of the Carstairs from her mind, but now anxiety about Graciana's future returned.

Ellie stepped away from the window and faced Matthew. A pulse throbbed in her throat. "Did you call on Mrs. Carstairs today?"

30

Matthew wiped the nib and laid his pen next to the inkpot. In spite of his statement to Ellie when he left that morning, he'd deliberately avoided traveling along Hancock Street when he was in town. By not passing the Carstairs' home he could put off speaking to them about adopting Graciana.

Ellie watched him, one eyebrow raised in a question mark. She looked worried. "Well? Did you see Mrs. Carstairs?"

He cleared his throat. "Not today. I didn't have time. I'll go tomorrow." He waited to see how she'd respond.

"So Graciana may be with us a few more days."

"I'm afraid so. I hope you don't mind."

Ellie walked to the table and rested one hand on his shoulder. The warmth of her touch sent ripples down his arm.

"I don't mind at all."

Matthew blew out the candle beside the bed. Crickets trilled beneath the open window, their chirps vibrating in the darkness. Ellie stirred under the sheet next to him and turned on her side.

"Did you finish your report for Elder Meecham?"

"I did."

"When are you leaving for Quincy?" Her voice wavered. "I wish you didn't have to go."

"I'm not going to Quincy." He pushed himself upright so that his shoulders rested on the headboard. "In the morning I'll take the letter to the post office and send it off. Elder Meecham can do what he wants with me when he receives it."

"What if he dismisses you?"

"I'll still preach. He can't stop me." He chuckled. "Of course, he won't send me a salary, either."

Ellie's hand crept into his. "The Lord will provide for us. He always has."

Matthew turned his head in her direction, surprised at his wife's expression of faith. He slid back onto the feather tick, his heart joyful. He fell asleep still holding her hand.

The boys' voices awakened him the next morning. They clomped down the stairs, arguing over whose turn it was to do the milking. He rolled over. Ellie's half of the bed was empty.

He slipped on his trousers and work shirt and hurried down to the kitchen. The smoky aroma of fried ham greeted him, making his mouth water. Maria and Graciana stood beside Ellie, watching while she stirred something on top of the stove. Matthew blinked and took a closer look.

"Uncle Matthew."

"Papa."

Graciana and Maria ran across the room and wrapped their arms around him. "We thought you were going to sleep all day," Maria said.

Matthew scrubbed his hands over his face and grinned at them. "Sun's not even all the way up yet." He pretended to turn toward the stairs. "Guess I'll go back to bed."

Graciana giggled. "No, stay here with us."

His heart turned over at the happiness in her voice. The idea of taking her to the Carstairs filled him with sorrow.

"Breakfast is almost ready." Ellie paused in her stirring. "We're having cornbread and ham gravy."

"Sounds good." He hugged the girls and headed for the wash basin on the back porch, his thoughts in turmoil.

Mounted on Samson, Matthew held the reins and looked down at Ellie. "I'll be gone most of the afternoon. When I'm done at the post office, I want to go to Molly's and see James for myself. It's answered prayer to have him home safe."

"I felt the same way when I first saw him. Thankfully, Molly and Karl have been able to dissuade him from trying to enlist again." She moved closer and lifted her face in the way she used to do when she expected a good-bye kiss.

He hesitated, then bent and brushed her lips with his. She placed her hand on his cheek, holding the kiss for an extra second. When he straightened in the saddle, he saw a light in her eyes that he hadn't seen for months.

Matthew nudged Samson's side with his heels and backed away. "While I'm in town, I'll stop at Carstairs' too. Hope Orville's home so I can talk to both of them."

Ellie's smile faded. "Tell Penelope I said hello." Her voice sounded flat. She turned and hurried into the house.

On an impulse, Matthew directed his horse into the church-yard instead of continuing to the post office. The promised quiet of the sanctuary beckoned. When he tied Samson, he paused to study the compact white church that he and many other towns-folk had built. It felt as much like home as the farmhouse he'd left two miles back.

When he walked in, he noticed footprints and bits of debris on the dusty wooden floor leading up the center aisle. Matthew moved toward the platform, his eyes skimming over the empty benches, the cold iron stove, the half-burned candles in their sconces. Flies bumped and buzzed against the whitewashed ceiling. Being inside felt like visiting an old friend whose health had deteriorated in his absence.

Matthew strode to the cloakroom, where he found a broom leaning in one corner. While he was there he could sweep the floor. He noticed a stack of rags in a bucket and tucked one into his back pocket, planning to polish the altar.

As he left the storage area, the door to the church creaked open, laying a bar of sunlight across the rear benches. He turned to see an unmistakable figure silhouetted in the doorway.

"Mrs. Beldon?"

She stepped inside. Tipping her head in her characteristic way, she looked up at Matthew. "It's time you and I talked."

He glanced over her shoulder to see if her husband had followed her.

Evidently reading his action, Mrs. Beldon's mouth twisted into a smile. "You're wondering how I got here? I walked. I'm not quite the invalid my husband makes me out to be." She slid onto a bench and patted the space beside her. "Do sit."

Matthew complied, wondering what she felt they had to talk about. He leaned forward and rested his hands on his knees. "What can I do for you?"

"You can listen. There's something you need to know." She lifted her head and he looked directly into her penetrating brown eyes.

298

"I've watched while my husband has done his best to become the most important man in this town. He saw in you an influence that he had to suppress, and unfortunately it seems he has succeeded. But I can't sit by and let it happen." Mrs. Beldon tapped his hand briefly. "Marcus didn't come here because he believed Beldon Grove to be his birthright, or whatever twaddle he may have told you. He came here because he failed at everything he tried back home, and my father gave him a stake for one last chance." A flush tinted her cheeks.

"I recognize how difficult this is—"

"Please do me the courtesy of listening until I'm finished."

"Yes, ma'am."

"Now it seems he's failing at his scheme to take over your congregation. Some of the members called on him last week and told him to cease preaching in this church."

A feeling of relief swept over Matthew. "So he won't be back?"

"Marcus ignored them. He ignores everyone who doesn't agree with him."

Matthew looked down at his cracked and dusty boots. He'd be willing to preach at Wolcott's store every Sunday if he had to. But then he thought about the towns he'd visited on his circuit, and what church division had done to their inhabitants. He couldn't allow the current situation to continue. He closed his eyes. *Lord, guide me.*

In the silence, Mrs. Beldon drew a deep breath and held it for a moment, then released it in a sigh. "Marcus only married me because of my father's money. Who else would want me, with this crippled body?" She held up a twisted hand. "For a long time, I pretended he loved me, but I can't lie to myself any longer. I've sent word to my father to come take me home." Tears pooled in her eyes.

Matthew's heart softened toward the woman he'd always believed to be cold and withdrawn. Seething at Beldon's arrogance, he cradled her hands in his. "I'm sorry."

She pulled away, assuming her former brittle tone. "Don't feel sorry for me. I allowed it."

She stood and moved toward the door. With one hand on the latch, she turned and looked back. "Whatever happens, don't let him intimidate you. You belong in this pulpit."

Ellie sat near the kitchen window, removing the stitching from the cloth body of Graciana's doll. The child watched as tufts of cotton dropped onto the table. Once the stuffing in the arms and legs was removed, Ellie plucked at the batting that surrounded the doll's stiffened middle section. Sliding her hand inside, she closed her fingers around a wooden cylinder and drew it out.

Graciana leaned forward. "That's what Papa gave Aunt Polly to sew into Nora."

The carved object rested in Ellie's palm. A wax-covered cork closed one end. Ellie's fingers tingled with the desire to open the container, but she hesitated and then handed it to Graciana.

The child turned the cylinder over in her hands and tugged at the cork. "Do you think there's treasure in here?" Her eyes sparkled.

Ellie caught her excitement. "Why don't you find out?"

The cork held fast, no matter how hard Graciana pulled at it. Defeated, she gave the container back to Ellie. "There's too much wax on the outside. It won't open."

"Well, let's help it along." Ellie stood and selected a knife from a drawer in the worktable. Before cutting through the thick layer of wax, she glanced at the stove where a kettle filled with soapy water waited.

She set the knife aside and moved the kettle to the worktable, then lowered Nora's grimy fabric body into the water. After placing the cylinder on a cutting board, she rolled the wax under the knife blade. Using a twisting motion, she removed the cork and poked inside the opening with her index finger.

Graciana crowded close. "What is it?"

She plucked the cylinder from Ellie's hand and peered inside, then turned it upside down and tapped it on the edge of the table. A tube-shaped bundle of paper slid out. Once freed, it tumbled over and dropped to the floor, unrolling as it fell.

Disappointment clouded Graciana's features. She held the paper in one hand and studied the writing that filled the page. "No treasure." Her brown eyes met Ellie's. "I hoped maybe gold or silver."

Ellie concealed a smile. "Maybe this paper is a treasure map. Was your papa a pirate?"

"No!" Graciana looked offended. She thrust the paper at Ellie. "Read it to me, please."

Glancing over the closely written lines of text, Ellie saw it was a letter. She moved to the rocking chair beneath the stairwell and opened her arms. "Come sit on my lap. We'll see what it says."

Instead, Graciana walked to the worktable and peered at her doll soaking in the kettle. "I think she's clean enough. Can we get her out and dry her off first?"

Ellie laid the letter down and joined Graciana. Rolling up her sleeves, she tested the water temperature with one finger, then squeezed the soapy mixture through the fabric. After rinsing, she carried the wet, limp Nora out to the porch and draped her over the back of a chair.

"As warm as it is today, she'll be ready for new stuffing before suppertime."

Graciana examined the doll. "She does look better. Thank you." She took Ellie's hand. "Now, let's read."

The rocker creaked when Ellie settled Graciana onto her lap.

My very dearest Graciana,

The child smiled and snuggled closer.

When Aunt Polly takes you to my old home, you will hear stories about me. I wanted to tell you those stories myself when you were older, but I don't have much time left, so I have to write this down and hope you will understand someday.

A long time ago, when I was a young man, I had another daughter. Her name was Eleanor. Her mama died when she was very little, just like your mama did. I didn't know how to take care of a child. It shames me to tell you this now, but I left her behind with my family and followed Mr. Austin's men to Texas. I never saw her again.

Hot blood rose in Ellie's cheeks. "'Eleanor'?"

"What?" Graciana asked.

Instead of replying, Ellie bent closer to the paper as though

302

she could draw hidden meaning from the script. Tracing the lines with her finger, she read rapidly to the end of the page.

> Then you were born in my old age, a blessing
> from God. After your mama died I promised
> I'd never leave you, but now I can't keep my
> promise. It makes me very sad to know that I
> won't see you grow up.
>
>   After I'm gone, always remember I love you.
>
> You are my heart.
>
> Your papa.

Ellie leaned back in the chair. He couldn't be the same man, could he? Her heart pounded as she reread the words. *Eleanor. Austin. Texas.* She drew a quivering breath and squeezed Graciana close to her chest. He must be.

"Aunt Ellie? What's wrong?"

"What was your papa's name?"

"Everyone called him Largo. Just Largo."

Palms sweating, Ellie studied Graciana's face, taking in the shape of her eyes, her slender, high-bridged nose, her soft, rounded lips.

She cupped the child's chin in her hand. "Do you remember me telling you my papa was dead?"

Graciana nodded.

"He died last winter." Ellie had trouble getting the words out.

The child patted her hand in a sympathetic gesture. "So did my papa."

Ellie took a deep breath. "My name is Eleanor. Ellie's a pet name. My papa left me behind when he went to Texas, just like this letter says. Graciana, maybe we're sisters."

Little hands pressed Ellie's cheeks. Graciana's mouth opened in an "O", then she whispered, "Truly?"

Ellie's tears ran over the child's fingers. "Oh, I hope so!"

Footsteps clattered up the porch stairs and the twins dashed into the room.

"When's dinner—" Johnny stopped, staring at his mother. "What's wrong?"

Ellie stood Graciana on the floor but kept an arm around her. "Do you remember last month when I told you I wondered whether my father had other children when he lived in Texas?" She fought to keep from crying.

Both boys nodded.

"See this letter?" Ellie handed it to Jimmy with shaking fingers. "It's from Graciana's father, and it sounds like he's talking about me."

Heads together, the boys read through the message. Their eyes grew wide and they stared at Graciana. Johnny was the first to speak.

"Her last name's Largo. It's not the same."

Ellie rose from the chair. "Maybe he changed his name when he went away. Sometimes people do." She lifted the paper from her son's hand and tucked it into the pocket of her skirt. "I know the Lord sent Graciana to us. How else can you explain Papa discovering her on a dock next to the Ohio River? She's meant to be part of our family."

"Then God gave you the desires of your heart, didn't he, Mama? You have a sister," Jimmy said. He put his hands on Graciana's shoulders. "I'm glad you're going to live with us."

She blushed. "Me too."

Ellie's breath caught in her throat. "Oh my word!" She swung around and looked at Johnny. "I have to go to town right now."

"How? Papa's gone." He looked bewildered.

"I'll walk. You boys stay in the house and mind the children." Ellie snatched her bonnet from its peg near the door. "Tell Harrison and Maria about Graciana's letter."

31

Ellie ran until her sides ached, then she slowed to a walk. Once she caught her breath, she ran again. Sweat trickled down her forehead and stung her eyes. She had to stop Matthew before he reached the Carstairs' house. *Please, Lord, help me.*

Breeze from the northeast rustled through the leaves of Wolcotts' corn crop as she passed their farm. Ellie loosened her bonnet and let it flop against her back, swiping at her forehead with the back of her arm.

Precious minutes ticked by. If only someone would come along and offer her a ride the rest of the way—provided it wasn't Mr. Beldon.

The road remained deserted.

Finally, she saw the church ahead. Blinding glare from the afternoon sun bounced off its white clapboard siding. Ellie paused in the shadow of the building until her breathing slowed. Trying to think where Matthew would have gone first, she stepped back into the light and hurried to the corner of Adams Street. She squinted across the town square toward the post office. Samson wasn't tied out front.

Her shoulders drooped. Ellie slowed her steps and trudged toward Hancock Street, eyes on the ground. What if Matthew had already promised Graciana to Penelope? Molly's cabin lay up the road on the right. Ellie turned in that direction and noticed Matthew's horse waiting at the hitching rail. Dreading the news he'd have for her, she crossed the road and tapped on the doorframe, then walked inside.

The house was empty. Ellie stood, fighting dizziness. Her head ached and the bodice of her dress was soaked in sweat. She heard voices coming from the rear of the building. When she walked out back, she found Matthew seated in the shade of the silver maple tree with Molly and her family. Luellen had a book open in her lap. Lily sat close to her side, evidently listening while her sister read aloud. Behind them, James and Franklin played mumblety-peg. A jackknife blade glittered in the sun as it arced through the air and landed point first in the ground.

Matthew noticed her first and jumped to his feet. "Ellie. How on earth did you get here?" His face reflected alarm. "What's happened?"

Ellie shook her head, unable to speak. She'd been so eager to stop him, and now it was too late. Her joy at learning Graciana might be her half-sister turned to pain. She couldn't face the thought of going to Penelope and telling her she couldn't take the child after all. But it must be done, and quickly.

Molly came to her side. "You look like you're going to collapse. Why did you walk all the way here in this heat?"

"I had to stop Matthew." She turned to him. "What did the Carstairs say?"

"I still haven't gone." Matthew flushed. He slid his arm around her shoulders and turned her toward a seat in the shade.

Ellie slumped against him. She tightened her arms around Matthew's waist and held on, face buried against his chest. The smooth cotton of his shirt felt cool against her cheek. After a moment she drew back and met his questioning gaze.

"What is it? Tell me."

Molly's children and Karl all gathered around. Curiosity filled each face.

Ellie glanced at them, then focused again on Matthew. "After you left, I decided to wash Graciana's doll. When I pulled out the stuffing, I found a wooden tube inside that contained this message from her father." She took a deep breath and handed the letter to him. "I believe Graciana could be my half-sister."

"How—" Matthew scanned the contents. When he looked up, his face was a mixture of hope and puzzlement. "He mentions your name, and a detail about Austin, but that doesn't tell us much. Graciana gave her last name as Largo—your father's name was Long."

Karl put his hand on Matthew's shoulder, interrupting them. "I studied languages in school. Largo is Spanish for Long." He took the page from Matthew, read it, then handed it to Ellie, shaking his head. "There must be hundreds of men named Long in this country."

"How many of them went to Texas?" Ellie folded her arms across her chest and tilted her chin upward.

"Could be any number. We don't know."

"Matthew just finished telling us about that little girl when you arrived," Molly said to Ellie, using a peacemaking tone of voice. "Please, sit here and tell us why you think she's your sister."

She turned to Luellen. "Bring your aunt a cup of water before she faints dead away from this heat."

"Don't tell the story until I get back." Luellen sped for the house.

When she returned with the water, Ellie surveyed her family, her eyes resting briefly on each face. "I'll start at the beginning. Just listen before you make up your minds."

She held out the letter. "Graciana's father tells of his shame at leaving his little daughter, Eleanor, behind when he left for Texas. I was only three when Aunt Ruby took me in."

"Wait a minute," Karl said. "He doesn't say when he left. Could've been any time."

Ellie lifted a hand to cut him off. "Aunt Ruby said my father followed Austin's first call for settlers. Graciana told us her papa was old. If we have the same father, he'd have been almost sixty when she was born. Graciana's father, and mine, died last winter. True, he used the name Largo." She searched Matthew's face, hoping she wouldn't see Karl's doubts mirrored there. "But I think Largo was probably what people called him. After all, Texas was part of a foreign country when he arrived. He must've learned the language to fit in."

A smile trembled on her lips as she studied the faces surrounding her. "Now do you see why I think she's my sister?"

Matthew seized her in a fierce hug. "I've been trying to decide how to tell you I want Graciana to stay with us." He grinned. "Looks like you don't need convincing. No wonder you ran all the way to town."

Keeping an arm around Ellie's shoulders, Matthew turned to Karl. "We'll never know if she's related or not, but I believe God brought Graciana safely from Texas for me to find."

"Sounds almost like the ending to a play, doesn't it?" Karl asked, a sly grin on his face.

"We need to tell your aunt right away. Graciana is her niece too." Matthew's arm around Ellie's waist held her steady as they rode Samson toward home. Warmth from his body radiated through her dress. She couldn't remember the last time they'd been this close.

Whose fault is that? a voice inside seemed to say.

Mine. But I don't know how to undo it.

Matthew shifted in the saddle. "What do you think Ruby will say?"

"No telling. I can't wait to see her face when she finds out."

Once they reached the Newberrys' farmyard, Ellie noticed that the curtains were drawn across the windows. The back door hadn't been opened to capture the breeze.

She turned sideways and looked at Matthew. "Do you think something's wrong?"

"We'll find out soon enough." He slid to the ground and walked to the house. When he raised his hand to knock, the door opened before his knuckles struck the wood.

Aunt Ruby stood inside the shadowy kitchen, wearing a black dress covered with an apron. "What brings you here?"

"Something unbelievable has happened."

Aunt Ruby blinked at him, saying nothing.

"Can we come in?"

She stepped to one side. "Please do."

Matthew helped Ellie down and led her into the house. She hurried to her aunt and seized her hands. "Are you ready for another niece?" Ellie heard the excitement bubble in her voice.

Aunt Ruby's eyes slid to Ellie's waist. "How do you know it's a girl?"

Ellie darted a glance at Matthew, heat rising in her cheeks. "I'm talking about little Graciana. You met her at our house when you arrived on Thursday."

"Graciana? Are you saying—"

"Let Ellie talk." Uncle Arthur's voice sounded from the rear of the room. His crutches thumped as he made his way toward them.

Ellie felt tension vibrate in the air between her aunt and uncle. She stepped back. "Let's sit. We'll explain everything."

Once the story had been told, a strange expression crossed Aunt Ruby's face. "With that dark skin and hair, she doesn't look anything like the rest of us. People will talk. What if the child isn't accepted here?"

Ellie's heart stirred at the fear in her aunt's eyes.

Matthew squeezed Aunt Ruby's hand. "It doesn't matter what others think. Graciana will be part of our family. We accept her, and that's enough." He stood and walked to the door. "We'll stop by in the morning and take you to church with us."

"Are you daft?" Aunt Ruby rapped the tabletop with her fist. "I can't face those people. Me and Arthur will stay right here."

Uncle Arthur pushed himself to his feet. "We ain't going. Save yourself a stop." The expression on his face left no room for argument.

Ellie reached for him. "But, Uncle . . ."

"Ellie." Matthew spoke in a gentle voice. "Give them time." His gaze encompassed both Ruby and Arthur. "When you're ready, we'll stand with you. You're part of our family too."

He slid a hand around Ellie's waist. "Now we need to get on home and have a proper welcome for our little gift from heaven."

Once the excited children were settled for the night, Matthew slid onto a kitchen chair and rested his head on the top rail. "This has been quite a day. First Mrs. Beldon, then the news about Graciana."

"Mrs. Beldon?" Ellie's heart skipped a beat. In her exhilaration over Graciana, she'd forgotten about Mr. Beldon. She turned her face away so he couldn't see the guilt she felt sure was written there.

"She came to the church this afternoon and told me some interesting things about her husband."

Ellie closed her eyes and took a deep breath. The lingering taste of boiled beans from their supper filled her throat. She flinched when she felt Matthew's hand on her arm.

"According to Mrs. Beldon, coming here was her husband's last chance to make something of himself. It had nothing to do with his father founding the town. It's *her* father who's been paying their way, and she's tired of it. Tired of him." Matthew squeezed her arm. "She urged me to take back my church."

Ellie lifted her head. "Now you listen? I've said that all along. So has Mr. Wolcott."

He looked embarrassed. "I know, but . . . Beldon makes me feel small—like I'm no match for him."

"You're worth a hundred Marcus Beldons."

Matthew blinked at her, surprise showing in his eyes. "I didn't know you felt that way."

"I forgot it until . . . recently." She assumed a brisk tone. "So, what are you going to do?"

"We'll go to services at Ben's store tomorrow. I'm eager to introduce Graciana to our community." A smile flitted across his face. "Afterward, I'll decide."

32

On Sunday morning, the Craig farmhouse rustled with activity. While Matthew helped Harrison button his jacket under the rounded collar of his shirt, he listened to Ellie fuss over Maria and Graciana across the hallway.

"Graciana, with your pink dress on, you two look alike," Ellie said.

"We don't look alike. Maria has blonde hair, and mine is black."

"Your faces are the same. Your eyes, your noses. Go see in the mirror."

Matthew leaned against the doorframe of the boys' room and watched as the two pink-clad girls scampered into his and Ellie's bedroom and giggled in front of the mirror. They dashed back to Ellie.

"You're right, Mama. We do look like sisters," Maria said. "But isn't Graciana my aunt now?"

Matthew stepped into the hall so he could better follow the exchange.

"I don't want to be your aunt." Graciana spoke so softly he had to lean forward to listen. "I want brothers and a sister . . . and a mama and papa."

Tears formed in Matthew's eyes. He stepped into the girls'

bedroom. He took Graciana's hand, then used his free arm to draw Maria and Ellie into his embrace. "You have us all, Gracie. Aunt Ellie and I will be your mama and papa."

"Then I'm your sister." Maria kissed Graciana's cheek. "Now come on. Let's beat the boys downstairs."

When everyone had gathered in the kitchen, Ellie and the girls served breakfast, their pink calico dresses covered with full aprons. The aroma of hot apple butter swirled upward from a bowl placed in the center of the table. After asking a blessing on the food and their day, Matthew scooped a generous portion of the warmed sauce over his cornmeal mush.

Ellie's words last evening, that he was worth a hundred Marcus Beldons, kept repeating in his mind—a song that couldn't be forgotten. In spite of the uncertainty awaiting him in town, he believed he could do anything, even face down his formidable adversary, if he had Ellie by his side.

Although he was no longer responsible for opening the church building and preparing it for the service, Matthew couldn't shake his Sunday morning habit of rushing out the door. While Maria dawdled over her breakfast, he slipped his watch out of his pocket and checked to see that they were on schedule.

Ellie's laughing eyes met his across the table. "We'll get there. I'm sure Mr. Wolcott's had everything ready since last night."

In spite of the uncertainty that awaited him in town, Matthew noted with satisfaction his six-foot-high corn crop as they left the farm. The rain they'd had earlier seemed to have boosted the growth by several inches.

He turned to his sons, who sat shoulder-to-shoulder on the back seat. "We should have a bountiful harvest this year. Good job, boys."

"What about me and Mama?" Maria asked. "We worked too."

"So you did." He reached out and patted her hand, then stretched past her and squeezed Graciana's also. "Looks like you girls might get some new dress goods when the crops are in."

Ellie shot him a wry smile. "Right now, I'd settle for a sack of wheat flour."

Matthew nodded. "Can't think why Elder Meecham didn't send any support money. I hoped for at least a few dollars' credit at the mercantile." He drew a deep breath, his nose tickling at the dust that rolled up around the horse's hooves. "We can get by until harvest time, I expect."

"We'll have to."

August sun pressed down around them. Holding the reins with one hand, Matthew slipped out of his black coat and draped it over the seat. The movement of the wagon drew a cooling breeze over his linen-clad shoulders.

He glanced at Ellie. "Too bad the Lord can't spread this heat out a bit. We could use it in January."

She grinned. "That's when he gives us the ice we'd like to have right now." They chuckled together at their long-standing joke.

Matthew felt a surge of hope. He'd missed the easy companionship of their marriage almost as much as he missed the physical intimacy.

When Matthew walked into the back room of Wolcott's Mercantile, he saw dozens of familiar faces from his old congregation.

People crowded around, welcoming him, patting him on the back, shaking his hand. He glanced at Ellie and motioned her to come forward with Graciana and the other children.

After she reached his side, he put an arm around Graciana's shoulder. "This is our newest family member, Graciana. The Lord has blessed us by bringing her all the way from Texas to our home."

A brief hush fell over the gathering. People's eyes shifted between Ellie, Graciana, and Matthew.

Molly moved forward. Kneeling, she wrapped her arms around the little girl. "Welcome to our family. I'm Reverend Craig's sister, your Aunt Molly."

Before Molly stood, Charity Wolcott joined them. She lifted Graciana's hand and patted it. "How do you do. I'm Mrs. Wolcott."

Another woman came up, smiled at Graciana, and complimented her shiny black hair. Soon she was surrounded by a group of twittering ladies, all trying to outdo one another's greetings.

Matthew sighed in relief.

Ben stepped beside him. "We were just about to start." He draped his arm over Matthew's shoulder and propelled him to the front of the room. He pointed to an empty bench. "Got a spot for your family right here."

After an opening hymn and prayer, Ben stood and addressed the audience. "I know all of us are tickled to have Reverend Craig back. Since he's a better preacher than I'll ever be, I'm thankful to have him here to give us a message from God's Word."

"Yes!" someone called.

"We missed you, Reverend," said another.

Their encouraging voices flowed over Matthew like balm. He stood and faced the room. Familiar faces smiled a welcome—Orville and Penelope Carstairs, Mattie and Hettie Sims, even Jack Bryant from the hotel. Near the front, Molly and Karl beamed in his direction. Their children lined the bench next to them.

Matthew smiled back. In that moment, he felt as planted among these people as an oak tree in a thicket. He imagined roots growing from his feet into the soil of Beldon Grove, and his arms spreading like tree limbs around his congregation. Carrying his Bible, he walked to the makeshift podium.

"Wait!" Ellie stood and dashed to his side.

Mouths opened in shock. Matthew stared at her as though she'd lost her senses. A woman didn't speak out in church, much less occupy the pulpit.

She tucked her arm through his and faced the crowd. He felt her trembling.

"We all want my husband as our pastor, but not here. This isn't a house of worship, it's Mr. Wolcott's storeroom. I say, let's take our church back."

Ben hurried forward. "Beldon will be there."

"I don't care. 'Greater is He that is in us, than he that is in the world,' and Mr. Beldon is definitely of this world."

Matthew studied his wife's flushed face. Where had she gotten such courage?

Nods of agreement spread through the room. "Let's go!" a voice shouted.

His children were already on their feet. "Come on, Papa," Johnny said. "We can do it."

Matthew clapped his hat on and strode for the door, stepping out into the radiant morning. When he started walking, thick dust from the street lapped over his shoes and settled on the hem of his trousers. He shook his head. He never seemed to face Beldon without looking like a hayseed. Why should today be any different?

Then his thoughts turned to Ellie, who kept pace with him on his right. Their children flanked his other side, Maria and Graciana hand in hand. For a moment he felt invincible. *Man looketh on the outward appearance, but the LORD looketh on the heart.* A flush prickled his bearded cheeks. *Forgive me, Father. I've been worried about all the wrong things.*

As they moved past the deserted town square, Matthew glanced over his shoulder, expecting to see Ben and Charity and maybe a few of the others following. Instead, everyone who'd been in the mercantile had joined him. The procession quickly covered the remaining blocks of Madison Street leading to the church he'd left many weeks earlier.

When he entered the sanctuary, his confidence plummeted. Elder Meecham sat next to the aisle at the rear of the sparsely filled room. Had he come to install Beldon as pastor?

To Matthew's astonishment, Meecham winked at him. "I reckoned you'd be here today," he murmured.

He gestured toward the pulpit where Marcus Beldon stood gaping as the crowd of people pushed their way inside. "Go on up. You're just in time."

"See here." Beldon's voice thundered into the uneasy silence that filled the room. "You can't interrupt this church service."

He wore one of his tailored suits, the golden watch chain glinting against his waistcoat. His meaty hands gripped the sides of the pulpit, defying Matthew to take it from him.

Stepping onto the platform, Matthew eyed his rival. Beldon was as well turned out as ever, but now Matthew noticed the desperation behind his threatening expression.

Beldon laughed—a harsh sound that tore through the sanctuary. "You're nothing but a farmer, Craig. Why don't you go tend to your crops? Leave the preaching to someone with a proper education."

Matthew's response rose from deep inside. "It's not education that gives a man the right to carry God's Word. It's his heart. My heart's been right with the Lord since I was a boy. I doubt we can say the same of yours."

Beldon stepped close to him and lifted his hand, palm out, as though he intended to shove him off the platform. He was near enough for Matthew to notice beads of sweat on the big man's forehead.

"Do your worst. You'll find us farmers are a tough lot." He brushed past him as though he were invisible, and slapped his Bible down on the pulpit.

Beldon's gaze darted over the congregation, then back at Matthew. After a tense heartbeat, his hand fell to his side. "You want this bunch of clodhoppers, you can have them."

Face the color of an angry sunset, he stalked off the platform and out of the church. The door banged shut behind him, rattling the windowpanes.

In the shocked stillness that followed, Zilphah Beldon stood. Instead of accompanying her husband, she made her way up the aisle and joined Ellie. Together, the two women moved to the front row. Matthew and Ellie's children followed. Other members of the congregation settled onto the empty benches. Faces upturned, they waited for their pastor to open the service.

Matthew bowed his head. "Let's pray."

33

"You have to admit, it *is* kind of humorous," Molly said.

The two families sat on the porch of the Craig's farmhouse later Sunday afternoon, sipping buttermilk and enjoying the warm Scotch bread Molly provided.

Ellie stopped in mid-reach for another slice. "What is?"

"You thought you had grown brothers or sisters, and the Lord sent you a little girl younger than Maria." She chuckled. "He always surprises us, doesn't he?"

"Indeed. He's able to do exceeding abundantly above all that we ask or think," Ellie quoted, sighing with satisfaction as she looked at Graciana. The child sat on the top step between Maria and Lily. Each girl held a doll.

Ellie pointed at Graciana's. In a low voice she said to Molly, "I stayed up late last night repairing and restuffing Nora. I put the message from our father back inside. That's where he meant it to be."

The two women exchanged a look that said more than words.

Molly patted Ellie's hand, then turned to her older daughter. "Luellen, it's time."

Luellen rose and walked to her parents' buggy. When she returned, she carried a bulky package. Matthew and Karl broke off their conversation to watch as she climbed the steps and laid the bundle at Graciana's feet.

Molly stood. "Luellen has a special gift to welcome your Gracie into the family." She dropped to one knee behind the child. "Go ahead, open it."

Brown paper rustled as Graciana unfolded the corners and lifted out the contents. The honeycomb quilt blossomed in the sunlight, its colors spilling over her legs and down the steps.

"For me?"

Startled, Ellie glanced between Molly and Luellen. "This is supposed to be for your bridal chest. Are you sure?"

Luellen stroked the back of Graciana's head. "I'm positive. I remember how it felt being in your house after my papa died. You made a home for us. Now I want to help make a home for Gracie."

Molly hugged her daughter to her. "We'll start another quilt soon, won't we?"

That night after supper, Ellie and Matthew faced each other across the kitchen table. An Illinois State Bank note for twenty dollars, more than three months' salary, lay between them. Matthew touched it with his index finger.

"Meecham knew all along I'd be back. He sent me to those towns on purpose." He shook his head.

Ellie blinked back tears. "With everything else that's happened, it's almost too much to take in." She patted her eyes with a corner of her apron. After glancing up the stairs where the children slept, she pushed her chair back and then flashed him a smile. "Let's go down by the creek and watch the stars. It's a beautiful evening."

Once out in the soft night air, they were enfolded in the sound of crickets and frogs calling from the nearby cornfields. Ellie slid her arm around Matthew's waist and leaned against him while they walked along the familiar path. Upon reaching the creek bank, they sank down into a cushiony patch of wild mint. Lightning bugs glittered around them.

Ellie caressed Matthew's face, her fingers tickling in his beard. The fragrance of mint filled his senses.

"I was so proud of you today."

"I couldn't have done it without you beside me."

She leaned back, resting on her elbows. He saw the light of the half moon reflected in her eyes. Ellie reached up and pulled him close. Her lips moved against his ear.

"I'll always be beside you," she whispered.

Acknowledgments

A novel doesn't come to life without many helping hands. I'd like to thank everyone who participated in the creation of *The Promise of Morning*.

As always, I'm indebted to the sharp eyes and multiple talents of my critique partners: Bonnie Leon, Billy Cook, Diane Gardner, BJ Bassett, Julia Ewert, and Sarah Schartz. Each of you possesses a particular gift, and I'm grateful for your help over the past months.

I can't say enough good things about my editors, Vicki Crumpton and Barb Barnes, and the entire team at Revell. Every step of the publishing process has been a blessing, thanks to their godly spirits and creative energy.

My agent, Tamela Hancock Murray, is my number one cheerleader. Thanks for being there with the answer whenever I have a question.

Craig Harms, a fellow author and ACFW member, has been my "man on the ground" in Illinois. He lives near the city limits of the fictional community of Beldon Grove and has helped tremendously with details about that part of the country. Thank you, Craig, for being so willing to share your knowledge. Any mistakes are my fault, not yours.

My husband, Richard, has encouraged me every step of the way. Without his support I couldn't have accomplished the task of researching and writing this novel. Thank you, my love.

Highest praise goes to my heavenly Father, who holds me by my right hand—always.

Ann Shorey has been a story collector for most of her life. Her writing has appeared in *Chicken Soup for the Grandma's Soul*, and in the Adams Media Cup of Comfort series. She made her fiction debut with *The Edge of Light*, released in January 2009. When she's not writing, she teaches classes on historical research, story arc, and other fiction fundamentals at regional conferences. Ann lives with her husband, Richard, in Sutherlin, Oregon. *The Promise of Morning* is the second book in her At Home in Beldon Grove series.

Contact Ann through her website at www.annshorey.com.

When tragedy strikes, how will Molly McGarvie survive?

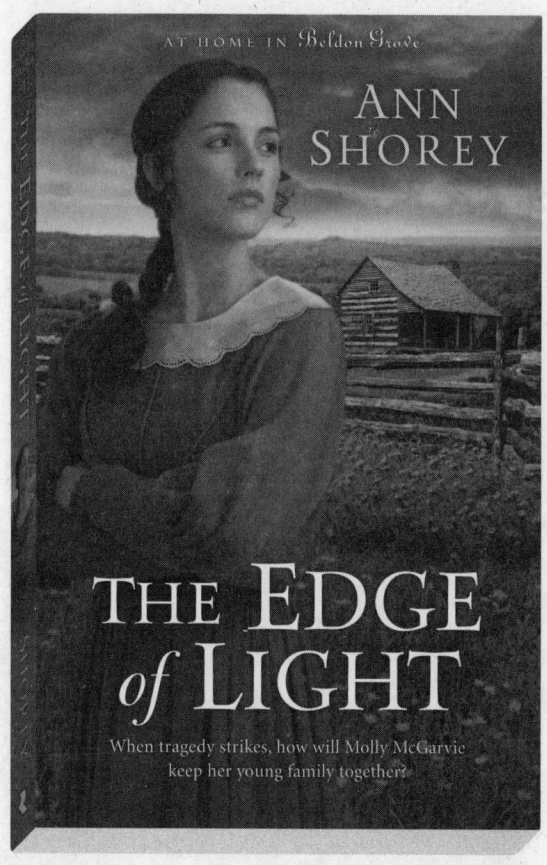

Experience the wonder and hardship of life on the prairie with Molly McGarvie
as she fights to survive loss and keep her young family together.

Journey into the
Heart of the West

MAGGIE BRENDAN

HEART of the WEST · 1

NO PLACE
FOR A *Lady*

A NOVEL

Can a Southern belle tame the heart of a rugged cowboy?

Can a Southern belle tame the heart of
a rugged cowboy?

Revell
a division of Baker Publishing Group
www.RevellBooks.com

Sweet Romances
That Capture the Heart

The Big Sky Country holds two treasures worth pursuing . . . which will he choose?

Her father's money could buy her anything except true love.

Coming June 2010

If You Loved This Book,

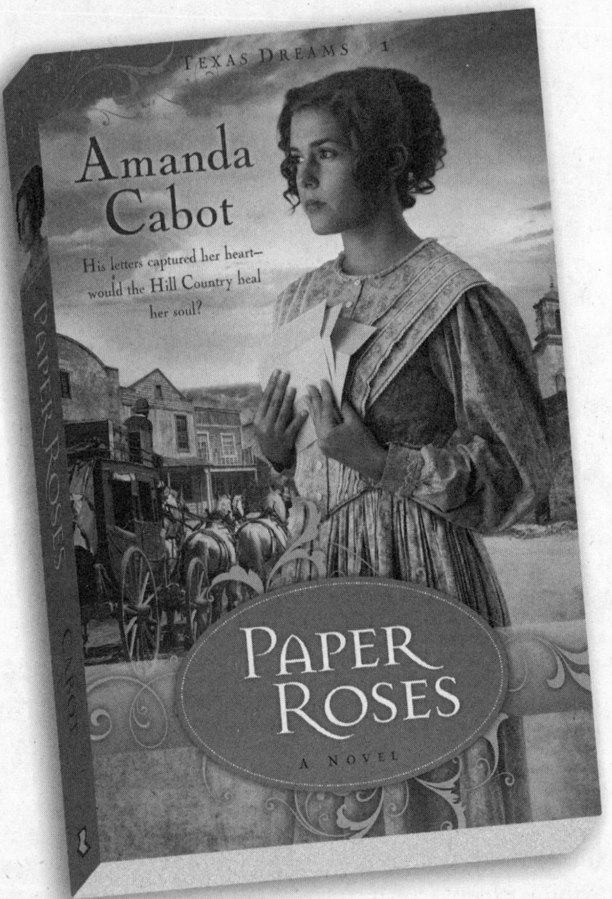

His letters captured her heart—
would the Hill Country heal her soul?

You Will Love the Texas Dreams Series!

Tragedy broke her spirit.
Will love mend her heart?